By Shirley Jackson

The Road Through the Wall

The Lottery and Other Stories

Hangsaman

Life Among the Savages

The Bird's Nest

The Witchcraft of Salem Village

Raising Demons

The Sundial

The Haunting of Hill House

We Have Always Lived in the Castle

The Magic of Shirley Jackson

Come Along with Me

Just an Ordinary Day

Let Me Tell You

Let Me Tell You

RANDOM HOUSE / NEW YORK

Let Me Tell You

NEW STORIES, ESSAYS, AND OTHER WRITINGS

SHIRLEY JACKSON

Edited by
LAURENCE JACKSON HYMAN
and SARAH HYMAN DEWITT

Foreword by
RUTH FRANKLIN

Illustrations, quotations, and all previously unpublished text by Shirley Jackson copyright © 2015 by Laurence Jackson Hyman, J. S. Holly, Sarah Hyman DeWitt, and Barry Hyman

Biographical Note, compilation, and Afterword copyright © 2015 by Penguin Random House LLC

Foreword copyright © 2015 by Ruth Franklin

Published in the United States by Random House, an imprint and division of Penguin Random House LLC, New York.

Random House and the House colophon are registered trademarks of Penguin Random House LLC.

The following pieces have been previously published: "Paranoia," "The Man in the Woods," and "It Isn't the Money I Mind" in *The New Yorker* and also in *Shirley Jackson: Novels and Stories,* edited by Joyce Carol Oates (New York: The Library of America, 2010); "Mrs. Spencer and the Oberons" in *Tin House;* "The Lie" and "The Sorcerer's Apprentice" in *McSweeney's;* "Let Me Tell You" in *Tin House's Open Bar;* "Bulletin" in *Fantasy & Science Fiction;* "Root of Evil" in *Fantastic;* "Clowns" in *Vogue;* "Good Old House" in *Woman's Day;* "In Praise of Dinner Table Silence," "Questions I Wish I'd Never Asked," "What I Want to Know Is, What Do Other People Cook With?," "Mother, Honestly!," and "Out of the Mouths of Babes" in *Good Housekeeping;* "How to Enjoy a Family Quarrel" and "The Pleasures and Perils of Dining Out with Children" in *McCall's;* and "Homecoming" in *Charm.*

Library of Congress Cataloging-in-Publication Data

Jackson, Shirley, 1916–1965.
[Works. Selections. 2015]
Let me tell you: new stories, essays, and other writings/Shirley Jackson; edited by Laurence Jackson Hyman and Sarah Hyman DeWitt.
pages cm
ISBN 978-0-8129-9766-8
eBook ISBN 978-0-8129-9767-5
I. Hyman, Laurence Jackson, editor.   II. DeWitt, Sarah Hyman, editor.   III. Title.
PS3519.A392A6 2015
818'.54—dc23
2014036656

Printed in the United States of America on acid-free paper

randomhousebooks.com

246897531

First Edition

Book design by Susan Turner

To the grandchildren and great-grandchildren of
Shirley Hardie Jackson and Stanley Edgar Hyman:

*Miles Biggs Hyman, Gretchen Anne Cardinal Hyman, Shiloh Alexis
Webster Elias, Maxwell Dervin Schnurer, Bodie Jackson Hyman,
Millie Noyes Stephenson, Ethan Lazarus Webster Elias, Rubin
Santiago Elias, Jamilah Sophia Parker, Nathaniel Nicholas
Jackson Hyman, Juliette Maï Theresa Hyman, Charlotte Rose
Josepha Corinne Hyman, Eliot Augustin Stanley Hyman, Rowan
Newbold Stephenson, Freya Helen Stephenson, Indie Sphere
Hyman, Sophie Joy Hyman, and Thomas Achita Hyman.*

Margaret stood all alone at her first witch-burning. She had on her new blue cap and her sister's shawl, and she stood by herself, waiting. She had long ago given up on finding her sister and brother-in-law in the crowd, and was now content to watch alone. She felt a very pleasant fear and a crying excitement over the burning; she had lived all her life in the country and now, staying with her sister in the city, she was being introduced to the customs of society.

—SHIRLEY JACKSON

Shirley Jackson

SHIRLEY JACKSON, WHOSE SHORT STORY "THE LOTTERY" FIRMLY established her as a master of the American short story, was born in San Francisco on December 14, 1916. She grew up in the affluent suburb of Burlingame, California, a community whose prejudice and wickedness Jackson savaged in her first novel, *The Road Through the Wall* (1948). Upon graduation from Syracuse University in 1940 she married fellow student (and future literary critic) Stanley Edgar Hyman and eventually settled in New York City. In 1945 Hyman joined the faculty of Bennington College, and the couple moved with their growing family to North Bennington, Vermont. Jackson artfully chronicled the joys and difficulties of bringing up four garrulous, rambunctious children in *Life Among the Savages* (1953) and *Raising Demons* (1957), two works that place her among the front ranks of contemporary American humorists.

"I find [writing] relaxing," Jackson once remarked. "There is delight in seeing a story grow; it's so deeply satisfying—like having a winning streak in poker." Her first nationally published short story, "My Life with R. H. Macy," appeared in *The New Republic* in 1941.

Jackson's most famous story, "The Lottery," was printed in *The New Yorker* on June 26, 1948. It prompted an unprecedented reaction from readers, most of whom felt betrayed by the story's unexpected, gruesome ending. "I have been assured over and over that if it had been the only story I ever wrote or published, there would be people who would not forget my name," confessed Jackson. "Of the three-hundred-odd letters that I received that summer I can count only thirteen that spoke kindly to me, and they were mostly from friends. Even my mother scolded me." Her first collection of short fiction, *The Lottery; or, The Adventures of James Harris,* came out in 1949. In the children's book *The Witchcraft of Salem Village* (1956) she attempted to explain in simplified terms the seeming madness that swept seventeenth-century Salem.

Jackson enhanced her reputation as a literary master with a succession of Gothic novels. *Hangsaman* (1951) tells of a shy, sensitive adolescent who escapes parental oppression by retreating into a nightmare fantasy world. *The Bird's Nest* (1954), a psychological thriller about a woman with multiple personalities, was made into the 1957 film *Lizzie*. In *The Sundial* (1958) Jackson offered up a satirical, apocalyptic novel about a group of people who await Armageddon in a secluded country estate. *The Haunting of Hill House* (1959), a bloodcurdling ghost story hailed by Stephen King as one of the greatest horror novels of all time, and a finalist for the National Book Award. *We Have Always Lived in the Castle* (1962) is the macabre tale of two sisters ostracized by a community for allegedly murdering the rest of their family. "Jackson was a master of complexity of mood, an ironic explorer of the dark conflicting inner tyrannies of the mind and soul," observed *New York Times* book critic Eliot Fremont-Smith.

Shirley Jackson died unexpectedly of heart failure on August 8, 1965. Stanley Edgar Hyman subsequently edited two omnibus collections of her work, *The Magic of Shirley Jackson* (1966) and *Come Along with Me* (1968). *Just an Ordinary Day,* a volume of

Jackson's unpublished and uncollected short fiction, appeared in 1997. "Everything this author wrote . . . has in it the dignity and plausibility of myth," said *The New York Times Book Review*. "Shirley Jackson knew better than any writer since Hawthorne the value of haunted things."

"I Think I Know Her"

by Ruth Franklin

In 1966, Stanley Edgar Hyman received a letter asking if he would consider donating his "literary manuscripts and personal papers" to the Library of Congress. At the time, Hyman was one of the most distinguished critics in the United States: a longtime staff writer at *The New Yorker*, former chief book reviewer for the opinion magazine *The New Leader*, and author of several erudite works of scholarship. As an aside, the letter mentioned that the Library would be interested also in the papers of Hyman's late wife, the writer Shirley Jackson, who had died suddenly the previous year at the age of forty-eight.

How taste changes. Today Hyman's rigorous, insightful work has been largely (and unjustly) forgotten, his once-admired books out of print for decades. Jackson's star, meanwhile, is steadily rising. At the time of her death, she was hardly unknown: the author of six completed novels, two memoirs, and dozens of published short stories, including, of course, "The Lottery," which became an instant classic upon its publication in *The New Yorker* in 1948 and remains a touchstone of midcentury American fiction. She was also an in-demand lecturer on the college circuit and at writers' conferences such as Bread Loaf, as well as a highly compensated contributor to *The Saturday Evening Post* and other glossy magazines. Yet—perhaps in part because of her popular appeal and her frequent appearances in women's magazines rather than the prominent intellectual organs of the time—Jackson's work, unlike her husband's, was not yet perceived as an essential piece of American literary history, important to preserve. That, too, would change.

The Shirley Jackson Papers at the Manuscript Division of the Library of Congress fill more than fifty boxes. (Hyman's archive, which followed after his own early death, in 1970, is now stored off-site.) Like many creative thinkers, Jackson thrived amid chaos, and her files mimic her overstuffed desk: pencil sketches and watercolor paintings; meticulously kept diet logs and appointment calendars; postcards, magazine clippings, and other visual sources of inspiration; multiple drafts of novels and stories; scattered dream notes and diary entries, often stashed among the pages of whatever else she was working on at the time; even Christmas and grocery lists ("5 lbs top round, 12 lamb chops, box minute rice, can pineapple chunks, Pepperidge French bread, Puilly-Fuisse"). In the lecture published here as "How I Write," Jackson comments that the "storeroom" in her mind for the "hundreds of small items" and ideas she might someday use in her fiction "must look a good deal like my desk drawers, which also contain all kinds of things I am sure I am going to need someday." In the preliminary stage of her writing process, she continues, she likes to keep "pads of paper and pencils all over the house," so that if an idea comes to her while she is doing something else, she can "race to the nearest paper and pencil and write it down, frequently addressing it to myself, in my own kind of short-hand dialect." Many of those scribbles, too, survive, puzzling the researcher with their cryptic notations: "Grock—pantomime/

pathos/ex tempore . . . Harpo Marx, Chaplin." Indecipherable when I first encountered it a few years ago, this particular note now reveals its meaning as part of the writing process for "Clowns," published in *Vogue* in May 1949 and reprinted here.

Most significant, Jackson's files contain also an astonishing amount of unpublished material, nearly all of it neatly typed on her signature yellow copy paper. The pieces range from fragments of a page or less to works that were completed but not published during her lifetime. Nearly two decades ago, two of Jackson's children, Laurence Jackson Hyman and Sarah Hyman DeWitt, gathered fifty-four stories in *Just an Ordinary Day*, bringing together powerful works of literary fiction such as "The Possibility of Evil" with lighter stories and humorous household chronicles beloved by their mother's women's magazine readers. Now *Let Me Tell You* showcases Jackson's work in even greater depth and variety. A few of these stories appeared recently in *The New Yorker* and other magazines; others have not seen the light of day since their publication in the 1940s or '50s; still others have never been published before at all.

A brief note on Jackson's several modes of writing is in order here. She herself distinguished between her serious fiction and the less complex, cheerier pieces demanded by her editors at *McCall's*, *Collier's*, and other "slicks," as they were called at the time. "At a thousand bucks a story, I can't afford to try to change the state of popular fiction today," she responded when her mother remarked that a few of those stories weren't up to Jackson's usual standard. Yet it's worth remembering that this was an era in which women's (as well as men's) magazines published significant literary fiction: Readers of *Mademoiselle* might find a story by Jackson in one issue and stories by Truman Capote or Jean Stafford in another. Many of Jackson's stories blurred the line between literary and popular: One of the stories here, "The Lie," about a woman's lingering guilt over her betrayal of a former classmate, was considered for publication by both *The New Yorker* and *Good Housekeeping*. Jackson also had a tremendous gift for warm, funny chronicles of life with children, represented in this collection by pieces like "Out of the Mouths of Babes," in which the children inadvertently spread gossip about the family ("You should have heard what Mommy said when the car wouldn't start"). Long before Jean Kerr's *Please Don't Eat the Daisies* or Erma Bombeck's *At Wit's End*, Jackson essentially invented the form that has become the modern-day "mommy blog." Her sympathetic, open-minded perspective on children and their imagination is evident in the homage here to Dr. Seuss, in which Jackson complains of her frustration when a publisher who had asked her to contribute to a series of children's books presented her with a list of "suitable" words : " 'Getting' and 'spending' were on the list, but not 'wishing'; 'cost' and 'buy' and 'nickel' and 'dime' were all on the list, but not 'magic.' . . . I felt that the children for whom I was supposed to write were being robbed, persuaded to accept nickels and dimes instead of magic wishes." Jackson must have had her way: The book she would write was called *9 Magic Wishes*.

Jackson wrote many of the stories in *Let Me Tell You* during the earliest years of her career, a period of impressive productivity as well as inspiring persistence. In 1943 and 1944, she published a dozen stories in *The New Yorker*, an astonishing achievement for an up-and-coming writer; yet for every piece the editors accepted, two or three others were sent back. Though the rejections stung, Jackson maintained her confidence in her work: A number of the pieces here, including "Remembrance of Things Past," "Gaudeamus Igitur," and the war stories, were earmarked for a short-story collection she shopped around in the mid-1940s. After she hit upon the organizing principle for the book of short fiction that would appear as *The Lottery; or, The Adventures of James Harris* (1949), some of those early stories dropped out. But Jackson never abandoned them entirely: After her great success with *The Haunting of Hill House* in 1959, her agent dusted off a few from the drawer and sold them.

Not surprisingly, more than a few of Jackson's early stories are preoccupied with World War II. Like the husband in "4-F Party," Hyman was rejected from the Army as physically unfit, owing to his poor eyesight (though he liked to joke that the Army doctor had told him he had the organs of a forty-year-old). But a number of the couple's friends served, and Jackson watched the war news closely. As a Gentile married to a Jew, she was well aware that if she and Hyman had been living in Europe, the whole family—their first child, Laurence, was born in 1942—would have been sent to a concentration camp. (Something of Jackson's parents' antipathy to her marrying a Jew appears in "I Cannot Sing the Old Songs," in which a girl's parents disparage her plans to marry a man of whom they do not approve.) Jackson also sent food and clothing to a French exchange student she had befriended in college who wound up in a Paris prison for her work with the French Resistance. Still, the war appears in these stories primarily as a backdrop to the human dramas: the wives (loyal and less so) left behind, the children taken aback by a father's sudden reappearance. In "As High as the Sky," the mother inspects her children as they sit together on the couch, "with just the table lamp turned on in back of them, the light softly touching the tops of their heads and the bowl of flowers behind Sandra's shoulder," anxious that their father be greeted by a model tableau of family life. "Homecoming" emphasizes the wife's anticipation of her husband's return and the pleasure she takes in the necessary housekeeping duties: "This is the part of the house he never sees, that no one ever knows about," she muses before her open linen closet. "The laundry when it comes back, the wash on the line fresh from the tubs. . . . Women with homes live so closely with substances, bread, soap, and buttons."

Jackson, too, considered herself at least a part-time housewife, and the life of a house—what is required to make and keep a home, and what it means when a home is destroyed—is important in just about all of her novels. ("I love houses" is the opening line of "The Ghosts of Loiret," a humorous take on Jackson's real-life search for a haunted house she could use as a model for Hill House.) But the organized linen closet was more a fantasy than a standard she strived to uphold. More often than not, housekeeping done too perfectly in a Jackson story is a sign that something is wrong. In "Mrs. Spencer and the Oberons," it is the disagreeable Mrs. Spencer whose kitchen is "immaculate, dinner preparing invisibly"; the bustling hospitality of the unconventional Oberons, which Mrs. Spencer cannot appreciate, signals comfort and cheer. As the nonfiction collected here demonstrates, Jackson made no pretense of being a flawless housekeeper, "trim and competent"; unlike her neighbors, she inevitably found herself as she does in "Here I Am, Washing Dishes Again"— with the dishpan heaped high, inventing stories to carry her through the task. Close readers of "The Lottery"—Jackson's tale of a ritual stoning carried out in an ordinary village, which was written around the same time as that essay—will remember that one of the main characters arrives late to the village square because she was finishing her dishes. Another echo of "The Lottery," and its warning about the dangers of conformity, appears in the unlikely setting of "Mother, Honestly!," a humor piece about raising a pre-teenager. In Jackson's hands, the classic adolescent complaint—"Everyone else is allowed to"—becomes an alarming sign of groupthink: Even to write the phrase "everyone else," she confesses, gives her "a little chill."

A highlight of this collection, especially for aspiring writers, is the craft lectures, in which Jackson, via anecdotes and analyses of her own work, shares succinct, specific advice about creating fiction. Her diversity of themes notwithstanding, Jackson's style remained consistent from her earliest stories to her late novels. One of its hallmarks is her uncanny ability to seize the telling detail—what she calls, in the lecture "Garlic in Fiction," the accent that when used "sparingly and with great care" gives a little extra emphasis to certain moments in a story. In "The Arabian Nights," the way a couple pick up and set down their cocktail glasses tells us everything we need to know about their marriage; in "Paranoia," the light-colored hat worn by the man following Mr. Beresford takes on its own malevolent power. Jackson explains that she generated credibility for Eleanor, the protagonist in *Hill House*, by carefully layering symbols—the cottage with the white cat on the step, the little girl who insists on drinking out of a cup painted with stars—to ease the transition from "the sensible environment of the city to the somewhat less believable atmosphere of the haunted house." ("This was hard," she admits.) In "Memory and Delusion," she emphasizes that the writer's intelligence must be constantly alert: "I cannot find any patience for those people who believe that you start writing when you sit down at your desk and pick up your pen and finish writing when you put down your pen again; a writer is always writing, seeing everything through a thin mist of words, fitting swift little descriptions to everything he sees, always noticing." For the writer, "all things are potential paragraphs," but their emotional valence remains to be determined. When a green porcelain bowl on the piano suddenly shatters during a bridge game, Jackson keeps the image of the scattered pieces in her memory storeroom, waiting for the right moment to deploy it: as a symbol of destruction ("what I can remember is the way the little pieces of the bowl lay there so quietly after they had been for so long parts of one unbroken whole"), or as an illustration of a sudden shock, or to represent the loss of a treasured possession. This image would appear, in different form, in *We Have Always Lived in the Castle*, her last completed novel, when one of the characters discovers the family's heirloom sugar bowl—an important symbol—in pieces.

Let Me Tell You contains a multitude of Shirley Jacksons. The whimsical fantasy of pieces like "Six A.M. Is the Hour" (about a poker game played by the Norse gods in which the jackpot is Earth) and "Bulletin" (a science fiction depiction of how a future society will understand life in 1950) may surprise readers who are expecting more fiction in the suspenseful mode of the Kafkaesque tale "Paranoia." Some of the pieces here are alternate versions of published material: "Company for Dinner," in which a man accidentally comes home to the wrong house, anticipates the more complex spin Jackson would give to a similar theme in "The Beautiful Stranger," and both "Still Life with Teapot and Students" and "Family Treasures" are variations on scenes she would develop differently in *Hangsaman*, her second novel. A notable absence from the fiction in this collection is the interest in the supernatural that would characterize so much of her work: There is nothing here along the lines of "The Daemon Lover," her retelling of the James Harris legend, in which a woman is jilted by a fiancé who may or may not actually exist. Only "The Man in the Woods," a fable incorporating different strands of mythology, hits some similar notes.

As her biographer, the question constantly on my mind is which Shirley Jackson was—as one of the pieces here is titled—"The Real Me." This collection alone offers a multitude of possibilities. The professional who stood at the lectern, delivering confident advice to her rapt audience? The housewife dreaming up a paean to her fork? The mother who laughs over her children's idiosyncrasies even as she chides them for their bad behavior? The amateur witch who lovingly enumerates her collection of curiosities ("I have a crystal ball and a deck of tarot cards and a lot of tikis and eleven Siamese gambling house tokens and a book by Ludovico Sinistrari listing all the demons by name and incantation") and writes only half-jokingly of digging for mandrakes in the backyard? The engaged parent who cheerfully creates and produces a play for her children's school, or the semi-recluse who confesses at one point, "I don't think I like reality very much"? In an early diary, Jackson once referred to "this compound of creatures I call Me." Of course, they are all one— which is the central mystery of any personality.

In the end, I return to the mental image of Jackson that has come to me over the years I have spent examining her papers. I imagine her at her overstuffed desk, its surface crowded with all the usual tidbits: an old postcard or two, drafts of three different stories, part of an unfinished letter. She might have only a few minutes—perhaps the children are about to arrive home from school, or her husband might call out from his study to ask for her opinion on something, or she has to start dinner. Absently she pulls out a note from the pocket of her dress and examines it. Then she rolls a blank sheet of yellow paper into her Royal typewriter and begins.

RUTH FRANKLIN is a book critic and author of *A Thousand Darknesses: Lies and Truth in Holocaust Fiction*, which was a finalist for the 2012 Sami Rohr Prize in Jewish Literature. She has written for many publications, including *The New Republic, The New Yorker, The New York Review of Books, The New York Times Magazine, Bookforum,* and *Granta.* She is at work on a biography of Shirley Jackson.

"I just like the binding, that's all."

Contents

I
Sudden and Unusual Things Have Happened
Unpublished and Uncollected Short Fiction

. . .

II
I Would Rather Write Than Do Anything Else
Essays and Reviews

III
When This War Is Over
Early Short Stories

IV

Somehow Things Haven't Turned Out Quite the Way We Expected

Humor and Family

• • •

V

I'd Like to See You Get Out of *That* Sentence

Lectures About the Craft of Writing

• • •

I

. . .

Sudden and Unusual Things Have Happened

Unpublished and Uncollected Short Fiction

"I have never liked the theory that poltergeists only come into houses where there are children, because I think it is simply too much for any one house to have poltergeists and children."

Paranoia

MR. HALLORAN BERESFORD, PLEASANTLY TIRED AFTER A GOOD DAY in the office, still almost clean-shaven after eight hours, his pants still neatly pressed, pleased with himself particularly for remembering, stepped out of the candy shop with a great box under his arm and started briskly for the corner. There were twenty small-size gray suits like Mr. Beresford's on every New York block, fifty men still clean-shaven and pressed after a day in an air-cooled office, a hundred small men, perhaps, pleased with themselves for remembering their wives' birthdays. Mr. Beresford was going to take his wife out to dinner, he decided, going to see if he could get last-minute tickets to a show, taking his wife candy. It had been an exceptionally good day, altogether, and Mr. Beresford walked along swiftly, humming musically to himself.

He stopped on the corner, wondering whether he would save more time by taking a bus or by trying to catch a taxi in the crowd. It was a long trip downtown, and Mr. Beresford ordinarily enjoyed the quiet half hour on top of a Fifth Avenue bus, perhaps reading his paper. He disliked the subway intensely, and found the public display and violent exercise necessary to catch a taxi usually more than he was equal to. However, tonight he had spent a lot of time waiting in line in the candy store to get his wife's favorite chocolates, and if he was going to get home before dinner was on the table he really had to hurry a little.

Mr. Beresford went a few steps into the street, waved at a taxi, said "Taxi!" in a voice that went helplessly into a falsetto, and slunk back, abashed, to the sidewalk while the taxi went by uncomprehending. A man in a light hat stopped next to Mr. Beresford on the sidewalk, and for a minute, in the middle of the crowd, he stared at Mr. Beresford and Mr. Beresford stared at him as people sometimes do without caring particularly what they see. What Mr. Beresford saw was a thin face under the light hat, a small mustache, a coat collar turned up. Funny-looking guy, Mr. Beresford thought, lightly touching his own clean-shaven lip. Perhaps the man thought Mr. Beresford's almost unconscious gesture was offensive; at any rate he frowned and looked Mr. Beresford up and down before he turned away. Ugly customer, Mr. Beresford thought.

The Fifth Avenue bus Mr. Beresford usually took came slipping up to the corner, and Mr. Beresford, pleased not to worry about a taxi, started for the stop. He had reached out his hand to take the rail inside the bus door when he was roughly elbowed aside and the ugly customer in the light hat shoved on ahead of him. Mr. Beresford muttered and started to follow, but the bus door closed on the packed crowd inside, and the last thing Mr. Beresford saw as the bus went off down the street was the man in the light hat grinning at him from inside the door.

"*There's* a dirty trick," Mr. Beresford told himself, settling his shoulders irritably in his coat. Still under the influence of his annoyance, he ran a few steps out into the street and waved again at a taxi, not trusting his voice, and was almost run down by a delivery truck. As Mr. Beresford skidded back to the sidewalk, the truck driver leaned out and yelled something unrecognizable at Mr. Beresford, and when Mr. Beresford saw the people around him on the corner laughing he decided to start walking downtown; in two blocks he would reach another bus stop, a good corner for taxis, and a subway station; much as Mr. Beresford disliked the subway, he might still have to take it, to get home in any sort of time. Walking downtown, his candy box under his arm, his gray suit almost unaffected by the crush on the corner, Mr. Beresford decided to swallow his annoyance and remember that it was his wife's birthday; he began to hum again as he walked.

He watched the people as he walked along, his perspective sharpened by being a man who had just succeeded in forgetting an annoyance; surely the girl in the very high-heeled shoes, coming toward him with a frown on her face, was not so able to put herself above petty trifles, or maybe she was frowning because of the shoes; the old lady and man looking at the shop windows were quarreling. The funny-looking guy in the light hat coming quickly through the crowd looked as though he hated someone . . . the funny-looking guy in the light hat; Mr. Beresford turned clean around in the walking line of people and watched the man in the light hat turn abruptly and start walking downtown, about ten feet in back of Mr. Beresford. What do you know about that?, Mr. Beresford marveled, and began to walk a little more quickly. Probably got off the bus for some reason; wrong bus, maybe. Then why would he start walking uptown instead of catching another bus where he was? Mr. Beresford shrugged and passed two girls walking together and talking both at once.

Halfway from the corner he wanted, Mr. Beresford realized with a sort of sick shock that the man in the light hat was at his elbow, walking steadily along next to him. Mr. Beresford turned his head the other way and slowed his step. The other man slowed down as well, without looking at Mr. Beresford.

Nonsense, Mr. Beresford thought, without troubling to work it out any further than that. He settled his candy box firmly under his arm and cut abruptly across the uptown line of people and into a shop; a souvenir and notions shop, he realized as he came through the door. There were a few people inside—a woman and a little girl, a sailor—and Mr. Beresford retired to the far end of the counter and began to fuss with an elaborate cigarette box on which was written SOUVENIR OF NEW YORK CITY, with the Trylon and the Perisphere painted beneath.

"Isn't this cute?" the mother said to the little girl, and they both began to laugh enormously over the match holder made in the form of a toilet; the matches were to go in the bowl, and on the cover, Mr. Beresford could see, were the Trylon and the Perisphere, with SOUVENIR OF NEW YORK CITY written above.

The man in the light hat came into the shop, and Mr. Beresford turned his back and busied himself picking up one thing after another from the counter; with half his mind he was trying to find something that did not say SOUVENIR OF NEW YORK CITY, and with the other half of his mind he was wondering about the man in the light hat. The question of what the man in the light hat wanted was immediately subordinate to the question of *whom* he wanted; if his light-hatted designs were against Mr. Beresford they must be nefarious, else why had he not announced them before now? The thought of accosting the man and demanding his purpose crossed Mr. Beresford's mind fleetingly, and was succeeded, as always in an equivocal situation, by Mr. Beresford's vivid recollection of his own small size and innate cautiousness. Best, Mr. Beresford decided, to avoid this man. Thinking this, Mr. Beresford walked steadily toward the doorway of the shop, intending to pass the man in the light hat and go out and catch his bus home.

He had not quite reached the man in the light hat when the shop's clerk came around the end of the counter and met Mr. Beresford with a genial smile and a vehement "See anything you like, mister?"

"Not tonight, thanks," Mr. Beresford said, moving left to avoid the clerk, but the clerk moved likewise and said, "Got some nice things you didn't look at."

"No, thanks," Mr. Beresford said, trying to make his tenor voice firm.

"Take a look," the clerk insisted. This was unusually persistent even for such a clerk; Mr. Beresford looked up and saw the man in the light hat on his right, bearing down on him. Over the shoulders of the two men he could see that the shop was empty. The street looked very far away, the people passing in either direction looked smaller and smaller; Mr. Beresford realized that he was being forced to step backward as the two men advanced on him.

"Easy does it," the man in the light hat said to the clerk. They continued to move forward slowly.

"See here, now," Mr. Beresford said, with the ineffectuality of the ordinary man caught in such a crisis; he still clutched his box of candy under his arm. "See *here*," he said, feeling the solid weight of the wall behind him.

"Ready," the man in the light hat said. The two men tensed, and Mr. Beresford, with a wild yell, broke between them and ran for the door. He heard a sound more like a snarl than anything else behind him and the feet coming after him. I'm safe on the street, Mr. Beresford thought as he went through the door into the line of people; as long as there are lots of people, they can't do anything to me. He looked back, walking downtown between a fat woman with many packages and a girl and a boy leaning on each other's shoulders, and he saw the clerk standing in the doorway of the shop looking after him; the man in the light hat was not in sight. Mr. Beresford shifted the box of candy so that his right arm was free, and thought, Perfectly silly. It's still broad daylight. How they ever hoped to get away with it . . .

The man in the light hat was on the corner ahead, waiting. Mr. Beresford hesitated in his walk and then thought, It's preposterous, all these people watching. He walked boldly down the street; the man in the light hat was not even watching him, but was leaning calmly against a building lighting a cigarette. Mr. Beresford reached the corner, darted quickly into the street, and yelled boisterously "Taxi!" in a great voice he had never suspected he possessed until now. A taxi stopped as though not daring to disregard that great shout, and Mr. Beresford moved gratefully toward it. His hand was on the door handle when another hand closed over his, and Mr. Beresford was aware of the light hat brushing his cheek.

"Come on if you're coming," the taxi driver said; the door was open, and Mr. Beresford, resisting the push that urged him into the taxi, slipped his hand out from under the other hand and ran back to the sidewalk. A crosstown bus had stopped on the corner, and Mr. Beresford, no longer thinking, hurried onto it, dropped a nickel into the coin register, and went to the back of the bus and sat down. The man in the light hat sat a little ahead, between Mr. Beresford and the door. Mr. Beresford put his box of candy on his lap and tried to think. Obviously the man in the light hat was not carrying a grudge all this time about Mr. Beresford's almost unconscious gesture toward his mustache, unless he was peculiarly sensitive. In any case, there was also the clerk in the souvenir shop; Mr. Beresford realized suddenly that the clerk in the souvenir shop was a very odd circumstance indeed. Mr. Beresford set the clerk aside to think about later and went back to the man in the light hat. If it was not the insult to the mustache, what was it? And then another thought caught Mr. Beresford breathless: How long, then, had the man in the light hat been following him? He thought back along the day: He had left his office with a group of people, all talking cheerfully, all reminding Mr. Beresford that it was his wife's birthday; they had escorted Mr. Beresford to the candy shop and left him there. He had been in his office all day except for lunch with three fellows in the office; Mr. Beresford's mind leaped suddenly from the lunch to his first sight of the man in the light hat at the bus stop; it seemed that the man in the light hat had been trying to push him *onto* the bus and into the crowd, instead of pushing in ahead. In that case, once he was on the bus . . . Mr. Beresford looked around. In the bus he was riding on now there were only five people left. One was the driver, one Mr. Beresford, one the man in the light hat, sitting slightly ahead of Mr. Beresford. The two others were an old lady with a shopping bag and a man who looked as though he might be a foreigner. Foreigner, Mr. Beresford thought, while he looked at the man. Foreigner, foreign plot, spies. Better not rely on any foreigner, Mr. Beresford thought.

The bus was going swiftly along between high dark buildings. Mr. Beresford, looking out the window, decided that they were in a factory district, remembered that they had been going east, and decided to wait until they got to one of the lighted, busy sections before he tried to get off. Peering off into the growing darkness, Mr. Beresford noticed an odd thing. There had been someone standing on the corner beside a sign saying BUS STOP and the bus had not stopped, even though the dim figure waved its arms. Surprised, Mr. Beresford glanced up at the street sign, noticing that it said E. 31 ST. at the same moment he reached for the cord to signal the driver that he wanted to get off. As he stood up and went down the aisle, the foreign-looking man rose also and went to the door beside the driver. "Getting off," the foreign man said, and the bus slowed. Mr. Beresford pressed forward, and somehow the old lady's shopping bag got in his way and spilled, sending small items, a set of blocks, a package of paper clips, spilling in all directions.

"Sorry," Mr. Beresford said desperately as the bus doors opened. He began to move forward again, and the old lady caught his arm and said, "Don't bother if you're in a hurry. I can get them, dear." Mr. Beresford tried to shake her off, and she said, "If this is your stop, don't worry. It's perfectly all right."

A coil of pink ribbon was caught around Mr. Beresford's shoe; the old lady said, "It was clumsy of me, leaving my bag right in the aisle."

As Mr. Beresford broke away from her, the doors closed and the bus started. Resigned, Mr. Beresford got down on one knee in the swaying bus and began to pick up paper clips, blocks, a box of letter paper that had opened and spilled sheets and envelopes all over the floor. "I'm so sorry," the old lady said sweetly. "It was all my fault, too."

Over his shoulder, Mr. Beresford saw the man in the light hat sitting comfortably. He was smoking, and his head was thrown back and his eyes were shut. Mr. Beresford gathered together the old lady's possessions as well as he could, then made his way forward to stand by the driver. "Getting off," Mr. Beresford said.

"Can't stop in the middle of the block," the driver said, not turning his head.

"The next stop, then," Mr. Beresford said.

The bus moved rapidly on. Mr. Beresford, bending down to see the streets out the front window, saw a sign saying BUS STOP.

"Here," he said.

"What?" the driver said, going past.

"Listen," Mr. Beresford said. "I want to get off."

"It's okay with me," the driver said. "Next stop."

"You just passed one," Mr. Beresford said.

"No one waiting there," the driver said. "Anyway, you didn't tell me in time." Mr. Beresford waited. After a minute he saw another bus stop and said, "Okay."

The bus did not stop, but went past the sign without slowing down.

"Report me," the driver said.

"Listen, now," Mr. Beresford said, and the driver turned one eye up at him; he seemed to be amused.

"Report me," the driver said. "My number's right here on this card."

"If you don't stop at the next stop," Mr. Beresford said, "I shall smash the glass in the door and shout for help."

"What with?" the driver said. "That box of candy?"

"How do you know it's—" Mr. Beresford said before he realized that if he got into a conversation he would miss the next bus stop. It had not occurred to him that he could get off anywhere except at a bus stop; he saw lights ahead, and at the same time the bus slowed down and Mr. Beresford, looking quickly back, saw the man in the light hat stretch and get up.

The bus pulled to a stop in front of a bus sign; there was a group of stores.

"OKAY," the bus driver said to Mr. Beresford, "you were so anxious to get off." The man in the light hat got off at the rear door. Mr. Beresford, standing by the open front door, hesitated and said, "I guess I'll stay on for a while."

"Last stop," the bus driver said. "Everybody off." He looked sardonically up at Mr. Beresford. "Report me if you want to," he said. "My number's right on that card there."

Mr. Beresford got off and went directly up to the man in the light hat, standing on the sidewalk. "This is perfectly ridiculous," he said emphatically. "I don't understand any of it, and I want you to know that the first policeman I see—"

He stopped when he realized that the man in the light hat was looking not at him but, bored and fixedly, over his shoulder. Mr. Beresford turned and saw a policeman standing on the corner.

"Just you wait," he said to the man in the light hat, and started for the policeman. Halfway to the policeman he began to wonder again: What did he have to report? A bus driver who would not stop when directed to, a clerk in a souvenir shop who cornered customers, a mysterious man in a light hat—and why? Mr. Beresford realized that there was nothing he could tell the policeman; he looked over his shoulder and saw the man in the light hat watching him, then Mr. Beresford bolted suddenly down a subway entrance. He had a nickel in his hand by the time he reached the bottom of the steps, and he went right through the turnstile; to the left was downtown, and he ran that way.

He was figuring as he ran: He'll think if I'm very stupid I'd head downtown, if I'm smarter than that I'd go uptown, if I'm really smart I'd go downtown. Does he think I'm middling smart or very smart?

The man in the light hat reached the downtown platform only

a few seconds after Mr. Beresford and sauntered down the platform, his hands in his pockets. Mr. Beresford sat down on the bench listlessly. It's no good, he thought, no good at all; he knows just how smart I am.

The train came blasting into the station; Mr. Beresford ran into one car and saw the light hat disappear into the next car. Just as the doors were closing, Mr. Beresford dived, caught the door, and would have been out except for a girl who seized his arm and shouted, "Harry! Where in God's name are you going?"

The door was held halfway open by Mr. Beresford's body, his arm left inside with the girl, who seemed to be holding it with all her strength. "Isn't this a fine thing," she said to the people in the car. "He sure doesn't want to see his old friends."

A few people laughed; most of them were watching.

"Hang on to him, sister," someone said.

The girl laughed and tugged on Mr. Beresford's arm. "He's gonna get away," she said laughingly to the people in the car, and a big man stepped up to her with a grin and said, "If you gotta have him that bad, we'll bring him in for you."

Mr. Beresford felt the grasp on his arm turn suddenly into an irresistible force that drew him in through the doors, and they closed behind him. Everyone in the car was laughing at him by now, and the big man said, "That ain't no way to treat a lady, chum."

Mr. Beresford looked around for the girl, but she had melted into the crowd somewhere and the train was moving. After a minute the people in the car stopped looking at him, and Mr. Beresford smoothed his coat and found that his box of candy was still intact.

The subway train was going downtown. Mr. Beresford, who was now racking his brains for detective tricks, for mystery-story dodges, thought of one that seemed foolproof. He stayed docilely on the train, as it went downtown, and got a seat at Twenty-third Street. At Fourteenth he got off, the light hat following, and went up the stairs and into the street. As he had expected, the large department store ahead of him advertised OPEN TILL 9 TONIGHT, and the doors swung wide, back and forth, with people going constantly in and out. Mr. Beresford went in. The store bewildered him at first—counters stretching away in all directions, the lights much brighter than anywhere else, the voices clamoring. Mr. Beresford moved slowly along beside a counter; it was stockings first, thin and tan and black and gauzy, and then it was handbags, piles on sale, neat solitary ones in the cases, and then it was medical supplies, with huge almost-human figures wearing obscene trusses, standing right there on the counter, and people coming embarrassedly to buy. Mr. Beresford turned the corner and came to a counter of odds and ends. Scarves too cheap to be at the scarf counter, postcards, a bin marked ANY ITEM 25¢, dark glasses. Uncomfortably, Mr. Beresford bought a pair of dark glasses and put them on.

He went out of the store at an entrance far away from the one he had used to come in; he could have chosen any of eight or nine entrances, but this seemed complicated enough. There was no sign of the light hat, no one tried to hinder Mr. Beresford as he stepped up to the taxi stand, and, although he debated taking the second or third car, he finally took the one in front and gave his home address.

He reached his apartment building without mishap, and stole cautiously out of the taxi and into the lobby. There was no light hat, no odd person watching for Mr. Beresford. In the elevator, alone, with no one to see which floor button he pressed, Mr. Beresford took a long breath and began to wonder if he had dreamed his wild trip home. He rang his apartment bell and waited; then his wife came to the door, and Mr. Beresford, suddenly tired out, went into his home.

"You're *terribly* late, darling," his wife said affectionately, and then, "But what's the matter?"

He looked at her; she was wearing her blue dress, and that meant she knew it was her birthday and expected him to take her out; he handed her the box of candy limply and she took it, hardly noticing it in her anxiety over him. "What on *earth* has happened?" she asked. "Darling, come in here and sit down. You look terrible."

He let her lead him into the living room, into his own chair, where it was comfortable, and he lay back.

"Is there something wrong?" she was asking anxiously, fussing over him, loosening his tie, smoothing his hair. "Are you sick? Were you in an accident? What *has* happened?"

He realized that he seemed more tired than he really was, and was glorying in all this attention. He sighed deeply and said, "Nothing. Nothing wrong. Tell you in a minute."

"Wait," she said. "I'll get you a drink."

He put his head back against the soft chair as she went out. Never knew that door had a key, his mind registered dimly as he heard it turn. Then he was on his feet with his head against the door listening to her at the telephone in the hall.

She dialed and waited. Then: "Listen," she said, "listen, he came here after all. I've got him."

Still Life with Teapot and Students

COME OFF IT, KIDS, COME OFF IT, LOUISE HARLOWE TOLD HERSELF just under her breath. She smiled graciously at her husband, Lionel's, two best students, noticing with an edge of viciousness that they both held their teacups exactly right, and said lightly, "You're going to have a pleasant summer, then?"

Joan shrugged perfectly, and Debbi smiled back, as graciously as Louise had smiled, but with more conviction. "It will be about the same as the others, I guess," Debbi said. "Sort of dull."

They're both too well bred to tell me what they'll be doing, Louise thought, and asked deliberately, "You'll be together, of course?"

"I suppose," Joan said. She looked inquiringly at Debbi, and Debbi, who was the talkative one, said "We're going to my family's summer place, most of the time."

"You won't be home, then?" Louise said to Joan, a remark first to one, then to the other; how perfectly they guided her.

"Mom's in Europe, of course," Joan said. "I may go to my brother's for a while."

Joan's brother, Louise knew perfectly well, was the well-known painter. Her mother was the dress designer. Debbi's father owned the meatpacking company that provided all the tinned meat Louise Harlowe bought at her grocery. Another of Lionel's students was the daughter of the family that owned the newspaper Louise and Lionel read. Still another had a father who directed the movies Louise and Lionel saw when they could afford it. We must have been crazy to let Lionel take this job, Louise thought briefly, and smiled again at Debbi—was it Debbi's turn?—and said, "Going to do any writing this summer?"

Debbi grinned, her own grin and not the polite smile she reserved for tea parties with faculty wives. "I hope," she said.

It cleared the air a little; the question had been so patently ridiculous. Louise's own picture of the summer Debbi and Joan would find so dull involved a montage of sailboats, country club dances, expensive evening gowns, and good scotch. What cleared the air was that Debbi and Joan knew she knew.

"Okay," Louise said. "You know I can't offer you a drink. So you might as well drink tea."

"I'll have some more then, if I may," Joan said. No matter what happens, Louise thought, touching the teapot lightly with her hand to test the heat, no matter what happens, they can't ask for more tea without the grace of those years of training, that subtle polish that comes from a lifetime of custom, in houses where nothing is finger-marked and nothing is chipped and the tea is always hot.

"It's not awfully warm," she said to Joan, mocking herself for saying "warm" instead of "hot"; who do I think I am? she wondered—Mrs. Astor? *My* brother sells insurance in New Jersey.

"That doesn't matter," Joan said. She accepted her cup and set it down on the table next to her; it doesn't matter a damn, Louise thought, she just won't drink it.

"So?" Louise said, leaning back against the couch cushions.

"So?" Debbi said. She and Joan looked at each other again, almost experimentally. Louise watched.

"You still making passes at my husband?" Louise asked deliberately of Joan, and was gratified to see them both blush. "Well?" she said.

"Look, Mrs. Harlowe," Joan said with a mild little laugh. "You know perfectly well—"

"I do indeed," Louise said. She waited again, still watching. The girls were tense, but not as tense as she was; they showed it more because they were younger and unprepared, and all of their training had not taught them what to do when they were attacked, because none of their training had ever anticipated that they might be exposed for anything, anywhere, at any time.

"Look," Joan tried helplessly, again. "Mrs. Harlowe, there's nothing between—"

Debbi decided to attack in her turn. "I don't think you have any right to say something like that to Joan, Mrs. Harlowe. After all—"

Louise laughed. "Listen," she said. "If I were someone like Ellen Thorndyke, Joan and I would be having a little heart-to-heart talk right now. Wouldn't we?"

Joan and Debbi both smiled reluctantly.

"Not that *that* did much good," Louise said, and then they all laughed aloud.

"It didn't, either," Debbi said. "That girl Dusty was so mad after Mrs. Thorndyke told her to lay off that—" She stopped abruptly.

"Exactly," Louise said.

"But, Mrs. Harlowe," Joan said. "Really, Mr. Harlowe and I—"

"Never mind," Louise said, perhaps a little too quickly. "Anyway, I won't be seeing either of you again, will I? I probably won't be at commencement tomorrow, and after that . . ."

"We won't be doing any writing this summer," Debbi said, with that same grin.

"I just wanted you to know," Louise said slowly, "that I'm glad you're going, even if I like you."

"I know you are," Joan said. There was a small silence, and then she went on. "I mean, I can see where you'd be glad to have—" She stopped, floundering.

Louise laughed, her first genuine laugh since she had opened the door for them. "You won't ever get out of *that* sentence," she said to Joan.

"Mrs. Harlowe," Debbi began suddenly; Debbi had been thinking. "Can I ask you something? I mean, would you be offended?"

"I don't think so," Louise said. Now it comes, she thought; now if I can't carry it off, I'm through.

Debbi searched for words, her alert, pretty face worried. "Why?" she asked. "Why don't you and Mrs. Thorndyke and Mrs. Crown and all the others just overlook it? I mean, the students all graduate and go away and there's no more to it. I mean, it's not anything serious, ever, is it?"

Please God, Louise thought, in the split second she had before she answered. "No," she said slowly, "it's certainly never serious—at least not for the teacher. I know that Lionel has told me about you, Joan, without ever thinking I'd mind anything so harmless as his being obsessed over one of his students. I know that Ellen Thorndyke was concerned because she thought that the girl was getting seriously involved." Louise remembered Ellen Thorndyke's face and thought, I could kill all these girls. "And I suppose we all feel pretty much the same way. Even though many of us aren't really much older than you are, we've all lived with these men for quite a while and we know a good deal more about them than you do, only seeing them occasionally." Keep it light, she told herself; keep it faintly patronizing. "It's very possible, you know, for a girl your age to get herself into serious trouble—with the college, with her family—"

"With his wife," Debbi said. "Bill Thorndyke's wife was so jealous she couldn't see."

Louise ran her finger softly along the design in the couch cushion. "I don't want to quarrel with you," she said. "Ellen Thorndyke is worth the whole pack of you."

"But she was jealous," Debbi said. "Dusty told us she cried."

I *could* kill them, Louise thought. "I hardly think that girl Dusty is any competent judge of emotions," she said, hearing her voice go full of hatred.

"Well, we've talked about it a lot," Debbi said seriously. "We've decided, among the students, that none of you could see your husbands go off to an office every day without worrying about his secretary. I mean, wives just *are* jealous, aren't they?"

Come off it, come off it, Louise thought; in my own country I was accounted quite a killer. "You may be married yourself someday," she said. "It's just possible."

"It's because you don't have anything to *do*," Joan said. "Anything better, I mean."

"What do *you* have to do?" Louise asked. Ellen Thorndyke was making a patchwork quilt, Jean Crown was growing orchids, Roberta Ewen had gone back to the piano. Suddenly Louise was aware that she had said all she had to say, that any more talking would destroy the handsome invulnerability she had set up for herself with such care, and she shrugged, as perfectly as Joan had shrugged a few minutes ago. "Well," she said. "There's no point in our arguing about it. After all, you two are leaving tomorrow."

She gave them the correct pause of attention to indicate that they might go. They needed no prompting—not two girls who were going to spend the summer drinking scotch on yachts. They both rose, getting out of their chairs as though they were at home and the chairs were handsome antiques. They both said "Thank you so much" in the correct tones and, without looking at each other, got themselves gracefully to the door. It was clearly understood between them that before they left they were going to have to say goodbye for good; Debbi started it.

"Mrs. Harlowe," she said, "I do want you to know that we appreciate all you've done."

"You've been very tolerant and sympathetic," Joan said.

"I've enjoyed it all so much," Louise said. "Being here at the college has been quite an experience for both Lionel and me." She laughed. "I think a year is enough, though."

"Lionel says he won't ever give up teaching," Joan said innocently.

Louise smiled at her beautifully. "Lionel," she said, emphasizing the word heavily, to make sure it carried to Joan, "Lionel has apparently been flattering you," she said.

She closed the door behind them, feeling ashamed of herself and afraid of seeing Lionel. There was still time for them to get to him before he came home; there was still time for Joan to tell him sweetly, "Mrs. Harlowe asked me —"

She went out into the kitchen and made herself a drink. So I did it, she told herself defiantly. He can't say a word without admitting everything. No more respect for his wife than that, she thought, every fat-faced little tomato who walks into his class. She took her drink back with her to the couch, and picked up the history book she was studying.

The Arabian Nights

ALICE WAS TWELVE; TO BE PRECISE, ALICE WAS TWELVE AND A DAY when she went to a famous nightclub with her mother and father and Mr. and Mrs. Carrington. The Carringtons were friends of her family's, and had just arrived that day from Chicago. "So Alice was twelve years old yesterday?" Mr. Carrington had said, looking down at Alice and grinning. "Don't you think that calls for a little celebration?" Mr. Carrington was big and cheerful and red-faced; when he said "a little celebration" it meant he wanted to spend money and show someone a good time.

Mrs. Carrington had red hair and was big and cheerful, like Mr. Carrington; Alice was very fond of both of them. "A girl's only young once," Mrs. Carrington had said. "This ought to be the finest celebration this old city has ever seen."

Alice's mother and father were cheerful people too, and they had seen to it that Alice had a very pretty twelfth birthday party; her father gave her a charm bracelet with a tiny silver cocktail shaker and glasses on it, which made her feel daring and sophisticated, and her mother gave her a manicure set with natural-color polish. Because Alice was an only child she felt very close to her mother and father, in spite of an uneasy feeling at times that they had a complete life apart from her. She knew that they were immensely popular people, that their friends were witty and charming, and that their books were good and their ideas modern; only occasionally did she wonder what they talked about all the time when they were with their friends, since they had so little to say to each other.

"Alice has never had a real grown-up celebration," her father said. He reached for Alice, who was standing next to him, and pulled her down onto his knee. "She's not a little girl anymore," her father said. "She's a young lady. What am I going to do," he asked Mr. Carrington, "when some young man comes along and wants to take her away from me?"

"Make sure he's rich," Mrs. Carrington said. "If I had a daughter I'd make sure she married a man who could support Charley and me in our old age."

"Stop mauling the child, Jamie," Alice's mother said. "She's too big, and it's undignified."

"Two days ago I could still hold her on my lap," Alice's father said, "but now that she's twelve I can't?"

"On my fiftieth birthday," Alice told her father, "I'll come around and sit on your lap."

Alice's father began to laugh. "See, honey," he said to his wife, "not everyone thinks it's undignified to sit on my lap."

Mrs. Carrington said quickly, "But what about this celebration? I propose that all of us go out somewhere to dinner, wherever Alice wants to go."

"I want to go to the Arabian Nights," Alice said, quickly. Everyone looked at her, and she blushed.

"What on earth?" her father said. He turned Alice's face around. "Why do you want to go there?"

Mr. Carrington was trying very hard not to laugh. "I don't blame her," he said. "I'd like to go there myself. Always did want to."

Alice held her breath. The Arabian Nights was a very big, very noisy, very famous nightclub; if she went there for dinner she could wear her new bracelet and her nail polish.

Alice's mother was laughing too. "She must have heard Jamie talking."

"I always wanted to go there," Alice said to Mr. Carrington.

"If that's where you want to have your birthday celebration," Mr. Carrington said. "Only there must be places you'd *rather* go?"

"Nowhere else," Alice said breathlessly. "I've been reading about it and hearing about it for a long time."

Mr. Carrington looked at Alice's father, and Alice's father nodded. Then Mr. Carrington looked at Alice's mother, and she hesitated, and then shrugged and smiled at Mrs. Carrington. Then Mr. Carrington turned to Alice. "I guess that's it, then, Alice," he said. "Shall I phone for a reservation?"

"Wear your blue dress," Alice's mother said, "and the bracelet your father gave you."

Alice sat between her father and Mr. Carrington with her nails shiny and pink beyond the bracelet, in the lavishly decorated Arabian Nights, at a table that had been especially reserved. She sat with her elbow on the edge of the table, and her chin in her hand, with her shoulders pulled tight together, and she looked disdainfully at the people sitting nearby. They're just like everyone else, she thought; I'm not afraid of any of them. When everyone had a drink—Mr. Carrington had ordered a glass of sherry for Alice—she picked it up and took a sip from it just like everyone else, and she watched how her mother toyed with the stem of her glass, and did the same thing. Seen through the glass, her fingers were long and thin.

When the floor show started, Alice had just begun her soup; her father and Mr. Carrington ate right on through in the almost-darkness and so did she. It's canned tomato soup, like at home, she thought with surprise. They were sitting very close to the stage, and everyone had taken care that Alice should sit where she could see everything. The comedians embarrassed her because it was necessary for her to pretend not to understand them when she saw her mother glance at her and then tighten her lips to keep from smiling. Her father and Mr. Carrington were watching her too, and she was proud when she realized she was acting exactly like everyone else. The dancers delighted her; one of them came down to the edge of the stage with a bowlful of gardenias to throw to the audience, and he saw Alice and tossed her one.

"We should have thought to get her some flowers," Mr. Carrington said as he pinned the gardenia onto Alice's shoulder.

Intermission arrived just in time for Alice to eat her steak. The lights all went on again, and everyone turned to Alice at once and began to talk.

"Do you like the show?" her mother said.

"How are you enjoying yourself?" Mr. Carrington asked.

"Want to go home yet?" her father said.

"You look very pretty, Alice," Mrs. Carrington said. Alice looked around at everyone and said: "I'm having a wonderful time. Everything's wonderful."

"Cigarette?" Mr. Carrington said to Alice very solemnly. Alice looked at her mother, and her mother shook her head. I suppose I can't have everything, Alice thought. "No, thank you," she said to Mr. Carrington. "I don't smoke." And Mr. Carrington, smiling, put the cigarette case away.

Alice's mother was staring off at the entrance, her eyes narrow and interested, and at the same time her hand was feeling around on the table for her bag; when her hand found it, she took out her compact, still without looking, then her lipstick and comb. Finally she dropped her eyes and hurriedly opened the compact and looked at herself, touched her nose with the powder puff and her hair with the comb, turning the compact to see the sides of her hair, and then she put on a little more lipstick, and raised her eyes again to the entrance. While she looked, her hands were busy again, putting everything back into her bag and the bag back onto the table. Then suddenly she turned to Mrs. Carrington. "Look," she said excitedly, "isn't that Clark Gable, coming in with that party? Over *there*." She gestured for Mrs. Carrington to look. "About three tables in back of Alice? I'm certain it is." Mr. Carrington and Alice's father were listening by this time; Mrs. Carrington gave one quick glance to the side.

"It certainly does look like him," she said.

Alice's father and Mr. Carrington both looked. "Sure, it's him," Mr. Carrington said.

"Major Gable," Alice's father said, "volunteered to be a top gunner during the war."

"Frankly, my dear, I don't give a damn," whispered Mrs. Carrington to Alice's mother.

Alice didn't turn around, because everyone else at the table had; people all over the room were looking too, and she felt oddly conspicuous because she was so close to Mr. Gable and at a table where everyone was turning around to look.

"How soon does the floor show start again?" she asked her father.

"Pretty soon," her father said absently. He was looking sideways at the famous man's table.

"I've always thought I'd like to be an actress," Alice's mother said gaily. Everyone laughed.

"Look over here, Gable," Mr. Carrington said softly, "I could use a million dollars."

"A man like that means glamour to a lot of people," Alice's father said. "Made six, eight movies with Jean Harlow!"

"I remember you playing Romeo in college," Alice's mother said. She took her eyes off the nearby table for a minute and looked at Alice's father. "You might be pretty," she said, "but you sure can't act."

Alice's father laughed again, unhappily. "I never had a chance to learn to be an actor anyway," he said. "By the time I was married and had a wife and baby—"

"Shh," Alice's mother said, "he's looking this way." She looked at Mr. Carrington and smiled vivaciously. "Aren't we silly," she said, and threw back her head and laughed. Mrs. Carrington joined in, nudging Mr. Carrington, and Mr. Carrington sat back and guffawed. Alice's father didn't laugh; he sat quietly with one hand over his eyes and the other before him on the table. Alice reached out and touched his hand. When he looked up she smiled embarrassedly, and he sighed and dropped his head to his hand again. Suddenly, Alice's mother stopped laughing and sat back in her chair. Mrs. Carrington looked around once, then picked up her glass and took a long drink from it.

Alice's mother said across the table to Alice's father: "You look like you just lost your last friend."

Alice's father dropped his hand from his eyes and sighed. "Just thinking," he said.

"About what you might have been if you hadn't had a wife and baby?" Alice's mother asked. Alice looked up, surprised at her mother's voice.

"'It seems too logical . . . I have missed everything, even my death,'" Alice's father said softly. He looked at Mrs. Carrington. "Cyrano," he said apologetically, then laughed sadly again.

"It's all right," Alice's mother said. "He isn't looking this way anymore."

"I'd like to meet that man," Mrs. Carrington said. "He looks so intelligent."

Alice's father looked up. "Alice!" he said, and everyone listened. "Why don't we have Alice go over and ask Gable for his autograph?" he said.

"She's only a child, she could do it," Alice's mother said.

"Say, you might even ask him to join us," Mr. Carrington said to Alice. "You know, just for a drink or something."

"Charley," Mrs. Carrington said reprovingly, "how could the child ask a man like that over for a drink? Anyway, he wouldn't dream of coming."

"He might," Alice's father said.

They're all thinking he'd look over here anyway, Alice thought, and see all of them and notice them, and maybe even bow to them on his way out. "I couldn't do that," she said.

"Don't be silly, darling," her mother told her. "You're only a child, it wouldn't look funny."

"She could say her mother—her mama—didn't want her to come over," Mrs. Carrington said, "but it's her birthday and she wanted to meet Clark Gable."

"I won't do it," Alice said.

"Alice!" her mother said.

"When I was your age," Mrs. Carrington said heavily, "little girls minded their mothers."

"Yes, indeed, Alice," her mother said. "You're not usually a disobedient child."

"Honey," her father said, "it's just a joke. You only pretend, don't you see?" He looks like the devil, she thought.

"I couldn't pretend to want his autograph," Alice said.

"Just tell him it's your birthday, then," Mr. Carrington said.

"I should think," Mrs. Carrington whispered, "that when a little girl gets taken out to a nice party and then someone asks her to do something, she'd do it and not be so silly about it."

"He's leaving," Alice's mother said in a flat voice. Everyone turned around to look. Then they looked back at Alice.

"It's too late now anyway," her father said.

"Well, it doesn't matter after all," Mr. Carrington said finally. "It wasn't important, Alice. Don't worry about it."

"I'm sorry," Alice said to her mother.

"It doesn't matter," her mother said.

The lights began to dim for the second half of the floor show. Alice put her hand on Mr. Carrington's arm. "Mr. Carrington," she said, "I've got a lot of algebra to do for tomorrow, so as soon as we finish dinner could we go home?" Mr. Carrington was moving his chair to see the floor show, but he stopped for a minute and looked at her. Alice put her hands under the table and began to work the fastening of the charm bracelet. "I've got all my French to do, too," she said.

Mrs. Spencer and the Oberons

THE FIRST SIGN THAT THE OBERONS WERE COMING MIGHT HAVE been early blossoms on the peach tree, but Mrs. Spencer did not know until she got the letter. It came on Thursday, when Mrs. Spencer was already beginning to feel the first tensions of anxiety over the day, with guests invited for dinner and Donnie's dentist appointment at three—itself requiring split-second timing at the school— and then there was the shopping to be done and the flowers to be arranged and the lemon cream to be made *early* this week to avoid the near catastrophe of last time, when people actually had to eat it with spoons. Now here was a strange letter in the mail.

Mrs. Spencer distrusted letters on principle, because they always seemed to want to entangle her in so many small, disagreeable obligations—visits, or news of old friends she had conveniently forgotten, or family responsibilities that always had to be met quickly and without enjoyment. If she had not persuaded herself that it was ill-bred to throw away a letter without opening it, Mrs. Spencer might very well have given up mail altogether, except for important things like Christmas cards from the right people, and announcements for the Wednesday Club, and invitations correctly engraved.

The letter from the Oberons looked, even on the outside, as though it carried some request, and Mrs. Spencer regarded it with distaste. The address straggled across the envelope, there was a dirty finger mark on the flap, and the stationery was obviously cheap; sighing, Mrs. Spencer opened it daintily. "Why would anyone with handwriting like this try to write a letter?" she asked irritably, and frowned up at her husband. "I can't even *read* it." Annoyed, not wanting to touch the letter, she threw it down onto the breakfast table.

Harry Spencer, who breakfasted in a mingled fragrance of good coffee, good shaving lotion, and the printers' ink of his morning paper, reached for his orange juice and said lazily, "Couldn't be anything very important, anyway." He smiled pleasantly at his wife. "Throw it away," he said.

"Nothing is *ever* important to *you*." The lemon cream, and the dentist, and the flowers, and the silver to be polished; Mrs. Spencer sighed. "I have enough on my mind for one day," she said. "*You* read it."

Mr. Spencer reached over and took up the letter and looked curiously at the sharp black handwriting. "It's not really so bad," he said. "A kind of puzzle, actually. He makes his *e*'s Greek style, and that funny little wiggle is an *s*. John Oberon—who is he, anyway?"

"*I* certainly could not tell you. No one I know, I'm sure."

Mr. Spencer laughed. "You may *get* to know him," he said. "This fellow wants you to find him a house."

"A house?" Mrs. Spencer stared as though she had not spent all her life in one house or another, adorning, cleaning, enriching. "A *house*?"

"They liked our town when they drove through," Mr. Spencer said, studying the letter. "Old friends of your sister's."

Mrs. Spencer set the marmalade down abruptly. "Of *Charlotte's*?"

Mr. Spencer glanced up at her briefly, curiously, and then back to the letter, and Mrs. Spencer sighed again. "I can't *help* it," she said, almost apologetically. "*You* know I'm fond of my sister, and I do have them here every Thanksgiving, and I'd do just anything in the world for them—"

Mr. Spencer glanced up again. "I never said a word," he remarked mildly.

Mrs. Spencer looked away. "It's just," she said helplessly, "that I feel it's important for you, and your position at the bank, to have a house and a family you can point to with pride. I'm really *terribly* fond of Charlotte, you *know* I am, but even I can see that she's not exactly the sort *we* want to know socially, and her husband is loud and coarse and vulgar and—"

"I always liked him," Mr. Spencer said.

"Really? Would you want him working with you in the bank?"

"He hasn't asked me." Mr. Spencer smiled across the table. "Never mind," he said. "Throw the letter away if you want to."

"Some people really have no consideration for other people," Mrs. Spencer said, touching the letter with one finger.

"They only want to know if you've heard of any summer places nearby," Mr. Spencer said. "Three bedrooms."

"Really," Mrs. Spencer said. "*Really*, Harry." She pushed away her half-finished coffee. "What earthly *right* . . . "

"That old house down by the river is for rent," Mr. Spencer said idly. "I heard the other day that Mrs. Babcock is very anxious to get a tenant this summer, and heaven knows she could use the money. Might just ask her," he told his wife.

"But why?" she demanded, staring. "Why?"

Mr. Spencer gathered his newspaper and rose. "I don't know why," he said, not looking at his wife. "Why does anybody do anything?"

Obscurely troubled, somehow defensive, Mrs. Spencer watched as her husband gathered his letters and left the breakfast room.

"Don't forget we're having guests for dinner," she said after him, but he did not turn. "Today, of *all* days," she told herself, and took up the intruding, unreadable letter and carried it out to the garbage pail. She was putting the dishes into the washer when Mr. Spencer called goodbye from the front door, and she answered him absently, thinking lemon cream, silver, flowers; when she dropped the coffee grounds into the garbage pail the unreadable letter was covered, safely hidden away. I must try to get in a half hour of rest sometime during the day, Mrs. Spencer was thinking; I really cannot drive myself like this.

The phone rang at about eleven, when the lemon cream was safely in the refrigerator and the living room was dusted and the silver polished, and she answered it upstairs, where she was mending a tiny rip in her dinner dress. Mrs. Spencer never allowed her clothes, which were expensive, to fall into disrepair, and the tiny rip infuriated her, since it had not been there before she sent the dress to the cleaner, and this meant that now she would have to remember to speak sharply to the cleaner's delivery man when he came on Monday. When the phone rang she immediately assumed that it was Harry calling from the bank to say that he would be home for lunch after all, and that would be too much, altogether too much, this day of all days. "Yes?" she said into the receiver.

"Mrs. Harry Spencer? Long distance calling."

Her sister, Charlotte, had been in the back of her mind since breakfast, and Mrs. Spencer told herself that if this was really Charlotte calling just to chat over family news she would absolutely hang up; Charlotte ought to have more consideration, she thought, and tapped her finger irritably against the phone table. I will tell Charlotte frankly, she thought, I will tell her frankly that I simply have no *time* for—

"Hello?" The voice was far away, truly a long-distance voice. "Hello?" it asked faintly.

"Charlotte?" Mrs. Spencer said. "Hello?"

"Maggie?"

No one except Charlotte called Mrs. Spencer "Maggie" anymore, not since she had implored her husband to introduce her to his friends in this new town as Margaret. *Margaret Spencer*, it said on her stationery and her personal checks, *Mrs. Harry Elliott Spencer*. "Hello?" she said.

"Maggie? It's John. John Oberon."

"Who?"

"Driving home today . . ." The voice was really very faint; perhaps there was something wrong with this upstairs phone. Mrs. Spencer raised her eyes to heaven, thinking, I will have to call the man to check the phone. "Drop in about four . . . say hello . . ."

"I can't hear you," Mrs. Spencer said, speaking louder. "I really can't hear you, I'm sorry. We must have a bad connection."

"Just a minute." The voice came more faintly still. "Rosie wants to say hello." Distantly, like that of tiny people talking thinly in a dollhouse, or a dream, the little voice said, "Here's Rosie."

"I really cannot hear you at *all*," Mrs. Spencer said firmly, and put the receiver down on the small little "Hello?" from a long, long distance. "Good heavens," she said aloud, "why people think they have the *right* . . . "

She rarely lunched improperly, because she felt that it was important to do things correctly even if one was alone, and she had her pretty salad and her cup of tea every day by the kitchen window, where it was sunny. Today, however, with the shopping and the dentist still to do, she had only a cup of tea, standing up to drink it, looking out over the handsome wide lawn that surrounded the house, making a mental note to locate the Carter boy and get him to trim the edges *correctly* next time if he wanted his money. After her cup of tea she forced herself to lie down on her bed for half an hour, dutifully going over in her mind the things she still had to do.

———

The Oberons must have come while she was waiting for Donnie at the dentist's office, chafing over the magazines, impatient at the leisurely, reassuring tone of the dentist's voice and Donnie's half-nervous giggle. She had bought Donnie his usual ice cream cone on the way home and he was still toying with it, delighted that with the novocaine freezing his lip he could not feel the cold ice cream. When she drove into the driveway and hurried him out of the car to play on his swing until the ice cream was gone, she was brought up short by the sight of a note tacked to her front door. It had been put up with a pin, and there was a tiny scratch on the white paint where the pin had gone in; she set her lips thinly and tore down the note, remembering at once the angular, unreadable black writing. "Those *frightful* people," she said, and then, to her son, "Look what they've done to our door."

Donnie pressed closer and his ice cream dripped onto the steps; it was really too much. Mrs. Spencer never slapped her children, or permitted them to be abused with any violent punishment, but today of all days she almost raised her hand to Donnie. Finally— because of course taking out one's annoyance on children was unfair, and unladylike—she wiped up the ice cream with her handkerchief, which she must now remember to drop into the hamper when she went by it, and sent Donnie quietly around to his play set in the back. The note she had taken from the door she dropped into the kitchen wastebasket without trying to read it.

The trash would not go out to be burned until morning, so the note stayed there, covered by the papers from the groceries and the wrapping from the candles for the table, and eventually Harry's evening paper. Mrs. Spencer gave Donnie and her daughter, Irma, their supper, and chilled the wine, and checked the lemon cream, which had come out admirably, and got the steak ready to broil, and whipped the potatoes, and made shrimp sauce. When she went upstairs to dress and say good night to her children, her kitchen was immaculate, dinner preparing invisibly, her table set and lovely in a quiet stillness of shining glass and white damask, and her living room, charming and so very like Margaret Spencer, people said, ready for the entrance of guests.

By the time her first guests arrived, Margaret Spencer's children slept, clean and warm and dreaming correctly, and she was waiting in the hall, as calm and lovely as always, gracious and elegant. "How well Margaret always manages," her guests told one another on their way home. "Entertaining seems no effort to her, somehow; she's done wonders for Harry's position in town." And one or two of the women reflected that Margaret Spencer might really be a very good choice for president of the Wednesday Club.

Before she went to bed, Margaret saw to it that the ashtrays were emptied and the glasses washed and the chairs moved back where they belonged, and she put salt on a wine stain on her tablecloth (and even if the tablecloth was permanently stained, it was a small loss, since the wine had been spilled by old Mack Ramsey; this was the first dinner invitation the Ramseys had accepted from the Spencers, and Mrs. Ramsey had really been *most* gracious about the living room drapes) and checked that the windows in the children's bedroom were open four inches from the top.

She had not remembered to tell Harry about either the telephone call from the Oberons or the note on the front door. She had so completely forgotten the Oberons by the next morning that she only stared blankly when Mrs. Babcock—a plain woman, and not one of the sort who dined with the Spencers—stopped her on the street by actually putting a hand on her arm. "I was going to call you," Mrs. Babcock said. "I saw the Oberons—" She waited, but Mrs. Spencer, moving her arm slightly away, still stared. "I thought I'd ask you," Mrs. Babcock explained, "seeing as they're friends of yours, and your family. About the *house*."

"What house?"

Mrs. Babcock laughed. "I guess they never told you they looked at it, even though I thought they were pretty taken with it. My old house down by the river. Heaven knows it's big enough for them, and they thought having the river right there would be nice for the children. Not," she went on consideringly, "that it's any kind of a fancy, dress-up place, but then they didn't look to me like fancy people." She glanced quickly at Mrs. Spencer and then away. "But of course I like to make sure," she finished.

"I'm really afraid—"

"I thought," said Mrs. Babcock, as though spelling it out, "that I would ask you what kind of people they are, these Oberons. They said they are old friends of yours, and it's not as though I'd need references or anything, with the kind of people they seemed to be, so nice and friendly and all, but I did think I ought to mention it to you and you could tell me if you know anything against them. Anything that would mean I oughtn't to rent them the house."

"Really," Mrs. Spencer said. Mrs. Babcock was a dreadful person, she thought, always coming and putting her hands on people. "I assure you," she said, "I know nothing against these people."

"Well, then, that's all right, isn't it?" Mrs. Babcock was clearly relieved. "It's a nice house," she explained, "and we've put some work in it, fixing it up, and it's belonged to Carl's folks for over a hundred years, and I wouldn't want to see anyone living there who might let it go down."

"Yes, I can quite understand," Mrs. Spencer said. "Goodbye." I am such a busy person, she thought, moving quickly down the street; why does everyone come to me with their problems? Irma had to have shoes, the lawn furniture must be repainted; would it be wise to look around for a new dress to wear when the Ramseys returned the dinner invitation, or would a new dress look ostentatious, eager? She sighed, and hurried.

She always did her own shopping, checking quality and price with care; it did not pay, she believed, to buy food for a family without considerable caution, and with prices on clothes and furniture and magazines and even Harry's newspaper going up all the time, a good housekeeper had to watch carefully to be sure she was not cheated, or deceived, or foolish. Consequently, when Mrs. Spencer went into the supermarket across the street from Harry's bank, she did not move idly but neither did she seize exciting novelties from the shelves or hurry to snatch the top head of lettuce or the special for the weekend. She walked slowly, pushing the shopping cart with the pride of one performing perfectly an exacting and delicate chore, and hesitated and debated and even, when the clerk was not looking, prodded at the melon with the tip of her gloved finger. It would not fit her position as Harry's wife to serve poor food to her family. Her children must bear visibly on their faces the healthy evidence of the very best; no unripe fruit must mar the smooth curve of little Irma's cheek or the growth of Donnie's sturdy legs. Rapt, devoted, Mrs. Spencer was considerably annoyed at the interruptions from her neighbors, who bade her good morning or asked about her health or stood in her way before the shelves. When she moved to the counter where old Sanson added and made change, she answered his good morning with only a nod; did that can of peas look slightly swollen? had she by some chance taken down a faulty container?

"That can doesn't look sound, Mr. Sanson. Will you please get me another?"

He glanced up at her, so briefly that she barely saw, and left the counter to fetch her another can of peas. "It's such a nuisance," she said to the woman waiting behind her in line. "These days, everything's so poorly made." The woman turned her head aside and looked impatient; *she* doesn't care what she feeds her family, Mrs. Spencer thought, and shrugged as Mr. Sanson returned with a sounder can of peas. As he added up the prices of her groceries, she followed his gestures for any absentminded blunder; he might charge her twice for something, perhaps for two cans of peas. Then, at last, surveying the slip that listed the items, checking as each went into the box for the boy to carry to her car, she was astonished when

Mr. Sanson said, as casually as he took her money, "Friend of yours was in yesterday, Mrs. Spencer. Moving into town for the summer."

"A friend of mine? Of *mine*?"

"Mrs. Oberon. Nice-talking lady."

"A friend of *mine*?"

"Said she was." His old eyes lifted, shrewd. "She didn't have any money with her," he said.

"Really—" Mrs. Spencer gasped, shocked. "You don't expect *me* to pay . . . ?"

Mr. Sanson smiled oddly. "Seen a lot of people come through here," he said, looking past Mrs. Spencer to the woman waiting behind her. "Back when this was a little country store, I used to know the ones I could trust. Still do. Can tell them every time. *Her*, I could trust. Being," and he looked again at Mrs. Spencer, "as she was a friend of *yours*."

"I absolutely refuse—"

"Besides," Mr. Sanson went on reasonably, reaching past Mrs. Spencer to pull the cart behind her, "Liz Babcock rented them Carl's old farm down by the river, and I guess they'll be around for a while."

"Those new people moved in," Mrs. Finley said, breathing heavily as she leaned to take up the pail and mop. "Thought sure you'd be down there helping out."

"What new people?" Mrs. Spencer asked. "I want all those shelves washed today, Mrs. Finley."

"Those friends of yours. Down to Liz Babcock's old man's farmhouse."

"Those people are not—"

"Half the town's down there anyway. They likely don't need *you*." Mrs. Finley's eye, on the bare edge of insolence, turned to her mop. "Nice folks," Mrs. Finley said. "Easy to get along with, I'd think."

Mrs. Finley is really too old and too heavy for this kind of work, Mrs. Spencer thought; I ought to start looking around for someone younger.

"New kid in my class," Donnie announced over his supper. "Nice guy."

"Donnie, dear. 'Guy' is not a civilized word."

"Nice fellow," said Donnie primly. "He's got a two-wheel bike. And a microscope. And a dog. A *dog*."

"Animals are very well for the open country, dear. But with our lovely lawns and our pretty flowers— Imagine what a dog would do, digging and scratching!"

"And he's got a big brother who's teaching him to pitch. He's already the best marbles player in the school."

"What's his name?" Irma asked. "Donnie? What's his name? Donnie?"

"Irma glirma," Donnie said. "Irma dirma epiglirma."

"Donnie? Donnie?"

"Joe," Donnie said, reverently. "Joe."

"Joe what, dear?"

"*I* don't know. Joe something. You know what? He's got a base-ball with all the Yankees' autographs on it. He's going to bring it to school."

"Really, Donnie." Mrs. Spencer spoke with some distaste. "Do you know what his father does? What kind of clothes does he wear? Does he speak nicely?"

"Sure," her son said, "sure," and bent his head over his pudding.

After considerable hesitation, and without quite knowing why, Mrs. Spencer brought herself reluctantly to speak to her husband. She put her slim dessert spoon down on the edge of her plate, touched the handle of her coffee cup, and said, not raising her eyes, "Harry, I'm worried about something."

"Money?" He looked up, concerned. "Money, Margaret? Surely there's no need—"

"No." She smiled, a little. "Not money, Harry. No, I'm worried about these people, the ones who have just moved into town."

"The Oberons?" He was puzzled.

"You *know* them?"

"Sure," he said. "Joe and Rosie. They've been in the bank. What worries you about *them*?"

"They've been using my name. Nothing serious, of course, and I'm sure everyone around town knows me well enough to recognize the kind of people I know, but they told Mr. Sanson at the market that they were friends of mine, and today I was disturbed when the florist just happened to mention that Mrs.—what *is* the name? Oberon—was buying white roses because they were my favorite flower and she was expecting me to call—"

"You ought to, as a matter of fact," Harry said. "Common courtesy."

"But I don't even *know* them," Mrs. Spencer said.

"If they're friends of your sister's—"

"Really," Mrs. Spencer said. Her fingers tensed on the handle of her coffee cup. "Harry," she said, then stopped. Finally she said, "If I call on them, then they'll expect to visit *here*."

"Why not?" Harry said. "You could buy *her* favorite flowers. They are very pleasant people, anyway."

"Introduce them to *my* friends?" Mrs. Spencer was astounded. "*My* friends, Harry?"

"Then do as you think best," Harry said slowly. "I just thought they were very pleasant people."

Mrs. Spencer lifted her chin regally. "I do not call on people who capitalize on my name," she said.

Harry glanced up, sardonically. "It's my name, too," he said, "and I'm honored."

———

Pamela Worthington was quite surprised, she told everyone, to find that the Spencers had not gone to the Oberons' housewarming; it was certainly *the* party of the summer, although probably the Oberons would surpass it themselves, the summer being young. At any rate, one would surely have expected the Spencers, of all people, to be there with their old friends.

"I simply couldn't understand it," Pamela Worthington said at last to Mrs. Spencer. "You, of all people."

"We were not invited," Mrs. Spencer said. "We don't know the people."

"Margaret, *honestly.* Rosie Oberon will simply *die* when she hears you thought you weren't invited. She'll simply *die.*"

"We were not invited."

"But, my dear, *of course* you were invited. Rosie told me herself she was expecting you, and all evening they were absolutely *watching* for you."

"We do not know the people."

Pamela stared. "But Harry *introduced* me to them, right there in the bank." Then she stopped, and lowered her voice. "Really, Margaret," she said, "whatever this is all about, I *do* think you're making too much of it. I don't know what they ever could have done to offend you."

Mrs. Spencer snapped her pocketbook open, and then shut, with finality. "Furthermore," she said, "I do not *want* to know them."

"It's your business, after all." Pamela's tone had grown definitely colder. "I always knew you could carry a grudge, Margaret, but I do think that in this case you're just carrying one too far. Rosie Oberon is one of the sweetest people I ever met, and I just don't see how it's *possible* to carry on a feud with her."

Mrs. Spencer turned away. "I said I do not know the people," she said. "That should be enough for any of my friends."

"Maybe," Pamela said, perhaps not quite loud enough to be heard, "maybe you don't have that many friends to spare."

The blossoms fell from the peach tree and were swept up by the boy who did the Spencers' lawn; dandelions sprang up, Donnie and Irma were released at last from school, the weather turned almost warm enough for swimming. On a Thursday, just two weeks after the Oberons' first letter had come, Mrs. Spencer was late getting home, held up by a tiresome woman who could not understand why the country club dances had to be kept small and exclusive and thought an important committee meeting was the place to argue about it; people should be more discriminating, Mrs. Spencer had been telling herself crossly all the way home; after all the work we've done to keep things nice, someone always turns up without any appreciation or understanding. Because she was angry and in a hurry she ripped her stocking getting out of her car, and *that* meant she would have to change stockings before dinner, and that meant she would be even later; almost running, she went quickly into her house. Surely one might get by without these petty irritations, she was thinking.

"Dorothy?" she called. "Dorothy?"

The high school girl who watched over Donnie and Irma in the afternoons when Mrs. Spencer had her committee meetings and her book club meetings and her Wednesday Club meetings unwound herself from a chair in the living room. She had been watching television, Mrs. Spencer saw with one shocked glance; there was an apple core in the ashtray on the end table. "*What?*" Mrs. Spencer said, gasping, "*Dorothy?*"

"Mr. Spencer—"

"Garbage in my living room? Where are the children?"

"They're not here," Dorothy said. Carefully, daintily, she took up the apple core. "I'll wash the ashtray if you like," she said sweetly.

"Watching *television?*"

"I only stayed around," Dorothy said, giving Mrs. Spencer one level, rude stare, "because Mr. Spencer asked me to. He said to tell you that he had taken the children out to the picnic. He said to tell you that they would be expecting you to join them when you got back. That," said Dorothy, "is what I stayed here to tell you."

"A *picnic?*"

"Everyone in town is going. At the Oberons'. I'm going too." For a moment Dorothy's voice trembled with adolescent outrage. "I could even be late," she said, "just because I wanted to do you a favor."

"Really, Dorothy." Mrs. Spencer lifted her chin. "I don't need people doing me favors. You could have left a note."

"Mr. Spencer asked me to, and I could have been at the picnic a long time ago." Dorothy stopped, schoolbooks and jacket in her arms, one hand fumbling for the front doorknob. "My mother says I don't have to babysit for you anymore if I don't want to," she said, with enormous dignity. "So I just guess I won't be back anymore."

"Just as you please, Dorothy," Mrs. Spencer said, but the door slammed behind Dorothy and her words trailed off. The house was very still; Mrs. Spencer's planning had somehow never taken into account the fact that someday she might come home and not find Harry and the children. Uncertain, she turned toward the stairs, thinking to go and change her stockings, and then hesitated. She had told Harry and the children, had she not, that the Oberons were socially unacceptable? This was just like her sister, this pushing and climbing and refusing to take no for an answer, until nice people were forced to visit out of sheer weariness; they will be making a great fuss over Harry and the children to get at *me*, Mrs. Spencer thought; I must go at once and put a stop to it.

Running again, not even sparing time to change her stockings, she went out to her car. It's like everyone back home, she was thinking, picnics and last-minute invitations, and everything confused and grimy and noisy, taking people away from their homes and their dinners without ever stopping to think how inconvenient it might be for the orderly routine of their houses. Mrs. Spencer remembered, with a little shiver of fury, the troops of laughing friends her sister was always apt to bring home, always, somehow, when the house was freshly cleaned and things put in order.

Potluck, Mrs. Spencer thought, as though it were a word from a nightmare. A picnic at dinnertime. Children being fed all kinds of things they shouldn't have. Grown-ups laughing and drinking and probably never getting anything to eat until all hours. People trampling through the house, wrinkling rugs, upsetting ashtrays, pressing into the kitchen to help make a salad, dropping cigarettes, putting glasses down on polished furniture, making noise. It's vulgar, Mrs. Spencer whispered fearfully to herself, vulgar and untidy and nasty.

She did not often drive along the river road; many of the houses along there were only shacks set by the water, and Mrs. Spencer had been on a committee that stopped the people living in them from throwing their garbage into the river. She had to follow the main highway to the edge of the town, and then turn off, and as she came to the entrance of the river road she slowed down, watching for the abandoned, derelict gas station that marked the turn; it's just *like* them to live along here, she thought, just *like* them.

She could hear the sound of a waterfall through the still night, even over the soft sound of her car. She had not perceived how dark it had grown until she realized that the moon was rising; under other circumstances she might have slowed down briefly to admire the light across the water, as she admired all things done in an orderly manner, but tonight she had to hurry. The thought had crossed her mind that one of these days she might open her front door to find the Oberons and their friends crowding in for a visit, expecting hospitality in the style of their own; she could not get Harry and the children away quickly enough.

Driven by the thought of the Oberons crossing her trim threshold, Mrs. Spencer drove faster. The Oberons' house on the river was not far past the waterfall, but tonight—perhaps because of the darkness growing steadily along the road, with only an occasional glimpse, now, of the moon through the trees—it was difficult to find. Once, Mrs. Spencer slowed down at a curve in the winding road, thinking she heard voices singing, and saw lights through the trees, but when she stopped her car there was nothing but silence, and she drove on.

The Oberons' house was set back from the road, down the slope to the river, and only a ramshackle fence post marked the turnoff that served as a driveway; peering through the darkness, Mrs. Spencer went on, and then found herself without warning on the broad highway that marked the end of the river road on this side; this highway would only lead her back home, alone. She had come too far, and must turn and go back. As she started back, she decided that she had taken enough. Tomorrow she would tell Mr. Sanson at the store, and Mrs. Babcock, and the florist, and all the rest that the Oberons were not to be trusted. "They used my name without any authorization from me," she would say. "I wouldn't let them owe *me* money; you may be sure that Mr. Spencer and I do *not* accept responsibility."

The winding road was very dark now, and she had to turn on the car's headlights; all they showed her were trees and quiet leaves. Far away was the sound of the waterfall and then, even more distantly, laughter. Mrs. Spencer stopped her car again and listened. She thought she could hear what might be children shouting, even one high voice that could have been Donnie's, and above the thin noise of the children was music, perhaps a radio, with that peculiarly clear sound that music has near water. She sat in her car, head bent forward intently, and heard—she was positive—Harry's voice singing. "Oh, my darling," he was singing, "oh, my darling, oh, my darling Clementine," and the children's voices joined him, rising in glad disharmony, "Oh, my *darling* Clementine . . ." and the laughter went on.

Unsteadily, Mrs. Spencer opened the door of her car and got out, the stones of the road hard and rough under her thin high-heeled shoes. Somewhere along here, she thought, and moved, stumbling, to the side of the road. Even if she could not see the lights of the house through the trees, the driveway must be along here somewhere, and time was pressing; she could not, *could* not, endure to hear her husband singing and her children laughing somewhere down there at the Oberons' house.

There was a fence going along the side of the road, almost certainly a fence that led to the post that marked the driveway, and she took hold of the top rail—she had forgotten her gloves—to steady herself as she followed it. Even with the car's headlights shining it was dark on the side of the road, among the trees, and the distant singing and laughter faded sometimes until it was only the sound of a very soft breeze going through the leaves. Walking almost blindly, Mrs. Spencer made her way along the fence, slipping into a ditch once, almost losing a shoe in a pile of dead leaves, straining to see lights down by the river. Then, turning at a curve in the road, she was halted; the fence ended in a tangle of fallen boards, and there ahead was the derelict gas station, and the other road home.

I've been going the wrong way, she thought, realizing that there were tears on her face, I've walked all this time the wrong way; the way in is somewhere behind me. Groping, she found her way back to her car, and sat for a minute on the seat, the door open beside her. When she sat still she could hear the singing distinctly, "Oh, my darling, oh, my *darling* Clementine," and a voice—surely Irma's—shouting, "Popcorn! Popcorn!" I'll have to turn around again, she thought; I must have missed it somehow. Her shoes were ruined, she knew, and it was just as well that she had not changed her stockings; her hands were filthy and scratched from the fence; she knew that her hair was draggled and her lipstick worn away. All of this the Oberons will pay for, she thought. The Oberons will suffer for every single bit of this; I'll have Harry run them out of town tomorrow; you just wait and see, she told the Oberons silently, you just wait and see what I am going to do with you.

She started the car then, fired with anger, and turned around by the gas station and started back along the road, driving very slowly and close to the side of the road. When she came to the spot where she had heard the singing she went even more slowly, her head partly out of the car window. It was possible—considering the haphazard Oberons, it was even probable—that the fence post that marked the driveway had been allowed to fall down, but even so, the driveway ought to have been visible as an opening between the trees. From far away she could still hear the laughter and the singing, as though the guests wandered now all along the river, perhaps in boats, going up and down the river and singing. If those people have put my Donnie into a boat, she thought fiercely, they'll have to account to me—and found herself again at the end of the river road where it joined the other highway home.

Why can't I find it? Why can't I find the house where the Oberons live? Everyone else has gotten there all right. No, she thought, sitting and staring at the streetlights going along in order toward her home, no, it isn't possible.

Then, beginning to feel frantic, she turned her car quickly and drove back along the road until she came again to the other end, to the abandoned gas station, and, turning again, back once more to the lighted highway. Once, she stopped, hearing first only silence and then, far away, the voices singing and the laughter. It seemed to her that she had spent hours, perhaps years, searching up and down a dark and empty road, following the distant merriment, never able to find a way to get closer to it. At last, tired and worn, tears drying on her cheeks, she accepted the highway home and left the river road behind. They will be waiting for me at home, she said over and over, they will be there waiting for me, they will have been waiting all this time.

The town was deserted; only an occasional light showed on a porch or in a hallway, as though most people had gone off by daylight, forgetting that it might be dark when they came home. No one was walking on the sidewalks, and Mrs. Spencer wondered if the movie theater and the restaurants and the drugstores and the bars downtown would all be empty, closed and dark, because all the town was down by the river laughing and singing and dancing. I'm the only one who didn't go, she thought with dismay; they all went off and left me behind.

In her haste she had not left any lights on in her own house, and it was dark and forbidding as she drove into the driveway and walked up to the front door. No one was waiting for her. She looked eagerly, pointlessly, through the downstairs rooms, calling "Harry? Donnie? Irma?" into the silence, then sat tiredly on the bottom step of the staircase. More than anything else, more even than welcoming her family home, she wanted to shower and change, make herself clean again, and yet she had not the will to get herself upstairs; I'm the only one who didn't go, she thought again.

At last she moved, alert, hearing suddenly the sounds of movement; cars going down the street, people walking, voices calling to one another. They're back, she thought, everyone has come home again; I must hurry and change before they get here. Harry and Donnie and Irma must not find Margaret Spencer sitting bedraggled on the bottom step of her own staircase; she must be neat and ready for them, and then, running up the stairs, she realized that they would be coming home dirty and sticky and perhaps wet from the river, perhaps tracking mud across the white doorsill, putting grimy hands on the stair rail, bringing their filthy shoes into the living room, and she sighed irritably. It's too *much*, she thought; it's more than I can stand. I spend my whole life keeping things nice for them, and what thanks do I get?

She heard Harry's car pull into the driveway, and doors opening and closing.

Then, irrepressibly, Irma giggled and said in what was almost a whisper, "Oh, my darling Clementine," and Donnie began to laugh and then Harry was laughing too. "Oh, my *darling* Clementine," they said to one another, as Harry unlocked the door, and then they were all inside.

Watching them helplessly, angry and bewildered in the face of their joyful, happy laughter, Mrs. Spencer could only think, It's too much, it's too *much*; I spend my whole life keeping things nice for them, and this is the thanks I get.

It Isn't the Money I Mind

IT WAS A SUNNY AFTERNOON, AND THE PARK WAS NEARLY FULL. OLD men and women sat on the benches; mothers sat idly beside baby carriages or watched children run shrieking over the grass. There were a lot of dogs walking up and down the paths on leashes or lying next to the benches. Except for the children, there was little conversation and not much noise.

A man came into the park from one of the side entrances. He stopped just inside the entrance to pat a dog on the head and speak to the owner, and then walked on slowly, looking for a place to sit down. He was middle-aged, partly bald, and, judging by his clothes, not very well off. As he walked he watched the people in the park with a bright interest, stopping to listen to an argument between a mother and child, and later to pick up a ball for a group of older boys. One of them said, "Throw it back here, mister," and held out his hands. The man threw the ball clumsily and it bounced twice before the boy scooped it up. The boy said, "Thanks," and turned and threw it easily far across the grass to another boy.

The man watched for a minute and then walked on. Finally he stopped in front of a bench with an empty place at one end. Beside it sat a woman with a baby carriage. "May I sit here?" he asked. She looked up and said, "It's not taken," and the man sat down. He sighed and sat still for a minute before reaching into his pocket for a cigarette.

The woman looked at him irritably and then turned away. A baby was lying in the carriage on its stomach, asleep, wearing only a diaper. The baby's back was brown, except for a sharp white edge where the diaper began. The woman was tirelessly rocking the carriage back and forth.

"Will the smoke bother the baby?" the man asked.

"I just got her to sleep," the woman said. "Just about anything wakes her."

The man leaned over and dropped the cigarette onto the ground and put his foot on it. "She looks like a fine, healthy baby," he said.

The woman smiled. "She's only six months old," she said, "and never even had a cold."

"A fine baby," the man said. "You see so many around here looking pale and white."

"They're not healthy," the woman said. "Some of the children in this park are really unhealthy."

"It's hard for children in the city."

"Their mothers should keep them out of the park if they have things other children can catch," the woman said.

While he was talking, the man had been fingering his billfold, riffling through the papers in it absentmindedly. Now he pulled one out—a magazine clipping. "Want to see my little girl?" he asked.

The woman reached out with the hand that was not rocking the carriage. "Of course," she said. "I could tell from the way you talked that you had one of your own."

The clipping was of a little blond girl of about six, with a pretty, adult face and a lot of makeup. "She's lovely," the woman said. "She has such a sweet face."

"She's a nice kid," the man said. He hesitated. "Know who she is?" he asked finally.

The woman shook her head.

"Her name's Angela Foster now."

"Of course," the woman said. "In the movies!"

"That's right." The man took the clipping and looked at it fondly. "It used to be Martin—that's my name. Her mother changed it. Angela Martin's not good for the movies," he said.

"What a lucky little girl!" the woman said, reaching over to adjust the hood of the carriage. "In the movies!"

"She'll be a second Shirley Temple someday," the man said. "She's got talent—everything."

"You must be very proud of her."

"I'll tell you," the man began carefully, "I'm proud of her, of course. And it isn't the money I mind, either. She's making plenty right now, and I don't grudge it to her. But it's like this. Before her mother took her out to Hollywood, I was always kicking about the dancing lessons and the singing lessons and the costumes and the late nights when her dance class gave a recital. And now I know I just didn't have sense enough to see the baby had talent."

"It's hard to tell," the woman said. "All children have a natural sense of rhythm. Even at six months—"

"It isn't the money I mind," the man said again. "I don't think a six-year-old girl *should* have to support her father."

"Well, there's a lot of luck connected with it," the woman said.

"I saw this article about her in a movie magazine," the man went on. "It said she was five years old, but she must be six now. And she's already getting fan mail."

"Really?" the woman said.

"I thought of writing to her and asking for a picture," the man said. "Her own father."

"I'm sure you'll be very proud of her," the woman said. He reached into his pocket again for his cigarettes, and she frowned and shook her head. The man rose.

"I'll just finish my walk while I smoke this," he said. He smiled at the woman and leaned over the carriage for a minute. "Such a pretty baby," he said. He bowed slightly to the woman and went rapidly down the path.

When the man got around the next turn, he began to walk more slowly. A little boy just learning to walk staggered out from a bench and grabbed him by the leg. The man said, "Where you going, champ?," turned the little boy around, and started him back to his mother. The man stopped for a minute to watch a checkers game and then went on again, only to stop a minute later and help a little girl of about two push her stroller around a difficult turn. The man called her "honey." Her mother, who was standing nearby, thanked him, and he said, "Lovely little girl." The mother smiled and went on, pulling the little girl and talking to her as she went.

The broad circle the man had been making had by now taken him back in the direction he had come. As he passed the group of boys playing ball, he saw the ball strike a tree and bounce in his direction. He scooped it up awkwardly and, holding it in his hand, walked over to the boys. They were waiting impatiently for the ball, and as he stepped across a low railing and handed the ball to the nearest one, he smiled apologetically and said, "Don't have the muscle I used to."

"Thanks," the boy said. He threw the ball, and the boys began to scatter. One of them caught the ball and threw it to another. The man said, "Bud," and the nearest boy turned around. The man, taking out his billfold, said, "Know who this is?" He pulled forth a newspaper clipping and held it out to the boy.

The boy glanced over his shoulder at his friends and then went over to the man. "Sure," he said, looking at the clipping, but without making any attempt to hold it. "Nicky Lopez. The middleweight challenger."

A couple of the boys nearby had also turned when the man

called, and now they came slowly over. "Nicky Lopez," one of them said. "Let's see Nicky Lopez." The man handed him the clipping, and the boy looked at it and said professionally, "There's a guy that can fight."

"He's pretty good," another of the boys said, taking the clipping in turn.

"I used to manage Nicky," the man said, watching the boys' heads turn slowly toward him. "Yeah," he said reminiscently, "I used to manage Nicky, until the syndicate got him away from me." He looked around at the boys and then went on, "It isn't the money I mind, you understand, but I sure hated to lose that boy."

Company for Dinner

Mr. Shapiro came whistling down the street, swinging his briefcase cheerfully. Getting dark early these days, he thought; mustn't forget to tell Marjorie what Hargreaves said to me today. "Hi, fellows," he said to the kids sitting on the curb, their faces turned around to watch him go down the street. Streetlights are on already, he thought, sure gets dark early these days. He trotted briskly up the steps of number 1018, saw that the door was open a crack, let himself in, and slammed the door behind him.

"Dear?" he called experimentally toward the kitchen at the end of the hall.

The sound of the can opener stopped, and she said, "That you, dear? Dinner's almost ready."

"Good," said Mr. Shapiro, and stopped at the hall closet to hang up his coat. Gray hat's getting sort of shabby, he thought, looking at it where it sat on the shelf; wish I could persuade Marjorie to hang up her coat in here instead of leaving it on the bed. Have to speak to Marjorie about getting a new gray hat. Wonder what's for dinner.

"Dinner almost ready, dear?" he called as he passed the kitchen door.

"Ready in a minute."

Dining room looks pretty good, he thought, on his way to the living room. He took an olive from the dish on the table, then stood looking at the table, thinking: Something different, something. New long scratch in my chair, must be the kid; something else different, though. New dishes? New silverware? Clean tablecloth? That's it, best tablecloth. Company for dinner? Only three places . . . Probably the laundry didn't come.

Must speak to Marjorie about the laundry, he thought, going into the living room, three of my handkerchiefs last week . . . "'Lo, fella." The little boy in the middle of the living room floor was making a toy dump truck go back and forth, back and forth, and barely looked up. "'Lo," he said.

"Got a kiss for Daddy?" Mr. Shapiro asked.

"No," the little boy said.

Mr. Shapiro sat down in his chair. Something wrong, he thought. The whole house is on edge tonight. Pictures a little crooked, chairs not quite in place, carpet a little more faded near the window. Bridge club come today? he thought; no, that's Thursday. Girl, that's it. Girl came to clean.

"Dinner almost ready?" he called out.

"Yeah, when's dinner?" the little boy yelled. "When's dinner, Mom?"

"It'll be on the table in a minute."

"Meat loaf tonight," the little boy said.

"Good," Mr. Shapiro replied absently. He was looking at the books on the table next to his chair. *They Were Expendable*—must have brought that home from the office, he thought, must have brought that home a few nights ago and meant to read it. Ought to read that book tonight, talking about it at lunch today.

"Dinner's on the table!"

"Yaaay," the little boy shrieked, shooting past Mr. Shapiro, who walked slowly through the dining room. "Got to wash my hands," he explained to the kitchen door.

"One night in your life you might wash your hands before I . . ." Her voice followed him into the bathroom, and he closed the door gently on it.

When he reached the dinner table and pulled back his chair, his eyes fell onto the bowl at his place.

"Didn't we have tomato soup last night?" he asked. He lifted his eyes to the woman at the head of the table, and then turned to the little boy. They were staring at him.

The woman rose. "I *thought* you were early tonight," she said blankly.

"Why . . ." said Mr. Shapiro. He put down his napkin, went over to the hall closet, and took out his coat and hat. Gray hat looks a little shabby, he thought. The woman and the little boy watched him until the door closed behind him.

Mr. Shapiro went swiftly down the steps and then up the steps of number 1016. He let himself in with his key and slammed the door behind him.

"Dear?" he called out. "The funniest thing . . ."

The sound of the can opener stopped, and she said, "That you, dear? Dinner's almost ready."

I Cannot Sing the Old Songs

THE GREATEST GUY IN THE WORLD, SHE THOUGHT, LOOKING AT HER father. She glanced over her shoulder a moment. The couch, she thought. I sat there last time.

"I think you owe us an explanation," her father said.

The easy start, she thought. Allowance for excitement or backtracking. Better not say anything.

"Your mother and I are terribly disappointed in you."

The catch in the voice, she thought, the appropriate quaver.

"I don't suppose there's any way we can tell you how we feel; you don't seem to have any consideration for us or for anything but your own selfish plans."

Don't get mad, she thought. They're only just starting to work on me.

"I suppose you think it was very gracious of you to come home for two days to tell us about this young man?"

A long pause. Better say something, she thought. This is getting one-sided.

"You knew about him a long time ago," she said.

"But why do you have to—" her mother asked. She began to cry.

"We think you could have shown us a little more consideration, that's all," her father said.

The greatest guy in the world, she thought. And he's letting her crying work on me for a while right now. Better not talk again for a few minutes.

"After all," her father was saying again, "you know that we don't like this young man."

What do you want me to do? she thought, say okay, the whole thing's off, I won't get married?

"If it were only someone—" her mother began again.

"Well, Mother," her father said, "I never thought we'd be ashamed of her, did you?"

Wait now, she thought. Go very slow on this one. Her mother was crying again.

"Why, for God's sake?" her father said, slamming his hand down on the arm of the chair. "If it were only someone fair and honest and aboveboard . . ."

He just thought up those words, she thought. Take it very slow.

"I want to be proud of you," her father said. "I want to be able to tell the whole world how proud I am of my daughter. And now—"

Okay, she thought. Take it now. "I'll leave tonight," she said, "if you're too ashamed of me." I can work up a good quaver too, she thought.

"No, please, listen," her mother said.

"Don't get high-handed with me, young woman," her father said. "I won't listen to that sort of talk from you. You're still my daughter, you know, until . . ."

As long as she could hold on with both hands she could keep from laughing. You can't just walk out in the middle of it, she thought. They'd have to say it all to each other, then.

"Mother," her father asked, "what are we going to tell our friends?"

The greatest guy in the world, she thought. Jesus, you poor old man.

The New Maid

IT WAS THE FIRST GOLDEN WEEK OF SPRING, AND MRS. ARTHUR William Morgan was almost completely unaffected by it. To begin with, she rarely saw the spring weather anyway, since she got on a commuter train every morning before the weather had rightly settled itself for the day, and took a commuter train home again in the evening, after everything the weather could do with itself in one day was over with, and spent the time in between in her fancy air-conditioned office designing clothes for fashionable women to wear the following autumn.

On Saturdays and Sundays, Mrs. Morgan frequently caught a passing glimpse of the weather between getting up and running off to somewhere to see someone, but spring weather is a thing to soak in, and it had no time to do any real affecting of Mrs. Morgan. Mr. Morgan, who habitually caught a commuter train four minutes later than his wife's in the morning, and seven minutes earlier than his wife's in the evening, could hardly have been expected to call his wife's attention to the soft air, the gentle sun, or the warm breeze.

At any rate, in this first really golden week of spring, Mrs. Morgan had hired a new maid. Not actually hired, that is, and she wasn't really a maid, if you stopped to think about it, but Mrs. Arthur William Morgan was so indiscriminate about the persons in her employ, since they all merged in her mind, eventually, into one inferior character, that you might as well say that Mrs. Morgan had hired a new maid, and be done with it. The person had come in answer to an advertisement in the local paper: "Wanted, housekeeper and governess for twin children, seven years old. Good salary. Best of references required. Write for appointment."

Out of all the letters, Mrs. Morgan had selected one neatly written in a fine, old-fashioned hand on heavy, expensive paper; anything expensive appealed to Mrs. Morgan. She had gone so far as to give up one of her precious Sunday afternoons to an interview, and perhaps in some subtle way the spring weather touched Mrs. Morgan that day, because the applicant was no sooner seen than hired, and Mrs. Morgan felt that she had made her usual good bargain. The applicant was a smiling, cheerful woman, perhaps a shade older than Mrs. Morgan expected, but she certainly seemed lively enough to keep up with seven-year-old twins.

And, although it was not important, the twins liked her too. As Andy said to Anne, that strange spring night when the lights were out and only the moonlight enabled them to see each other, sitting up in their twin beds, "*I* like her because she smiles a lot."

"*I* like her," said Anne, "because she has candy in her pocket."

"Always thinking about candy and stuff," Andy said scornfully. "Anyway, she said she *always* has candy in her pocket."

"That's a good thing," said Anne. "I wish it was already tomorrow," she added wistfully. "I'm going to be tiny and live in the dollhouse all day."

"I'd like to be a squirrel, I guess," Andy said. "Maybe a bear, or a cowboy, only that's way out west, and I guess I better stay around home the *first* time. Maybe a tiger. Or I guess a squirrel."

"You could be a pig," Anne suggested hopefully. "I wish it was tomorrow. She said we could do anything we liked, and I'm going to be tiny and live in the dollhouse. Maybe you want to be a puppy?"

"Old Anne," Andy said.

"Or a cow?" Anne was getting sleepy. "Or a horse?"

"Old Anne." They began to giggle softly.

"Or a cat?"

"Old Anne."

"Or a pig," Anne said, her voice muffled in the pillow. "Pig," she added, and was asleep. Andy, with his masculine superiority, outlasted her valiantly; he heard her take two deep breaths before his own eyes shut. "Squirrel," he said, and smiled in his sleep.

Downstairs, Mrs. Arthur William Morgan said to her husband, in that soft and persuasive voice wives use sometimes, "After all, I have my work, too. Please let's not forget, dear, that my work is *almost* as important as yours. Almost," she said again, and her voice, slipping away into silence, implied strongly that she was being wonderfully flattering to his work.

"Aren't I ever going to hear about anything but your work?" Mr. Arthur William Morgan looked at his wife irritably. "I'm *tired* of hearing about your work."

"Not half as tired," Mrs. Morgan said softly, stepping into the advantage, "as I am, sometimes."

"All right," her husband said. "So you've got a very important job and you're a very important woman and everyone thinks you're wonderful, and no one, not even your husband, is allowed to think any different. Except sometimes," he added bitterly, "I get to wishing I had a wife who wasn't *quite* so important and who stayed home sometimes and—"

"I suppose you wish you'd married someone else?" his wife asked, still using her same soft voice. "I suppose you wish you'd married—"

Their argument, begun in a familiar strain, went on in channels already so smoothly worn by years of bickering that neither of them bothered any longer to think about what they were saying. Mr. Morgan remarked that other wives found it possible to stay home and care for their homes and children; Mrs. Morgan pointed out that other wives did not have important, responsible positions. Mrs. Morgan added to this statement its usual corollary, which was that other wives did not have weak-kneed husbands who couldn't take on half the responsibility their wives did. Mr. Morgan retorted that he personally didn't see what was so damned important about Mrs. Morgan and her tiresome work except that it seemed to make Mrs. Morgan feel she had the right to tell everyone, Mr. Morgan in particular, what to do. Mrs. Morgan said that *some*one had to tell him. Mr. Morgan said that he was capable of taking care of himself. Mrs. Morgan said that she had never felt that subservience was necessary in a wife. Mr. Morgan said . . . Their voices went on and on.

In the kitchen, the new maid, her pocket full of candy and her eyes twinkling wickedly at some secret knowledge, listened first to the voices of the children as they drifted down from the open window of their room; when there was silence upstairs, she was forced to listen to the monotony of the argument going on between Mr. and Mrs. Morgan. After she had put the last dish away, given a final polish to the sink, and surveyed her new kitchen one last time to make sure that everything was in perfect order against the morning, the new maid smiled at the door behind which Mr. and Mrs. Morgan were bickering and went soundlessly upstairs to the room where the children slept in identical positions, as befitted twins. They had both kicked their blankets off, and she covered them. Andy said *"Blugh?"* inquiringly, and Anne answered him, *"Mnh."*

Then the new maid, who had that day, by Mrs. Morgan's authority, been given full charge of the children, the house, the cooking, the laundry, and presumably the mice in the pantry and the pumpkins in the garden, went soundlessly on her small feet to the room Mrs. Morgan had assigned her and where she had unpacked her belongings that afternoon. Much, much later, Mr. and Mrs. Morgan resolved their argument at the same point of mutual weariness at which it had been resolved so many times before, and went to bed.

In the morning, the sun rose as usual, and sent its usual impertinent rays to glitter on the eyelids of Mrs. Morgan. She opened her eyes, stirred uneasily, blinked, and sat up in bed. The room was full of sun, it was emphatically spring weather, and Mrs. Arthur William Morgan leaped out of bed with a firmness and resiliency she had not employed for a very long time. She slid expertly through the formality of washing, dressed quickly, not bothering with her shoelaces, gave her hair a civil pat with the brush, and ran downstairs. It's morning, she was thinking, the sun is bright, the sky is blue, and I am hungry. She ran into the kitchen, and said, as she ran, "Can I please have a cookie?"

"No cookie," said the new maid, looking severely at the plates she was setting onto the kitchen table. "Not before breakfast."

"*What's* for breakfast?" said Mrs. Morgan. "Can I have mine now, right away, quick?"

"You can have it when it's ready," said the new maid. "Not before."

"But I'm *hungry*," said Mrs. Morgan. "I'm *starving*."

The new maid half smiled. She set a bowl of hot oatmeal down at one place, and beckoned with her head at Mrs. Morgan. "There you go," she said.

Mrs. Morgan sat down, twisted her feet comfortably around the rungs of her chair, and said "Oatmeal? Oatmeal *again*?" She slid her napkin out of the ring and onto the floor, bent to retrieve it, and dropped her spoon. "I *hate* oatmeal," she said. "I want to put my *own* sugar on."

"You mind your manners," said the new maid, "or you won't have any sugar at all."

Mrs. Morgan ate half her oatmeal in three spoonfuls, then lingered over the other half until it was clammy. She bit largely into a piece of toast, and broke the rest of the toast into small pieces, some of which she dropped into her fruit juice glass; some of them she hid inside her napkin ring. "Can I please be excused?" she asked finally.

The new maid looked down at the dish of oatmeal, sighed, and said, "Three more spoonfuls and you can run along."

Mrs. Morgan dawdled over her three spoonfuls until she was excused without them, and then, free of the ritual of breakfast and possessed of a cookie, she ran out into the garden. She wandered for a while just looking; the grass was unbelievably green, the flowers just beginning to show color in the bright spring morning. The sky was so blue it hurt Mrs. Morgan's eyes to look into it. When she looked up once, she saw a gray squirrel race happily up the trunk of the tallest tree in the garden; when he reached a high branch he stopped, looking curiously around and down at Mrs. Morgan, and winked his eyes at her amiably.

"Come on down, squirrel," Mrs. Morgan said. She held out her hands and called to him, "*Come* on, *come* on. I'll give you some peanuts," she added winningly, but the gray squirrel only winked mockingly at her and ran on, up the tree and out of sight.

Mrs. Morgan went on undiscouraged through the garden; when she turned a corner of the path she saw, suddenly, a small boy staring back at her. For a minute they regarded each other soberly, and then the small boy said, "Who're *you*? Think you're big?"

Mrs. Morgan stood on one foot and swung the other back and forth. "I'm bigger'n *you*," she pointed out. "I'm better'n you, too."

"I'm smarter'n *you*," the small boy said.

"I'm smarter'n *you*," Mrs. Morgan said, "and I can boss you if I want to."

"You can *not*," said the little boy.

"Let's play house," suggested Mrs. Morgan. "I'll be the daddy and you'll be the mommy and I must come home from my office and you must be cooking dinner and I must say—"

"I don't want to play house," said the little boy. "I want to play army."

"How do you play army?" said Mrs. Morgan.

"First I kill you and then you kill me," said the little boy, reasonably.

"I don't want to play *that*," said Mrs. Morgan. "That's a silly, silly game."

"It is *not*," said the little boy.

"It is *so*," said Mrs. Morgan.

She turned and ran away, through the garden and back into the kitchen. "Can I have another cookie?" she asked.

After lunch she was tired and ready for a rest, but the minute she was put into her room with the shades drawn and the door closed she got out of bed and crept softly in her bare feet over to the dresser. There she opened all the jars and bottles of powder and cream and perfume; most of these she rubbed onto her face and into her hair. She carefully removed all of her clothes and then, as carefully, put them on again, but backward. Then she wriggled under the bed and played there until the new maid came and said she could get up from her rest. And, the new maid added, tightening her lips, Mrs. Morgan could just keep her clothes on backward for the rest of the day.

Later in the afternoon, as she played and danced among the flowers, Mrs. Morgan met the little boy again in the garden, and he yelled at her from a distance, "Nyah, nyah, *youuuu* can't boss *meeee*." She chased him, but he escaped her and stood behind a bush and jeered at her, as the squirrel capered above their heads in the late afternoon sunlight. Mrs. Morgan began to cry, finally, and ran away herself, into another part of the garden. It occurred to her that she could go into the house and ask for another cookie, but she had just turned the corner to the front steps when the sun, which had been meditating on this scene unnoticed for quite a while, went down.

Mrs. Morgan, her foot on the first of the steps, turned when she heard a sound behind her, and saw her husband.

"Evening, Agnes," he said formally.

"Arthur," Mrs. Morgan replied as formally. Together, in silence, they went up the steps to the front door. He held the door open for her and they went inside. In the living room the lamps were on, and Mrs. Morgan thought briefly how comfortable and warm it looked after the chill that had followed the sun's setting. Then Mr. Morgan said, "Why, look at you. You've got everything on backward."

"Well, you've got mud all over yourself," she said angrily. After one more mutually disapproving glance, they turned their backs on each other.

"Dinner is served," said the new maid, from the doorway.

Mrs. Morgan sat down at the table, looked deeply into her bowl of consommé, and said, "Heavens, I'm tired."

"So am I," said her husband, as though the fact surprised him.

"What *do* you do all day?" asked Mrs. Morgan maliciously. "I mean, to get so tired?"

"More than you do." His voice rose to its familiar argumentative tone. "If you think—" he began.

"I think," Mrs. Morgan cut in smoothly, "that you are speaking to me as though I were one of your secretaries or some such thing. Remember," she pointed out icily, "you are not my—" She stopped abruptly.

"Well, you can't boss—" he began, and then he, too, stopped speaking. His face went crimson, and Mrs. Morgan, her own face reddening, stared back at him. "You can't boss me," he finished weakly. His mouth stayed open as he stared at his wife.

"*You,*" Mrs. Morgan said helplessly, "can't boss *me,*" and then they both began to laugh, guiltily at first, and unwilling to look at each other, but then, finally, holding on to each other weakly while the tears rolled down their cheeks, until they were no longer able to laugh out loud but could only gasp.

"Arthur," Mrs. Morgan said finally, barely able to speak. "Oh, Arthur."

Mr. Morgan wiped his eyes with the back of his hand. "And your clothes!" he said, "Agnes, your clothes!" Together they burst into laughter again.

The new maid, peering through the swinging door between the dining room and the kitchen, watched the couple for a quick minute, and then, grinning, returned to her dishwashing. From upstairs, the voices of the children drifted down to her through the open windows.

"And when you're right on top, in the little tiny branches"— Andy's voice rose—"you can swing, and hold on tight, and swing way out over the ground!"

Anne giggled softly. "I had five cookie crumbs and a grape," she said. "You know the little cups in the little tiny china closet? Well, they leak. Everything leaks out of the bottoms of them. And the beds look soft, but really they're not."

"And the ground looks so far far far away," Andy went on dreamily, "and you have to hold on tight."

"And I rode on the little fire engine," Anne said. "She wound it up for me and I rode around and around and around the playroom, and it's miles and miles and miles . . ." Her voice faded.

"Swinging back and forth, up in the sky," Andy said. His voice softened abruptly. "Up in the sky," he said once more, and then all was quiet.

The new maid finished her washing, took the untouched soup bowls off the table in the dining room, and glanced into the living room, where Mr. and Mrs. Morgan sat on the couch holding hands and talking earnestly, and still laughing occasionally.

When the kitchen was clean and tidy, the new maid took off her apron and hung it up with a sigh. She went upstairs soundlessly,

72 • SHIRLEY JACKSON

stopping at the room where Anne and Andy slept in identical positions. When she covered them, Anne said "*Graa?*" inquiringly, and Andy reassured her, "*Wssh.*"

Then the new maid went back downstairs, still without sound on her small feet, to the room Mrs. Morgan had assigned her and, stopping now and then to smile wickedly to herself, began to pack.

French Is the Mark of a Lady

SHE CAME IN VERY QUIETLY, STANDING IN THE DARKNESS OF THE huge polished room until I noticed her. She was very small, and her dark curls were tied up in a red bow. When she walked, the bow shook back and forth on her head.

"Hello," I said to her politely.

"What do you want here?" she asked.

"I've come to see your mama."

"My *mother*"—the emphasis was very marked—"is still dressing."

"I know. I'm waiting for her."

"Have you come about a charity?"

"No. I used to know your mother a long time ago, and now I've come to see her."

"Did she invite you?"

"No."

The red bow shook vigorously. "My mother doesn't talk to people unless she invites them here."

I was annoyed. "Nevertheless, I strongly suspect that your mother will be down to see me in a minute."

"Oh." Large dark eyes regarded me steadily. "Why do you want to see my mother?"

"I used to know her a long time ago."

"How long?"

"Oh . . . ten years. Before you were born."

"I'm eight."

"I've known your mother since she was a little girl."

The topic seemed to bore my companion. She stood perfectly still, her eyes looking over my shoulder. When I finished speaking, she looked at me again and said: "I've got a boyfriend."

I didn't laugh. "Aren't you rather young?" I asked.

"No."

I tried again. "What's his name?"

"John. He drives a car."

"How old is he?" I was a little startled.

"Thirty-three." She nodded vigorously. "He drives me around."

"That's very convenient."

"I need someone to drive me around," she said, looking at me.

"Where do you have to go?"

"Everywhere." She made a vague gesture with her hand. "I have to go around everywhere."

A sudden thought struck me. "I suppose you have a great deal of charity work to do, like your mother."

Her voice took on a heavy lifelessness. "It's such a bore," she sighed.

"But tell me about your boyfriend," I said. "What else does he do besides drive you around?"

"He delivers ice," she said.

I kept my face sober. "That must be very interesting."

"Sometimes it is," she said. "Sometimes it's inconsistent."

I thought. "Do you mean inconvenient?" I asked.

"Inconsistent," she said firmly.

"Oh. Well, are you going to marry your boyfriend?"

"What?" she said blankly.

"No. Well . . . what does your mother think of him?"

"She thinks it's good for me."

"What, your having a boyfriend?"

"She says she used to ride on ice wagons when she was a girl."

"She did," I said. "I used to ride on them with her. But I don't recall our having any boyfriends among the drivers. We always felt that they were a little . . . well . . . old. I recall that we preferred younger men . . . say, the boys we met in school."

"They're so puerile," she said.

I jumped. "I suppose they are," I said faintly.

"It's nice having a *man* around," she added.

"Has your mother met him?"

"No," she said, looking at me. "You don't deliver ice to the front door."

"Where do you go to school?" I asked desperately.

"I go to a private school," she said. Her voice took on that lifelessness again. "School is such a bore," she said.

"What do you learn there?"

"French. And music."

"Do you like French? I remember I used to hate it, in college."

She looked at me severely. "French is the mark of a true lady."

"Your mother doesn't speak French. Is she a true lady?"

"My mother does so speak French. She learned when we were in Paris after her divorce. She said she would have to know a few words anyway. You don't need more than that."

"And music?" I said.

The opening of the door interrupted her, and we both turned to see her mother entering. The little girl held out her hand to me, and I shook it weakly, and then, smiling at her mother, she went to the door, stopping to say: "Mother, this lady and I have had such a nice chat, while we were waiting for you." Then she smiled again at me, and closed the door quietly behind her.

"Such a sweet child," I said.

"And so clever, too," murmured her mother. And then to me, gaily: "But, *you*, my dear! How are *you*?"

Gaudeamus Igitur

ALTHOUGH SHE WENT FIRST OF ALL TO THE HILL BEYOND THE OLD cemetery, it was too wet to sit on the ground and there were children walking sedately up the hill in a long line, following one another in solemn procession; five of them. She put her scarf on a rock and sat down, realizing it would be difficult to sit there for even as much as the few minutes she owed the hill, seeing already as she sat down the uneasy perching, her feet braced in the mud, and the ungraceful rising, with the hem of her dress caught in the grass, her self-conscious duty completed, nothing solved.

I've got to think, she had told herself; decide what to do. Go somewhere and sit down quietly and think sweetly and logically and come home at peace. Not, however, on this wet, windy hill with children eyeing her cautiously in a long row against the sky. Five of them, three boys and a girl and a small, unidentifiable one; she disliked getting up from the rock while they watched her.

Now, she thought, putting her shoulder up to hide the children. Now what are we going to do? There was nothing to do, turning to see if the children were still watching, nothing to do but what she was going to do anyway. "Might as well go ahead, then," she said aloud, and stood up quickly, realizing when she was standing that the children were watching and her skirt was swinging mud against her stockings. "Nothing to do," she said as loud as she dared, and started down the hill, hurrying, as she felt the children moving down slowly to inspect the rock where she had been sitting, possibly shouting something unkind after her.

She knew how to go, and where, but she minded going with her hair uncombed and mud on her clothes. "They'll have to get used to it," she said, and felt her footsteps going slower on the pavement. There was no one around she knew; she might be going to call on someone in the city, or to the American consul in a strange country. The houses passed by her quickly; they registered faintly against her mind, trying to delay her. She had been inside many of these houses in three years; as she passed them, her mind swiftly set up a partial interior for each: one had heavy walnut furniture and antiques in a dark room; another was just a hall, with a copy of *Life* on a table; one was a room cleared for a fraternity dance, a punchbowl set on a bench against large windows, and lights around the walls.

On the corner was the house she was going to, smaller than the others, but her mind refused this one, stopping obstinately with a picture of the front door set back in its narrow white frame, solidly closed around the familiar rooms within. "It will all be different now," she said, and hesitated at the foot of the path across the lawn. No one had seen her; she could walk right on past, except then where would she go? Not back to the hill, and she felt the five children following her, so vividly that she turned and looked behind her, but there was nothing but the row of houses she had been in.

I'll look like a fool now unless I do, she thought, and walked up to the door, stopping to admire the front of the house as though she had never seen it before, had not come here many times in wonderful fear and excitement. In the small panes of glass on either side of the door she saw halves of herself; her untidy hair clouded her glimpse of the hall within, but the oak umbrella stand was still there.

("It makes me look academic," he had told her once; they were reading Keats.) I'll say I've been out walking, she thought, and rang the bell.

He opened the door himself and she said "Hello, Mr. Harrison," very timidly, not knowing if he would feel right about letting her in; realizing, suddenly, that she had come alone.

He was pleased to see her, he said, happy she had come; they had returned only a week ago, he said, had she come only today? Ashamed to say that she was here to see them her first day back, she let him lead her into the living room, too quickly for her to be prepared to meet his wife again.

Barbara was just getting up from the couch; she was wearing an unfamiliar blue dress. (Back in the dormitory, only last year, she had worn a tweed skirt and a sweater; she used to have a black dinner dress with a full net skirt.) "Gloria," she said, "I'm so glad you came." They had been reading; his book was open on the arm of his chair, and Barbara was putting her magazine down on the table. "You've no idea how happy I am to see you," Barbara said. She looked at her husband, and then said, "Sit down, won't you, Gloria?"

For a minute it was easy to say, "I wanted to be the first to congratulate you. And welcome you back," and then he was pushing a chair up to her and she sat down, suddenly, and there was a long silence.

Barbara said, "I was hoping you'd come right away. I've been so eager to see all of you. But Stephen said . . ." And she stopped.

"I was eager to come," Gloria said. I sat on that hill wondering if I ought to, her mind went on.

"Can't we offer our guest some tea?" he said abruptly. "I'd like to have tea."

"Of course," Barbara said, and stood up. "I'll get it right away."

Gloria was beginning, slowly, to realize that the house was still the same: There was a bowl of asters on the mantel now, but the bookshelves still stood firmly on either side; the chairs were still wearing green-and-white chintz, although Barbara's black leather pocketbook now lay on one; the windows still looked over the lawn to the college street. "It's so nice to be here again," she said, leaning back.

"I'm always glad to get back," he said. "Summers are fine for a week or two. Always happy to get away from enthusiastic young students." They both laughed. "But I'm glad to be back," he said. "I was out west all summer wishing I were sitting here in my own house."

"I thought Barbara would have this whole room changed around by now," Gloria said.

"She always did like it this way." He seemed surprised. "I don't know why it should be different."

"I was writing you a letter this summer. Just before Barbara's letter came, with the news. Then I didn't know whether I ought to write you or not, so I kept the letter."

"I'd like to see it," he said. "What was it about? You could have sent it."

"I finished my long poem," she said, watching him to see if he remembered. "I wrote asking if I could send it to you, or if you'd rather have me wait and show it to you this fall. I wasn't sure what to do, so I kept the letter."

"Barbara wrote you?" he said. "She didn't tell me."

"She wrote all of us," Gloria said. "We were all very close friends last year in the sorority, and she thought we'd like to know."

"She should have told me," he said. "So you finished the poem; when will I see it?"

Barbara was coming into the room managing a large tray awkwardly through the doorway. Gloria lifted the magazine and an ashtray from the coffee table and stood holding them while Barbara put the tray down. "I thought you were going to drop it," she said.

Barbara, sliding onto the couch behind the table, nodded and said, "I thought I was too." She began to pour the tea, eagerly, and as though she were very conscious of being a hostess. "Sugar?" she said, looking up at Gloria.

"Please," Gloria said, and Barbara smiled.

"I remember, of course," Barbara said. "Stephen?"

Gloria balanced her teacup carefully; it's important to Barbara now, she thought, remembering how they would put full cups on the floor of their room between books and ink bottles and never think about it, and she stirred her tea cautiously.

"In Arizona," Barbara began gracefully, "we used to have cocktails every day on the balcony of our room, because it was the only cool place we could find. Stephen, wasn't that fun?"

"Lemon?" he said suddenly.

"How did you like Arizona?" Gloria asked. "Did you learn to ride a horse? Did she, Mr. Harrison?"

"She learned to ride quite well," he said. "Lemon, Barbara?"

"I thought I brought some," Barbara murmured, leaning forward to look over the tray. "I knew you wanted it, Stephen," she said.

He hesitated and then said, "Never mind."

"You got a beautiful tan," Gloria said to Barbara. They both looked at him, pale against his dark hair, quiet, never dared by the sun. "Stephen never tans," Barbara said gaily.

"I was on the beach all summer," Gloria said, "and lost it all after a couple of weeks in New York."

Barbara's hand moved nervously from the teapot handle to the spoon in her saucer, then up to her hair, smoothing it back over her ears. "We were in New York for a few days."

He put his cup delicately on the table, and the small sound encouraged Gloria to put her cup down too, next to his. "I ought to be getting back. I haven't even unpacked." I came here right away, she thought, before I opened my suitcase.

"Did you do any writing at all this summer?" Barbara asked. "We thought of you so often."

She looked at her husband expectantly, and he said, "We haven't finished unpacking even after a week. Barbara shipped back boxes of junk from the west."

"Souvenirs," Barbara said. "Everything they sell tourists."

Gloria stood up, feeling again the mud on her skirt, her hair still wild from the wind outside. "I went up and sat on the hill past the cemetery," she said to Barbara. "It was cold and wet and horrible and a pack of kids chased me away."

"You'll come to see me, won't you?" Barbara said. "I want all of you to come."

She rose and followed Gloria into the hall, and stood waiting with her husband while Gloria hesitated, her hand on the door latch. "I'd love to come, if I may," Gloria said. They looked incredibly married, she thought, standing there next to each other. "I'll see you in class Monday, Mr. Harrison?"

"Try to get to my office Monday afternoon," he said, "and bring my letter. I worry," he went on, "that Barbara is already afraid of being bored living as a faculty wife, out of touch with her old friends."

"*Will* you come see me?" Barbara asked urgently.

"Of course," Gloria said, smiling. "We all want to—Mrs. Harrison," and realized as she said it how dreadful it sounded.

"You were so nice to come," Barbara said.

Gloria felt the door close behind her; it doesn't matter anymore how I look, she thought, I can go unpack now. She thought of the children on the hill perhaps still waiting, expecting her back, and it pleased her to disappoint them by turning down the street toward the campus.

It doesn't make any difference at all, she thought, as she walked quickly away from a house that was a warm living room full of books, past a house that was a hallway and a copy of *Life* on a table; he hated having her ask about my writing.

The Lie

JOYCE DUNCAN'S DECISION TO GO BACK WAS CRYSTALLIZED BY THE receipt of a letter from her mother, saying, in part, "Dear, your last letter sounded so lonely and sad; remember they say that whenever a woman feels low she can always cheer herself up by buying a new hat or a new dress, or both, so am enclosing a small check. Buy yourself something *silly.*" The check was just small enough not to matter enormously against the rent or the phone bill, and just large enough to make the trip a reality instead of the dim temptation it had been for so long.

"Jed," she said, "I think I *will* go back. Just for a day or so."

"It's your money," he said, not even lifting his head to speak to her.

Perhaps if I can explain somehow, she thought, relate it to something *he* understands; perhaps then when I come back there might be a way we can start to talk to each other, perhaps even start over . . . "You see," she said inadequately, "everything is so *wrong,* somehow. Maybe if I went back to where I started from, just for a while . . ."

"Go ahead," he said.

"Maybe I'd be happier if I tried it," Joyce said. "You see," she went on, not wanting to explain but hoping that somehow it might make him turn at last and look at her, "there's a sort of mix-up that happened a long time ago that I'd like to straighten out. A . . . a lie."

"I didn't know one lie more or less mattered to *you*," he said, and turned a page of his book.

She knew by now that if she let the tears come into her eyes or her voice, Jed would only take his book and go into the bedroom to read. Helplessly she said, "I can't help feeling that if I go back and straighten things up *there*, maybe things *here* will be better. Maybe I've been off on a wrong track all these years just because of that one thing. Maybe when I come back, maybe you and I can . . ."

He stood up, his finger between the pages of his book. "Look," he said tiredly, "maybe if you go back to that town, wherever it is, and un-lie yourself, you'll cancel out every lie you've told since. You might even cancel out all the unkind things you've *done* since. But I doubt it."

"If you'd try to understand—" she began, but he closed the bedroom door so gently that he might not have heard her. I'll leave early in the morning, she thought; I'll leave before he's up and he can make his own stupid breakfast, and when I come back . . .

In the car the next morning, headed finally back exactly the way she had come here nearly ten years before, she found herself almost chanting, in a rhythm made up partly of the sound of the car wheels on the pavement, and partly the pulse of her own excitement: I'm going back, I'm going back. I should have done it much much sooner, she thought suddenly; things wouldn't have been as bad as this if I'd gone back before. Once it's done, I realized with triumph, I won't ever need to go back again. She tried to imagine what Jean Simpson's face was like, and found she thought instead about the pictures on the wall of the office; she thought she could remember Jean Simpson's voice, but all she could hear when she tried to think about it was her own voice, level and positive, saying "I saw her, it was Jean Simpson. I recognized her."

I will tell her, she thought, recognizing that although she was driving on a wide and nearly empty highway she was going very slowly; I will tell her that I am more sorry than I can say, that I was wrong, that I realize now the injustice I did her. I could offer a public apology, she thought, and then: No, why submit her to that?

Milltown. Seventeen miles to Prospect, and it was barely ten-thirty. Perhaps Jean Simpson had moved away? Her family could not have afforded to leave Prospect; the only way a girl like that could get out of town was to move into a worse environment, and Jean had never been—this thought was oddly reassuring—a particularly *good* girl, not at all the sort of person one might be concerned about for the past ten years. She was not, actually, worth a second thought, but nevertheless Joyce Duncan, scrupulously honest, was coming back after all this time to right an old wrong.

I'm being ridiculous about this, she thought, driving more slowly still past Milltown and East Milltown; I'm thinking in terms of a major disaster and it *was* only a trifle. Perhaps I ought to take her something, some small thing to show I hold no grudge, a pretty scarf, perhaps, or a box of candy? She could hardly expect me to give her *money*, but perhaps a couple of pairs of stockings? Better let it wait until I've seen her, she told herself; she may be angry still and not want anything from me.

She had thought she would not remember this town after ten years, but she turned automatically onto the street that led to her old house without recognizing anything strange about her memory of it. When she stopped the car, she found it hard to look at the old house and imagine that it could have changed. "So that's it," she said, half aloud. "Still here, after all."

Until she stepped out of her car it was difficult to imagine herself as a stranger, trying to go back, but the minute she put her foot down onto the familiar sidewalk in front of her old house it was suddenly so surprising, so odd a combination of ten years gone and yet still present in her mind, that she had to turn and rest her hand upon the side of the car to steady herself. Joyce Richards, she thought, little Joyce Richards, not Mrs. Jed Duncan at all.

She felt wary of going too close to her old house, although she had been anxious to see it again; perhaps if she came within its reach it would capture her again, and never let her go this time. Or perhaps it was only because she was embarrassed about being seen by people looking out their windows and telling one another, "There's Joyce Richards come back. Thought she was doing so well in the city?" The sight of the house had reminded her of Mrs. Random, so she turned on the sidewalk and started up the path to the house next door. Once on the overgrown little path with Mrs. Random's house ahead of her, she realized at last that this was indescribably real, and it seemed to her for a moment that perhaps all this time she had been living in unreality, and waiting to awaken here again, where things were solid and the colors of the sky and the flowers and even the path were actual, real, unfaded. The door of the house was blue, and she thought that for years she had not known how blue that color could truly be.

Going up the path, she almost tasted the richness of color and form, and stopped—which she could never remember having done before—to look at, and finally touch, a rose, which bent slightly toward her and gave back to her touch a strong and soft pressure. She bent to see if it smelled as she remembered roses ought to smell, and it was heavy, rich, and lovely. Even the white doorstep amazed her eyes, and the knocker—had she ever seen another one like it?—was possessed of an actual weight of its own, so that it fell back from her hands and crashed loudly in the still morning.

Waiting on the shiny doorstep—was there city dirt on her shoes to soil its whiteness?—she listened to the odd, echoing house inside, and thought that within the city there was never any sense, even though people lived so close together, of that intimate knowledge of walls and floors and ceilings, and she remembered the distant sharp sound of voices in another room when she was a child and supposedly asleep in bed. She heard a footstep inside and then the door opened.

"Hello," she said, wondering at the sound of her own voice, "it's Mrs. Random, isn't it?"

"Yes." The eyes were not precisely suspicious; wary, rather, as of one who had dealt with personable salesladies and been taken in by supposed bargains.

"I'm Joyce Duncan. I used to be Joyce Richards."

"Yes?"

"Don't you remember me?"

"No."

"I used to live next door."

The information was taken in and discarded. "Did you?"

"I used to play in your yard." Desperately, she was spending information she had meant to use sparingly, dwelling on each remembered moment, hoping Mrs. Random might help her reconstruct her lost childhood. "Don't you remember?"

"So many people." Mrs. Random waved vaguely at the house next door. "Can't remember *every*one, you know."

"Well, I remember *you*." She looked again at the clean housedress, pink imprinted with thousands of small flower sprigs, and thought that in that long-dead time Mrs. Random had worn either this, or one astonishingly like it, and that the same wisp of white hair had been lying against her cheek for all these years; had Mrs. Random, she wondered, then been this vague-eyed creature, hiding nervously behind her own door? "When my mother was sick you brought us a little roast chicken, and you came over when my father died," she said, unwillingly. She was forced into this conversational coin; one had always collected news of deaths and miscarriages and broken legs for Mrs. Random's pleasure. She thought deeply. "I had pneumonia," she added.

Mrs. Random's interest was caught and she frowned, trying to remember. "Williams?" she asked.

"Richards. I was Joyce Richards. My father was John Richards, and he was the clerk in the railroad station. You used to say that I could hardly wait to get away from town, the way I used to spend all my time at the station watching the trains."

"Richards?" said Mrs. Random wonderingly. "You must have gone away at last, then," she added intelligently. "I heard it said you were in the city."

Joyce smiled, thinking that her smile, warm and proud and altogether the secret pleasant smile of a woman happy and secure, was not entirely a lie; by Mrs. Random's standards she had certainly done very well for herself. "I'm married now," she said, still smiling. "My husband's a wonderful man."

"Girls ought to get married," Mrs. Random said, with a sudden odd, perceptive glance at Joyce. "Keeps them out of trouble. Your old house is still there," she went on, "but no one's living in it. Probably open."

"I may still have a key to it," said Joyce, ashamed to admit that she had carried it on her key ring all these years.

"Go on in, then," said Mrs. Random generously, free with any invitation except one into her own house. "Been a lot of people in and out of there, all these years."

Joyce lingered on the doorstep, even though Mrs. Random showed signs of wanting to withdraw and close the door. "Whatever happened to the Collinses, used to live on the other side of us?"

"Collins?" said Mrs. Random vaguely. "Can't recall the name. It was Williams lived *there*."

"The Cartwrights across the street?"

"Moved, I suppose," said Mrs. Random.

"And Bob Cartwright?"

"Now," said Mrs. Random, "I *do* recall a Bob Cartwright. Married that plain girl. Got a little grocery or some such down on Railroad Street."

"Bob is married?"

"I get *my* groceries at Wingdon's," Mrs. Random pointed out, as though it were necessary to establish this fact clearly and immediately. "Come back again sometime," she said.

This time she closed the door flatly, obviously having concluded that otherwise there would be no end to this conversation, and perhaps feeling that there was no harm in closing the door against the face of someone she would probably never see again.

The roses turned slightly away from Joyce as she went down the path, and she wondered that she had ever felt free with them or if it could be true that she had once been punished for the desecration of picking one. She could see the house next door, but the hedge between had grown so dense that it did not seem likely her private path through it still existed. Nothing, she realized now, had been tended for years; she could see that on the house next door a second-story window frame sagged against the shingles, and bricks were gone from the chimney.

I certainly won't go in there *now*, she thought, not with Mrs. Random peering out from behind her curtains to see if I'll try to steal the doors or make off with part of the fence; I'll come back later. Perhaps, too, if she visited other old acquaintances and checked on other landmarks, she might approach this house again, later in the day or perhaps even tomorrow, more in the spirit in which she had left it, less as a stranger whom Mrs. Random could not remember. She realized that she had not asked Mrs. Random about Jean Simpson, and wondered if there were anything about her that Mrs. Random might have remembered.

She got back into her car, aware of Mrs. Random's critical eye from the downstairs window, and drove down the street, thinking, as she passed the streetlights and the curbs and the paths into gardens, of how many times, and always alone, she had walked and run and scuffled and skipped rope down this street. She would idle with one foot in the gutter and one on the curb, stepping gingerly in high-heeled shoes, hoping someone would notice her and speak to her, afraid sometimes, and sometimes elated, on her way to school, or to play alone in the park, and always thinking of the time when she would be rich and successful and would come back to walk with scorn past the people who had never noticed her then.

She had always come this way, because the street ended shortly beyond her old house and fell away into fields and trees, although it might be that they had put a road through there now, since there were certainly new houses farther down the street than she remembered. Even though she was driving, which she had never done here before, she found that she was turning the car along the same old ways. She watched along the sidewalk, as she drove slowly, for her old footprints, perhaps even expecting that—as though they had told her that the old Joyce had gone on ahead, and could probably be caught up with on the way—upon turning a corner she might see, halfway down the block ahead, herself in a pink sweater and a white linen skirt, on her way to the library, carrying a book or a white patent leather purse, striding along—was she not always a little bit late?—and not turning to look at cars passing by. "Joyce," she wanted to call, "Joyce, wait a minute, I want to tell you something."

Abruptly, because these streets were shorter and narrower and less alive than she had once known them, she turned a corner and found the high school facing her, and she felt swiftly, without at all wanting to, the old familiar dismay; was she late for class, were they all looking at her, was she being laughed at? Then, stopping the car and putting her chin down on the wheel, she looked the high school slowly up and down, half-smiling, as one whom it no longer had power to terrify. "So there you are," she told it, "and I'm safe from you now, forever. I got away after all, didn't I?" The high school stared back, square and blank and uncommunicative, as though even now what happened to Joyce Richards was unimportant.

Beyond the red brick and the wooden facings of the school building, she could see the straight lines of the goalposts on the football field, and the long wooden bleachers. She remembered

walking quickly along the path alone, on her way to a game, knowing that she went to the games, even alone and without friends, because the mere sense of being where everyone else was made her
feel somehow almost a part of the crowd. Names came into her
mind, and she smiled again. Katharine, she thought, pretty Katie.
Married some local boy, probably, and is sitting somewhere in this
town today with a pack of children and lines in her face. . . . Dot,
the most popular girl; had she stayed popular and successful, or
failed miserably at some appealing career? . . . Was it actually possible that all these girls (Katie wearing her green skirt, Dot always a
cheerleader, sarcastic Marian, and Wendy) had wandered off in different directions, and perhaps married and had children, and lived
in different houses, unfamiliar and remote? Was it possible that
those girls were no longer a source of laughing danger to Joyce
Richards, that they were now powerless? Then what had they known,
so long ago, that Joyce had not known? What power had they ever
really had?

She shook her head, amused at her own silliness, and restarted
the car. No sense parking in front of the high school, where everyone would only pass by and wonder what you were doing, and she
did not think that she could safely sit here and watch the new Katies
and Dots and Marians come arm in arm down the walk, staring at
her briefly and curiously, before turning to go toward the village.
Perhaps, though, it might be Jean Simpson who came down the
walk, proudly and not turning her head; not, in fact, seeming to
hear anything said to her, although it was always clear from her face
that she had been crying.

Hastily, Joyce drove the car around the corner at what was almost
a dangerous speed and turned onto the main street of the village; was
it possible that in all these years the brightness of the Sunrise Dairy
had not faded? She could see its sign halfway down the main street,
past the jeweler's, and she could see the railroad station beyond. "I
should have come by train," she told herself unreasonably, "like the

way I left." She parked the car halfway down the main street, directly in front of the Sunrise Dairy, and stepped out onto the hot, unshaded sidewalk, remembering as she did so that farther up the street, near the gas station, there was a handprint in the cement and the initials JRS. The younger children had always believed that the unknown JRS had been sent to prison for defacing the sidewalk, and the more sophisticated older children told one another cynically that he had later been elected the town's first mayor.

The Sunrise Dairy, with its black and white tiles and its familiar smell of chocolate syrup and toast and strawberry ice cream, was for a moment loud with remembered voices, and then suddenly quiet with a late-morning silence. As she sat down at the counter she saw that actually she was alone in here, except for the counterman—could it still be Red, after all these years?—busy with something at the far end of the counter. "Lettuce and tomato and a chocolate shake," she said, without thinking. Perhaps she had ordered these things in soda shops and drugstores and restaurants during the past ten years, but it was certain, as she said the words and then smiled reminiscently, that the correct inflection had been missing ("*lettuce* and tom*a*to and a *choc*olate shake"), and she wondered if perhaps the general inferiority of lettuce and tomato and chocolate all these years had been due to that lost rhythm.

"Lettuce and tomato and a chocolate shake," the counterman said in confirmation, and she knew that she could not have forgotten his voice with its faint lisp, so she said, "It *is* Red, isn't it?"

"That's right," he said.

"I thought I remembered you. But I imagine you've forgotten *me*."

He looked at her, his head to one side, frowning; she realized that she had remembered him as lean and young, but he was stouter now, as though the dairy had done well since she left, and his red hair was graying. "Mary?" he said. "Mary Something?"

"No," she said, unwilling to let him guess names she perhaps would not like to hear. "I used to be Joyce Richards."

"Joyce what?"

"Joyce Richards."

He shook his head and smiled. "Well, you know," he said, "I guess a hundred people come in here every day. And all those kids from the high school—"

"I used to go to the high school."

"Sure," he said.

He turned away to make her sandwich, and because he was not looking at her she said boldly, "I'm trying to get in touch with a girl I used to know. Jean Simpson."

He selected a piece of lettuce and looked at it thoughtfully. "Simpson," he said, as though she had ordered something.

"Jean Simpson. Has she left town or anything?"

"I couldn't say, I really couldn't say."

"You see," she said, "she got into trouble once, and it was my fault, and I wanted to come back and sort of fix it up with her."

He nodded approvingly, and laid another piece of tomato on her sandwich. "Right thing to do," he said. "What kind of trouble was it?"

"Nothing important, just something I'd like to get straightened out."

"Look," he said, glancing up at her, "what do you mean, trouble? You fight over some fellow or something?"

"No, no," she said.

He hesitated, pausing with her sandwich in his hand. "Nothing serious, I suppose?"

She thought that perhaps he would not give her the sandwich until she told him, so she said, "Well, she made a kind of mistake, and it turned out that I had to be the person who told on her." That's as much as he deserves to know, she thought, and it isn't a lie if I don't tell *him* the truth.

"I *did* hear," he said elaborately, "that there was a girl couple of years ago got into trouble with some man out at that roadhouse."

"It certainly wasn't anything like *that*. Is that my sandwich?"

"Lots of girls—"

"Nothing serious," she said. "If you don't know her, it wouldn't even interest you. It happened a long time ago."

"Jean Simpson," he said reflectively. "Now you mention it, it seems to me that I heard she did something pretty bad. Not *killing* anyone, you understand." He looked at her eagerly. "I might just happen to know what it was, after all," he said.

"You couldn't know," she said. "I don't believe anyone knows anymore."

He grinned unpleasantly. "Never mind," he said. "She got into some kind of trouble and you're back now to try and fix it up. What do *you* get out of it?"

"Don't be silly," she said. "It's a trifle, and all I want is to see that it's straightened out."

"Oh, sure," he said knowingly, and set the sandwich down before her. "You wouldn't be here trying to square it unless it was something pretty important," he said.

"It's a private matter," she said, and tried to smile at him; surely it was not going to be necessary to discuss this with people like Red? If he did not remember Jean Simpson, was there any reason for telling him about old scandals? Why, after all, should she and Jean Simpson suffer because Red was curious? "You know how these things are," she added stupidly.

"Sure," he said. "Right. I know." And he winked at her.

She lifted half of her sandwich; was not the lettuce faded and the tomato yellowed? "What do I owe you?" she asked, sliding off the stool.

"Ninety. Might be able to help you, after all, if you'd let me know what *happened*."

"It doesn't matter," she said. "Nothing happened. Keep the dime."

"Thanks, lady," he said ironically as she went toward the door. "I'll be asking around for your Jean Simpson."

Next time I'll know, she thought, jabbing her key viciously at the car's starter; next time I'll know not to open my mouth and not to humiliate myself, and not to order lettuce and tomato, and next time I won't even come back, and Jean Simpson can take care of herself. Next time, she thought, I hope Red is dead, or gone crazy or poor and starving or something.

Well, she thought further, in a moment of utter clarity, I've seen my old hometown and I've visited my old neighbor and my old school and Red's, and there isn't another soul in this town who'd remember me, and *that*'s what I came back for—to see a crazy old woman and a gossiping old man and a fallen-down old school, and I haven't even told Jean Simpson I'm sorry.

There might be one more place to look, and she realized that she might have saved time and gone there earlier, as she turned the car toward the railroad station. A little grocery down on Railroad Street, Mrs. Random had said.

Trying to fix the probable location of the grocery in her mind, she found that although she could remember the station side of Railroad Street very clearly, she had only the dimmest picture of what the other side of the street looked like. She knew that the station offices and the post office should be on her right as she approached the station, but on the left she could remember only a row of dirty little houses and perhaps a bar and grill. Hadn't Jean Simpson lived in one of those houses? It seemed reasonable, at any rate, to turn left when she reached the station, and as she swung her car around the corner she saw ahead of her a faded sign, stiff and colorless under the hot sun. SQUARE DEAL GROCERY, it said. MEATS.

Now, she told herself, sitting in her car in front of the grocery and staring straight ahead to where the railroad tracks disappeared between the quiet hills, now I am Joyce Duncan who used to be Joyce Richards, and I am twenty-nine years old and I live in the city with my husband. I am not nineteen, and I do not live in this town, or owe anyone here any kind of loyalty, and I do not have any crush on any Bob Cartwright, and all I am doing is trying to perform a generous act that nine people out of ten would never think about doing. I am here, she told herself, sitting in the car and not looking out at the grocery, because a long time ago I did a silly thing where I lost my head and said Jean Simpson took that money. She has every right to think I deliberately tried to get her into trouble just to save myself, and even if this *is* Bob Cartwright's store he is probably married, and I am certainly married, and I am going inside only to see if he knows how I can find Jean Simpson.

I hope he isn't in the grocery, though, she thought, deliberately fixing her mind on a picture of him in a white apron, holding a butcher's cleaver, probably haggling over small change; I hope the store is closed for the day.

It was dark inside, and for a minute she hesitated just within the store, making out vague shapes, which were of course a counter and bins of fruit and vegetables, and rows of cans on the shelves. Then, as she let the screen door close behind her and moved toward the counter, a woman emerged from the back room brushing her hair out of her eyes and not looking up. "Yes?" she said.

What was there to say? I would like a can of corn, please; how much do you charge for hamburger? "I'm looking for Mr. Cartwright."

The woman looked up at her and then away again. "He's not here. I'm his wife."

It was not possible to stop and think, to remember Bob Cartwright and how he had once been too proud to speak to Joyce Richards. It was only possible to stop for a second and look again at the woman, at her dull hair and her dirty dress. But the woman was waiting, and her stance suggested strongly that unless this business with her husband was legitimate, it might be better to hurry and do whatever purchasing was necessary and then leave at once. "I actually wanted to ask him," Joyce said hesitantly, "that is—perhaps you could tell me—I want to know whatever happened to an old friend of mine, a girl named Jean Simpson."

"My name used to be Jean Simpson," said the woman. "Was it me you wanted?"

"I guess it was," said Joyce Duncan, dazed. Although she had never really intended to run up and embrace her long-lost friend, the idea that they might not recognize each other had not, up till now, occurred to her. "I didn't remember you," she said, with a false little laugh.

"I don't remember *you.*"

"My name is Joyce Duncan now. I used to be Joyce Richards."

"That so?" said the woman indifferently. "Doesn't come back to me."

"I guess you'll remember when I tell you what I came for." Now it was surprisingly easy to say. "Before I left this town, ten years ago, I did something I've always been sorry for, and I've been hunting for you all day to try and fix it up."

"What's it got to do with me?" The woman glanced at the back room from which she had come, as though she wished this interminable conversation over and herself safely back in her rocking chair, or on her bed, or watching her soap operas on TV.

"You don't remember? The money that disappeared during gym class during senior year, and I said I saw you take it?"

"I never took any money."

"I know you didn't," said Joyce Duncan. "I took it. It was two dollars and seventy cents and I spent it on a pair of stockings and a box of candy and a cheap pearl necklace from the five-and-ten. I said I saw you take it because I was scared, and they almost expelled you from high school. It was the dues from the Girls' Club."

"We run an honest store," the woman said. "Business is tough, but we've always been honest."

"I know. What I mean is, I once accused you of stealing, and you didn't, and even though it wasn't important I wanted to come back and tell you I was sorry."

"We give people a square deal," said the woman dully, "and they mostly give us a square deal. That's why we call it the Square Deal Grocery. Because we give—"

"Don't you mind anymore? I mean, I remember how you must have felt that day in old Martinson's office when you kept saying you didn't and I kept saying I saw you, and they believed me because they knew you wanted the money more than I did."

"I guess everyone wants money," the woman said, with what was almost a smile.

"But I want to make it up to you," Joyce said helplessly.

This time the woman did smile. "Seems as though I did remember your face there for a minute," she said. "I remember once just seeing you come up to some other girls at some class party or something and they laughed and walked away and you were just standing there. I just remember your face there for that minute, just standing there."

"Really?" said Joyce. "Well, of course, *now* . . . "

"Why worry about it?" said the woman. "I never did anything I'm sorry for, and me and Bob, we got our own little business here, and even though costs—"

"Well, I'm sorry anyway," Joyce said irritably. "Will you give my regards to Bob—if he remembers me, that is?"

"I don't suppose he would remember you," the woman said thoughtfully. "Seems like he would of mentioned you sometimes if he did."

Joyce hesitated, half turning away, and then thought that it was not enough to leave like this. "Are you *sure* you don't remember?" she asked, and the woman, already turning toward the other room, said wearily, "Look, lady, we keep a grocery here. I already told you that whatever's bothering you is *your* worry, not mine."

"Well, perhaps I'd better get some cigarettes before I leave," Joyce said. "I'll take a carton, please. And one of those boxes of candy and a dozen oranges." She watched silently as the woman put them into a bag. "How much is that?"

"Two-thirty."

Looking around desperately, Joyce said, "Then give me—oh, say, eight—ten packs of gum."

Without comment, the woman counted them out and put them into the bag with the candy and the cigarettes and set the bag next to the bag of oranges on the counter. "How much?" asked Joyce.

"Two-seventy-three, with tax."

"Fine," said Joyce. She gave the woman a five-dollar bill, and counted the change carefully, thinking, after all, a person who has once been accused of stealing doesn't always worry afterward about being *too* careful.

"Will that be all?"

"Yes, thank you."

"Come again," said the woman tonelessly, and this time she moved purposefully toward the other room and waited in the doorway while Joyce went to the outer door and the street. Is she afraid that *I'll* steal something?, Joyce wondered, and called back, "Don't forget to give my regards to Bob."

"I'll tell him."

She doesn't even know my name any longer, Joyce thought, how could she ever tell him? She put the packages into the backseat of the car and sat down gratefully behind the wheel. "Well," she said aloud, *"that's* done."

It was not until she was almost in Milltown, nearly seventeen miles from Prospect, that she recalled that she had not returned, after all, to look at her old house again. I'll never see it now, she thought, knowing that she would never go back again, but everything's all right anyway; I didn't need to worry at all; I told that woman I took the money, but it was a long time ago and she doesn't even remember my name. Lucky I didn't take her any flowers or anything; she would have been suspicious.

Stopping the car in front of her own apartment and seeing the light upstairs that meant Jed was home, she laughed aloud, thinking of her triumph, and she ran upstairs because the elevator would be too slow.

"Jed," she said, as the door opened before her, "it's all right, I fixed it all."

He raised his eyes calmly to regard her. "No more lie?" he asked.

"I saw her and I told her all about it and she said it was perfectly all right, and she wouldn't take the money so I bought some cigarettes and things—she runs a little grocery, I forgot to tell you—and gave her the money back *that* way. And we can always smoke the cigarettes."

"I hope you got our brand," Jed said without humor.

"Of course, idiot. And what do you think? She married my old boyfriend, and I went back and saw my old high school and my old house and a few old neighbors, and I told everyone about how I was married and everything."

She looked at him, at his serious eyes apparently waiting for her to say something more, and her voice faltered. "So now," she said, "everything's going to be all right—isn't it?"

She Says the Damnedest Things

"She's bats, that girl," said Dottie. "I mean, honestly, bats. She does the *damnedest* things."

"She must be charming," I said.

"Honestly, though!" said Dottie. "You should see her. She'll sit down here and talk about the craziest notions she's got, like buying the university and turning it into a pig farm because no one would ever notice the difference."

"Already I like her," I said.

"Yeah," said Dottie, "and she'll read all the time, or go banging away on that damned old typewriter of hers, and then she'll talk and talk. She can spout poetry by the hour, honest."

"When can I meet her?" I asked.

"God, you don't wanna," said Dottie. "She says the damnedest things, honest. She's liable to get you into an argument on some screwy subject like religion, and then make you talk all night, or she'll tell you about some damned book she's been reading, about logic or pyramids or some other crazy thing, honest, and you'll go nuts."

"That strikes a chord," I said.

"Really," said Dottie. "But she can tell some swell stories, I'll say that for her. She's all the time got some wild line about something. Honestly, you'd die if you heard her."

"She sounds familiar," I said.

"Oh, and yeah!" said Dottie. "I almost forgot the screwiest thing of all. She's gonna be a writer! Honest—can you imagine? A writer? God, the things some people will think of. She's some screwy dame, I'm telling you, honest."

"I think I know her," I said.

Remembrance of Things Past

Mr. Waggoner came wearily into the living room. His wife was sitting by the fireplace, knitting. Mr. Waggoner realized with some surprise that he had forgotten his wife's name.

"Good morning, my dear," Mr. Waggoner said to his wife.

"Good morning, William," his wife said.

Mr. Waggoner sat looking at his wife, wondering what her name was. He found himself thinking of a lot of names, none, he knew, belonging to his wife.

Sandra?, he thought tentatively. He wished he had married a girl named Sandra.

"Was your breakfast all right, William?" Mrs. Waggoner asked casually. "I told the maid only one egg this morning. You ate a little too much last night."

"I had an excellent breakfast, thank you, my dear," Mr. Waggoner said. Annabelle?

"And what are you going to do today, William?" Mrs. Waggoner asked.

"I really hadn't thought." Clarice?

"A little gardening, perhaps? Or some golf?"

"I played golf yesterday," Mr. Waggoner said, annoyed.

"You want to be playing your best when we go south this year, William."

Like birds, William thought. What *was* the woman's name? Lucrece?

This has gone far enough, Mr. Waggoner thought. His first concern had changed to anger. This woman had no right to go on being anonymous.

"My dear," he said.

"Yes, William?" said his wife.

Mr. Waggoner thought deeply. "You remember when we were first married?"

Mrs. Waggoner thought deeply. "Not very well," she said.

"*You* know," Mr. Waggoner said. "When we were first married."

"Yes?" Mrs. Waggoner said.

Mr. Waggoner took a deep breath. "Remember how silly we were? What did I used to call you?"

Mrs. Waggoner frowned. "I used to call *you* Bubbles," she said.

Mr. Waggoner winced. "Ah, but what did I used to call *you*?" He made his voice deliberately coy.

Mrs. Waggoner compressed her lips. "Bumpo," she said.

"I see," Mr. Waggoner said. "Well . . ." he began.

Evidently considering the subject closed, Mrs. Waggoner said briskly, "I had a letter from Becky this morning. She and the baby will be here on the tenth."

"Very nice," Mr. Waggoner said. Becky. Rebecca. That was his daughter. Had she been named after her mother?

Reba?

"You must get your hair cut this week," said Mrs. Waggoner.

Delilah?

The phone rang.

"Will you answer it, William, my dear?" said Mrs. Waggoner.

William my dear went to the phone. "Hello," he said vaguely.

"Oh, *William*," said a female voice. "May I speak to Jane, please?"

Jane. Jane. Furiously angry, Mr. Waggoner put down the phone. "Jane," he bawled. "Telephone. Oh, *Jane* . . . "

Let Me Tell You
(An Unfinished Story)

LET ME TELL YOU ABOUT THIS GIRL, SHE'S PRETTIER THAN I AM, BUT she's my best friend. We have fun together. When we go to a party or to the country club dancing or horseback riding—we ride at Becket's; no one rides at Wilson's anymore—or ice skating or even just out for a walk, we make jokes together and tell each other everything. She's got dark hair and dark eyes and she wears black a lot; her mother doesn't mind. Her name's Hilda. She's fourteen, like me, and neither one of us believes in going steady. That's no fun.

I try to do a lot of the things she does, but of course she's always better. When I steal something from a store I always get caught and they call my father. Hilda has lots of things like slips and sweaters that she's stolen from stores, and once she even stole a coat but of course she never wears it. We get all our clothes from the fashion shop. Everybody does. You just don't wear a coat from anywhere else. She's allowed to drink gin; her father's a psychiatrist. I'm allowed champagne and a pink lady if my father makes it. My father's a lawyer. It's important what your father is. Also it's important to have a swimming pool, only not the biggest swimming pool. One family moved into our part of town and right away they built the biggest swimming pool of all and of course no one would dream of going near it. But the most fun Hilda and I have is with the common people. The riffraff. The hoi polloi.

The way we have fun is this: We get a ride into town with someone, usually Hilda's mother or mine, when they are going into the doctor's or to a matinee, or on one of their shopping trips. Then we make all kinds of promises about when we will be home, and how, and usually when to meet somewhere to get home. Then we take a streetcar to some part of town where the common people live and go around and eat and talk and all the other things that people without advantages like them do. They drink beer—we've watched them do that—and buy clothes in department stores, and they talk to each other a lot. That's where we have our fun, talking to the common people. They all have bad teeth. They don't take care of themselves. They bathe, of course—everybody does, after all—but they don't know how to cook. They eat hamburgers and French fries.

One day we rode into town with Hilda's mother and said we would meet her on the corner of Nation and Main at five o'clock, and I guess she thought we were going to a movie. She said did we have enough money and Hilda said sure, and then she said well, have a good time, and we said sure. She never worries about our meeting bad men or something the way my mother does. My mother always wants to know exactly where we've been and whether any dirty men spoke to us, and Hilda and I always have to think of something to tell her, although I don't remember ever seeing a dirty man in my life. Once we told her a man had spoken to us because Hilda had read about it in a book. She's allowed to read anything she likes. My mother told my father and for a while they wouldn't let me go anywhere except with people they knew. Now that I'm fourteen, though, my father says it's time I got used to the idea of the world being the way it is. My mother just says if any men speak to us we must run, unless there is a policeman nearby. Hilda's mother doesn't care, Hilda's allowed to speak to anyone she wants to.

This day Hilda's mother drove us into town, she was annoyed because Hilda was wearing her brown coat, and Hilda couldn't tell her that where we were going she couldn't wear her fur. Anyway she let us off and said did we have enough money? and then she drove away, and Hilda and I stood on the corner for a minute arguing. I wanted to go downtown to some of the stores first, but Hilda had it in her mind that she wanted to go far out on the streetcar to the end of the line. Hilda won, of course; she always does because she says she won't be friends anymore. We got on the streetcar and Hilda sat down next to a girl about twenty who was really dressed in a most ghastly fashion and I sat down next to an old man who smelled. We never got to the end of the line because Hilda kept looking at the girl next to her out of the corners of her eyes and kind of smiling, and when the girl got up to get off Hilda waved her head at me and got up and we followed the girl off the bus. We like to follow people sometimes and this girl had taken Hilda's fancy. "Did you ever see such clothes?" Hilda whispered to me when she got off the streetcar and I had to admit I never did. She was all kind of cheap perfume and everything too tight. "I think she's a prostitute," Hilda said, "and when we follow her we'll find out where prostitutes go."

She was a very disappointing prostitute if she was one because she didn't stop anyone or talk to anyone or anything, just went on down the street, and we walked along some distance behind her, talking and trying to pretend we weren't following. We were in a very common neighborhood; there were little dirty stores and little dirty houses, and everything close up together and dirty in the streets. There were a lot of people, probably because it was a Saturday afternoon, and Saturday afternoon is when the common people come out and sit on their front porches and watch ball games on television and drink beer. The girl we were following went right down the street without stopping and then she turned suddenly as though she had just thought of it and went into a little grocery store, so we hurried and went right into the store after her. It was a small store, and dark, and we stopped near the door because there were quite a few people inside and our girl was standing waiting her turn.

I don't much care for getting up close to people, and I certainly don't like being close enough for them to touch me, but Hilda doesn't care about anything, so I kind of stayed near the doorway while Hilda went a little farther in, kind of touching things and looking as though she had something she wanted to buy. Hilda has nerve, and she's fun, and I wouldn't do some of the things she does. If my mother ever found out, I wouldn't get a car for my birthday.

Anyway, Hilda was poking at loaves of bread and taking down cans and putting them back and no one was paying any attention to us because they were all talking and even the girl we followed had turned around to listen because one woman was doing most of the talking and she was mad.

"No right," she kept saying, "they hadn't any right. I never knew the boy myself but his mother and father were decent people and they brought their kids up decent and no one had any right to accuse him without the facts."

"They go to church, the Andersons," someone else said, and the girl we followed said, kind of hesitating, "Wasn't it in the paper? They found some of the stuff in his room?"

"He never did a thing," the woman who talked so much said. "I know for a fact that boy was brought up right, and when he says the other kids gave him those watches, I for one believe him."

Now I'll show you how Hilda has fun. She kind of stepped up to the woman talking and shook her head, and when the woman noticed her, Hilda said, very little-girl, "Please, I couldn't help hearing what you said, and I guess you don't know everything about it because we used to know the Anderson boy and he stole things all the time."

"What?" said the woman, and then, "I just simply don't believe it."

"It's true," Hilda said, nodding. "When I saw about it in the papers I just said, 'So they caught him finally.' He used to steal anything he could find. He stole from other kids. And once he tried to steal his own father's car but he couldn't get it started. I was right there and I saw him."

"I don't believe it," the woman said. "I just don't believe it." Then she turned to Hilda and said, "What Anderson boy are you talking about? Are you sure you mean Johnny Anderson?"

"I certainly do," Hilda said. "The one who stole the watches and said the other boys gave them to him and it was all in the paper. I used to know him and he stole things all the time."

"Hard on his people," another woman said, and someone else said, "No matter how much you try to bring kids up right . . ."

"Well, I just never would have believed it," the first woman said. She sighed and turned away to look at some things on a shelf. "He was always so polite, too."

Someone started asking to have oranges weighed and the grocery clerks were putting things into bags, and Hilda came over to me. "Come on," she said, and we sneaked out. No one paid any attention to us, of course, and we went on down the street and Hilda squeezed my arm hard. "How was that?" she said, and I said, "Ghastly," which of course is our word meaning pretty wonderful. "Let's do some more," I said, and then Hilda said, "Well, it's your turn next," and I began to get nervous because I can't do it anywhere near as ghastly as Hilda.

I thought I would try the newsstand on the corner because usually they're easy, and I cheated by using an old game although of course it's always fun. Hilda kind of stood back and I went up to the newsstand and the man behind it was selling a paper so I waited till he finished and then when he looked at me I said, "Please, we're lost, my friend and I. We don't have enough to telephone."

He looked at Hilda standing a little in back of me, and then he looked at me again and finally he said, "Well, where do you live?"

I told him on Manica Street, which was all right because we had been there once and people lived there, and he looked surprised and said, "Well, what are you doing all the way out here?"

This was where Hilda was always better. She would tell him something like we were trailing her father's divorced wife, or we had seen a man kill someone and we were following him, and maybe he wouldn't believe her but he'd kind of laugh and give in. I never had that kind of courage, so I'm not as good as Hilda. All I could think of to say was "We got on the wrong streetcar and kept thinking it would be time to get off at the right corner, but it was going the wrong way."

You could tell he thought I was kind of foolish at my age to get on the wrong streetcar and come so far away from home, but there was no real reason for him not to believe me, so at last he said, "What do you want me to do?"

"We don't have enough to telephone," I said.

He looked at Hilda again and then at me and finally he reached into the moneybox under the stand. "Well," he said, "I guess your folks will be worrying." He took out two quarters. "Think you can find your way home without getting lost again?" he asked me, and I could tell he was still a little doubtful because I had done it so badly. I took the quarters and said, "Oh, thank you, mister. We can get home now."

"See that you go straight home, too," he said.

"Thank you," I said, and Hilda said, "Thank you," and we went off toward the streetcar stop because he was still looking at us. "How did I do?" I said, and Hilda said, "Ghastly," but we both knew it really wasn't because no matter how I try I can never think of things the way Hilda can.

"I'm going to do a house," Hilda said all of a sudden, and that really scared me because in all the time we had been having fun we had never tried a house before, but then I saw the house she was going for and I could kind of see what she had in mind. This was a little house, and it was unusual, because instead of being right on the street with a little fence and all it was set far back, and it had almost a garden, and on one side of it was a house that was clearly empty with no one living there and no curtains and the steps falling down, and on the other side was just a vacant lot.

[*This story was left unfinished by the author. We include it here because we feel the characters she has created are unique and the work warrants it.*]

Bulletin

(ED. NOTE: THE TIME TRAVEL MACHINE SENT OUT RECENTLY BY THIS University has returned, unfortunately without Professor Browning. Happily for the University Space Department, however, Professor Browning's briefcase, set just inside the time travel element, returned, containing the following papers that bear ample evidence of the value to scientific investigation of sending Professor Browning on this much-discussed trip into the twenty-second century. It is assumed by members of the Space Department that these following papers were to serve as the basis for notes for the expected lecture by Professor Browning, which will now, of course, be indefinitely postponed.)

(From a newspaper, torn, heading reading only ". . . ld Tribune, May 8, 2123":)

. . . indifference in high quarters which has led so inevitably to this distressing result. Not only those directly affected—and they are many—but, indeed, thoughtful and reasonable persons everywhere, must view with extreme alarm an act which has given opportunism an advantage over intelligent planning. It is greatly to be regretted that, among those in power who were in a position to take action, none except the unpopular Secretary chose to do so, and his opposition was, as so frequently it must be, disregarded. In any case, let us unite in hope that the possible consequences will not take place, and prepare to guard ourselves with the utmost vigilance against a recurrence of such incidents.

(From what appears to be a private correspondence:)

June 4

Dear Mom and Dad,

I am haveing a fine time at camp. I went swiming and dived, but Charley didnt. Send me a cake and some cokies and candy.

Your loveing son,

Jerry

(A mimeographed sheet:)

American History 102
Mid-Term Examination
April 21, 2123

1. Identify twelve (12) of the following:

Nathan Hale
Huey Long
Carrie Chapman Catt
Merry Oldsmobile
Cotton Mather
Robert Nathan
George Washingham
Oveta Culp Hobby
Sinclair (Joe) Louis
Alexander Hamilton

Grover Cleveland
Woodrow Wilson I
Joyce Kilmer
Edna Wallace Hopper
Chief Sitting Bull
Old Ironsides
John Philip Sousa
Sergeant Cuff
R. H. Macy

2. The historian Roosevelt-san has observed that "Twentieth-century man had both intelligence and instinct; he chose, unfortunately, to rely upon intelligence." Discuss.

3. Some of the following statements are true, some are false. Mark them T and F accordingly:
    A. Currency was originally used as a medium of exchange.
    B. The aboriginal Americans lived above-ground and drank water.
    C. The first American settlers rebelled against the rule of Churchill III and set up their own government because of the price of tea.
    D. Throat-scratch, the disease which swept through twentieth-century life, was introduced to this country by Sir Walter Raleigh.
    E. The hero Jackie Robinson is chiefly known for his voyage to obtain the golden fleece.
    F. Working was the principal occupation of twentieth-century humanity.
    G. The first king in America, George Washingham, refused the crown three times.
    H. The cat was at one time tame, and used in domestic service.

4. Describe in your own words the probable daily life of an American resident in 1950, using what you have learned of his eating, entertainment, and mating habits.

5. In what sense did ancient Americans contribute to our world today? Can we learn anything of value by studying them?

(A narrow card, identifiably from a machine:)

YOUR WEIGHT AND FORTUNE
Your weight is . . . 186
Your fortune for today: Expect permanent relief in minor domestic problems, but avoid too-hasty plans for the future. Try not to

dwell on the past. You are determined, clear-sighted, firm: use these qualities. Remember that you can be led but not driven.

(Ed. Note: This last item seems of great significance. It is well known that Professor Browning's weight when he left the University in the time travel element was better than 200 pounds. The evident loss of weight shown indicates clearly the changes incident to time travel, and points, perhaps, to some of its perils; there is possibly a hint here of an entirely different system of weights and measures than that currently in use. We anticipate that several learned and informed papers on this subject are already in preparation.)

Family Treasures

ANNE WAITE WAS A MOST UNFORTUNATE GIRL, ALTHOUGH SHE WAS, of all the girls living in the small women's dormitory, the only one who might not be persuaded to agree that she was unfortunate. More than any of the other girls in the house, Anne felt herself to be free and unconfined, accepting the ordinary regulations of institutional community life as a concession to the authorities, rather than as an imposed obligation. The university was large, and Anne was small, yet the university was more strictly bound by iron rules than Anne, and was, on the whole, Anne would have said, more unfortunate. The university authorities had been brought to recognize Anne particularly because of the death of her mother during the last term of her freshman year; Anne, returning to college as a sophomore, was without one surviving relative except for the university. Her college education had been paid for in advance, along with a regular, although small, allowance, that duly provided for—in case the university should not extend its paternal benevolence—the purchase of Anne's clothes.

The university provided Anne with a small, fairly well-maintained room in one of its more comfortable living centers, where, as did fifteen other girls, Anne had a bed and a chair and a desk and a dresser. She was required to present herself for breakfast at seven, arrive promptly upon call at fire drill, and be in the house with the front door locked behind her no later than eleven on weeknights, twelve on Saturdays. She was also required to be reasonably friendly with the other girls, a friendship in no cases to extend to extreme devotion, pointed whispering in the dining hall, or sleeping two in one bed; she was expected to rise when the house mother entered the room, and be decently civil to the maids.

Anne's mother had died shortly after the end of the football season, and long before the season of spring dances, and although Anne was at that time a shy and rather friendless girl, everyone in the house, from the house mother to the three girls on the first floor who had received permission to set up a darkroom in the first-floor bathroom for developing photographs, had sought Anne out either in the gloomy weather before she had set out for home, or in the bright warm days that followed immediately after her return, to offer both sympathy and a quick, friendly curiosity for details of the funeral. Anne had a vague comprehension, although naturally she could never investigate the fact fully, that several of the girls—Helena, for instance, on the second floor, and Cheryl, who was of course the house president—who had sat with her, choking up and saying "I know how I'd feel if it was *my* moth—" before dissolving into tears with her, had gone directly from Anne to dates with well-dressed boys who parked their cars, as a matter of hallowed custom, on the hill near the lake, where Cheryl certainly, and Helena probably, had sat laughing, and drinking beer, and what else?, Anne wondered.

Anne minded none of this particularly; what she did mind, and found insulting, was the immediate decrease of her value in the eyes of the other girls in the house shortly after her mother was buried. It was no longer in good taste to commiserate with Anne, because, as was generally known, Anne was Trying to be Brave. With her bravery clearly established by her anonymity, Anne faded back into the colorless girl on the third floor who lived alone, had no friends, and rarely spoke.

It was too much to hope, naturally, that Cheryl and Helena would introduce Anne to any of their young men just because her mother had died, or that the three girls on the first floor would allow her to develop pictures in their bathroom darkroom, but Anne had cherished a hope, along with so many other people to whom sudden and unusual things have happened, that after it was all over she might be changed—her face a little prettier, perhaps, or her hair a more decided color, or at *least* an interesting sadness in her manner, and the ability to think quickly and effortlessly of things to say when she passed the other girls in the hall.

At the beginning, then, of her sophomore year at the university, Anne was doing as well as might be expected in her studies, had an unblemished record at fire drill, could certainly not be accused of any disproportionate friendships, and was, in fact, very little better off after her mother's death at all.

It did not take long for Anne to recognize this, since she was, in her silent and veiled manner, very agile; consequently it was in only about the third week of the school year that Anne stole Helena's ankle bracelet and hid it in her mother's trunk. It went under her mother's books and papers and the ancient fur cape, which was of no value but had become Anne's in the disposal of Anne's mother's private things, during which the bank holding all of Anne's money had, with the air of an impersonal machine humanizing itself through a sentimental understanding of a small detail, sent it neatly wrapped to Anne as a memento.

Helena's ankle bracelet was of solid gold, and had been given to Helena by a young man in whom she no longer had any profitable interest. Anne had seen it during the glorious days of her bereavement, in a blue china trinket box on Helena's dresser, where it would be difficult to discover its loss casually out of the mess of necklaces and compacts and odd little items donated to Helena by various young men whose names Helena could remember easily when she looked over their honorary insignia in the box on her dresser, although in most cases she had forgotten the occasions when she had received her trophies. The ankle bracelet was neither the greatest nor the least of Helena's treasures, and Anne, stealing it and hiding it safely away, was confident that in all the mixture of young men's gifts in the box, Helena would forever be unable to recall the name on the ankle bracelet without its presence to remind her.

One evening, several days after the ankle bracelet had joined Anne's mother's fur cape in the trunk in Anne's closet, Anne passed Helena's room, full of noise and chatter, with six or seven girls inside, and after hesitating for a minute in the doorway, she slipped inside and sat down on the floor near the door. Although everyone noticed her and greeted her amiably enough, no one asked her any questions or addressed any particular remarks to her; nor did the tenor of their conversation change materially with her entrance. While Anne was there, Helena several times consulted the trinket box, twice to put things away and once to determine the year in which a young man under discussion had made the university's scholastic honorary society. Not in all this evening did Helena notice that she no longer had one of her gold ankle bracelets.

The day on which a notice appeared on the dormitory bulletin board announcing the date of the university's winter dance, Anne went quietly, in her slippers, into Cheryl's room while she was in class. In the top drawer of Cheryl's desk—Anne had seen it before—was an inexpensive black pen-and-pencil set, which, in its particular box, had been awarded to Cheryl when she graduated from high school by the members of her class, whom, as class president, she had inspired to be exactly the same as every other class graduated from that academy. Anne had heard Cheryl telling about the pen-and-pencil set (the pen no longer worked) with becoming modesty:

they had voted her most likely to succeed, and given her the pen-and-pencil set, and there were shy little jokes about the great books she had been expected to write with the pen and the great pictures she had been expected to sketch with the pencil but how, as a matter of fact, she used neither, although she was the house president and a member of the senior council of the university. Along with her name, on both the pen and pencil, was written "Voted Most Likely to Succeed."

Anne put the pen-and-pencil set with the ankle bracelet, on the bottom of her mother's trunk, and if Cheryl noticed that it was gone, she said nothing to Anne about it, although Anne had taken of late to joining the other girls in the living room after the house was closed for the night, where, in pajamas and bathrobes, they drank Cokes ordered from a neighboring drugstore and ate sandwiches barely inferior to the college food.

There was a girl named Maggie, who was accounted a great wit, and from her room Anne stole a stuffed gray bear that Maggie ordinarily kept securely hidden under her pillow; by the time the bear had settled comfortably into Anne's mother's trunk, Maggie had probably discovered her loss but, after a noble battle with herself, had apparently decided to say nothing about it, but to sharpen her sarcasms against the world until her errant bear should return, wending his individual way back as he had taken his secret way of going.

Anne's usual method was to watch, pressing herself softly against the slight crack in the door of her third-floor room, or leaning back beside a window with the curtain before her, until the girl whose room she had chosen to violate had left the house. Then, wearing felt slippers and usually a bathrobe over her clothes, and sometimes carrying a bath towel to avert suspicion and to cover any bulky objects, Anne would move softly out of her room, her heart shaking deliciously, biting her lips to keep from smiling. In the early afternoons, when the house was most quiet, Anne could go from one floor to the next by the backstairs, without being seen or attracting attention if she were. If anyone noticed her, she could say that the tub on the third floor was occupied and she had come to the second floor to take a bath, or to the first floor to answer the phone; if she were seen coming out of someone's room—which never, to her knowledge, had happened—she could say, with perfect truth, that she was looking for something.

Before the snow had fully melted, in the inexorable round of the university year, Anne had, besides the ankle bracelet and the pen-and-pencil set and the gray teddy bear, a black satin slip she had found on the floor of a closet and washed carefully and folded neatly before setting it away in her mother's trunk; she had a carbon copy of a sonnet, neatly typed and dated (it had been sent away, Anne knew, to a poetry magazine not long before, but the rejection notice was not attached to the carbon), and a small leather-covered note-book, virgin except for the first page, on which was written largely: "BUY ASPIRIN. WRITE HOME. GET SPANISH ASSGNMT. DRESS FROM CLEANERS."

Also by this time, of course, many of the losses had been discovered. Cheryl, going one day to her desk drawer to make a shy point about her own worth, was not able to find her pen-and-pencil set inscribed "Voted Most Likely to Succeed," and after much thought and consideration, she mentioned the fact cautiously to several of her friends.

"Not that I think it's been *stolen*, or anything," Cheryl insisted over and over again. "I don't think anyone in the house *steals*. I just can't imagine where my pen-and-pencil set has gone."

"Perhaps you left it somewhere," one of the girls might suggest incautiously, to which Cheryl would reply with indignation, "*Naturally* I'd never take it anywhere—not with 'Voted Most Likely to Succeed' written all over it. But I just *know* it hasn't been *stolen*."

When the loss of the black satin slip became a topic of conversation, Cheryl's apprehensions became "But who around here *steals*?" and "I just can't *believe* it of anyone in the house." Maggie, who had lost the gray teddy bear, never mentioned it, although she did say she was almost positive that a silver signet ring was gone from her top right-hand drawer, and she was fairly certain that she had seen one of the maids hovering near the dresser shortly before she'd discovered that the ring was gone. The girl whose carbon copy of a sonnet was missing admitted blushingly that she could not say for sure how many copies of the sonnet she had made. One of the girls managed to recall that at one time she had owned a compact with her name on it, which she was no longer able to find; another believed that the yellow blouse she had blamed the laundry for losing had most likely been stolen. Anne softly contributed, during one discussion, the additional fact that she herself had lost a couple of things, but no one noticed particularly, probably on the theory that Anne's possessions were so anonymous anyway that loss of any of them would be superfluous.

"I can't believe it of the *maids*," Cheryl was saying by now. "Surely not the *maids*."

"Someone must have come in from outside, then," said the girl who had lost the black satin slip. "Imagine, if anyone sneaked into the house and went through our *clothes*." She shivered delightedly.

"I don't think anyone could have come in," Helena said firmly.

They circled joyfully around the fact that it might be one of themselves, and eyed one another with pleased suspicion. There was a group, made up of Helena, Cheryl, and several of the others, who believed excitedly that Maggie was doing it, and Cheryl said feelingly, "I can't believe it of *Maggie*."

"Well," someone offered hesitantly, "she doesn't have a lot of money, you know. She could have sold some of the jewelry."

"She has a new sweater," Helena said. "You know—the red one. And you can take my word for it, that sweater cost a lot more than anything Maggie's ever worn before."

"Of course," Cheryl said thoughtfully, "she wouldn't *dare* wear any of those things—*you* know. But still, I can't—"

There was another group, made up of Maggie and several others, including the three girls with the bathroom darkroom, who believed Cheryl was responsible.

"Of course," Maggie said charitably, "if it *was* Cheryl, you couldn't really blame her. I mean, sometimes people have something wrong with them and they've *got* to steal."

"Dipsomania," one of the darkroom girls contributed knowingly. "It can only be cured by psychoanalysis."

The girls moved closer to one another, listening, and someone offered, softly, "Do you suppose her family knows? And let her come back to college?"

"*Her* family," Maggie said, "probably they don't want her stealing *their* stuff."

There was still another group, of course, with shifting ringleaders, who believed that Helena had done it. "She can't *stand* anyone having something she doesn't have," one girl said. "It drives her crazy just to see one of us with a new coat or something."

"Not that she doesn't have *enough*, as it is," said another. "I can't really *imagine* Helena touching anything that didn't belong to her. Except, of course, she's really *terribly* jealous."

The remaining girls, who believed that the three girls with the bathroom darkroom had stolen the property, based their case on incontrovertible facts: 1) that people who have permission to turn a first-floor bathroom into a photographic darkroom think they own the world, anyway; 2) no one could really tell whether they were in their darkroom at any given time, no matter what they *said*; they could be anywhere in the house; and 3) one of the three girls had been heard expressing a most enthusiastic admiration of a china cat on the dresser of another girl in the house, and although the china cat was not missing yet, a pack of cigarettes she had put down next to it was, and anyone could get rattled and grab the first thing she saw.

No one, for a minute, suspected Anne. Anne, in all of the suspicion and confusion, went from one to another of the little talking groups, offering her disregarded opinions, and at night, when the house was quiet, she took out her treasures and counted them over, setting the teddy bear next to the sonnet and the ankle bracelet next to the leather notebook, weighing the pen-and-pencil set in her hands and regarding its motto until she could have drawn from memory the peculiar angular script of it; trying on the black satin slip and walking silently around her room, with its door never locked.

Eventually, it was Anne who brought a formal complaint to the house mother.

It had occurred to Anne that the house mother, whose name was Miss McBride, had worn at various times a pair of dangling jet earrings, which Anne knew were kept in a cardboard box in Miss McBride's dresser. As a result, one afternoon, in her bathrobe and carrying her towel, Anne approached the quiet, bookless room that Miss McBride had only just vacated to go shopping, and had, fortunately, only just stepped inside when Miss McBride returned unexpectedly. In the still atmosphere of the room Anne was speechless for a minute, as Miss McBride looked at her, and then Anne, making the best of her situation, said urgently, "Miss McBride, I was looking for you."

"Yes?" Miss McBride said, not prepared to commit herself. She was a fairly young, well-set-up, incredibly romantic woman, and was fond of the big-sisterly admiration she received from her girls; she was partial to sympathetic smiles and knowing nods, and allowed the rumor to circulate uncontradicted that she had permitted — even encouraged — one of her girls to elope several years before with an extremely wealthy chemistry major. Although she had heard the stories of thievery, and was completely aware of the many rumors going around in her house, she was not yet prepared to commit herself on the subject, and did not intend to take any action until she knew better what kind to take without offending anyone. By telling her precipitately, Anne would force her to do something immediately, and so Miss McBride's tone when she said "Yes?" again to Anne was cold, and almost ominous.

"Miss McBride," Anne said, allowing her words to come almost in a rush, so that later, when Miss McBride questioned her, the easygoing mind would remember only her emotionality, "Miss McBride, I don't know what to do. Really, it's *awful*. I couldn't have *believed* it of her," Anne said, borrowing freely from Cheryl; "it must be some kind of a mental disease, or something," borrowing freely from Maggie. "I mean, when I *saw* her I tried to think of something to say, and she looked so guilty. So I came right down to tell you and ask you what to do." Anne hesitated for a minute, then added plaintively, "Please, can't we sort of keep it quiet, not have a scandal?"

"Who?" Miss McBride said, having fastened accurately on the one essential fact.

Anne dropped her eyes. "I'd rather not say, please, Miss McBride."

"You won't tell me?" Miss McBride's voice rose. Anne blushed and remained silent.

"Of course," Miss McBride said, embarrassed for a minute at her own forwardness. There was no further attempt made by either of them to discuss the thievery. After a few minutes' thought Miss McBride said, "I'll post a notice on the bulletin board, for a house meeting tonight."

By some odd coincidence every girl at the house meeting—in fact, every girl in the house—knew by the time Cheryl called the meeting to order that Miss McBride knew who the thief was, or had a clue, or meant to find out that night. Delicious apprehension made each girl tremble separately; many of them hoped that their most intimate friends would prove to be innocent; if a vote had been taken, the most likely candidate would have been Cheryl herself, just as she had been elected president of the house. As she stood in the center of the room, with the other girls around her draped over chairs and lying on the sofas and sitting on the floor, Cheryl knew perfectly well that each girl watching her imagined she saw some sign of guilt on her face.

Miss McBride spoke, soberly and earnestly. "Look, kids," she said, "this is a terrible thing. Everyone, all over campus, knows about it by now. They're beginning to talk about us, how we've got someone in this house who borrows things that don't belong to her and then forgets to return them. It's not good for any of you. I know you all want to protect your own reputations, and all together we want to keep this a clean and decent house. I think that the girl who is responsible for all this doesn't quite realize that she is hurting all of us by not stepping forward." Miss McBride stopped for a minute, but no one came forward, hand raised. "Do you think," Miss McBride went on, "that if I said we'd all go to our rooms quietly, and then I'd wait in mine until the girl came to me—do you think that would do any good?"

There was a silence, and then one of the girls in a corner, who wanted action, said, "Not if she's gotten away with it this far, she won't."

"I think I ought to tell you," Miss McBride said significantly, "that the name of the girl is known."

There was a dead silence of anticipation.

"I'm not going to tell you her name," Miss McBride said firmly. "And I'm not going to tell you who saw her. All I'm going to say is that I'm going to take steps to stop this business, once and for all."

There was another silence; Miss McBride was the one who had to take action. Miss McBride took a deep breath. "I'm going to search every room in this house," she said with relish. "Tonight."

There was another long silence, finally broken when one of the girls said timidly, "I don't think you have the right to do that, Miss McBride."

"Anyone who has anything to hide," Miss McBride said emphatically, settling the matter once and for all, "can easily see the position she puts herself in."

Anne, unappalled, hugged herself secretly. This was the best of all; she was perhaps the only person who had read the diary in Cheryl's desk, seen the letters in Helena's dresser, penetrated the secrets buried in handkerchief boxes, under beds, in the darkest corners of closets, the secrets known to be there, yet believed inviolate until a good excuse made them common currency, sometimes shocking, sometimes laughable.

"You can start with *my* room," Cheryl said with dignity. There was a strong shift of sentiment toward Cheryl after this statement— unless, several of the girls wondered privately, Cheryl, as house president, had had warning of the search?

Miss McBride rose purposefully and went to the stairs, where she stopped again. "Kids," she said, her voice lacking eagerness, "isn't there some other way of doing this?" As she spoke, she started up the stairs. Cheryl first, and then the whole roomful of girls, followed her. Miss McBride went up to the second floor and then, after another minute's thought, up to the third floor. Here there lived only Anne and three others.

"Whose room shall I start with?" Miss McBride asked indecisively.

"Mine," Anne said firmly. Miss McBride, looking at Anne across the line of girls standing still in the hall, tried to make her glance meaningful. "Anne," she was trying to say, "I know it's all right, you're not the thief because you won't tell me who is; I've got to search your room." Miss McBride's gesturing eyebrows tried to say eloquently, "But we know, you and I, that it's only a formal gesture." She looked at Anne until all the other girls looked at her too, and then, unseen, Miss McBride shrugged helplessly at Anne.

Miss McBride, with the advice and the occasional help of the other girls, searched quickly and ineffectually. All of the drawers in the dresser and the desk were opened and their contents stirred around. "Some of the stuff was too big to really *hide*," one of the girls contributed, and Miss McBride, adopting this theory into her concept of searching, made only perfunctory gestures at the bookcase and the bedcovers, although she lifted the mattress to look underneath, and one of the girls took the pillow out of its case. Anne, standing near the door, watched the girls showing curiosity about her for the second time in her life, saw a girl whom she rather admired poke hastily and surreptitiously at Anne's dresses in the closet, saw another girl stop by the desk to read a letter Anne was writing to a high school friend. Miss McBride, at the lid of Anne's mother's trunk, said superfluously, "This yours, Anne?"

"My mother's," Anne said quietly. Miss McBride let the corner of the fur cape fall immediately from her fingers, and said questioningly to the other girls "I don't think . . . ?"

"Of course not," someone said uncomfortably, and the girl who had been reading Anne's letter hurriedly dropped it back onto the desk.

"Well," Miss McBride said, and smiled at Anne. "That's that," she said. She moved with purpose out of the room, and the girls followed her in a flock. Although Miss McBride moved into the next room on the floor, some of the girls separated themselves from her and could be heard, farther down the hall, instituting a search of their own in another room. Miss McBride, her searching growing more and more haphazard, went through all the rooms on the third floor; by the time she had done all four rooms she was only opening drawers and glancing into closets, but the rest of the girls were going over the rooms like locusts, reading, confusing, examining everything they could find. Talk was circulating among the group ("Did you *see* what they found—" "I should think she'd *die*—"), but the girls held together. Miss McBride said occasionally, "Now, let's play fair, kids. No one running off to her own room." And always, when she said this, she counted them, rapidly, at a glance.

On the second floor, Cheryl's diary turned up, and a collection of scandalous love letters in Helena's room, and a locket in which another girl had pasted a picture of one of her professors. The owner of the room always, without exception, stood by the door while her room was searched, ready to run if anything too awkward (something she never knew she had? perhaps something she had borrowed and not returned? perhaps something everyone would find unanimously, irresistibly funny? the stolen things, perhaps?) or too shaming turned up.

Naturally the darkroom was not searched, but Miss McBride insisted on having the girls go through *her* room, which, carefully prepared, disclosed nothing except a picture of a handsome young man whom Miss McBride blushingly refused to identify as either a brother or a fiancé.

When the search was over and they were all gathered together in the living room again, Miss McBride gave voice to the prevailing suspicion by saying, "Well, kids, it looks like one of you was warned in time and got rid of the stuff. But, as I told you before, we know who it is. *Now* I am going to say that if the girl who took these things that didn't belong to her will come to me secretly in my room tonight, nothing more will be said." She started for her room and then stopped to turn back and add, "Needless to say, if nothing comes of this tonight I shall have to take further steps. I had hoped"—she sighed lightly—"I had hoped to settle this here among ourselves, but if that is not possible I shall have to take further steps." She took herself with dignity into her own room, and the girls, knowing more now than they did before, separated and went silently off to their own. No one cared to speak; each one knew the secrets of all the others; no one was inviolate any longer. It would be a long and painful process to build new privacies, secure them safely against intrusion, learn to trust one another again; there was a great destruction that went on in the house that night, of ruined treasures being burned, torn, cut with nail scissors. The wastebaskets taken out the next day were filled with loose torn pages and destroyed photographs, and for many days after that the girls in the house spoke rarely, and very politely, to one another.

When the house was finally quiet, Anne took out her ankle bracelet, her teddy bear and her sonnet, her pen-and-pencil set, her black slip and her leather notebook, added to them Miss McBride's dangling jet earrings, which she had slipped into her pocket while helping search Miss McBride's room, and set them in a row on her bed. All together, they were barely enough to fill a tiny overnight bag, so Anne stopped off in the house living room to slip three or four metal ashtrays into the bag with them. She stood for a minute just inside the front door, surveying the house, which was silent, with all its doors shut; it was her first minute of unalloyed pleasure since her mother's funeral. Then she slipped quickly out the front door and down the street, carrying the overnight bag; mighty, armed.

Showdown

Visitors, if there had ever been any, would have said that the little town of Mansfield was haunted. It didn't *look* haunted, hidden comfortably away among green hills, with its placid houses and cheerful-looking inhabitants, but nevertheless a visitor, if there had ever been any, would have said that it was definitely, but definitely, haunted.

Some notion of this entered Billy Manners's head as he sat on the front porch of his house looking down Mansfield's only street. Billy's father was the storekeeper, schoolteacher, and preacher in the church on Sundays, and Billy, at fifteen, felt that he had a responsible place in the community as the son of his prominent father. From his porch Billy could look down to his father's store, where school was held in the back room, and over to the church next door, and then past a few houses to where the hills began again. About three hundred people lived in Mansfield, but it took only one to be haunted. And Billy had begun to feel that he was it.

Golly, Billy thought, golly. There ought to be some way for a smart guy like me to figure this out.

Uneasily he went into the house, and out to the kitchen. He looked at the mail-order calendar on the wall, which read JULY 16,

1932. That's fine, Billy thought, Saturday. Pop will still be at the store. Mother is out visiting Mrs. Baxter. I'll go fishing.

As though Billy's father had heard this thought, Billy heard his name being called. Billy ran out the front door and saw his father outside the store, calling him.

Golly, Billy thought, what did I forget to do? Full of apprehension, he hurried down the street to the store.

"Billy," his father said as he approached, "your mother wants you to hurry right over to the church and help her clean it out for tomorrow."

"Going to be a good sermon tomorrow, Ray?" old Thad Ruskin called from the end of the store porch. "Full o' hellfire?"

"Pop always preaches good sermons," Billy said with dignity. He detested Thad Ruskin; everyone in town did. Thad drank—where he got it no one knew; rumor had it that he ran a still up in the hills somewhere—and he had ruined his pretty daughter Susy's romance with Tom Harper, who had subsequently left Mansfield and had not been heard from since. Rumor also had it that Tom Harper had made a million dollars in the city, and was coming back someday to face down Thad Ruskin and carry off Susy. Susy was still waiting, on the off chance. Nowadays, Susy spent all her time at home sewing towels and pretty clothes for her hope chest, while Thad, usually drunk, sat among the loafers in front of the store, repeating over and over that no Tom Harper was going to come into *his* home and steal off *his* daughter. Everyone hated Thad, sympathized with Susy, and hoped that Tom Harper would bring his million dollars back to town.

"—And your mother wants you, first of all, to run over and help Mrs. Baxter get the ladder up from the cellar so's she can get down her top row of preserved peaches and see if the cat's had her kittens back there."

"Then can I go fishing, Pop?" Billy asked without much hope.

"Promised me you'd help in the store this afternoon, didn't you?" Billy's father said.

"Yessir," Billy muttered. As he started despondently across the street to Mrs. Baxter's house, a sudden commotion behind him made him turn. Voices were raised. A stranger was walking down the street. He was a ragged, tired-looking figure—looks like he's been walking for three days, Billy thought—and he was heading for the store. The loafers on the porch of the store were all standing, old Thad Ruskin well in front peering at the stranger and murmuring.

Why, it's Tom Harper! Billy thought. All ragged, and poor! Billy stood watching while Tom Harper—it *was* him—walked up to the steps of the porch and stood facing Thad Ruskin.

"You ruined my life once, Thad Ruskin," he said. "Now I'm going to finish yours."

No one stepped forward to help Thad as Tom Harper went slowly up the steps, but as he closed in on Thad, the old man moved swiftly. "Come back to kill me?" he demanded, and Tom's body slipped to the ground. "Ain't nobody that smart."

Billy had been hurrying across the street toward Tom for what seemed an eternity. By the time Tom's body lay on the ground, Billy had gotten there, and stood peering with the others at the man who was supposed to have made a million dollars, and who now lay with Thad Ruskin's knife in his chest.

"Go call Susy, someone," Thad said. "I want her to see what happens to people who try to cross me."

"He's still breathing," Billy's father said. "Here, let's make him more comfortable."

Someone had found Susy, who came running over to the store, and she sank down beside Tom's figure on the ground, crying.

Tom opened his eyes halfway. "Didn't forget me, did you, Susy?" he whispered.

"I won't ever forget you," Susy cried passionately, "and neither will anyone else. They all just stood here and let my father kill you! I'll see that they don't get off easy!"

"I don't want anyone punished for this," Tom said weakly, "not even your father. Just don't forget me . . ."

"Guess he's dead, Susy," Billy's father said gently.

Billy went fishing after that. In the general excitement it was easy for him to slip away. But he was late for dinner, and as he opened the front door warily, he heard his father's voice from the kitchen, calling, "Billy!"

Billy went into the kitchen and saw that there was fried ham and applesauce for dinner. He hoped his mother would sneak some up to him later.

"You were supposed to help your mother and Mrs. Baxter and then help me in the store, Billy," his father said sternly. "I think you'd just better run along up to bed."

Billy turned meekly. It was no more than he had expected. "Pop," he said as he left the kitchen, "Pop, what did they do to Thad Ruskin?"

"They're going to settle that tomorrow," his father said. "And I don't want you hanging around the store while we men talk about it, either."

Billy went upstairs to bed. The excitement of the day, combined with the hot sun and the walking he had done in the afternoon, had made him tired. He fell asleep before his mother could manage to escape his father's eye and sneak upstairs with a plate of ham and applesauce.

It took a few days for Billy to decide that Mansfield was haunted. He never thought about it consciously, but now and then a shadow of a troubling idea seemed to come over him, like the next morning, as he sat on his front porch looking down the street. Golly, he thought. Golly. There ought to be some way for a smart guy like me to figure this out.

Soon after, he went into the kitchen, and saw that the date was July 16, 1932; Billy thought he might go fishing and forget about work. Just then he heard his name being called, and he hurried down the street to where his father was standing in front of the store.

"Billy," his father said, "your mother wants you to hurry right over to the church and help her clean it out for tomorrow."

Old Thad Ruskin piped up, "Going to be a good sermon tomorrow, Ray? Full o' hellfire?"

Billy said, "Pop always preaches good sermons," and then his father added: "And your mother wants you, first of all, to run over and help Mrs. Baxter get the ladder up from the cellar so's she can get down her top row of preserved peaches and see if the cat's had her kittens back there."

Without hope, Billy asked his father if he could go fishing and was reminded he had agreed to work in the store that afternoon. He started across the street, then heard a commotion and turned to see ragged Tom Harper walking toward the store. Billy watched Tom Harper approach old Thad, and Billy was across the street in time to see Tom fall at Thad's feet. When Susy promised Tom that no one would ever forget him, Billy murmured assent, as did everyone else, and then he went fishing.

When he got home late for dinner his father was angry and sent him to bed without anything to eat, and Billy fell asleep before his mother could sneak him a plate.

And the next morning Billy sat on his front porch and thought about it again. Somehow it always evaded him, the secret of why Mansfield was haunted. Nothing ever happened there, just the same things over and over every day, ever since Billy could remember.

Let me see, Billy thought. What happened yesterday?

He had gone fishing, he remembered, and had gotten home late for dinner. What else? Probably just fooled around all day, he thought. Was today Saturday? He went in and looked at the calendar. He thought he might go fishing again today.

But when Billy ran down to the store after his father called, he found that excitement had really come to Mansfield; he saw Tom Harper, home from the city, try to kill old Thad Ruskin, but Thad killed Tom instead. Billy saw the whole thing. Afterward, he went fishing.

The next day, just as Billy was crossing the street to go to Mrs.

Baxter's, he thought, Something's going to happen in a minute! And something did. The day after that, as he ran across the street to see Tom Harper die, he thought, Haven't I done this before?

And the next day, as he ran down the street in answer to his father's call, he thought, How many million times have I done this?

It was several hundred thousand times, anyway, and always on July 16, 1932, and in all that time something had been growing in Billy's head. From his first thought, as he ran across the street to see Tom Harper's body the first time, that here was something he wasn't going to forget in a hurry, there had grown in him a definite conviction that there was something wrong going on. Particularly since he could never remember what he had done the day before. Finally, Billy had a realization.

I do these things again and again, he thought one day, running across the street to the store to see Tom Harper die. I bet I've run from Mrs. Baxter's over to the store lots of times for lots of reasons, but I don't remember ever running across for anything but to see Tom Harper.

The next thought, of course, was: Suppose I *don't* run across to see Tom Harper? It didn't work. Every time Billy turned around and saw Tom Harper walking up onto the porch to meet Thad Ruskin he began to run, and he always got across the street just in time to see Tom's body topple at his feet.

Suppose I hurry?, Billy wondered. He tried to speed himself up crossing the street. With a prodigious effort he managed to reach the store porch before Tom had started to fall. Everything else was the same, but Billy had arrived a fraction of a second sooner.

He hurried home from fishing a fraction of a second earlier, that afternoon, but was still too late for dinner.

The next morning he really tried to hurry. He went into the kitchen a fraction of a second sooner than he felt he ought to; he thought, I'll go fishing, then had to wait for his father to call him; he said, "Pop always preaches good sermons" to Thad Ruskin just as

Thad was finishing "hellfire"; and he crossed the street in time to see the knife go into Tom's breast.

He was still late for dinner, though. He entered his house, knew his father was sitting at the kitchen table eating ham and applesauce, and went right on upstairs. He had just reached the top of the stairs when he heard his father begin: "You were supposed to help your mother and Mrs. Baxter . . ."

All this time, Billy didn't quite know what he was doing. He was still going on with the same motions every day, but his doubt—something that made him know the whole business was fishy—also made him go faster. After three or four days of speeding up, he was beginning to arrive at the store several seconds before his father stepped out front and called "Billy!" He was answering Thad Ruskin's remark before Thad said it.

He was beginning to remember more, too. When he heard his own voice saying "Pop always preaches good sermons" to thin air, and then a minute later heard Thad Ruskin's remark, Billy was beginning to realize what was going on. By this time he had managed to get across the street in time to walk up the store steps with Tom Harper and stand next to him as the knife went in.

The idea that was coming to Billy was vague. It finally materialized into a strange thought, one morning as he sat on his front porch. If I should see a murder somewhere, he thought suddenly, and if I could be there in time, what I should do is step between the two guys and grab for the knife.

The Trouble with My Husband

"THE TROUBLE WITH *MY* HUSBAND," MRS. SMALLWOOD SAID, nodding profusely, "is that he thinks he's God almighty. He thinks he's God almighty." She reached out inaccurately for Mrs. James. "Let me fill your glass for you."

"No thank you," Mrs. James said quite firmly. She looked uneasily across the room to where her husband sat trying to talk art with Mr. Smallwood.

"My husband," Mrs. Smallwood went on, "thinks he's God almighty. That's the only trouble with him. He thinks he's—"

"I understand he's a very fine painter," Mrs. James said vaguely. She looked at her own husband again; he was leaning forward, gesturing eagerly; Mr. Smallwood was leaning back, arms folded; both of them were very much absorbed. Mrs. James turned back to Mrs. Smallwood. "You have such a lovely place here," she said. "So attractive." She laughed deprecatingly. "I'm afraid I don't know very much about art—"

"They're all his," Mrs. Smallwood said. "Every damn one of them is his, except the little one by the door."

Mrs. James leaned forward.

"You can't see it from here," Mrs. Smallwood said. "It's mine."

"Yours?"

"I painted it," Mrs. Smallwood said. "You can't see it from here." She got up and reached again for Mrs. James's glass. "Let me just fill," she said, and went toward the kitchen.

"Arthur," Mrs. James said. "Arthur, dear." Neither of the men heard her; they were both talking at once, watching each other intently. "Arthur?" she said again, raising her voice a little.

"He won't listen," Mrs. Smallwood said. "They both think they're God almighty." She sat down and took a long drink from her glass. "It's his house, his paintings, his kids, his money, his every goddamn thing."

"How *are* your children?" Mrs. James asked. "Such dear boys, both of them. I saw them walking up the hill the other day with their father, and they all looked as if they were having such a wonderful time."

"His kids, his house, his money," Mrs. Smallwood said. She swayed over and put a confiding hand on Mrs. James's knee. "You know," she said, "I *love* children. I wanted to have children and Harry didn't. It was *my* idea to have children. And you know, the minute I saw those goddamn little helpless little things I had such a real *feeling* for them; you'll never know how I feel about kids."

"They're such . . ." Mrs. James thought for a minute. "Such interesting little fellows," she said.

"I really feel for those kids," Mrs. Smallwood said. "I spend the whole goddamn day cooking and cleaning and washing and wiping their noses, and I really love those kids. Don't let Harry say anything to you about *that*."

"I suppose they'll be painters, too, won't they," Mrs. James said brightly.

"Like me," Mrs. Smallwood said. "You go over and look at that little picture I painted. You can't see it from here. I'll tell you something," she said, catching hold of Mrs. James's arm, "let me just tell you this. Watkins in New York called me the other day. Offered me their whole advertising campaign, just like that. That's two hundred a picture."

"That sounds perfectly wonderful," Mrs. James said.

"I'm not sure whether I want to do it," Mrs. Smallwood said. "You know, I think when a woman has a home and children she ought to give up art. Would you think I ought to give up my painting just for a home and a couple of lousy children with running noses?"

"Arthur," Mrs. James said, "Arthur dear, I think—"

"And the rest of it is," Mrs. Smallwood said. "I think I'll go on down to New York for a few weeks and see Watkins. He ought to pay my expenses." She nudged Mrs. James. "I could have a time," she said.

"It must be wonderful to be able to paint," Mrs. James said. "To be able to express yourself. I've often wished—"

"Let me just show you," Mrs. Smallwood said. She stood up and went unsteadily across the room to a stack of papers piled untidily in a bookcase. "Let me show you," she called over her shoulder to Mrs. James. "Pour yourself a drink while you're waiting."

"What are *you* looking for?" Mr. Smallwood said suddenly. He and Mr. James had stopped their conversation to watch Mrs. Small-wood, and now Mr. Smallwood stood up and walked over to his wife. She was a small woman and had to look far up at him when he stood next to her. "What in hell do you think you're doing?" he said. "Going through my stuff."

Mrs. Smallwood put back the papers she was holding. "I was looking for the sketches I did for Watkins," she said.

Mr. Smallwood looked down at the drink in his wife's hand and then gave her a soft tap on the shoulder. "You go back and sit down," he said.

Mrs. Smallwood came sullenly back to sit down next to Mrs. James. "He hates to have me talk about my painting," she said in a whisper. "I didn't hurt any of your old paintings," she said aloud.

"That's all right, Diana," Mr. Smallwood said. He turned to Mr. James, but Mrs. Smallwood said loudly, "Think you're God almighty. You just can't stand it if Watkins wants me to do a big contract. I might get more money than you do, you and your godalmighty paintings."

"Arthur," Mrs. James said, "don't you think we'd better—"

Mr. James looked at his watch. "Indeed, yes," he said. "Mr. Smallwood and I were just having a very interesting—"

"I suppose he told you all about how good he is," Mrs. Smallwood said. "His painting his money his house his kids. I take care of those goddamn kids all day long while he sits there and says he's painting and he's so scared I'll make more money than he does. I have a real feeling for kids," she said to Mrs. James. "I *love* those kids. You'll never know how I felt when I first saw those little helpless things—so goddamn *helpless*."

"I know how you felt," Mrs. James said. She went over and stood beside her husband's chair. "I'm afraid we really must—"

"And now you've got to drive out these people, too," Mr. Smallwood said to his wife. "Any nice people who come to see us, with your Watkins and your money talk."

"No, really, it's late," Mrs. James said, and Mr. James added, "No, certainly not."

"He really did call me," Mrs. Smallwood said. "He called me on the phone, long-distance from New York, and he said he wanted me to do their whole setup this year. He certainly did call me."

"One day while I was out, probably," Mr. Smallwood said. "Watkins never talked to you since that trash you sent him three years ago."

"I did do some good pictures," Mrs. Smallwood said. "I was looking for them."

Mr. Smallwood turned to Mr. and Mrs. James. "I feel as though I ought to apologize," he said.

"Not at all," Mr. James said.

Mrs. James added hurriedly, "If you would just show us where our coats—"

"Don't go," Mrs. Smallwood said. She came over to Mrs. James and put a hand on her shoulder. "*Please* don't go on account of me. I want to show you those pictures I did for Watkins. They're really good, I promise you."

"You won't be able to find them," Mr. Smallwood said.

"I'm afraid we haven't time," Mrs. James said.

"Where did you put them?" Mrs. Smallwood asked her husband, and then, to Mrs. James, "It's so early yet. You only just got here. Where are they?" she said to her husband insistently.

"I'll tell you where they are," Mr. Smallwood said. He walked over to the table and picked up his drink, and went on, with his back to his wife. "You tore them up," he said, "the last time we had company."

Six A.M. Is the Hour

Six A.M. IS AN HOUR WHEN DUDE RANCH COWHANDS ARE STILL ABLE to play at being real ranchers. Even the tired nags after a night in the fields are frisky, and there will be a half hour for coffee after the herd is locked in the paddock and before the earliest guest is out. But this morning the horses balked at the gate and, instead of crowding through to the feed troughs, turned, reared, and finally stood milling in obvious terror.

Six A.M. is, too, the hour when tired jazz musicians, tired of other people's voices and other people's liquor, are finally able to play at being people themselves. After a night at the clubs, there is a half hour for coffee after the celebrants are sent home and the doors are closed at last.

But this morning the sun did not rise clearly, and the early-morning passersby on the street turned apprehensively, hesitated, neglected bus schedules and trains, spoke nervously to one another, and waited.

The front pages of the morning papers were given over, as if by common agreement, to the solemn but vague proclamation written for the President urging "every citizen to have faith." The vague statement asserting that "the best scientists of the nation are cooperating with the Army" trailed off into a general assurance that instructions would be announced, possibly tomorrow. The radio pundits had retired, and the air sounded alternately with symphonic recordings and prayer.

The fact that the sun did not shine was incidental, although there were those who felt that it was the main contributing factor to the air of general hysteria that was growing slowly and inexorably, in spite of the open doors of the churches, and the hymns sung on street corners by stars of stage, screen, and opera. There was a sizable portion of the population who felt that the sun's vagueness was the beginning of the end; these people gathered on mountaintops previously decided upon, and spent the hours on their knees. There was a small select group among the panic-stricken who believed that their own personal destruction was the object of the general wholesale violence, and these few alternately repented and became brazen, depending upon whether it looked as though their own private deaths might save the rest of the country, or might only involve it in a great unending ruin.

When the first hour of that day had passed, therefore, citizens began to watch for some sign. Apparently no one noticed that the clocks still said six o'clock. No one, that is, except Sossiter. In his luxurious midtown apartment, nothing stirred until noon. And then Sossiter awoke, looked at his watch, scratched his head, rose, dressed, and rang for his breakfast.

That the bell should have rung at all is one of the minor miracles of that morning, when no sounds moved in an orderly fashion, when standard cause-and-effect were suspended in favor of a great, more supremely logical cause-and-effect; at any rate, when Sossiter rang, the bell also rang, and only the fact that the bell was not answered disturbed the regular routine of Sossiter's well-paid existence. He rang again, and a third time, consulted his watch again, looked out at the sunless sky, and debated. The cigarette that he selected from the package on the dresser came to reach his hand already lighted; this he did not consciously observe. With his cigarette in his hand, he sat in the overstuffed chair in his bedroom and considered.

How much time went by while he pondered, neither he nor his ornamental clock could say. All that is sure is that Sossiter smoked and waited. "It must have stopped," he said. "The clock is stopped. But my watch stopped too. That is unlikely." He was a logical man. He set himself to solving the mystery. So he went to the clock and heard it ticking. Still, it said six o'clock. It must have been some time since he had wakened. "Nevertheless," he said, "it does move."

It *had* to move; all things moved and that was the secret of life. "Conservation of energy," Sossiter told himself. "Admit no entities beyond necessity, all things have their opposites, a stitch in time saves nine." He felt tremendously reassured by these incontrovertible facts, and he glanced at his watch with contempt; it must have stopped, after all. It occurred to him finally that, six o'clock or not, man must eat. Ignoring the bell, he put on a heavy figured silk dressing gown and opened his bedroom door. That, possibly, was when Sossiter first began to believe that perhaps thesis does not necessarily imply antithesis; birds of a feather, even, might not flock together. It was not even absolutely certain to Sossiter, after that first moment, that water seeks its own level. Because surely there had been a hall outside his bedroom door the night before? Surely, when he had retired with a highball and a mystery story at eleven o'clock the night before, surely there had been stairs going down to the first floor of his home? Surely, Sossiter thought, surely, without any doubt, there was something illogically, terribly wrong.

Martians, he thought. Those crazy physicists that spend all day cooking themselves under an atomic reactor and all night writing stories for *Weird World* have done it. Spoiled my day completely. One of those idiots has hung the world up like a celluloid ball in an airstream. Serve him right if the moon fell in his lap. So Sossiter drew a breath, testing it. And sure enough, to his superdelicate senses the air plainly was the same he had breathed last night upon retiring. Now the problem became clear. He must find the crux of this hiatus and give the globe a shove before something slipped. "Think fast," he said, "and don't anybody move."

Move? Was movement one natural law that had been suspended for the duration of Sossiter's supreme test? He lifted his hand tentatively, made the thought that indicated movement in the fingers, and was happy to see that where he dictated turning to the thumb, it was the ring finger that moved, in a particularly impossible gesture, and the hand itself that made the decision. This is it, then, Sossiter thought, and nodded gravely. Without any conscious weighing of his act he stepped firmly out into the infinite space that lay outside his bedroom door, and floated without fear down to the ground and the street that lay outside his house. Actually, it was not the street that lay outside his house normally; it was, to all appearances, the main street of a western ghost town; Sossiter noticed a sign saying SILVER DOLLAR SALOON, and nodded again. This is most certainly it, he thought. The Time is upon us.

And Sossiter, leaving no footprint in the dust, marched blithely backward until his elegant back had entered through the swinging doors. Of course, the doors did not swing. If they had, he would have known the game was up. But the doors hung dead center. "Stranger," a voice intoned, "the game is about to start. Yer jest in time." (Pretty shrewd, Sossiter noted.) "You may not know the rules. I cut, deal, and call. Don't peek at the dealer. Lay yore poke out. And name yore pizen." Sossiter seemed to shrink with the effort of his concentration.

"I usually decline a game unless I know who I am playing against," he said courteously, hoping to delay until he found some inkling of the rules, if any, that governed this game, if it could be called a game, when so obviously it seemed that more than Sossiter was at stake. "Would you consider telling me your names?"

The voice that had spoken to him before made a sound of derision and said, "I cut, deal, and call; do you want to know my name too?"

"I do indeed," Sossiter said firmly.

The voice laughed and said, "Thor. The gent on your right is named Loki; we don't let him touch the cards, and you'll soon know why, if you don't already. The other gent is Wotan; he runs the bank in this game. If you don't like our rules, you can quit. Anytime, anytime at all."

The way the voice said "anytime at all" gave Sossiter a small icy chill down his back, and he caught his breath before he could say, "Sure, buddy. Play it any way you like." Even in his own ears the words lacked conviction, had no authentic ring at all.

Then, cautiously, Sossiter turned to find the table, his eyes obediently lowered but high enough to see that the three figures were seated—rather, were in a seated position—around a huge spinning iron pot suspended in air. Already it was warm enough to give off a slight acrid scent. With studied nonchalance Sossiter reached for his wallet and found a fistful of cartwheels, heavy-looking but weightless. He flipped one, and the rest followed in a cascade into the pot. Loki tittered, "Now the kitty." And a soft cry followed by the odor of burned hair issued from the pot.

"Good, brave man," said Thor. "But you'll make one of us in spite of that, I trow. This is going to be a brand of poker you never knew."

"I'm sure," Sossiter said fervently. "Deal, bud." Thor looked up sharply and seemed about to speak, but thought better of it and began solemnly to deal the cards; these were as large as slabs of marble, and seemed equally heavy, although Thor dealt them effortlessly. Next to him, Loki was examining each of his cards as they came, breathing quickly and laughing in a shrill, high giggle. Sossiter turned his cards up laboriously, and then said, "How do I bet?"

A shout of laughter from Thor and Wotan greeted him, and Loki turned slightly and giggled again. "You've already bet," Thor said, laughing still. With a quick memory of the lost sun, Sossiter was silent. "Well?" Thor said sternly, eyeing him.

Casually Sossiter indicated his cards. "Straight flush," he said. "To the jack."

"Straight flush to the king," Loki said, next to him. "In spades." With dismay Sossiter turned and saw Loki grinning evilly at him.

"Next bet?" Thor said. "I'm ready to deal, mortal. Bet."

Sossiter's mind, which had been relied upon in crises involving billions, in solving disputes on which hung issues of war and peace, behind great public and greater private plans a thousand times—Sossiter's massive brain seemed to rattle in his aching skull. The decision, however, came in an instant: "New York," he drawled. "Nine million people, and a tenth of America's wealth." The three sneered. "Silence, vermin," said Thor. Then courteously to Sossiter, "I'll see you a millennium of scalding lead and raise you a comet's tail. Call it."

"Right," said Sossiter. "Chicago. Almost as big as New York, but farther west."

"As far as Hollywood?" asked Loki with the first real interest he had so far shown.

"Not quite," said Sossiter, and Loki turned away crossly. Again Thor dealt the cards, and Sossiter, looking eagerly at his, found that he had four aces; this time he returned Loki's sneer with a sneer of his own, and casually turned his cards over. "Four aces," he said with vast indifference.

"Five," said Loki.

"Five what?" said Sossiter.

"Five aces, mortal fool," Loki said.

"The mortal loses," said Wotan.

"Bet, mortal," Thor said.

This time Sossiter in his agony looked up at the place where Thor was sitting. Only the happenstance that Loki in his writhing of delight at that moment tipped a whiskey bottle into the pot, raising a bitter cloud of smoke and steam, shielded our champion and saved us all. To gain a moment, Sossiter snickered. "You guys run a cheap game. You mean there's no piano player, no girls?"

Thor uttered a Beelzebubbling roar. "Lunkheads! Scuttlebumpkins! Suffering sulphuroids, didn't I tell you to have the damned minstrels on hand? Bring out a fresh stinger for our guest and a brimstone daiquiri for me. Fly!"

"And the girls?" said Sossiter insidiously. Loki waved a hand casually, and Sossiter found a lovely girl sitting, most abruptly, in his lap; she was smiling and dark-haired and seemed most agreeable, except that she seemed to be made of white stone, probably marble, and her weight made Sossiter's knees buckle. He slid her off, she landed on Loki's toe, and Loki, rising with an immense shout of rage, aimed a blow at Sossiter that might have crushed him onto the floor; Sossiter ducked, the blow hit Wotan, and as Wotan, with a casual gesture of his left hand, let loose a lightning stroke at Loki, Sossiter fled. He ran, as silently as he could in his bathrobe and slippers, down the corridors of time, through the invisible barriers of space, back into his own apartment, where, sitting on his bed, he smoked a cigarette. He glanced at his watch. Six o'clock.

He took a deep draft of the scented Turkish blend, briefly smiled at the remembrance of his days as a student at Beirut, when he smoked a true Middle East blend of camel droppings, mahorka, and goat's hair . . . and rang for his breakfast. When it came, he studiously avoided looking at Thornton, the immaculate Thornton, whose clear eye and slender though aging figure was a reproach that Sossiter kept to scourge himself for his own sybaritic ways. "Thornton, get that clock fixed today, you knave. Do it, or you'll find there's the devil to pay."

"Clock, sir? The clock?" Thornton picked up the clock and examined it as though he had never seen a clock before.

"Certainly," said Sossiter, "the clock; what did you think I meant when I said 'clock'? Have it fixed today."

"Yes, sir," said Thornton indignantly. "What would you care to have done to it, sir?"

"I want it fixed," said Sossiter. "It says six o'clock."

"So does mine, sir," said Thornton. "So do all of them."

"Is it only six o'clock, then?" Sossiter asked.

"No, sir, no indeed," Thornton said. "But they said on the radio that time has been suspended until the god Thor decides what to do with us. It seems he won us, sir, in an . . . er . . . a poker game."

Root of Evil

MISS SYBIL TURNER OPENED THE ENVELOPE AND TOOK OUT THE EN-closure, glanced at it, started to set it down on a stack of similar mail, and then took it back and glanced at it again; then she giggled. "Listen to this, Mabe," she said, and her friend Mabel Johnson, working at an identical desk, but typing at the moment, said, "Wait a minute," and finished her line before looking up. "What?" she said.

Sybil was still holding the letter. "Listen," she said. "Here's a guy wants us to run an ad for money."

Mabel laughed shortly. "*That*'s no way to get it," she said, look-ing down again at her typewriter. "Better he should go to work."

"No, *listen*. He says, 'Money to give away' and he's got a post office box to write to and two dollars enclosed for the ad to run all week, and everything. Can you imagine?"

"He must be crazy," said Mabel Johnson.

"Crazy it *is*," Sybil Turner agreed devoutly.

"Here's something funny," Mr. George Carter commented to his wife the next evening. He had been quietly reading his evening paper and his wife was doing needlepoint; they sat peacefully in front of their living room fire, with the children soundly asleep upstairs. "Here's a real good one," George Carter said again, and his wife looked up patiently. "'Money to give away,'" George Carter read, once he was sure he had her attention. "Right here in the paper. People think of the screwiest things."

"But so many people are taken in by a thing like that," Ellen Carter said in her soft voice. "People writing to him, hoping."

"Paper has no right to print a thing like that," George said.

Ellen started to speak and then paused, her eyes lifted to the ceiling and her mouth open, listening. Then, reassured, she looked again at her husband and said, "Probably they run a thing like that to test how many people read the classified ads. Couldn't that be it?"

George was obviously sorry that he had not thought of this himself. "Maybe so," he said grudgingly. "Wish they'd send some of that money along to us, though. *We* could use it."

"Oh, dear," Ellen agreed with a sigh. "With prices the way they are, and meat . . ." She dropped her scissors onto the arm of the chair, and folded her hands in her lap, and sighed again. "George," she demanded, as one who begins a long and intricate story, "just try to guess how much they had the nerve to charge for lamb today? *Lamb!*"

"Things are pretty bad." Mr. Carter hastily elevated the paper before his face. "Screwiest idea I ever heard," he muttered.

"The fact is perfectly plain," Mrs. Harmon said severely to her daughter. "Your own mother's sewing, weeks and weeks of work, isn't good enough for you to wear out in public. So you can go without."

"Without clothes?" said Mildred sullenly.

"You know *perfectly* well what I mean. You picked out the style of this dress yourself and I spent three weeks making it and it looks just beautiful on you and—"

"I *didn't* pick out the style," Mildred said.

Her mother sighed. "I sometimes think you are the *most* unreasonable—"

"I wanted the dress in the *store*," Mildred wailed. "Not for you to *copy* it."

Her mother took a deep breath, as if determined to be reasonable in spite of everything. "Dresses in the store cost a lot of money," she said. "This dress cost less than—"

"If I only had some *money*," Mildred said hopelessly. "I'll write to this guy in the paper says he's giving money away. I'll get *married* or something." She tossed her head defiantly. "*Then* I can have dresses."

Mrs. Harmon shifted her ground abruptly and began to weep. "Three weeks I took to make that dress," she said mournfully, "and now it's not good enough for you, and you want to run away and get married, and all these years I've tried to keep you looking nice and worked to buy pretty things and spent three weeks—"

"Oh, *Mother*," said Mildred. She blinked to keep tears out of her own eyes. "I'm not going to get married, *honestly*. And the dress is *beautiful*. I'll *wear* it, honestly I will, I'll wear it all the *time*."

"It's no good," her mother said. "I know all the other girls—"

"It's *beautiful*," Mildred said. "It's just like the one in the store. It's the prettiest dress I ever saw, and I'm going to put it on right *now*."

Mrs. Harmon lifted her face briefly from her handkerchief. "Watch out for that pin I left in the shoulder," she said.

"For the last time, I'm afraid I find it necessary to say," Amy Nelson said emphatically, "that I do not wish to go to any movie."

"But—"

"Indeed I do not," Amy said. She set her shoulders and looked extraordinarily stern. "Movies last night," she said. "Movies the night before. I'm so tired of going to movies I don't know what to do. And anyway there's nothing left to see."

"But, Amy—"

"*Some* girls," said Amy pointedly, "like to go to the theater. *Some* girls like to go to a nightclub and dance. *Some* girls even like to ride in taxis and wear gardenias. Of course *I'm* always happy at the movies, though. Good old Amy."

"I can't afford—"

"*That* point," said Amy delicately, "is the one I was too polite to refer to. Let me just remark, however, that I know of only one grown man who has not got enough initiative to get out and *do* something for himself. He works heart and soul for this organization and comes around every week and says thank you to them so gratefully for— What is it they pay you? Seventeen cents a week?"

"Now listen—"

"*Some* men are making good money at twenty-four. *Some* men have good jobs and *they're* not afraid to assert themselves and keep up with other people and not let everyone else get ahead of them, and *their* girls don't have to go to movies every night of the week and see the same old—"

"But when I've worked there a little—"

"And *some* men," Amy continued icily, "do not expect girls to wait around until they are sixty-five and drawing old-age pensions before they can get married."

"Well, to hear you talk—"

"Here," said Amy in her sweetest voice, "perhaps *this* will help you. Here, in the classified section of tonight's paper. Perhaps *this* is the lucky break you've been waiting for. Let me just give you this copy of tonight's paper, since I am sure it would take your entire weekly earnings to buy one for yourself."

"You don't have to talk like—"

"And now, good night," said Amy, less than graciously.

"He shouldn't of done it, that's all," said Ronald Hart, who was fifteen years old and felt utterly responsible for his mother and ten-year-old brother. "He's going to get us all in trouble, that's what."

"Dickie," said his mother, "tell me again what happened."

"I wrote the man like I said," Dickie told her. He looked nervously from his mother to his brother. "I didn't think he'd *answer*," he said, his voice trembling. "I never thought he'd *answer*."

"I'm afraid we ought to send it back to him," his mother said. She had tight hold of the shining bill, and she twisted it between her fingers as though afraid to let it go.

"Well, *we* haven't really done anything," Ronald said. "Maybe we ought to tell the cops."

"No, no," said his mother hastily. "That's the *most* important thing of all. We're not going to tell *any*body, you hear? Ronald?"

"Okay," said Ronald, "but maybe he's a gangster or—"

"Dickie, you hear me?"

"Yes, but suppose they catch us?" Dickie said.

"We haven't *done* anything," his mother said again. "I don't even know if it's any good. I don't dare take a hundred-dollar bill into the bank and ask them if it's any good."

"Counterfeit," said Ronald wisely.

"But what if it isn't?" said his mother. "Suppose it's real?" She sighed, and looked down at the hundred-dollar bill. "They have our address, of course."

"I had to put the address in for him to know where to send the money," Dickie said miserably.

His mother reached a sudden decision. "I'll tell you what we'll do," she said. "We'll put it right in Dickie's piggy bank. Then if they come and ask us about it, we can say we just put it away for safekeeping. And if no one comes after a while, why, I guess it's ours. But don't *tell* anyone."

"Don't you tell, Dickie," his brother said warningly.

"Don't *you* tell," Dickie said.

"*You*'re the one always blabs out everything."

"I was the one thought of writing him in the first place, wasn't I?"

"And look what you got us into."

"Boys," said their mother warningly, "we've got enough trouble without you quarrelling. Now, Dickie, there's one more thing I want you to do."

"What?"

"Just in case it *is* all right," his mother said, "I want you to sit right down and write that man a nice letter saying thank you."

"Oh, *Mother!*"

"No one is ever going to say my boys weren't brought up right," she said firmly.

Mr. John Anderson let himself into his apartment, carrying his mail, and sighed deeply as he closed the door behind him. He was hungry and tired, and his day had gone poorly. He had succeeded in persuading a newsboy to accept ten dollars, and he had slipped a hundred-dollar bill into the cup of a blind beggar, but otherwise he had had no success at all. He winced when he remembered the way the truck driver had spoken to him, and the thought of the giggling shopgirls made him almost ill.

He took off his coat and sat down wearily in the easy chair. In a few minutes he would take care of the mail, then have a shower and dress and go out to some nice restaurant for dinner; he would take a vacation for this evening and carry only enough to take care of his own expenses. He could not decide whether to take a taxi uptown to a fancy steakhouse, or to go to the seafood restaurant nearby and have a lobster. Lobster, he rather thought.

After he had rested briefly he got up, went to the desk, and picked up the mail he had brought home with him. Absently he stared at the stacks of ten-dollar bills in the pigeonholes of his desk: the fives, the fifties, the hundreds. The mail under his hand was typical—one offensively humorous request for a million dollars, badly written in capital letters, and unfortunately including no return address; one circular from a loan company featuring on the envelope a man pointing toward the reader and the statement "YOU need no longer worry about money." There was a terse note from the newspaper saying that his week was up today, and asking if he desired to continue running his ad. One letter was signed by three hundred children in the Roosevelt Elementary School, saying thank you for the television set he had given the school library. One postcard read, "Dear Sir, If you really mean it please send ten dollars return mail." This last he answered, addressing the envelope quickly and enclosing, without counting, a handful of ten-dollar bills.

Then he sat down at the desk, looking with desperation and frustration at the stacks of money. Finally, in a fury, he took one of the piles of ten-dollar bills and threw it wildly against the opposite wall, where it scattered so that ten-dollar bills floated all about the room and settled gently down onto the furniture. "In the name of heaven," he wailed, "what am I going to *do* with it all?"

The Bridge Game

MRS. MURRAY WENT QUICKLY INTO THE LIVING ROOM CARRYING A dish of salted nuts in one hand and a dish of chocolates in the other, and hummed amiably to herself as she put them down carefully on diagonal corners of the bridge table, which stood already set up in the center of the room.

"I got out a large ginger ale and a large club soda," she said, her humming rising for a minute into words and then subsiding back to anonymity again.

"Okay," Mr. Murray said. He sat reading his newspaper, a large, cheerful, balding man like millions of others who sat peacefully of an evening in their own chairs, reading their own papers; like probably hundreds of other men whose wives had invited neighbors over for bridge, he still had his jacket and tie on. He would take them off when the Leghorns came, asking permission politely of the ladies, encouraging Mart Leghorn to do the same, but as long as he had to open the door to the Leghorns he must be correctly dressed.

Like millions of other wives, Mrs. Murray looked like her husband. She was plump and pleasant, and dieting, and would try to go very easy on the candy and nuts while she played bridge, she and Mrs. Leghorn both begging prettily to have the dishes put as far away from them as possible, "So I won't forget and just go on eating them; I just *can't* stop once I start!" Later in the evening she would serve coffee and a chocolate cake she had made herself, with a careful eye on the sugar.

The doorbell rang as she was standing vaguely looking around the room, rechecking everything. Mr. Murray rose heavily and put his paper down on the arm of the chair, and Mrs. Murray moved it to the bottom shelf of the end table and followed him out into the hall.

"Evening, evening," Mr. Murray was saying heartily. "Come in, come in, Roberta. Mart, old boy."

"Don't you look nice," Mrs. Murray said, and Mrs. Leghorn said, "How *nice* you look tonight," and "Dora, dear, we brought our daughter, Carol, I *hope* you don't mind, she was all alone at home and I told her I was sure you wouldn't mind."

"Of course not," Mrs. Murray said, making her voice sound pleased. "We're delighted, of course."

"She can just sit and read or something," Mrs. Leghorn said. "You really don't mind?"

"I hope you don't mind my barging in like this, Mrs. Murray," Carol said; she went over and put her arm around Mrs. Leghorn. "Mother said she was sure you wouldn't mind, and I said I'd just sit and read or something."

"We're delighted," Mrs. Murray said. "I hope we won't bore you."

Carol laughed. She was very tall and thin and very tan, and she wore her hair—it was black, as Mrs. Leghorn's used to be—over her forehead in bangs, and down her back in a smooth straight line. She put her hand out and squeezed Mrs. Murray's. "I *did* want to stop and say hello while I was in town," she added.

Breaking away from Carol, Mrs. Murray succeeded in leading everyone into the living room, where she and Mrs. Leghorn sat on the couch and Carol sat properly on a stiff chair slightly removed from the rest of the room, while the men walked around each other absently, like dogs settling down to sleep.

"How is college, Carol?" Mrs. Murray asked.

"Oh, grand," Carol said. She smiled brightly. "It's good to get home for a while, though."

"How long will you be here?" Mrs. Murray asked, nodding.

"Till Wednesday." Carol had started to answer almost before Mrs. Murray finished asking; it was a polite formality, like "How are you," that had to be gotten past before Mrs. Murray and Carol could size each other up afresh. Carol had been away for three months now, and this was her first trip home. Mrs. Murray noticed her thin leather sandals, her long bare legs. "You certainly have changed," she said, and Carol laughed easily.

"Bet it feels good to be home," Mrs. Murray said.

"Well?" Mr. Murray demanded abruptly, coming to stand in front of Carol. "Well, how does it feel to be back home?"

Carol looked up at him. "Gets pretty dull in the old hometown," she said.

"Well," Mr. Murray said, "ought to have some young men around to liven it up. Girl like you needs young fellers."

Mrs. Murray tightened her lips. She disliked her husband's use of vernacular just as she disliked his telling stories in dialect; she felt it sat awkwardly on a man of his age and dignity, and besides, he was apt, so often, to misuse a mechanical vocabulary. "I thought we might play bridge," she said to Mrs. Leghorn, gesturing at the card table. She allowed just the faintest hint of disappointment, plans upset, to creep into her voice. "But I'm afraid Carol . . ."

Carol turned away from Mr. Murray immediately. "Oh, *please*," she said. "I'll be just fine, honestly."

"Well," Mr. Murray said, looking at the card table as though he had never seen it before, "I don't know why we can't *all* play. Carol can take my place to start with, and then we can cut in."

"I don't think we ought to . . ." Mrs. Murray began.

"Oh, no, really," Carol said. "I can just sit and read, that's what I *came* for. I just didn't want to sit home all alone," she added to Mr. Murray.

"Mart," Mrs. Leghorn called, "tell them that Carol doesn't want to play bridge."

Mr. Leghorn turned around guiltily. "She can take my place," he said.

"Suppose we just give up bridge," Mrs. Murray said. This time her voice held an audible grievance. "We can sit and talk."

"Suppose I make everybody a drink," Mr. Murray said. He slapped Mr. Leghorn on the shoulder. "Drink, old man?"

"I'll help," Carol said, jumping up. "After making so much trouble I ought to do something useful."

"Never mind," Mrs. Murray called, but Carol had followed the men out to the kitchen.

"You know," Mrs. Leghorn began at once, "I could just *kick* myself for bringing Carol tonight, but the poor child gets *so* lonesome, and it seems like all her friends are out of town—the Raglan boy's in Maine, you know—and I can't just send her off alone to the movies or something."

"What's she been doing all the time she's been home?" Mrs. Murray asked flatly.

"Well," Mrs. Leghorn said, waving delicately, "she's been busy, of *course*. Out a lot, and shopping and all that. There are plenty of people who'd *like* to take Carol around, of *course*. But she won't go out with just anybody."

Mrs. Murray felt her social injury being passed over lightly. "I'll tell you what we can do," she said. "I don't care much for bridge anyway, you know. I like to play, but of course I'm not really terribly good."

"You're *much* better than I am," Mrs. Leghorn said. "If anybody's going to . . ." She stopped and listened to a roar of laughter from the kitchen. "You know, Oliver seems *such* a hand with young folks," she laughed. "I'll never forget him at the country club dance last Christmas."

Mrs. Murray nodded grimly. "But I don't mind sitting out at all," she said.

Carol came into the room, laughing and carrying two drinks. "Natch," she said over her shoulder to Mr. Murray, who was also carrying two drinks, and they both laughed.

"Mother, Mrs. Murray," Carol said. She handed them the drinks, then took hers from Mr. Murray. "Here's to fun," she said, and she and Mr. Murray laughed again.

Mr. Leghorn followed them finally out of the kitchen, carrying his own drink, which he sipped as he walked. "I like that dining room wallpaper," he said to Mr. Murray. "Who'd you get it from?"

"Our landlord," Mr. Murray said boisterously.

"It was here when we moved in," Mrs. Murray explained.

"Daddy can't think of anything but business," Carol said.

"I can't think of anything but pleasure," Mr. Murray said. Kittenishly, Mrs. Murray thought.

"We've settled the bridge problem," Mr. Murray said to his wife. He took a deep swallow of his drink. "You three are going to play, and Carol and I are going to play gin rummy."

"Oh, come on," Carol said, making a horrible frown. "I said I wasn't going to play anything, and you know it."

"Perhaps Carol would like to play in *my* place," Mrs. Murray said loftily. "I don't really feel like playing at all."

"Let's not have all that again," Mr. Murray said firmly. "It's all settled."

"You read this thing, Oliver?" Mr. Leghorn asked from across the room. "This book?" He held up a book he had taken from the end table.

"Never learned to read," Mr. Murray said. "Can't read a note."

Mr. Leghorn laid the book down and turned the pages absently. "I like music, now," Mr. Murray said to Carol. "I get a real kick out of that."

"Charge," Carol said. When he stared, she said, "*Charge*. You get a *charge* out of that."

"I get a *charge* out of that," Mr. Murray said.

Mr. Leghorn closed the book and came purposefully across the room. "Going to play bridge?" he asked. "Roberta, you play with Oliver. Dora and I will take you on."

"And Carol?" Mrs. Murray asked, before her husband could say it.

"She can sit and read or something," Mr. Leghorn said. "Good book over there on the table, Carol."

"See here," Mr. Murray said, "we can't just leave Carol out."

Mrs. Murray got up suddenly, said "Excuse me," and hurried out of the room.

"Are you all right?" Mrs. Leghorn called blankly after her, and then, to Mr. Murray, "She's feeling all right, of *course*?"

"Sure," Mr. Murray said, surprised.

"Mrs. Murray looks so *nice* tonight," Carol said eagerly, "I don't know when I've seen her looking handsomer."

"That blue dress has always looked good on her," Mrs. Leghorn said.

Mr. Leghorn was setting the usual chairs around the bridge table, silently and efficiently. He riffled the pages of the score pad, tested the point on the pencil, moved the candy dishes slightly, and finally sat down to shuffle the cards. "Come on, everybody," he said. "Got to get started."

Mrs. Leghorn and Mr. Murray moved obediently to the bridge table, and Carol walked over to Mr. Murray's easy chair and settled down, holding the book Mr. Leghorn had suggested.

"Where's Dora?" Mr. Leghorn demanded. "If we're going to get in more than a couple of hands . . ."

"She's been gone quite a while," Mrs. Leghorn said to Mr. Murray. "Do you think there's anything . . . ?"

"She'll be back," Mr. Murray said. "Here she comes now."

Mrs. Murray entered the room quickly, smiling brightly. Her nose had just been powdered. "Sorry, everyone," she said. "Oh, is *this* how we play?" She looked at the bridge table and then over at Carol. "Carol, honey," she said breathlessly, "I want you to take this." She circled the table and handed Carol a small box, then went back and sat down.

"Why, Mrs. Murray," Carol said. "You really *shouldn't.*" She opened the box and looked inside. "Really," she said, "I *can't* possibly . . ."

"Bring it here," Mrs. Leghorn said. "Let me see."

Carol took the box over, and Mrs. Leghorn looked. "Dora," she said, "isn't that nice, now." She tilted the box and held it for Mr. Leghorn to see. "It's awfully pretty," she said.

"Yes," Mr. Leghorn said. Insistently, he began to deal the cards.

"Try it on," Mrs. Murray said to Carol.

It was a piece of costume jewelry, a pin of gold leaves, each with a small pink or green or red stone set in the center; when Carol tried it on, it looked plain and matronly on the shoulder of her young cotton dress. "It's perfectly lovely," Carol said, looking down at it. She unpinned it and put it back into the box.

"I'll tell you," Mrs. Murray said quickly, looking down at the cards Mr. Leghorn was dealing her, "I really bought it for myself, but it's *much* too fancy for me, and then when I saw how Carol was growing up to be such a young lady, I thought she might like it. That's all."

"But I really couldn't take it," Carol said.

"I want you to, dear," Mrs. Murray said. "It *looks* like Carol, doesn't it?" she said to Mrs. Leghorn. Mrs. Leghorn stared up at Carol for a minute.

"Thank you very much, then," Carol said. "I'll let you get on with your game." She left the box on the corner of the table and settled back into the chair.

"Carol loves the pin, of *course*," Mrs. Leghorn said to Mrs. Murray. "It's a sweet thing."

"It gives her a *charge*," Mr. Murray said.

Mrs. Murray regarded her husband. "For heaven's sake, Oliver," she said finally, "don't talk like a child."

The Man in the Woods

WEARILY, MOVING HIS FEET BECAUSE HE HAD NOTHING ELSE TO DO, Christopher went on down the road, hating the trees that moved slowly against his progress, hating the dust beneath his feet, hating the sky, hating this road, all roads, everywhere. He had been walking since morning, and all day the day before that, and the day before that, and days before that, back into the numberless line of walking days that dissolved, seemingly years ago, into the place he had left, once, before he started walking. This morning he had been walking past fields, and now he was walking past trees that mounted heavily to the road, and leaned across, bending their great old bodies toward him; Christopher had come into the forest at a crossroads, turning onto the forest road as though he had a choice, looking back once to see the other road, the one he had not chosen, going peacefully on through fields, in and out of towns, perhaps even coming to an end somewhere beyond Christopher's sight.

The cat had joined him shortly after he entered the forest, emerging from between the trees in a quick, shadowy movement that surprised Christopher at first and then, oddly, comforted him, and the cat had stayed beside him, moving closer to Christopher as the trees pressed insistently closer to them both, trotting along in the casual acceptance of human company that cats exhibit when they are frightened. Christopher, when he stopped once to rest, sitting on a large stone at the edge of the road, had rubbed the cat's ears and pulled the cat's tail affectionately, and had said, "Where we going, fellow? Any ideas?," and the cat had closed his eyes meaningfully and opened them again.

"Haven't seen a house since we came into these trees," Christopher remarked once, later, to the cat; squinting up at the sky, he had added, "Going to be dark before long." He glanced apprehensively at the trees so close to him, irritated by the sound of his own voice in the silence, as though the trees were listening to him and, listening, had nodded solemnly to one another.

"Don't worry," Christopher said to the cat. "Road's got to go *some*where."

It was not much later—an hour before dark, probably—that Christopher and the cat paused, surprised, at a turn in the road, because a house was ahead. A neat stone fence ran down to the road, smoke came naturally from the chimneys, the doors and windows were not nailed shut, nor were the steps broken or the hinges sagging. It was a comfortable-looking, settled old house, made of stone like its fence, easily found in the pathless forest because it lay correctly, compactly, at the end of the road, which was not a road at all, of course, but merely a way to the house. Christopher thought briefly of the other way, long before, that he had not followed, and then moved forward, the cat at his heels, to the front door of the house.

The sound of a river came from among the trees. The river knew a way out of the forest, because it moved along sweetly and clearly, over clean stones and, unafraid, among the dark trees.

Christopher approached the house as he would any house,

farmhouse, suburban home, or city apartment, and knocked politely and with pleasure on the warm front door.

"Come in, then," a woman said as she opened it, and Christopher stepped inside, followed closely by the cat.

The woman stood back and looked for a minute at Christopher, her eyes searching and wide; he looked back at her and saw that she was young, not so young as he would have liked, but too young, seemingly, to be living in the heart of a forest.

"I've been here for a long time, though," she said, as if she'd read his thoughts. Out of this dark hallway, he thought, she might look older; her hair curled a little around her face, and her eyes were far too wide for the rest of her, as if she were constantly straining to see in the gloom of the forest. She wore a long green dress that was gathered at her waist by a belt made of what he subsequently saw was grass woven into a rope; she was barefoot. While he stood uneasily just inside the door, looking at her as she looked at him, the cat went round the hall, stopping curiously at corners and before closed doors, glancing up, once, into the unlighted heights of the stairway that rose from the far end of the hall.

"He smells another cat," she said. "We have one."

"Phyllis," a voice called from the back of the house, and the woman smiled quickly, nervously, at Christopher and said, "Come along, please. I shouldn't keep you waiting."

He followed her to the door at the back of the hall, next to the stairway, and was grateful for the light that greeted them when she opened it. He was led directly into a great warm kitchen, glowing with an open fire on its hearth, and well lit, against the late-afternoon dimness of the forest, by three kerosene lamps set on table and shelves. A second woman stood by the stove, watching the pots that steamed and smelled maddeningly of onions and herbs; Christopher closed his eyes, like the cat, against the unbelievable beauty of warmth, light, and the smell of onions.

"Well," the woman at the stove said with finality, turning to look at Christopher. She studied him carefully, as the other woman had done, and then turned her eyes to a bare whitewashed area, high on the kitchen wall, where lines and crosses indicated a rough measuring system. "Another day," she said.

"What's your name?" the first woman asked Christopher, and he said "Christopher" without effort and then, "What's yours?"

"Phyllis," the young woman said. "What's your cat's name?"

"I don't know," Christopher said. He smiled a little. "It's not even my cat," he went on, his voice gathering strength from the smell of the onions. "He just followed me here."

"We'll have to name him something," Phyllis said. When she spoke she looked away from Christopher, turning her overlarge eyes on him again only when she stopped speaking. "Our cat's named Grimalkin."

"Grimalkin," Christopher said.

"*Her* name," Phyllis said, gesturing with her head toward the cook. "*Her* name's Aunt Cissy."

"Circe," the older woman said doggedly to the stove. "Circe I was born and Circe I will have for my name till I die."

Although she seemed, from the way she stood and the way she kept her voice to a single note, to be much older than Phyllis, Christopher saw her face clearly in the light of the lamps—she was vigorous and clear-eyed, and the strength in her arms when she lifted the great iron pot easily off the stove and carried it to the stone table in the center of the kitchen surprised Christopher. The cat, who had followed Christopher and Phyllis into the kitchen, leaped noiselessly onto the bench beside the table, and then onto the table; Phyllis looked warily at Christopher for a minute before she pushed the cat gently to drive him off the table.

"We'll have to find a name for your cat," she said apologetically as the cat leaped down without taking offense.

"Kitty," Christopher said helplessly. "I guess I always call cats 'Kitty.'"

Phyllis shook her head. She was about to speak when Aunt Cissy stopped her with a glance, and Phyllis moved quickly to an iron chest in the corner of the kitchen, from which she took a cloth to spread on the table, and heavy stone plates and mugs, which she set on the table in four places. Christopher sat down on the bench, with his back to the table, to indicate clearly that he had no intention of presuming that he was sitting at the table but was on the bench only because he was tired, that he would not swing around to the table until invited warmly and specifically to do so.

"Are we almost ready, then?" Aunt Cissy said. She swept her eyes across the table, adjusted a fork, and stood back, her glance never for a minute resting on Christopher. Then she moved over to the wall beside the door, where she stood, quiet and erect, and Phyllis went to stand beside her. Christopher, turning his head to look at them, had to turn again as footsteps approached from the hall, and after a minute's interminable pause, the door opened. The two women stayed respectfully by the far wall, and Christopher stood up without knowing why, except that it was his host who was entering.

This was a man toward the end of middle age; although he held his shoulders stiffly back, they looked as if they would sag without a constant effort. His face was lined and tired, and his mouth, like his shoulders, appeared to be falling downward into resignation. He was dressed, as the women were, in a long green robe tied at the waist, and he, too, was barefoot. As he stood in the doorway, with the darkness of the hall behind him, his white head shone softly, and his eyes, bright and curious, regarded Christopher for a long minute before they turned, as the older woman's had done, to the crude measuring system on the upper wall.

"We are honored to have you here," he said at last to Christopher; his voice was resonant, like the sound of the wind in the trees. Without speaking again, he took his seat at the head of the stone table and gestured to Christopher to take the place on his right. Phyllis came away from her post by the door and slipped into the place across from Christopher, and Aunt Cissy served them all from the iron pot before taking her own place at the foot of the table.

Christopher stared down at the plate before him, and the rich smell of the onions and meat met him, so that he closed his eyes again for a minute before starting to eat. When he lifted his head he could see, over Phyllis's head, the dark window, the trees pressed so close against it that their branches were bent against the glass, a tangled crowd of leaves and branches looking in.

"What will we call you?" the old man asked Christopher at last.

"I'm Christopher," Christopher said, looking only at his plate or up at the window.

"And have you come far?" the old man said.

"Very far." Christopher smiled. "I suppose it seems farther than it really is," he explained.

"I am named Oakes," the old man said.

Christopher gathered himself together with an effort. Ever since entering this strange house he had been bewildered, as though intoxicated from his endless journey through the trees, and uneasy at coming from darkness and the watching forest into a house where he sat down without introductions at his host's table. Swallowing, Christopher turned to look at Mr. Oakes and said, "It's very kind of you to take me in. If you hadn't, I guess I'd have been wandering around in the woods all night."

Mr. Oakes bowed his head slightly at Christopher.

"I guess I was a little frightened," Christopher said with a small embarrassed laugh. "All those trees."

"Indeed, yes," Mr. Oakes said placidly. "All those trees."

Christopher wondered if he had shown his gratitude adequately. He wanted very much to say something further, something that might lead to an explicit definition of his privileges: whether he was to stay the night, for instance, or whether he must go out again into the woods in the darkness; whether, if he did stay the night, he might have in the morning another such meal as this dinner. When Aunt Cissy filled his plate a second time, Christopher smiled up at her. "This is certainly wonderful," he said to her. "I don't know when I've had a meal I enjoyed this much."

Aunt Cissy bowed her head to him as Mr. Oakes had before.

"The food comes from the woods, of course," Mr. Oakes said. "Circe gathers her onions down by the river, but naturally none of that need concern you."

"I suppose not," Christopher said, feeling that he was not to stay the night.

"Tomorrow will be soon enough for you to see the house," Mr. Oakes added.

"I suppose so," Christopher said, realizing that he was indeed to stay the night.

"Tonight," Mr. Oakes said, his voice deliberately light. "Tonight, I should like to hear about you, and what things you have seen on your journey, and what takes place in the world you have left."

Christopher smiled. Knowing that he could stay the night, could not in charity be dismissed before the morning, he felt relaxed. Aunt Cissy's good dinner had pleased him, and he was ready enough to talk with his host.

"I don't really know quite *how* I got here," he said. "I just took the road into the woods."

"You would have to go through the woods to get here," his host agreed soberly.

"Before *that*," Christopher went on, "I passed a lot of farmhouses and a little town—do you know the name of it? I asked a woman there for a meal and she turned me away."

He laughed now, at the memory, with Aunt Cissy's good dinner warm inside him.

"And before that," he said, "I was studying."

"You are a scholar," the old man said. "Naturally."

"I don't know *why*." Christopher turned at last to Mr. Oakes and spoke frankly. "I don't know why," he repeated. "One day I was there, in college, like everyone else, and then the next day I just left, without any reason except that I did." He glanced from Mr. Oakes to Phyllis to Aunt Cissy; they were all looking at him with blank expectation. He stopped, then said lamely, "And I guess that's all that happened before I came here."

"He brought a cat with him," Phyllis said softly, her eyes down.

"A cat?" Mr. Oakes looked politely around the kitchen, saw Christopher's cat curled up under the stove, and nodded. "One brought a dog," he said to Aunt Cissy. "Do you remember the dog?"

Aunt Cissy nodded, her face unchanging.

There was a sound at the door, and Phyllis said, without moving, "That is our Grimalkin coming for his supper."

Aunt Cissy rose and went over to the outer door and opened it. A cat, tiger-striped where Christopher's cat was black, but about the same size, trotted casually into the kitchen, without a glance at Aunt Cissy, went directly for the stove, then saw Christopher's cat. Christopher's cat lifted his head lazily, widened his eyes, and stared at Grimalkin.

"I think they're going to fight," Christopher said nervously, half rising from his seat. "Perhaps I'd better—"

But he was too late. Grimalkin lifted his voice in a deadly wail, and Christopher's cat spat, without stirring from his comfortable bed under the stove; then Grimalkin moved incautiously and was caught off guard by Christopher's cat. Spitting and screaming, they clung to each other briefly, then Grimalkin ran crying out the door that Aunt Cissy opened for him.

Mr. Oakes sighed. "What is your cat's name?" he inquired.

"I'm *terribly* sorry," Christopher said, with a fleeting fear that his irrational cat might have deprived them both of a bed. "Shall I go and find Grimalkin outside?"

Mr. Oakes laughed. "He was fairly beaten," he said, "and has no right to come back."

"Now," Phyllis said softly, "now we can call your cat Grimalkin. Now we have a name, Grimalkin, and no cat, so we can give the name to your cat."

Christopher slept that night in a stone room at the top of the house, a room reached by the dark staircase leading from the hall. Mr. Oakes carried a candle to the room for him, and Christopher's cat, now named Grimalkin, left the warm stove to follow. The room was small and neat, and the bed was a stone bench, which Christopher, investigating after his host had gone, discovered to his amazement was mattressed with leaves, and had for blankets heavy furs that looked like bearskins.

"This is quite a forest," Christopher said to the cat, rubbing a corner of the bearskin between his hands. "And quite a family."

Against the window of Christopher's room, as against all the windows in the house, was the wall of trees, crushing themselves hard against the glass. "I wonder if that's why they made this house out of stone?" Christopher asked the cat. "So the trees wouldn't push it down?"

All night long the sound of the trees came into Christopher's dreams, and he turned gratefully in his sleep to the cat purring beside him in the great fur coverings.

In the morning, Christopher came down into the kitchen, where Phyllis and Aunt Cissy, in their green robes, were moving about the stove. His cat, who had followed him down the stairs, moved immediately ahead of him in the kitchen to sit under the stove and watch Aunt Cissy expectantly. When Phyllis had set the stone table and Aunt Cissy had laid out the food, they both moved over to the doorway as they had the night before, waiting for Mr. Oakes to come in.

When he came, he nodded to Christopher and they sat, as before, Aunt Cissy serving them all. Mr. Oakes did not speak this morning, and when the meal was over he rose, gesturing to Christopher to follow him. They went out into the hall, with its silent closed doors, and Mr. Oakes paused.

"You have seen only part of the house, of course," he said. "Our handmaidens keep to the kitchen unless called to this hall."

"Where do they sleep?" Christopher asked. "In the kitchen?" He was immediately embarrassed by his own question, and smiled awkwardly at Mr. Oakes to say that he did not deserve an answer, but Mr. Oakes shook his head in amusement and put his hand on Christopher's shoulder.

"On the kitchen floor," he said. And then he turned his head away, but Christopher could see that he was laughing. "Circe," he said, "sleeps nearer to the door from the hall."

Christopher felt his face growing red and, glad for the darkness of the hall, said quickly, "It's a very old house, isn't it?"

"Very old," Mr. Oakes said, as though surprised by the question. "A house was found to be vital, of course."

"Of course," Christopher said, agreeably.

"In here," Mr. Oakes said, opening one of the two great doors on either side of the entrance. "In here are the records kept."

Christopher followed him in, and Mr. Oakes went to a candle that stood in its own wax on a stone table and lit it with the flint that lay beside it. He then raised the candle high, and Christopher saw that the walls were covered with stones, piled up to make loose, irregular shelves. On some of the shelves great, leather-covered books stood, and on other shelves lay stone tablets, and rolls of parchment.

"They are of great value," Mr. Oakes said sadly. "I have never known how to use them, of course." He walked slowly over and touched one huge volume, then turned to show Christopher his fingers covered with dust. "It is my sorrow," he said, "that I cannot use these things of great value."

Christopher, frightened by the books, drew back into the doorway. "At one time," Mr. Oakes said, shaking his head, "there were many more. Many, many more. I have heard that at one time this room was made large enough to hold the records. I have never known how they came to be destroyed."

Still carrying the candle, he led Christopher out of the room and shut the big door behind them. Across the hall another door faced them. As Mr. Oakes led the way in with the candle, Christopher saw that it was another bedroom, larger than the one in which he had slept.

"This, of course," Mr. Oakes said, "is where I have been sleeping, to guard the records."

He held the candle high again and Christopher saw a stone bench like his own, with heavy furs lying on it, and above the bed a long and glittering knife resting upon two pegs driven between the stones of the wall.

"The keeper of the records," Mr. Oakes said, and sighed briefly before he smiled at Christopher in the candlelight. "We are like two friends," he added. "One showing the other his house."

"But—" Christopher began, and Mr. Oakes laughed.

"Let me show you my roses," he said.

Christopher followed him helplessly back into the hall, where Mr. Oakes blew out the candle and left it on a shelf by the door, and then out the front door to the tiny cleared patch before the house, which was surrounded by the stone wall that ran to the road. Although for a small distance before them the world was clear of trees, it was not very much lighter or more pleasant, with the forest only barely held back by the stone wall, edging as close to it as possible, pushing, as Christopher had felt since the day before, crowding up and embracing the little stone house in horrid possession.

"Here are my roses," Mr. Oakes said, his voice warm. He looked calculatingly beyond at the forest as he spoke, his eyes measuring the distance between the trees and his roses. "I planted them myself," he said. "I was the first one to clear away even this much of the forest. Because I wished to plant roses in the midst of this wilderness. Even so," he added, "I had to send Circe for roses from the midst of this beast around us, to set them here in my little clear spot." He leaned affectionately over the roses, which grew gloriously against the stone of the house, on a vine that rose triumphantly almost to the height of the door. Over him, over the roses, over the house, the trees leaned eagerly.

"They need to be tied up against stakes every spring," Mr. Oakes said. He stepped back a pace and measured with his hand above his head. "A stake—a small tree stripped of its branches will do, and Circe will get it and sharpen it—and the rose vine tied to it as it leans against the house."

Christopher nodded. "Someday the roses will cover the house, I imagine," he said.

"Do you think so?" Mr. Oakes turned eagerly to him. "My roses?"

"It *looks* like it," Christopher said awkwardly, his fingers touching the first stake, bright against the stones of the house.

Mr. Oakes shook his head, smiling. "Remember who planted them," he said.

They went inside again and through the hall into the kitchen, where Aunt Cissy and Phyllis stood against the wall as they entered. Again they sat at the stone table and Aunt Cissy served them, and again Mr. Oakes said nothing while they ate and Phyllis and Aunt Cissy looked down at their plates.

After the meal was over, Mr. Oakes bowed to Christopher before leaving the room, and while Phyllis and Aunt Cissy cleared the table of plates and cloth, Christopher sat on the bench with his cat on his knee. The women seemed to be unusually occupied. Aunt Cissy, at the stove, set down iron pots enough for a dozen meals, and Phyllis, sent to fetch a special utensil from an alcove in the corner of the kitchen, came back to report that it had been mislaid "since the last time" and could not be found, so that Aunt Cissy had to put down her cooking spoon and go herself to search.

Phyllis set a great pastry shell on the stone table, and she and Aunt Cissy filled it slowly and lovingly with spoonfuls from one or another pot on the stove, stopping to taste and estimate, questioning each other with their eyes.

"What *are* you making?" Christopher asked finally.

"A feast," Phyllis said, glancing at him quickly and then away.

Christopher's cat watched, purring, until Aunt Cissy disappeared into the kitchen alcove again and came back carrying the trussed carcass of what seemed to Christopher to be a wild pig. She and Phyllis set this on the spit before the great fireplace, and Phyllis sat beside it to turn the spit. Then Christopher's cat leaped down and ran over to the fireplace to sit beside Phyllis and taste the drops of fat that fell on the great hearth as the spit was turned.

"Who is coming to your feast?" Christopher asked, amused.

Phyllis looked around at him, and Aunt Cissy half turned from the stove. There was a silence in the kitchen, a silence of no movement and almost no breath, and then, before anyone could speak, the door opened and Mr. Oakes came in. He was carrying the knife from his bedroom, and with a shrug of resignation he held it out for Christopher to see. When Mr. Oakes had seated himself at the table, Aunt Cissy disappeared again into the alcove and brought back a grindstone, which she set before Mr. Oakes. Deliberately, with the slow caution of a pleasant action lovingly done, Mr. Oakes set about sharpening the knife. He held the bright blade against the moving stone, turning the edge little by little with infinite delicacy.

"You say you've come far?" he said over the sound of the knife, and for a minute his eyes left the grindstone to rest on Christopher.

"Quite a ways," Christopher said, watching the grindstone. "I don't know how far, exactly."

"And you were a scholar?"

"Yes," Christopher said. "A student."

Mr. Oakes looked up from the knife again, to the estimate marked on the wall.

"Christopher," he said softly, as though estimating the name.

When the knife was razor sharp, Mr. Oakes held it up to the light from the fire, studying the blade. Then he looked at Christopher and shook his head humorously. "As sharp as any weapon can be," he said.

Aunt Cissy spoke, unsolicited, for the first time. "Sun's down," she said.

Mr. Oakes nodded. He looked at Phyllis for a minute, and at Aunt Cissy. Then, with his sharpened knife in his hand, he walked over and put his free arm around Christopher's shoulder. "Will you remember about the roses?" he asked. "They *must* be tied up in the spring if they mean to grow at all."

For a minute his arm stayed warmly around Christopher's shoulders, and then, carrying his knife, he went over to the back door and waited while Aunt Cissy came to open it for him. As the door was opened, the trees showed for a minute, dark and greedy. Then Aunt Cissy closed the door behind Mr. Oakes. For a minute she leaned her back against it, watching Christopher, then, standing away from it, she opened it again. Christopher, staring, walked slowly over to the open door, as Aunt Cissy seemed to expect he would, and heard behind him Phyllis's voice from the hearth.

"He'll be down by the river," she said softly. "Go far around and come up behind him."

The door shut solidly behind Christopher and he leaned against it, looking with frightened eyes at the trees that reached for him on either side. Then as he pressed his back in terror against the door, he heard the voice calling from the direction of the river, so clear and ringing through the trees that he hardly knew it as Mr. Oakes's: "Who is he dares enter these my woods?"

"I'll tell you, Mr. Covici—first I've got to get the baby's wash done, and then put dinner on, and I ought to write a couple letters, and then I'll sit down and start this new novel."

II

. . .

I Would Rather Write Than Do Anything Else

Essays and Reviews

. . .

"No one mentions the fact that I also write books, as though it were not polite to talk about it."

. . .

Autobiographical Musing

I LOATHE WRITING AUTOBIOGRAPHICAL MATERIAL BECAUSE IF IT'S dull no one should have to read it anyway, and if it's interesting I should be using it for a story. No one whose life is completely dominated by four children should have to recall her own childhood; mine was pleasant and swift and easygoing, and very little of it remains in conscious memory. I regard the shiny new mess kit that my son has just gotten for camp and recall, suddenly, long hot weeks and bluejays and the unmistakable smell of a canvas sleeping bag, but I would not otherwise ever remember that I, too, went to camp. So much is happening right now, and the present goes by so imperceptibly; summers are shorter than they used to be, but it is pleasant to reflect that no one, any longer, is in a position to insist that I learn to swim.

I like to think that my mind is bent on sterner things now. Writing, for instance, used to be a delicious private thing, done in my own room with the door locked, in constant terror of the maternal knock and the summons to bed; now that I am so luckily grown up and independent, there is no one to knock on the door and save me from my excruciating labors. Although I flatly refuse to reveal the plans I had for the future when I was fifteen, I may say that they were realized in only one or two major respects. I would have regarded my present situation in many aspects as frankly incredible. There is, of course, no question in my mind but that I am better off this way.

Since ninety percent of my life went on in my head anyway, I cannot see any point in remembering odd concrete items. I grew up near San Francisco—which means a suburb, and trees, and having to stop playing prisoner's base when the streetlights went on in the evening, and sitting on a fence eating pomegranates with my dearest friend, whom I now remember very imperfectly. I remember going to all kinds of public grammar schools, and two different high schools, one in the West and one in the East, which brings back to me the sick inadequate feeling of standing in a hallway holding a notebook and wondering without hope if I would ever find the right room.

I recall how the entire chemistry class halted one afternoon while everyone went to the window to show me my first snowfall, and the increasingly rare letters to my dearest friends back home, and the high-heeled shoes. I went to college, and I remember the mail coming in the mornings, and my first fur coat, and the frightful embarrassment of seeing a story of mine in the college magazine— worse, I believe, than the first day in a gym suit—and when my son asks me, after all of this, what it is like in camp, or whether people really ever get homesick, I remember my first night in the college dormitory, and a girl named Laura something, and I can only tell him no, everything is always all right, somehow.

A *Garland of Garlands*

MY HUSBAND REVIEWS BOOKS FOR A LIVING, AND I WOULD LIKE TO enter a protest. I know things are pretty hard these days, with the girls hanging around snatching the eligible males right out of the high school graduating classes, but I don't think I deserved a book reviewer. My mother raised me better, that's all.

I realize now, thinking back over the events of the last few years, that people marry book reviewers with the expectation that it is a temporary thing, that sooner or later the poor dear is going to find himself a better niche in life, such as selling vacuum cleaners. Book reviewing is just nothing for a healthy young woman to be married to. In the first place, a girl gets to reading. And then of course, there's everything else—"Reviewer's Complaint," "The Earmarked Pen," "The Development of the Theory of Universality in Art," and all the rest.

In case there are any eager young women hanging on my every word, and even in case there are not, I'd better go right ahead and bore all you people who have heard this before many times, and give out with the warnings. Let me, for instance, give you a rough idea what we are up against, we reviewer wives.

Take "Reviewer's Complaint," for instance. It starts from the theory that no book over five hundred pages long is worth more than three lines from any man's typewriter, and works from that into the theory that no book ever written is worth any number of lines at all, and eventually you find the reviewer turning the pages of the new bestseller rapidly, memorizing the names and the characters and the chapter headings, and then turning to see what Thompson in the *Times* had to say about it, and if there's anything worth disagreeing with him about. If there's nothing worth disagreeing with Thompson about, the reviewer is going to toss the book casually to his wife, and say, "Just read through this quickly tonight, will you, dear? Like to get another person's opinion before I commit myself on paper."

After the wife has plowed through nine hundred pages of the new historical novel, she is going to come out with some such comment as this: "I like it all right, I guess, but it does seem sort of dull for nine hundred pages."

Then her reviewing man will say, consulting his notes, "What do you think of this character . . . ah . . . Rosita?"

The wife thinks deeply, and answers: "Well, I don't know why she had to go and marry Cedric, I liked the other one much better."

"Oh, did she *marry* Cedric?" the reviewer will say, writing it down. "When, about the middle of the book?"

"No, toward the beginning, and then she kept on going back to him and leaving him and going back to him and leaving him, and I don't see why the other one wasn't much nicer. After all, he had all the money, and did keep sending her those plans for the new railroad to approve, didn't he?"

"What railroad?" the reviewer will say. "I don't seem to remember much about that . . ." And so it will go on.

A few weeks later the doting wife will pick up a copy of the very literary weekly her husband is reviewing for and find his name attached to a review that begins: "Although this book is fundamentally good structurally, it has grave faults, and one might almost go so far as to classify it as dull. Take, for instance, the character of Rosita, the heroine of the book, very ably drawn, whose marriage early on to Cedric, her husband, strikes a false note and does much to weaken the artistic integrity, or wholeness, of the author's intention to bring out the history of the development of the railroad in this country, always a good and interesting subject to this reviewer, although unfortunately overshadowed in the present volume by the author's disagreeable weakness of character portrayal, which, in Rosita, the ably drawn heroine of the book, appears to be . . ."

And then the wife has to sit across the dinner table from her husband and say: "It's all so *true*, what you said in the review. I wish I had the brains to review books."

Or consider "The Earmarked Pen." This is something that any writer whose works appear with some regularity in any one periodical is apt to fall prey to, but I think that it is most insidious in the case of the book reviewer, who has, at best, a limited number of words at his disposal, and is prejudiced against more than half of those from the start. (Who, for instance, ever heard of someone calling a book just "good"? If a book is good, it is "eminently readable.") Most reviewers, in fact, eventually find themselves with one or two, or at most three, personal words firmly established, like helpful relatives, in the book review as they write it; these are impossible to get rid of, and any attempt at substitution leaves the review uneasy and inclined to turn back on itself and bite.

Take, as an example, the word "heartrending." My own reviewer is particularly attached to this word, along with "delectable" and, to a lesser extent, "invidious" (which he cannot distinguish from "insidious") and "bailiwick." I can recognize one of my husband's reviews at fifty yards because somewhere in it there is going to be a paragraph beginning: "One of the most heartrending factors in this work derives from the lapse on the part of the hero, Cedric, into an invidious cad, a type of man most unsuitable for a book emphasizing the delectable character of Rosita. Removed from his own baili-wick, that of wealth and luxury, Cedric gradually deteriorates into a heartrending wreck of a man, driving Rosita into madness with his invidious insinuations. . . ." That is "The Earmarked Pen." I have never seen a book reviewer (or a movie reviewer or a music reviewer or an art critic) who didn't catch it, once his first signed review brought in a check for two cents a word. There is no cure that I know of. I once gave my husband a dictionary of synonyms and a game of anagrams for his birthday, hoping they would help some. "Delectable," he said, putting them back into the boxes, "positively heartrending."

"The Development of the Theory of Universality in Art" comes right along with "The Development of the Theory of Style"; in other words, once he gets the idea it's his, he's got to pretty it up. Sooner or later your two-cents-a-word reviewer is going to turn around to his wife some evening, when she is sitting there quietly with *The Unpleasantness at the Bellona Club* tucked inside the nine-hundred-page historical novel, and he is going to say: "Listen, I don't see any reason why all these guys should get so much money for these books they write; it seems to me that any one-page criticism is as good as any long novel ever written, and from now on I'm an artist too, see?" I call this "The Development of the Theory of Universality in Art," because it starts from the assumption in the re-viewer's mind that he is a writer too, only better, since reviewing can favor or condemn other artists. From that time on, the reviewer be-gins to think of himself as a stylist, and as a poet, too, if he can man-age it.

And his reviews begin to sound like this: "When, in the course of pursuing his own heartrending and thankless brand of livelihood, the reviewer finds himself confronted with such an isolated, invidi-ous, even incredibly desolate, comparison of his lot with that of such a delectably constructed piece of degradation as Cedric, it is not enough for one man occasionally to envy another: He must also be at some pains to suggest to himself the wicked, unhappily invidious bailiwick in which both are placed, that is to say, the *sine qua non* without which no book, and no reviewer, who necessarily builds from a book a new, finer, higher, and, in some cases, beautiful and lasting, form, can survive." This is style. The poet-reviewer still gets his two cents a word, and the poet-published still gets his substantial royalties. This leads to some bitterness and eventual bad feeling, and finally review-articles beginning: "The fundamental ecological principle of art is this: No work of art, no matter how lofty, vast, or highly poetical, no matter how successful financially, can possibly expect ever to exist without the diligent application of the critic's heartrending assistance. . . ."

All this time I haven't said anything about the *books.* That's the reviewer's wife's big problem, the books. Whether she sells them or whether she sends them to the library or whether she gives them to her kid sister, they pile up in the bookcases, in packing boxes, in the corners of the living room, all incredibly pathetic in their bright shiny dust jackets, all called "The Novel of the Year" or "The New Sinclair Lewis" or "The Finest Piece of Work This Young Author Has Yet Done." And after a certain number of books beginning:

> Rosita entered the room softly and closed the door carefully behind her. Was Cedric's presence here? Could he be? She breathed his name softly . . . "Cedric!" . . . and immediately, wonderfully, he answered! How achingly lovely, how ecstatic, it was, Rosita thought suddenly, blissfully. "Cedric," she murmured again, "Cedric!" The heavy fragrance of roses filled the air, seeming to carry her words to him where he waited . . . there.

Or:

> Rosie slammed the door behind her and walked over to the bed. Her high heels made a sharp clacking sound as she moved.
> Ricky was asleep.

Bringing up her foot, she caught him heavily on the back of the head with her heel.

"Listen, ya punk," she snarled, "I've taken enough from you, hear me? Sleep, sleep, sleep, all day long, and I'm working my fingers to the bone walking the filthy streets so you can have money to buy canned heat. Huh!"

Rosie laughed cruelly into Ricky's wide-eyed face.

"Huh!" she said.

As I say, after so much reading starting off like this, the reviewer's wife begins to wonder about it all. Maybe two cents a word isn't a living wage. Maybe vacuum cleaners aren't selling so well these days, but they're honest. Maybe she ought to have married Cedric. Maybe she'd better call the whole heartrending thing an invidious flop.

Hex Me, Daddy, Eight to the Bar

EVER SINCE I MET ONE OF MY GRANDMOTHER'S OLD CRONIES—THE one with the evil eye—down on Sullivan Street the other day, I have had an uneasy feeling that I am being followed by something supernatural and malignant. Twice since then I have narrowly escaped destruction by fire, and in addition I have developed a particularly severe case of hives—out of season, I might add. In order to combat the superstitious fear that is beginning to prey on my mind, I stopped the other day in a secondhand bookstore and asked the young man on the high stool what would be good for Visitations. After some misunderstanding, the thought of which still makes me hot and cold all over, I procured a copy of a slim paperbound volume called *Pow-Wows: Art and Remedies for Man and Beast.*

This is by way of testimonial for John George Hohman, who compiled the book. Since I first picked up your little collection, brother, I haven't needed another thing to keep me well and happy. From the very first remedy for mother-fits, right straight through to the punch line, the cure for wind-broken horses, it holds me. I tell you honestly that I couldn't stir out of my chair until I had finished it. Every page is packed full of thrills. Take, for instance, page 74, with its stirring recipe for destroying spring-tails or ground-fleas. Or page 62, which explains how to "Retain the Right in Court and Council." Let me pass *that* one on to all you poor devils who fear the law as I used to. It must only be employed, I might point out, when the judge is not favorably disposed toward you. You must stand in court, courageous and unabashed, and say slowly: "I appear before the house of the Judge. Three dead men look out of the window; one having no tongue, the other having no lungs, and the third being sick, blind, and dumb." O brethren, what a cure this has worked in me! No longer do I fear the light; the haunts of the underworld see me no more, lurking in the shadows and the hidden places. No indeedy!

Sometimes Mr. Hohman is pretty short with us neophytes, all things considered. For instance, on page 30—a particular pet of mine, since it also tells me how to make cattle return home and how to cause fish to collect—we have the plaintive request: "To Prevent Cherries from Maturing Before Martinmas." To which Mr. Hohman replies smartly: "Engraft the twigs on a mulberry tree, and your desire is accomplished." That's Hohman for you. No patience for the trivial.

Or take what we call "A Very Good Plaster," on page 26. Mr. Hohman points out that he doubts "very much whether any physician in the United States can make a plaster equal to this." Now it may bring the American Medical Association down on me in a fight to the finish, but I doubt also whether any physician could. You take two quarts of cider, a pound of beeswax, a pound of sheep tallow, and a pound of tobacco, and you boil it and dissolve it and strain it. The recipe doesn't say whether you wallow in it after that, or whether you use it in your fountain pen, or whether you take one jigger of it to a glass of plain water and lots of ice please, but I tried it with a pound of oleomargarine because the grocery was fresh out of sheep tallow and it didn't cure a thing.

Right now Hohman and I are having a lot of traffic with epileptics, always hanging around waiting for a good, quick cure. Hohman has several, provided the patient has never fallen into fire or water. Of course if the subject *has* ever fallen into fire or water he can take comfort from "A Safe and Approved Means to Be Applied in Cases of Fire and Pestilence" or "A Very Good Cure for Weakness of the Limbs, for the Purification of the Blood, for the Invigoration of the Head and Heart, and to Remove Giddiness, etc." Or, as a last resort, he can desert the field completely and go in for dropsy, for which we have no fewer than eight cures. Finally, as a precaution against *everything* troublesome, carry the right eye of a wolf with you at all times, hidden in your right sleeve. This last charm interests me particularly, but inasmuch as I wear loose sleeves most of the time, I can't get the right eye of anything to stay up them unless I have someone sew it in for me, and even then it would probably spoil the whole line of the shoulder.

And right near there, on page 78, there's a system for compelling thieves to return stolen goods that doesn't seem likely to fail: "Walk out early in the morning before sunrise to a juniper tree, and bend it with the left hand toward the rising sun, while you are saying: 'Juniper tree, I shall bend and squeeze thee, until the thief has returned the stolen goods to the place from which he took them.' Then you must take a stone and put it on the bush, and under the bush and the stone you must put the skull of a malefactor." I'm going to get back all the books I ever lost, if I can find enough skulls.

Who can tell what better world lies ahead, with John George Hohman leading the way—a world free from thieves, maledictions, lawsuits, and dropsy! A world where the cherries bloom on mulberry trees, and the good old-fashioned mother-fit has stolen off into the darkness! And in this clean new world, Hohman offers me, temptingly, the power "To Dye a Madder Red." I entertain visions of the giddier whirl, the more achingly poignant delight, the superlative, the madder red; or, possibly, the drab little madder, so quietly enduring its colorless web of days, suddenly transformed into a creature of glamour, vitality. I have dreamt of contacting herpetologist Dr. Ditmars, and bargaining with him for a few dozen (pecks? gallons? pounds?) of madders, in return for which I would dye his vampire bats or his ant colonies red, the madder red.

In the minor matters, Hohman and I can string along fine together, curing a wind-broken horse here, destroying a spring-tail there, but it all ends ultimately in disillusionment and mutual bitterness. Sand, Mr. Hohman, that's what you've built on, sand. It's page 22 that showed me—page 22, with its remedy for mortification and all. Here there is a charm to "Prevent Wicked or Malicious Persons from Doing You an Injury—Against Whom It Is of Great Power." This remedy is simply the phrases "Dullix, ix, us; Yea, you can't come over Pontio; Pontio is above Pilato," to be repeated over and over until they do something. Now, I had occasion to use this charm recently, and even though it may sore disappoint John George Hohman, I feel that I ought to report my findings on it.

There is a certain Mrs. Quilter, who, besides being one of the least pleasant persons I know, has had the additional bad taste to move into a house next to mine. Not long ago she left a note in my mailbox saying that unless things got quieter fast around here she was going to complain to the police (perhaps this was due in part to a cat of mine that used to go out my back window and into hers— a long and perilous journey for a cat). Since I very rightly took no notice of her letter, a few days later I found another note from her saying that she was good and sick of the whole thing, and that it was more than human nature should be asked to stand, and that if she heard one more sound out of me (or, I suppose, my cat) she was going to Take Steps. Referring to Mr. Hohman, I wrote out the magic formula, "Dullix, ix, us; Yea, you can't come over Pontio; Pontio is above Pilato," and dropped it into *her* mailbox. I thought that would be the end of it, but she came to the door last night, in curl papers, and said, Was this infernal racket actually going to keep on? "Dullix," I said to her quietly, "ix, us; Yea, you can't come over

Pontio; Pontio is above Pilato," and I closed the door. This morning, the doorbell rang, and when I answered it, there was a policeman. "Well," he remarked ominously, "what's this I hear about *you*?" "Dullix—" I said. "I hear you been annoying the neighbors again," he said. "Well, well, well."

Frequently, however—and this is the main reason I think Hohman and I perhaps weren't made for each other—I am made aware that maybe Hohman and his charms exist on a different level of culture from my own. And nowhere is this distressing fact borne home to me more tragically than in this recipe:

"You must go upon another person's land and repeat the following words: 'I go before another court—I tie up my 77-fold fits.' Then cut three small twigs off any tree on the land; in each twig you must make a knot. This must be done on a Friday morning before sunrise, in the decrease of the moon unbeshrewedly."

Now, leaving out the "unbeshrewedly," which I don't pretend to understand, I think I have a pretty good idea of what would happen if I gave this charm a good try. Suppose I were subject to fits—77-fold ones—and I wanted a good, quick cure. The only person I know with land and a tree with twigs on it is a gentleman some six houses down the block who has a good-size window box with a rosebush. Say some Friday morning I feel a fit coming on, so I take my little book under my arm and head down the street. Clambering ungracefully into the window box, I begin: "I go before another court—"

At this point the gentleman owning the window box, whose name, as I recall from the tag on the rosebush, is Pelargonium Capitatum, will open the window noisily and peer out at me nearsightedly. "What the hell do you think you are doing in that window box?" he will say. "Oh, just trying to cure a fit," I might toss off casually. Or perhaps I might say: "Well, I have this book by this guy and it says . . ."

In any case, if Mr. Capitatum is an impetuous man, he will by this time have left the window to go after a phone. Or, if he has the staying power, he will be saying: "What did you just say you were trying to do?" By this time I will have reached the part in my charm where I cut three small twigs off the tree, and when he lets this go by, I have him. Then I tie a knot in each twig, and if he is the man I vaguely remember him as being, he will tell me: "Say, I used to have a sister had a little boy had fits. Tried everything, but they never cured him that way. Doctor said—"

Any long story about someone's sister's little boy's fits is not best listened to in a window box; at this point I would feel constrained to slither down and say, "Well, I guess I'll go gargle a couple of aspirin in a glass of water," and saunter off, leaving Mr. Capitatum with his story poised in midair, his rosebush fearfully knotted, and himself with what I should diagnose, from here, as a severe—or 77-fold—convulsion.

In case anyone is interested in joining us in our work (there is still much to be done; we haven't even touched on radioactive elements yet, or phobophobia, or the harmful substances contained in inhaled cigarette smoke), come right on over. I will be in the back-yard, curing wind-broken horses and dyeing madders a madder red. And all my old superstitious fears will have been jauntily and unbe-shrewdly laid to rest.

Clowns

"Whᴀᴛ's sᴏ sᴘᴇᴄɪᴀʟ ᴀʙᴏᴜᴛ ᴄʟᴏᴡɴs?" I'ᴅ ʙᴇᴇɴ ᴡᴏɴᴅᴇʀɪɴɢ ᴛᴏ ᴍʏ-self. "What makes them so funny?" (Let me say here that I intend someday to ask a clown—for instance, Emmett Kelly, that mighty creature—about people. "What's so special about people?" I shall ask him.) Wandering around asking idiotic questions is not usually the best way to learn anything, I'd have thought, but with clowns it seems to be not how you introduce the subject but, once intro-duced, how you dismiss it.

"The one in the circus," said my son with whom I began it. "The one who sweeps up the spotlight."

"Grock," said our friend who is a musician. "The greatest clown who ever lived, and the *most* unfortunate fellow." He began to laugh reminiscently. "Let me show you," he said; he stood up and gestured widely. "Grock used to come onto the stage, walking like *this*. In his bag he found first a clarinet, which he played, singing the low notes the clarinet would *not sing*. Then, he finds a violin, and he wishes to play *that*, but it is a small violin, a toy. And Grock is wearing those great gloves of the clown, so he plays the violin anyway. Like *this*. The small violin, and the large gloves. And he tosses the bow into the air, but cannot catch it." The musician stopped for breath. Then, while he was tossing an imaginary violin bow into the air and pointedly not catching it, the writer interrupted.

"Remember the Marx Brothers? And the dancing scene in front of the mirror? Or Groucho's walk? Or Harpo swinging on the opera house scenery? Or—"

"Grock, then," the musician said, his voice rising. "He *will* play the piano, although it displeases him, and it plays badly, so he dismembers it. So he thinks he will play the accordion, and for a while it plays beautifully, but then he cannot make it squeeze back together again, and it grows longer and longer, until poor Grock is wound around and around. The most *unfortunate* fellow."

"Remember Emmett Kelly slouching along chewing on that loaf of bread?" demanded our neighbor who owns the coal business. "He walks—I can't describe it—like *this*, look."

"There was a little circus used to come around summers," my grocer told me. "Had a clown, funniest man I ever saw. He threw tomatoes. Didn't do anything else—just threw tomatoes." He made an easy throwing gesture. "Just threw tomatoes," he said.

"Watch *me*," my son said. He ran around in little circles, shouting, "I'm sweeping up the light, look! I'm sweeping up the light!"

"Grock?" said the lady whose business is cosmetics. "Yes, I remember Grock; he was a great man. He was the only clown I ever saw who wore almost no makeup. His face was natural, if you know what I mean, but like a clown's without paint."

It was like that right along. First the familiar, faraway look in the eyes, then the reminiscent smile. Then the urgent need to imitate, rather than describe—to be, for one minute, the clown himself. In the conversation of all the people I listened to, there was also an intensely *personal* remembrance of some clown whose gestures and actions were indelibly marked on their minds. The musician remembered Grock, the unfortunate, with his toy violin and his unwinding accordion, and yet kept insisting while he spoke: "He was a truly great musician, that Grock, a superlative musician. All the musicians used to attend Grock every night, and he made them cry." The lady who made cosmetics had no wistful smile for Grock's music, but recalled perfectly that he wore almost no makeup. That a writer should remember a mimic dance before a mirror is hardly surprising; that a grocer should remember a clown who threw tomatoes is an interesting sidelight on what must be one great repressed longing of grocers toward their customers. And—this, I believe, was the saddest of all—the child remembers how uproariously helpless Emmett Kelly was, sweeping up the spotlight into an enormous circle, so that he had constantly to start over.

Hearing all this, our friend who teaches sociology remarked, "Did you know that the Pueblo Indians have a special 'ceremonial clown' who joins in the dances and songs of the religious ceremonies, simply making fun of them? And while the ceremony is going on, the ceremonial clown wanders around among the performers, making faces behind their backs, or throwing things at the audience, or mimicking the dancers."

And, even in the sociologist, the nostalgic smile.

I think—although there are many people I should hesitate to ask about it—that almost everyone remembers, with that same longing, a moment when a conclusion of superlative importance emerged from the actions of the pathetic little man who was so funny. Is it because the clown seems so overwhelmed by the infinite pathos of life, so outlawed by complexity and confusion, that what overpowers us with laughter is the expression of our own futility or the sight of our own precious little concerns reduced to a proportionate stature? The businessman laughs over Emmett Kelly gnawing on the loaf of bread; the Indians, with a sound eye for the practical, encourage a mockery of their sacred performances, as though to remind the audience and the participants that they are only human and, consequently, silly.

Most of my friends were furiously indignant when I suggested that there could be women clowns. The idea was preposterous: The clown was a man and might, if he chose, dress as a woman, but only briefly, and to make a point. Perhaps the clown should be a man because, although he is allowed to retain a vast human dignity, he must be deprived of all human rights so that he is a valiant small figure at the very broadest part of universal experience, with an emotional aspect so unselfconscious that it can become personal to every member of his audience. His emotion *must* be impersonal—and impersonality is not a feminine characteristic.

If I had wondered whether any man might be a clown, a second glance at my clown-loving friends—one trying to show how funny it was that a man in enormous gloves should try to play a toy violin, another futilely trying to reproduce an irresistibly funny walk, a third explaining, in a voice shrill with giggling, the mechanics of a droll face or a funny turn of the head—would have convinced me that the gift of real humor is a rare thing, to be administered judiciously and guarded carefully against imitation. "Some people *have* to take life seriously," our neighbor with the coal business told me earnestly. "If they didn't, then there wouldn't need to be clowns at all."

What belongs to a clown, then? What, aside from the fact that he is born a clown and can never be anything else, are the essential things he must have to set up in business? A man can't just start out, apparently, with a funny face and a conviction that he is the local lowest common denominator and expect to make people laugh and cry; there are certain unchangeable factors on which any informed audience insists.

First of all, your clown must *look* like a clown. He must wear a distinctive dress. It may be the traditional clown costume, or some variation of it, or even, like Charlie Chaplin, a completely individual dress of his own. But it must be two things—constant and functional. Charlie Chaplin's shoes are a familiar example of the costume that looks always, and still is, an essential part of the act; they are distinctive, peculiarly adapted to him from the traditional clown costume, and they are the irresistible factor in his walk— without the shoes, there could not possibly be the Chaplin walk. Similarly, Grock's lack of makeup was an identifying characteristic, since it was unusual for that type of clown at that time to be without a heavy coat of whitewash, but Grock's singularly expressive face was, without makeup, one of his most eloquent assets.

Another thing that seems to be very important for all clowns, not even excepting the Indian ceremonial clown, is that he must be acting extemporaneously, or at least *seem* to be acting extemporaneously. No one will follow a clown who shows plainly that he has spent laborious hours perfecting some slight knack, or indicates by attaching any importance to it that the tiny trick of the hand is a product of endless practice. The clown, reacting universally to overwhelming provocation, must react immediately, impulsively, inevitably, as any of us might; he must not have a carefully prepared plan of action, since any one of us can have that.

Moreover, let him keep quiet, please. He may fall, climb, roll, dance, grimace, smash furniture, or do any number of idiotic and completely satisfying things, but he must, above all, do them without chattering at us. Perhaps this is our deep-seated mistrust of the spoken word coming out again; if the clown talks, he is vulnerable, like the rest of us, to reasoning, to argument, to correction, to the endless verbal tidal wave that has engulfed us. Also, if the clown is properly personal enough to his audience, his actions and his gestures are meaningful, more than any words can be. The breathlessness in a movie audience when it seems that perhaps Harpo Marx is going to speak at last is as much fear as it is expectation; it is the terror lest the clown weaken for the one moment that would lose him his invulnerability. Charlie Chaplin, speaking, has become a comedian, which is another thing altogether from a clown.

Everyone, by the way, who mentioned Grock to me added one important fact, which stayed with them past all meaning in the word "clown" itself; it was so important that it set Grock as the spirit of invulnerability on a very pinnacle of greatness. "He never came to America," they said dreamily. "He was asked to come many times, but he never came. He said he had enough money, and he didn't want any more."

There was a clown, that Grock, with an unbelievable depth of human sympathy; the man who had enough money, and didn't want any more.

I wonder, then, what a clown might say about people. "They wear a distinctive dress," he might say, "usually copied from other people. They seem to be futilely resisting a complexity of life far too great for them, they never *seem* to have any rational motive for their behavior. And they're so pathetic they make you cry, but above all"—and here, if he were a true clown, there would be an exaggerated gesture of despair—"they're unbelievably, irresistibly funny."

A Vroom for Dr. Seuss

THE SUBJECT OF CHILDREN'S READING, LIKE TAXES AND HAY FEVER and the fate of the New York Mets, is a matter upon which anyone, informed or not, feels the right to hold a positive opinion. I do not imagine that anyone really intends to come right out and propose that children *not* be taught to read, television and comic books being what they are, but how children read, and what, and when, are subjects of interest to all of us.

Many grade-school children can hardly read at all, or hate it if they can; many more can read words but not for sense. Reading for its own sake, for pure enjoyment, seems to be set aside as a waste of time in favor of reading as a vehicle for acquiring information, and for children today this knowledge is apparently supposed to extend from moral precepts (puppies who disobey their mothers get caught by the dog catcher) for the very young, to popular science and anthropology for the more sophisticated.

As the mother of four children who have somehow learned to read, I think back with no nostalgia at all to the seemingly endless parade of "good" current children's books that came into our house, were absorbed, passed on to the next child, read, torn, scribbled on, and that finally found their way, carton by carton, to the children's room of our local library. I remember the adventures of numerous bluebirds, airplanes, toy engines, clowns, rabbits, and walking-talking dolls, all of whom got into trouble by not obeying, or not conforming, or not going to bed on time. I read and listened to touching tributes to doctors and school-bus drivers and little boys and girls who live in far-off lands, and jolly old Dan the grocery store man. I could tell you how to build a treehouse, I could give you the latest word on how we might live in a pioneer village, or how far away the sun is, or the chemical composition of table salt. The major part of our children's reading was devoted, for more years than I care to remember, to an antiseptic and wholly misleading interpretation of the world we live in; I was heartily glad to see each carton of books leave the house.

Not all the books went, of course, but the only ones that stayed were the ones people wanted. These turned out to be almost exactly what might have been predicted: The real books remained, the ones that packed a sense of excitement and enchantment, that were *read* rather than skimmed, the books that led young minds into worlds of imagination and delight. These are still around, and they are still being read.

I recently was asked to write a children's beginning-reading book. All right, I thought; for years I have been deploring the quality of the kids' books we are forced to buy, hating the practical, every-day moral stories; now I could write my own. I thought to write a little fairy tale, simple and short, the kind of story I would have liked to have my own children sound out as beginning readers. I was given a word list, made out by "a group of educators," and asked to confine myself to this list, which included perhaps five hundred words of a basic vocabulary that was felt to be desirable for beginners. "Getting" and "spending" were on the list, but not "wishing"; "cost" and "buy" and "nickel" and "dime" were all on the list, but not "magic"; "post office" and "supermarket" were on the list, but not "Fairyland." I felt that the children for whom I was supposed to write were being robbed, persuaded to accept nickels and dimes instead of magic wishes. This is a very small quarrel; there are many groups of educators who feel that Fairyland is an unhealthy environment for growing minds, but in a choice between television ("television" was on the list) and Fairyland, I know where I would rather have my own children growing up.

In all the morass of children's books, Dr. Seuss stands out as a particularly welcome friend. He could not have worked from my basic word list ("snacks"? "bellies"? "slunk"?), but then, Dr. Seuss makes his own rules, and has managed somehow to cover every step of reading growth from beginning to almost-sophisticated with a rich deposit of nonsense.

Not all the nonsense is his own, of course. On the back of *Hop on Pop*, an "educator" is quoted as saying: "The rhythmic pattern of words and ideas will provide excellent 'sound-ear' basic training for the use of phonics," and another "educator" chimes in, saying: "With *Hop on Pop*, children not only get a chance to enjoy fine literature, but also have an opportunity to learn a number of phonic elements, painlessly and joyfully." Fine literature ("We like to hop on top of Pop." "STOP. You must not hop on Pop.") it may or may not be, but no reader, slowly mesmerized by rhythmic patterns, can avoid being caught by its charming silliness, which is, after all, far more of a recommendation for reading a book than any number of phonic elements.

I am mortally afraid of offending Dr. Seuss. If I did, a Grinch might steal my Christmas, or a Thnadner might turn up in my morning coffee, or I might find myself being pursued by a Sneetch or a Vroom or a Collapsible Frink. I've lost count of how many books Dr. Seuss has written, but I do know that his books are some of the rare bright spots in children's literature today. It is an honest pleasure to turn from a story about a dear little black-and-white kittycat who wants to make friends with a buttercup to *The Cat in the Hat*, with his effrontery and his casual joy in making a mess.

Dr. Seuss's A B C, the author's newest book, is the very beginning of beginner's reading ("BIG C, little c. What begins with C? Camel on the ceiling—C ... c ... C"), although I do not find "begins," "camel," or "ceiling" on my basic word list for beginners. And—after long ago dismissing "zebra" as the logical end of the alphabet—Dr. Seuss has found a substitute, "Zizzer-Zazzer-Zuzz," which makes Z far more persuasive than "zebra" ever did. *Dr. Seuss's A B C*, along with *Hop on Pop*, will give young readers a head start on reading for the sheer joy of it, which is no small accomplishment.

If there are faults to be found with Dr. Seuss—remember that Collapsible Frink—they are certainly very small ones. There is a certain appearance of haste that creeps into the later books; I am sure that Dr. Seuss writes, as he says he does, for fun and not for accumulated output, but perhaps he is too anxious to get the books finished and into the children's hands. The animals are beginning to look alike, for one thing, with less crazy invention; it is a sad comment on the state of things today when a Jo Redd-Zoff looks a lot like a south-going Zax, and both of them strongly resemble a High Gargel-orum. Also, I do quarrel with such lines as those in which Sneetches had "bellies with stars" and others had "none upon thars."

Nevertheless, why a mind that finds one alphabet inadequate for its needs should be expected to confine itself to standard grammar and spelling is a question I could not try to answer.

Perhaps this quibbling is only because it is a temptation to wish that anyone who has given us such a wealth of zoological misfits and thoroughly satisfying nonsense should go on forever without a slip. Dr. Seuss's slips are small and rare, and as for going on forever, I think he probably will.

Notes on an Unfashionable Novelist
(Samuel Richardson, 1689–1761)

IT IS DIFFICULT TODAY TO SUGGEST SERIOUSLY THAT ANY THINKING, responsible person sit down and read a book; the glorified comic magazine we call the modern "novel" has taken too firm a hold on our racing, bewildered minds. It is too easy to read a thin volume where everything is said only once, and seven or eight words suffice for a sentence, just as seven or eight pat phrases suffice for an idea; why read anything "long" or, worse still, "old"? Why, for instance, read a stuffy old character like Samuel Richardson, who looms only very vaguely back there beyond Henry James and past Thackeray and is more than obscured by Jane Austen; why read Richardson, who was certainly very moral and extremely long and, not to put too fine a point on it, dull?

I can think of, offhand, three reasons. I can find in someone like Richardson three attributes somehow lost today and intensely, humanly, valuable: peace, principle, kindness—three qualities as emphatically stuffy and old-fashioned as your grandmother's wedding gown, and as emphatically lost from general circulation.

Peace would come first today, I should think. Out of a time

when things moved slowly, and conversation was formal and, if you like, stilted, and when a man could, if he chose, write a book a million words long and expect people to have time for it, Richardson made three books. They move along like molasses; no small action is consummated in less than ten pages. They line up, volume after volume full of solid, meaningful words, and they are leisurely, relaxed, and gracious. Richardson was a fat little man who ran a fine printing business and worked hard at it; he sat daily at tea with groups of admiring ladies; he liked his cat and he liked his garden and he liked gossip about high life, and he had plenty of time. With all his interests and all his busy concerns—and he stayed plump; he liked his food—he wrote three novels, *Pamela; or, Virtue Rewarded*; *Clarissa; or, The History of a Young Lady*; and *The History of Sir Charles Grandison*, which, placed side by side, would fill up two mystery-story shelves in a modern library.

Page after page, volume after volume of intimate letters go into these novels, letters back and forth from one character to another, describing events, commenting on the descriptions, reflecting on the moral implications of several courses of action, requesting more comments, all taking plenty of time, with nobody hurrying. In any dramatic crisis, the heroine has time for a polysyllabic remonstrance, which she reports faithfully in her letters; the villain has time for a lengthy insincere apology, which *he* reports faithfully in *his* letters; and both explain their actions minutely, and ask for comments from their correspondents, which they get, along with recapitulations of what *might* have been done under the circumstances, and comments on *that*. And in all of it, there is a vast sense of leisure to reflect, to choose, to be graceful. Peace provides the opportunity to have time to think.

Principle is a great inspiration, too. Sir Charles Grandison (who may be the perfect man) cannot marry the woman he loves, or even let her suspect that he loves her, because he feels himself responsible to another woman who is devoted to him. Clarissa Harlowe is abducted and seduced, but she cannot marry Lovelace, her repentant seducer, although offered riches, a title, the forgiveness of her family, and perfect respect from all her friends, because her conception of herself as honorable has been destroyed. Pamela is kidnapped, besieged, commanded, bribed, tormented, and deceived, but cannot bring herself to yield to the irrepressible Mr. B. until she is offered a genuine wedding ring. It all sounds like the most outrageous nonsense, and yet what is it but Richardson's exaggerated notion of honor? And is it possible that honor, however exaggerated, can really be ridiculous? Pride of self, dignity, respect: these still exist today, one hopes, and although Pamela and Clarissa and dear Sir Charles keep their values in an area once removed from the area in which our values lie today, are they so foolish? Is a sinful man the less sinful because his crimes are against a standard more rarified than ours? Lovelace, who ruined Clarissa, is not perhaps as bad a man as Faulkner's Popeye, but Lovelace is certainly as real a sinner in his sphere; moreover, he has more time to be bad and to be subtle about it than Popeye.

The goodness of Richardson's good characters—and all his characters are very sharply divided, half being devils, half angels—is in the same terms as the badness: That is, they are good in a sense that, translated into terms we understand fully, comes out as qualities we like and admire and would like to own ourselves.

Kindness, the third attribute, is an outlandish word to use about a writer, or about writing, or about anything except people and the way they feel. And yet kindness is a strong quality felt in Richardson's writing, the sort of kindness that evokes the tremendous tenderness the man himself must have felt, and tossed about embarrassingly on everyone who came his way. His characters, for instance, are nice to one another. One of them may abhor another; some of them—again, like Lovelace—outrage every precious tenet of a rigid morality and bring this outrage to bear on others; frequently these precise, lazy people are cross with one another, and stirred to anger. Harriet Byron was completely out of patience by about volume eight, when Sir Charles was sedately making absolutely *sure* that no conceivable shred of formality had been inadvertently overlooked. Nevertheless, implicit in every word, in every comment upon a comment, is the deep conviction of sympathy: not "We are all from the same mind: Richardson's," but "We are all from the same people: the mortals." That is a valuable thing to record, and perhaps it takes ten volumes to put it across.

There is very little humor in Richardson, and, to be honest, some of the books are pretty heavy going—Pamela's reflections on the education of her children, or some of the long stretches in *Grandison* where everyone takes a breather from the burning question (is it honorable or is it not?) and they just sit back and write long letters scrutinizing themselves—but without every word of it you couldn't really be satisfied that Sir Charles ought to propose or that Pamela deserves her husband. The richness of it is in those long muddy sections, the dark background of the bright tapestry. After Pamela's prolonged musings on children, we are disrespectfully delighted to see Mr. B. contemplate an elopement with a designing widow.

It takes a long time to read Richardson, and even so, he is only that stuffy little man a long way back—down the length of years to the eighteenth century, standing beyond even Thackeray and just behind Fielding—but peace, principle, and kindness are qualities that may even survive our own distempered time.

Private Showing

WHEN THE PRIVATE SHOWING OF THE MOVIE *LIZZIE*, MADE FROM MY novel *The Bird's Nest*, was scheduled in New York, I could not see it because my small son Barry had chickenpox. I had put the bottle of calamine lotion down on the telephone table to pick up the phone and said, no, I could not come to New York because I had chickenpox—and, I could have added, because there was a button off my blue coat, and my only decent dress, the brown one, had a large spot on the front, and the living room had to be vacuumed, and I had so many letters to write, and anyway, the first meeting with my Lizzie was something I had been trembling over for nearly a year, and I honestly lacked the courage to make the first move. When I finally put down the phone I tried to pick up the bottle of calamine lotion and could not close my fingers around it; the stain is still there on the hall floor, but—I have met Lizzie.

Out of consideration for the chickenpox, the magicians in charge of such things arranged to send Lizzie to me, and so I met her face-to-face at last on my home field, as it were, in our small local movie theater here in Vermont. Out of my many conflicting reactions, the only one I can isolate clearly is excitement; nothing so surprising has ever happened to me.

As long as I can remember, the act of writing has been a private one. A book is a comfortable stack of pages of yellow copy paper, with typed words on them, a familiar and fitted country in which I am perfectly at home, able to find a paragraph or a line without difficulty, able to recognize from the look of a page just where it belongs. A book translated into galley proofs is no longer mine—the pages are different, the paper is not yellow, the words are printed and look smaller; the whole country has been tidied and set in order. When the book is bound, there is the unfamiliar jacket and the sudden odd weight of it, and other people—strangers!—are holding it in their hands. I can read my own books in print the way I read and reread old books from my childhood, and the difference between *The Bird's Nest* and, say, *Northanger Abbey* is one of literary skill, not degree of familiarity; I can remember more passages from *Jane Eyre* than I can from any of my own books.

I have never, in all the years I have been writing, heard my own words read or spoken aloud, except by myself, unwillingly, and under pressure. *That* translation is too much for me; I cannot imagine how these words will sound; on the yellow page they *look* as though they will sound all right, and since they are going to be read, I trust, in silence, it seems to me most important that they look as though they will sound all right. I once heard a tape of myself reading one of my own stories and it sounded silly. The voice, of course, was not mine, and the words had been subtly changed; they were not on yellow paper at all, they were *strange* on that infernal tape.

All this, of course, changed, because of my unnerving encounter with my own words spoken out loud, and my own people walking around, in the movie *Lizzie*. It was something like being hit on the head with a rock: Everything was very bright for a second, and then it got kind of wavy. I sat there watching *Lizzie* with my mouth half-open, thinking—and there is really no other sensation like it— Why, there is Doctor Wright; he is taller than I remembered. It was suddenly clear that through some gap in time *these* were the real people, and I had stolen them for my book. Elizabeth talked and looked just exactly as I remembered her (remembered her from where? from the movie, from the book?) and Aunt Morgen and Doctor Wright were there, and it was like a family reunion, although I kept wondering if *they* recognized *me*.

It was exciting, too, because—as in any family reunion—I knew pretty well how everyone was going to behave, but still I could not tell when the explosions were coming. At one point I wanted to tell Morgen to look out—if she kept on talking to Elizabeth like that there would be trouble, even though I *knew* that Morgen always talked like that. It isn't fair, I kept on thinking, the way Morgen keeps picking on that poor child, when everyone knows Elizabeth isn't well, and then I had to shake my head and tell myself not to worry, it's only a movie; everything will come out all right.

I took my four children to see what they were unashamedly calling "Mommy's movie," after explaining with some care that there would be no serial, no cartoon, no popcorn stand open, no candy, but that at least they could sit wherever they liked, because there would also be no audience. It was Barry's second movie—the other one having been *Cinderella*—and he approved wholeheartedly of the MGM lion at the beginning; he felt that I had achieved a kind of masterstroke by arranging to have my movie begin with that lion roaring. For the rest of it, he pointed out that it was not very much different from *Cinderella*, after all.

Sally broke into enthusiastic cheering at the sight of my name on the screen and had to be violently hushed by her horribly embarrassed father and brother, one on each side holding a hand over her mouth. The movie itself enchanted her; she screamed once when Lizzie threw a bottle at Aunt Morgen, and clapped wildly when Doctor Lone Ranger Wright came riding to the rescue.

Jannie, whose standards are noticeably more mature than her younger sister's, found the movie experience deeply disturbing. She sat through the entire show in silence, refused to join in the later discussion at the dinner table, and had nightmares all night. Under other circumstances, I had realized by then, it would not be the kind of movie we would take Jannie to at all; I could measure the extent of its disturbance to her by my own reactions.

Laurie, on the other hand, thoroughly enjoyed it; he is fourteen, and has spent perhaps an accumulated four or five years at Saturday matinees, regarding beasts from Planet X and alien minds plotting to take over Earth. He had no difficulty whatsoever in identifying the Mad Scientist, and a Monstrous Intelligence (though human, not movie prop construction) that disguises itself behind a smiling face, and a pretty good, even cool, piano. Our conversation at the dinner table that evening took the form of "Well, I think the best thing in Mommy's movie was the part where . . ."

Later, I went upstairs to investigate a suspicious silence in the playroom, and found Barry lying back in a chair with his eyes closed while Sally made mystic passes before his eyes. They explained that they were playing doctor.

Good Old House

When we came to occupy our present house, we were not at first accepted, although the neighbors welcomed us and took us in with the deep New England courtesy that is half tolerance and half humor. We shortly accustomed ourselves to trading at certain stores, and we bought our coal locally, and we found a doctor and a dentist and a dog, and we went to the local movie theater and enrolled Laurie in the local nursery school—still, the old house had grave reservations about us and would allow us to feel only provisionally at home. Twice, the first week we were there, I awoke with nightmares of the old house shaking over me, malevolent and cruel, and after that, during our first few months, I frequently found myself awake after having walked in my sleep toward the front door, and once I found myself out between the pillars, as if running away.

Our cats, who had lived with us for years in New York, could find no resting place in this house; all the hallowed places for cats to sleep—the spot behind the stove, the wooden rocker—would not countenance city cats, and turned them away, and our New York furniture had somehow become different, so that the armchair in which young Shax had always slept before was off in a cold corner and had no sun in the afternoons. Laurie went off pleasantly from the house to nursery school, he played happily in the yard and through the attics, but there was a corner of the hall where a wolf lived, and he would not go near it alone.

We had been there only about three weeks when I found an ad in the local paper for a woman who wanted to do housework, and such things being fairly rare in our town, I telephoned her immediately and asked if she could come to work for us. She was pleased to have an answer to her ad so quickly, and terms were quickly and easily settled between us. I agreed to her charges, she approved of the children, we reached an honorable agreement about laundry, and then she asked, her voice trim and clean over the phone, "I clean forgot to ask you, Missus, where do you live?"

"In the old Ogilvie house," I said readily. "The one with the pill—"

"Where?" she asked. "The old Ogilvie house, did you say? The Fielding place?"

"That's right," I said. "The one with—"

"I'm sorry, Missus," she said, and her voice sounded really regretful. "I guess I can't come work for you after all."

"Why not?"

"Well . . ." she said. "It's too far," she said.

"I'll take care of your transportation."

"Well . . ." she said. "I guess I better not."

"But *why?*" I asked, but she had hung up.

No one liked to come into the house. We discovered much later that the painters and plumbers and carpenters Mr. Fielding had hired before we came had demanded extravagantly high pay, and Mr. Fielding had agreed to stay with them all the time they worked in the house. My grocer, who was very helpful about delivering orders, could never find a delivery boy who would leave my groceries any closer to the house than the end of the lawn. Our neighbors would stand and talk interminably at the front door or the back door, but they would never come inside, and the attempts I made to invite them in for tea met with faint, but polite, incredulity.

Toward the end of our first month, the painter arrived to do the outside of the house. As always, we were not consulted. The house had always been white with green trim, as were all the other houses on the block, and I suppose all the other houses in New England, and the painter did not for a minute imagine that anything else would be required of him; indeed, I doubt if he owned any other colors of paint. The first day he worked I went out to talk to him, and took him out a cup of coffee; he was on a ladder painting the pillars.

"Nice to see the old house cleaned up," he said, after we had spoken about the weather and had taken care of such other conversational preliminaries as the rent we paid for the house, my husband's income, and our opinion of the town.

"I can't believe it's the same house we saw last year," I said. I turned, as I frequently did, to look through the glass panes of the front door into our pleasant light hall, with the dining room showing beyond and the bright curtains and the pretty rugs and the lines of plants against the windows. "I'm so happy here," I said, realizing as I said it that I was.

"You know," the painter said, applying himself industriously to the pillar, "it don't seem to matter much what folks get to thinking about a house; when you get people living there, it all changes."

"This house has seen a lot of people going in and out."

"It's a good old house," he said. "Spite of what they say, it's a good solid house; not many like it nowadays." He turned and waved the paintbrush at me. "Kids wouldn't go past it at night," he said.

"I didn't know that," I said. "Do they feel any different now?"

"Well, no," the painter said. He seemed afraid that he might have hurt my feelings, because he added quickly, "It's a good old house, though."

There was another strange quality to the house; it had an odd effect on the things in it—never the old things, of course; they seemed to belong and to understand—but only our newer things, such as the living room clock, which had been a wedding present and had worked perfectly well until we moved into this old house. It stopped every day at five minutes to five. For a little while I thought it was an eccentricity of my own, that perhaps I did not wind it enough, or perhaps I had noticed that once or twice it had stopped near five o'clock and so fell to believing that it stopped every day. I made a point of winding it carefully, and then I got so that I was checking it regularly, and I would glance at it every time I passed the living room, and finally I came to accept as natural the fact that it would stop every day at five minutes to five, and when the five o'clock whistles blew at the lumberyard I went in and restarted the clock. It became an almost habitual small gesture, like checking to see if the children were covered at night, and I timed myself by it, knowing that when I had to restart the clock it was time to start making the children's supper.

The window in the back bedroom was another thing. It was ordinary glass; I knew that because I had had a glazier in to change it once. But no matter when you looked out of it, and no matter what the weather was like outside, it was opaque, as though a cloth were over the outside of it. When the glazier was working on it and had taken out the glass, he had held the new glass outside the window and looked through it. I could see his face clearly, as though through an ordinary window, and then he set the new pane of glass into the frame and dusted his hands and closed the window, and we looked through it together, and it was opaque. When we opened the window and looked out again we saw the maple trees outside and the sky; the glazier, who was a local man, smiled and shrugged and refused his pay, and touched one of the pillars gently as he went down the steps.

Still another troubling thing was the way small articles disappeared. I realized that in a large house with small children, things are always disappearing anyway, but this was different; it was as though there were pockets of time in the house into which things dropped for a little while and then came back. Small things disappeared, such as scissors and pencils and spoons, all things you might expect to lose but of course do not expect to find again back in their accustomed places. Sometimes it was larger things that stepped out, such as kitchen utensils. I remember one evening I went into the pantry to get a strainer off the shelf, groping absentmindedly the way you do when a thing is always kept in the same place and you reach for it without looking, and it was not there. I spent the next two days taking the pantry apart to find the strainer, and I looked as far afield as the playroom and the tool chest, and at the end of the two days I went into the pantry absentmindedly and put up my hand to take down the strainer and it was there.

Once, a little round rug disappeared for almost a week from the study, as though it had been absorbed into the floor, and reappeared after a while looking the same as ever, and so natural that for a while we forgot to be surprised that it was there. Several times I left groceries on the kitchen table and found them later neatly put away in the pantry; one reason I am sure I do not do this myself in a sort of trance is that the refrigerator is never used—butter and milk and such are set on the pantry windowsill, where it is cool. Once, buttons appeared, newly sewn onto my son's jacket, and another time my daughter's stuffed lamb had a blue ribbon removed and a pink one substituted. A day or so later the blue ribbon was back, washed and ironed.

None of these things bothered us excessively; we have always been a family that carries bewilderment like a banner, and odd new confusions do not actually seem to be any more bewildering than the ones we invent for ourselves; moreover, in each of these cases it was easier to believe that nothing had happened, or that it was of no importance anyway. We spoke affectionately of poltergeists and pixies, and affected to believe that each single instance was of course some unconscious behavior on our own parts. Laurie, who believed in any case in good and bad fairies, adjusted quickly and easily to the oddities, and was completely unaffected after a while, although my husband and I received a little jolt when, on Christmas morning, Laurie found a second stocking hung up against the mantel, as though it had been feared that *we* might forget. And there was the time when he lost a tooth, forgot to tell us, and found, in the morning, two dimes under his pillow. However, after a while the house seemed to gain a certain amount of confidence in us, and only Laurie ever experienced this pleasing duplication, although Joanne's clothes are still mended occasionally, that being a field in which the house can have no legitimate confidence in me.

It is not hard, after all, to live with such things, and after a while they do not seem much more unnatural than that water should change its form when heat is applied, or that trees should change color in the fall; I recall that the first week with our first television set shocked us much more deeply. I have grown used to the tricks of the house as I have grown used to the dip in the kitchen floor beside the windows, or the stair that creaks, or the study window that will not open at all. My husband, who does not come into as intimate contact with the house as I do, is consequently less troubled, although he was quite surprised when a nearly empty bottle of whiskey disappeared and was lost to him for a day, then returned full. And once his muffler disappeared from the hall closet and returned some time later to its own hook, where we had both looked several times.

I think perhaps a great reason for our relaxing into this mild acceptance was the complete ease with which these small things were accomplished, frequently so unobtrusively that it was not until afterward that we realized something had happened. When Joanne's good silver spoon vanished, it disappeared from my hand in the dish towel: That is, I was drying it, as I do every night, and as I reached forward to slip it into the drawer along with the other silverware it was gone. I had seen it the moment before and then did not see it

the moment after. I looked for it, of course, but without much enthusiasm, knowing without admitting it that I need not bother. A
day or so later, after Joanne had become reconciled to using another
spoon, I was drying silverware, and as I was slipping it into the
drawer, Joanne's spoon fell into its place. I knew the spoon had been
gone and that I had been looking for it, but it was returned so naturally that I closed the drawer, then thought, then opened the drawer
and saw that the spoon was really there.

Perhaps it was exactly because we took this cheerful teasing so
well that one day, near the end of our first year in the house, the
doorbell rang at about eleven o'clock in the morning. Laurie was in
school, Joanne was in her playpen in the children's room, and I was
making dough for gingerbread men, which we would cut out in the
afternoon. I remember that when I went to answer the door I thought
idly that probably my mixing bowl and spoon, my cups and rolling
pin, would all be washed and returned to their places by the time I
came back. There was an old lady at the door, neatly dressed in
black and smiling.

"I'm so *very* sorry to trouble you," she said as soon as I opened
the door. "I hope I'm not disturbing you."

"Not at all," I said. "Won't you come in?" I added, because she
was obviously intending to come in anyway.

"Thank you," she said, and stepped daintily inside. She looked
around the hall curiously, then smiled. "I used to visit here very
often," she said. "I was passing by, and I thought how wonderful it is
to see the old house occupied again." She waved her hand apologetically. "I *couldn't* go on without stopping in for one more look at
the old house."

"I'm very glad you did," I said. "Won't you come in and look
around?"

She followed me into the living room, stopping once to touch
the shining wood of the old stair rail, and in the living room she
went directly to the old wooden rocker and sat down, turning her
head to look around.

"It's not really very much changed," she said.

"It's a lovely old house," I said.

"Do you think so?" She turned quickly to look at me. "Do you really think it's a lovely old house?"

"We're very happy here."

"I'm glad." She folded her hands and smiled again, as though to herself. "It's always been such a *good* house," she said. "The old doctor always used to say it was a *good* house."

"The old doctor?"

"Doctor Ogilvie." She smiled at me again.

"Doctor *Ogilvie?*"

"I see they kept the pillars, after all," she said, nodding. "We always thought they gave the house character."

"There was a hornet's nest in one," I said inadequately. Doctor Ogilvie had built the house in 1816.

"Which one?"

"The one on the right end."

She nodded again. "There always was," she said.

"What was it like when you visited here?" I asked.

"Oh, my dear," she said, and smiled on me as from a long way off. "It was very gay then, you know. There were no other houses for miles around, you know, and we all came in carriages—"

"But the Fieldings built the other houses in—" I began, and she interrupted me, her soft cheeks faintly pink.

"No other houses we *visited*, of course."

I was silent, a little anxious, and then Shax came into the room, without footsteps, but making his presence known the way a cat does. The old lady turned and looked at him for a minute and then said, "Fine fellow." She put down one black-gloved hand and Shax went to her, touched her glove with his nose, and poured himself into her lap. She stroked him comfortably while she said to me, "They've taken away the old wallpaper, and I suppose the front bedroom isn't blue anymore?"

"It's blue," I said, wondering. "Someone chose a very pretty blue paper for that room."

"I'm glad the Fieldings kept it up," she said. "So often you can't tell, when a young family buys into a home. Sometimes they change the old things."

"We've been trying to keep it comfortable," I said.

"I remember," she said, "I remember when the Fieldings first offered to buy it, we sat upstairs in the blue front room, Sally Cortland and I, and we tried to think what the Fieldings might do to the house. The Cortlands hadn't really been here *long*, of course; the Ogilvies built it. We brought the pillars from Boston."

I could think of nothing to say, and after a minute she put Shax down and said, "May I look at the rest of the house? Are you busy?"

She liked the way the bedrooms were still the same colors, and the children's room pleased her. "What a pretty child you are, indeed," she said to Joanne in the playpen, and Joanne looked up, considered, and smiled. "It *needs* children, this house," the old lady said, touching me on the arm as we went out the door. "It was the sorrow of Anne Ogilvie's life."

When we moved at last to the kitchen and she saw my half-finished gingerbread, she was amused, and picked up the bowl to examine the dough. "You'll get it good and short," she said. "It won't bake even, if you don't get it good and short. And put in a little coffee."

"The children are going to cut out the gingerbread men this afternoon."

"With raisin eyes," she added, and sighed. Then she laughed softly. "Still the same old house," she said.

I went with her to the door, and she stood for a minute looking back into the house, as I often do. Then she smiled at me once more, affectionately, and thanked me, and I watched her go off down the walk.

When I closed the door, I leaned one hand against the door

frame, and it seemed to me that for the first time the old house responded, turning in toward me protectively. When I went back into the living room, Shax was asleep on the wooden rocker, and that afternoon one of my neighbors dropped in for a cup of coffee, coming through the back door so naturally that neither of us thought of her never having come in before.

Small things still disappear, of course, and for a while Joanne spoke occasionally of a faraway voice that sang to her at night. Once I went into the kitchen and found a still-warm pumpkin pie on the table, covered with a clean cloth; we had it for dinner and praised it in voices that we hoped would carry throughout the old house.

The Play's the Thing

I CAME TO MY DESK ONE BRIGHT MONDAY MORNING RECENTLY, PLAN-ning to get right to work, and looked at the various things I had been working on, any one of which I could spend my Monday doing. There were four manuscripts, in different stages of progress, on my desk.

One was a novel, a story about a haunted house and what happens to the people who live in it; it emphasizes the idea that ghosts, like dreams and hallucinations, are figments of the human intelligence.

The second manuscript was a long story about a girl who runs away from home and tries so successfully to eradicate any aspect of her old personality that when she wants to go home again she can't get in; they don't know her.

The other two were, in a sense, nonprofessional pleasure work. One manuscript was a birthday present for my husband, the script for a ferocious dialogue to be tape-recorded by several of his bridge-playing friends. My husband is a most meticulous bridge player, and dislikes any form of clumsiness or carelessness about the game, so I wrote an account of a game in which every possible rule is broken, and all kinds of confusion goes on during the play of a hand. This was to be acted out by his friends, and recorded, and—just to make him feel happy—the fourth hand would be left out in the recording; a space of time was left for him to bid and play. We all called it "Play-Along Bridge" (and I may say that in a sense it has served its purpose; he has announced that he will never play bridge with any of us again).

The fourth manuscript on my desk was a one-act play for children, which I had not written voluntarily. My children and some of their friends had thought they would give a play, and they'd gone about it in the eminently practical fashion that children use for these things: First they'd chosen their costumes, then they'd decided where they would give their play and how much they would charge and who could be in it and who could not be in it, and then they'd started looking for a play to give. They'd asked me where you went to find a nice play with big parts for everybody, and I'd sent them down to the library, where I was sure they would find half a dozen volumes of plays for children. My older daughter came back to me, disconsolate. "Listen to this," she said, and read to me: "'I fear me, good husband, that our wretched hut will not again withstand the rigors of the winter wind.'"

"What's that?" I said.

She said, "It means their house is going to blow down, but that's the way I have to say it if we do that play."

"Well, why not do another play instead?" I asked.

"Do you like this better?" she asked. "'I am Lafayette, a French man of noble birth, and I have come to this new country to aid General Washington in his battle for freedom.' You know," she continued, "I'd be downright ashamed to get up on a stage and talk junk like that, and the other plays are just as bad. No one could remember the lines because they don't sound right, and you have to stand still and say them so you look silly on the stage because there's no way to act or sound natural."

"Why don't you make up your own play?" I asked her.

"We can't," she said, "but *you*'re a writer . . ."

Well, with half a dozen of them urging me on, I sat down that evening to sketch out a one-act play. I decided that it would be most suitable for the group who were going to act it if I used a familiar fairy story, rewriting it in language they could understand, with action that would appeal to them. I thought of Hansel and Gretel, which is a fairy story that has always annoyed me because I strongly resent that Hansel and Gretel eat the Witch's house and never get punished for it. I thought I might please myself by seeing that Hansel and Gretel got what was coming to them.

So I made the Witch into a fine crazy character, full of progressive ideas about the improvement of witchcraft. I put in an Enchanter, to accommodate an older boy in our cast, and made the Enchanter a lazy old creature who lets the Witch do all the work, and I made Hansel and Gretel into the two most objectionable children I could, whining and quarreling and insolent and greedy. Then I made the Mother and Father into a pair of bewildered, helpless parents who want their children to be well mannered and nice but find out that nothing seems to help: They have joined the PTA and the Little League, and bought Girl Scout cookies, and given the children bicycles for Christmas, and gone to the class play, and *still* their children are impolite and bad.

So the Witch does not want to capture the children at all, but has to shut them in her house to keep them from eating all of it, and when she tries to give the children back, the parents will not take them. The Witch begs and threatens, but the parents point out that the children are so unpleasant, they would *prefer* to have the Witch keep them.

I had a wonderful time writing it, though I had half an idea that I'd better keep my play away from the children, as it outraged all the tenets of fairy tales. Every time I thought of things my children do that I can't stand—and there are a lot of them—I put them in for

Hansel and Gretel. As I went along I thought of a little song that Hansel and Gretel could sing, a kind of echo song, in which one of them says, "You're mean," and the other answers, "*You're* mean," and it goes on "You're bad," "*You're* bad," "You're a pig, I won't play with you," "*You're* a pig, I won't play with *you*." I wrote the lyrics in, and when I'd finished the first half of my play I thought it over and decided that I would show it to the children after all and see what they thought.

Well, to my surprise, they loved it. There was an immediate wild demand to be allowed to play the parts of Hansel and Gretel, and the children took up my little song and chanted it to a tune adapted from a nursery rhyme, adding verses freely and shouting it from one end of the house to the other. They began quoting lines back and forth, and then I discovered a very odd thing: I had thought of the Mother and Father characters as sympathetic, but kind of mixed up and tired—the way I see mothers and fathers. However, once the children got hold of the play, the Mother and Father changed: They became slightly silly, and as the children discussed the parts, it became clear that the Mother and Father were going to become the comedic roles. When their lines were read in a slightly exaggerated fashion, they sounded self-pitying and foolish.

The Witch and the Enchanter became the powerful figures. From the Enchanter's first appearance, it is perfectly obvious that he is the kind of person who would drop dead before he would umpire a Little League game, and the Witch's main desire is to go on a television quiz program and make a lot of money, and spend it on fancy clothes and good things to eat. They are, in a word, not at all proper parent figures, and the children loved them.

We ran almost at once into further complications: The children were singing the echo song and thought they would like more music, particularly a song for the Witch to sing—that was my older daughter, who fancied herself onstage belting out a solo number—and another song to close the play. My son offered to write the music, and I wrote a couple of songs with simple jingling words, but then it turned out that although the echo song was all right in its simple form, like a nursery rhyme, no one wanted the older characters to have to sing "junk like that."

So it was unanimously decided that the song the Enchanter sings must be a real low-down blues, to be called "The Mean Old Wizard Blues" and to begin "I want a rich witch, baby; no others need apply." While I sat there with my jaw hanging, the blues got itself composed and firmly embedded in the family culture. I got in a couple of fast patter songs for the Witch and the parents, with a lot of rhymes that could be from Noël Coward, and then I found that what my children wanted to close the show was a good fast number, very rhythmic, with hand clapping and a chorus, in the manner of a fast spiritual such as "Ain't Gonna Study War No More."

I got that song written, then proposed that since the big moment in the play is the one in which the Witch and the Enchanter do a magic incantation and dance around the pot in which the magic is cooking, there might be a little musical number for that scene, too. Thereupon, my son composed "The Incantation Rock-and-Roll," which he said was a "good wailing rock song with a boogie bass and a crazy backbeat."

I was a little bit worried. Something had gone terribly wrong with my idea of making a silly little play for the kids to put on. Then I realized what it was: I had written it from my own viewpoint, hinting ironically that children ought to behave better, thinking I had a sound little moral lesson there that would really do the children good, hearing how unpleasant Hansel and Gretel sounded on the stage and how they distressed their parents. But when the children got hold of it, it turned into a general statement by the children themselves about the world. They wanted the fun of pretending to be bad children, the deep satisfaction of making fun of the parents and the laziness and self-indulgence of the Witch and the Enchanter, and the excitement and spirit of the modern kind of music, which, even in the blues, expresses a kind of young joy it is very hard for grown-ups to comprehend. Overall, I had thought that the sardonic humor of the play was mine, but it turned out to be the children's.

I did make one attempt to rescue my play: I rewrote the ending, so that by means of magic Hansel and Gretel are transformed into sweet, dear, good, kind little kiddies, but the children threw it right out. Hansel and Gretel stay horrible to the end.

Above everything else, I was desperately afraid that they would try to perform the play in public. I was quite sure that we would be everlastingly disgraced if that souped-up, cynical fairy tale ever reached a real stage, and the thought of being discovered as a fellow conspirator had me in terror. I managed to have any production of it put off until the fall school term, on the grounds that it was much too late in the year for any serious preparation, and I thought privately that the children had really had all the fun they wanted by just putting it together, and that by fall they would be interested in something else.

Unfortunately, they took the songs to school, then began repeating lines from the play, and inevitably, finally, I found that copies were being mimeographed and passed around the seventh grade. I wanted to take a firm stand, but before I could make up my mind what to say I received requests from two local high schools for permission to put on the play. While I was still reeling, the principal of a private school thirty miles away called me to say she had heard about this play, and was there *any* chance of their performing it?

I tried to tell everyone that it was a rather callous parody, cynical and full of slang, but all the teachers said the same thing: What a wonderful idea! The children will be really interested, and will actually *enjoy* a play that speaks their language.

Well, it certainly does speak their language—much more so than the play about the fisherman's wife who fears that her wretched hut will not withstand the rigors of the winter—and now that it exists I can't seem to get rid of it. It is a defiant statement by a pack of children about their world and their acceptance of it. I finally gave in as gracefully as I could—I had the play copyrighted, including the lyrics and music, and gave it to the children. It belongs to them, as it should. I am going to stick to ghosts and bridge games and haunted houses, where I belong.

The Ghosts of Loiret

I LOVE HOUSES. I LOVE TO LOOK AT THEM THE WAY THEY JUST STAND there, and I most particularly love old and big and fancy houses. My grandfather was an architect, and his father, and *his* father; one of them built houses only for millionaires in California, and that was where the family wealth came from, and one of them was certain that houses could be made to stand on the sand dunes of San Francisco, and that was where the family wealth went. I don't have any feeling, myself, about *building* houses; I don't need to own them or live in them or even go inside; I just like to *look* at houses.

I have an Egyptian scarab and I have a Japanese netsuke of a skeleton reading a book of poetry, and I have a crystal ball and a deck of tarot cards and a lot of tikis and eleven Siamese gambling house tokens and a book by Ludovico Sinistrari listing all the demons by name and incantation, and an Australian throwing knife and an incunabulum and a copy of Villon with shocking illustrations, and a small book by Currer Bell and an African boat harp and a skull from the Collyer mansion, and a wishing ring and three magic talismans—one for Thursdays only—and a necklace from the Congo made of tiny carved wooden skulls, and five black cats and an electric frying pan and four children, but I have had no good pictures of houses to look at.

This year, when I realized this, my husband had already ordered my birthday present, which was to have been a Japanese scroll on rice paper in eleven panels showing the gradual decomposition of a dead body, but he canceled it and wrote instead to a British bookseller and ordered a collection of picture postcards of houses. These had been put up for sale by the heirs of one of those intrepid British travelers; I think of the man himself as a fellow house lover, gentle, observant, with a lap robe and a notebook with a silver pencil on a chain, always ready to toss an urchin a coin or bow to a lady on a bridge. This distinguished old person had wandered far, gathering postcards, and his heirs must have been most surprised when an urgent offer arrived from my husband in Vermont. I do not think that I was so excited even when the assegai came. Like all the presents my husband gives me, the postcards were even lovelier than I had imagined.

With his hip bath and his bowler, my dogged friend had traveled extensively through England, France, and the United States, and had feasted those good British eyes on a vast range of great, old, and storied houses and taken their images home. The French houses were lovely slim châteaux rising above their little lakes, with magic names such as Annecy and Gruyères and Pontchardon, and the English houses were solid and straightforward, properly surrounded by lawns, and the American houses were lavishly decorated with gargoyles and classical pillars and gothic turrets. I dwelt lovingly on the Château de Menthon, on Beaumesnil and Nîmes; I gazed for a moment on the T. D. Stimson residence in Los Angeles, dreamed over Strawberry Hill, and looked into grottoes and Roman baths and summer palaces.

Every time my husband gives me a present, I have to go and look something up in the *Encyclopaedia Britannica*; this time, I had to know about the ornamental writing across the front of Villesavin, what it said and what it was called and why it was there at all, but the encyclopaedia did not know, any more than it had known why my thunderbird necklace was made out of old phonograph records or how to get the strings back on the zither.

Then, at a cocktail party, I met a French scholar, a charming native Vermonter who spends his holidays in France teasing the French people into thinking he has lived all his life in Paris. When I said to him "Can you tell me what it says, the writing on the front of the Château de Villesavin?" he stared at me, as, standing on the broad steps of Villesavin, overlooking the sweet gardens, he might have stared at a stranger approaching and saying "Can you tell me about the Elks' Hall in the country of Vermont in the U. S. of A.?" The poor exile—his world *did* exist, then?—brightened and smiled. "You know the country?" he asked at once.

"I have only pictures."

"Only pictures? But you must *go* there. To visit France . . ."

"Alas." I sighed. "I have an Egyptian scarab, but I have never seen a pyramid."

"A pyramid? In the south of France?"

"Can you tell me what it says on the front of Villesavin?" (What do they read in the land of the Lilliputians; what is the news in Islandia, Megapolis, Utopia?) "What does it really look like?" I asked inadequately.

He gestured at Vermont beyond the window. "Not like this," he said.

"Tell me about the houses."

"There is one place," he said. "That one is haunted, haunted by—"

"Well, old *fellow*," said someone who wore a plaid jacket and carried whiskey in a glass, "when did *you* get back? Paris just about the same?"

I finished my drink, and my husband took me home; they were singing "Auprès de ma blonde" in the corner. At home, looking my houses over again, I came to the château at Loiret and stopped, sur-prised. "Look," I said to my husband. "Here are two people on the balcony at Loiret."

"Why not?" my husband said. "They probably live there."

"But there weren't people in the picture before."

"M. R. James," my husband said wisely. "You've been reading that mezzotint thing."

"I haven't. And anyway *his* house was only a fine old English mansion. This is the Château du Loiret!"

"They're probably *all* haunted," my husband said.

"No," I said. "Not *my* houses. Not my lovely Menthon. Not Villesavin. Not Beaumesnil or the James Flood residence in Menlo Park."

"Well, perhaps not Menlo Park."

"There simply should not *be* people on the balcony at Loiret. The windows are all closed and shuttered and the house is clearly empty, and those people have no business whatsoever to be standing there on the balcony."

"Go to bed," my husband said unsympathetically.

The next night I looked again, and there were no people stand-ing on the balcony at Loiret.

When I had just finished my latest book, *The Sundial*, my hus-band and I were on our way to New York to spend three or four days talking to my publishers and such. It had been a long time since I'd last been to New York, and an even longer time since I'd been any-where at all without my troops of children tagging along, and I was excited and a little bit nervous. When the train stopped at 125th Street, I glanced out the window to get my first sight of the big city and found myself looking squarely at the most hideous building I have ever seen. It was altogether disgusting, and I have no idea why that particular word came into my mind. It was a tall tenement building, standing alone, and staring at it out the train window all I could think of was that I wanted to turn around and go back to Vermont; I didn't want to spend another minute in a city with that building in it. I pointed the building out to my husband, but he couldn't see it; there were a number of other buildings around and he could not pick out this one before the train started, so he told me to calm down and try not to be so excited; we would be in the hotel in half an hour. As long as I could, I looked back at that unspeakable building, just wishing I would never have to see it or think of it again as long as I lived. I cannot really describe it. No one else, I expect, has ever seen it the way I did that afternoon. It was horrifying.

I thought I had forgotten about it, in the confusion of arriving in the city and getting to the hotel, but that night I woke up from a nightmare about the building, one of those bad nightmares that get you out of bed to turn on the lights and make sure it was only a dream. All I could remember was that I had been dreaming dreadfully about that awful building, and from that time on I spent my entire time in New York dreading the moment when we would take the train home and pass the building again. It was so bad, finally, that we had to change our plans and take a night train, so that we would pass 125th Street in the dark and I wouldn't see the building. It troubled me still after we were home, and finally I decided I had to find out about it, so I wrote to a friend of ours who teaches at Columbia University and described the building, asking him to locate it and find out if there was any reason why it should give me such an impression of horror.

Finally, he wrote me that he had had trouble finding the building because it existed only from one particular point of view from the 125th Street station; from any other angle it was not recognizable as a building. Some seven months before, it had been almost entirely burned in a disastrous fire that killed nine people. What was left of the building was a shell. The children in the neighborhood said it was haunted.

Then a postcard of one of the California houses began to bother me. It was an ugly house, all angles and all wrong. It was sick, diseased, and the photograph of it on the postcard made it look yellow and flabby. "I don't like this house at all," I said, showing it to my husband.

"Very nice," he said, reading. I should perhaps say that after having gotten me a crystal ball, he wouldn't let me look in it while he was around, and, when the Sinistrari book came, he was unkind enough to refuse to translate the parts left in Latin, although he could have done it perfectly well; neither has he permitted me to put the Thursday talisman into his pocket on Thursday, which is his poker night, although every Friday morning he is forced to admit that he could have used it.

"I don't like this house at *all*," I said again. "I wish it would go away, and not stay with my other houses."

"Throw it away."

"But I can't, of course. That nice old man gathered it for a reason. He liked houses, and what would he think of me if I took his houses and started throwing them away? He might want them back."

"Very nice," said my husband, reading.

"And the encyclopaedia isn't any help, because this house is in California, and when *that* encyclopaedia was written there wasn't any such *thing* as California, and if only you didn't insist on having just the eleventh edition—"

"Amateurs," my husband said. "Nothing *after* the eleventh can properly be called an encyclopaedia."

"But suppose I want to find out about this house in California—"

"California?" said my husband, suddenly alert. "Are your mother and father coming again?"

"No," I said, "but of course you are right. I shall write my mother tonight about this house. If it exists in California, she may know of it. Thank you, my dear, for the splendid suggestion."

"Very nice," said my husband, reading.

I had not much time to look at my postcards for the next few days, after writing to my mother in California, because my husband gave me a book called *Some Haunted Houses of England & Wales* and I got involved in solving the mystery of Glamis Castle. As a matter of fact, I had almost forgotten writing her at all, and when her letter came I was pleased, because I thought she was sending me the recipe for my grandmother's nut cake, but she only wrote that yes, she remembered that horrid house in California very well, although she was surprised to know that there were any pictures of it still around. My great-grandfather had built it. She remembered when the people of the town got together one night and burned it down.

The next day, my husband and our older son, Laurie, came home from a walk and brought me a hickory leaf to use as a bookmark in *Some Haunted Houses of England & Wales*. There was no one on the balcony at Loiret.

I found out about a haunted house in England where they had an heirloom skull kept in a box on the mantelpiece, and I told my husband about it. "Whenever they try to get rid of it," I told him, "there are thunderstorms and the roof blows off and all the cows are barren until either they go and get it back again or it rolls back by itself and gets into its box."

"You have a skull from the Collyer mansion," my husband pointed out.

It sounded right. "We could get Laurie to put it in a bag or something and take it over and throw it in Lake Paran," I said. "Then we would have thunderstorms and the roof would blow off and I guess all the cats would be barren."

"That's good," my husband said jovially. "That part about the cats being barren. You call Laurie while I get the stepladder."

The skull sits on the top shelf of a bookcase, on top of a volume of Dr. Dee's *Actions with Spirits*. I called Laurie, and when he came his father said, "Help me with this ladder; we're going to take Mother's skull and put it in a bag and throw it into Lake Paran so there will be thunderstorms."

"All right," Laurie said. "Except we're going to look kind of silly throwing Mother's skull into Lake Paran. People *fish* in Lake Paran."

But it would not come down. Neither would John Dee. My husband pulled and tugged and tried to shake it loose, and then Laurie got up on the stepladder and hit it with a broom, but it would not come down.

"Well," my husband said at last, "I guess we'll just have to put up with the kittens."

"We're better off anyway," Laurie said. "If anyone had seen us going around throwing skulls into Lake Paran, they might not have liked it. People swim in there, too, you know."

"Let me show you the letter I got from my mother," I said. "She forgot about my grandmother's nut cake again. Laurie can throw something else into Lake Paran."

"Kittens," my husband said.

"Certainly not. Laurie, look and see if there are any people on the balcony at Loiret."

Laurie looked. "Yeah, there's a couple of people," he said. I raced to his side, and, indeed, the same two people were standing on the balcony.

I began to wish that my English colleague had chosen his postcards a little more carefully. For a long time I watched for the people to return to the balcony at Loiret, but no one appeared. A nun kept looking out the window of Ballechin House, and that crazy buttress on The Priory, where Charlie Bravo died, came loose at one end and was just hanging there, and when I used a magnifying glass I could see Mrs. Cox looking out from the upper window, and once she waved; I didn't like having Mrs. Cox wave at me. For one thing, the last person I seem to remember Mrs. Cox waving at was murder victim Charlie Bravo in 1876.

I had a postcard of Borley Rectory and another picture of Borley Rectory in *Some Haunted Houses of England & Wales*, and the picture in the book was all right, but on the postcard a dining room window kept coming open and all the careful bricking-over they had done was wasted, because I could see clearly into the dining room, and what they must have thought in there, with me looking into the dining room through a magnifying glass, I can't imagine. There was something gibbering on one of the battlements of Menthon, and over at Château de Kergrist the stones from that round tower at the end kept falling and falling.

"I wish that skull would come down," my husband said several times. "I don't like having it stuck up there."

"That skull was the first present you ever gave me that didn't have bookworms," I said.

"I just wish it would come unstuck," he said.

I was afraid that with the postcards going on the way they were, and the skull stuck up on top of John Dee, we might have some kind of trouble, even a poltergeist manifestation, but all that happened at first was that Laurie's goldfish died, and that could have been because there was too much chlorine in the water. I have never liked the theory that poltergeists only come into houses where there are children, because I think it is simply too much for any one house to have poltergeists *and* children, so one morning when everyone was out, and the cellar door began to bang itself open and shut regularly, I was so angry that I looked up an incantation for the demon Vapula, who appears in the form of a lion with griffin's wings and drives away evil spirits, and I typed up the incantation, the one beginning "*Cara, cherna, sito, cirna,*" and stuck it onto the cellar door with a piece of Scotch tape, and then I nailed the door shut and it stopped banging back and forth.

I had to get out another incantation, the one for the demon Andrealphus, when the sugar bowl got itself hurling back and forth across the kitchen, and I typed that one up and taped it to the sugar bowl, and then later another one on the toaster, which kept popping by itself, and when the children came home from school for lunch that day they went around the kitchen reading the incantations out loud and giggling. During lunch, a crashing started upstairs, and I sent Laurie up to see if we needed another incantation, but it was only my cat Kuili trying to get into the back copies of *The New Statesman and Nation*, which she likes to tear up and eat; she was pounding with her head against the screen I use to cover them.

My husband had a present for me when he came home, one that had come in the mail from Sotheby's; it was a two-handed Japanese ceremonial sword. One of the dogs came home with a bone he had dug up somewhere, and when I looked at the bone closely I saw that it had teeth.

"I am going to put my houses away," I said to my husband. "I can't get my housework done."

"They were not a particularly good present, were they," he said. "I'll try to get you something else instead."

"They were perfectly lovely," I told him. "I have been extremely happy with them; it's only that I kind of have to let everything else go because of them. And those people at Loiret never come back outside anymore."

"They were probably never there in the first place," he said unkindly.

"I wonder what they could have been looking for. The movie camera is broken, by the way."

"I thought it must be, from the things it was taking pictures of. I think you should put your postcards away, and I'll try to think of another present for you."

I put the postcards into a box with camphor and a copper coin, and my husband gave me a silver pomander, and in the encyclopaedia it said to take my pomander to an apothecary and get him to put civet into it, but Mr. Carter down at the drugstore said no. I have a reading copy of John Dee, so we left the skull where it was.

Well, that was not my last cocktail party, by a long way. You know the kind of party where some damnfool woman goes around cornering people and asking them questions like "What do you *really* think of the struggle between good and evil for the soul of man?" or "Do you know what I was reading the other day about the things they do to horses?" Well, these days it's me. "Do you believe in ghosts?" I ask them. "Let me tell you about a very strange experience I had with the Château du Loiret; these people . . ."

"Well?"

"WELL?" ASKED STANLEY FINALLY.

"I think that's the end," I said doubtfully.

"Aren't you sure?"

"Ye-es."

"Have you anything more to say?" Stanley inquired.

"No."

"Have your characters anything more to say?"

"Only," I giggled, "that they're very glad they met you."

Stanley shook his head. At last: "Well, it had a plot," he said.

"Stanley!"

"Yes?"

"I wonder which of us really wrote this."

"I refuse to take the blame," said Stanley.

"Well, it's yours, anyway. You *practically* wrote it."

"I might have written it."

"I'll give it to you."

"Don't want it," said Stanley nastily.

"'Love, with this tawny marigold . . .'" I began. Stanley stared at me.

"I'll dedicate it to you," I added.

We both laughed.

III

● ● ●

When This War Is Over

Early Short Stories

. . .

"I thought I was insane, and would write about how the only sane people are the ones who are condemned as mad, and how the whole world is cruel and foolish and afraid of people who are different. That was when I was still in high school."

. . .

The Sorcerer's Apprentice

MISS MATT WAS AT LEAST PARTIALLY CONSCIOUS THAT SHE LOOKED like the teacher everyone has had for English in first-year high school; she was small and pretty, in a rice-powder fashion, with a great mass of soft dark hair that tried to stay on top of her head and straggled instead down over her ears; her voice was low and turned pleading instead of sharp; any presentable fourteen-year-old bully could pass her course easily. She had read *Silas Marner* aloud almost daily for the past ten years, marked tests in a dainty blue pencil, and still blushed dreadfully at the age of thirty-four.

The year she was twenty-eight she had gone from New York to San Francisco through the Panama Canal with two other teachers from her high school (Gym and General Science), but none of them had found husbands. With her meekest expectations still unsatisfied, Miss Matt lived quietly alone in an inexpensive two-room apartment, with a tiny kitchenette and a Cézanne print over the sofa. She knew her landlady fairly well; they had a cup of tea together occasionally, two refined ladies, in the landlady's first-floor apartment, but in the six years she had lived in her apartment, Miss Matt had not met any of her neighbors.

On Wednesday afternoons, freed early from the high school,

Miss Matt came home and straightened her apartment and washed her hair, and then, her head wrapped in a towel, wearing a Chinese silk housecoat, Miss Matt sat down with a peaceful cup of tea and played *Afternoon of a Faun* and *The Sorcerer's Apprentice* on her small portable phonograph. Sometimes, when it had been a hard day at school and the future looked unusually dark, Miss Matt would permit herself to cry luxuriously for half an hour; afterward she would wash her face, and dress and go out to some nice restaurant for dinner.

Miss Matt was crying on the afternoon that Krishna came to see her. There was a sudden vigorous knock on the door, and while Miss Matt was still holding her handkerchief before her in surprise, the door opened a little and a small pretty head hooked curiously around the edge of the door and stayed, regarding Miss Matt.

After a minute Miss Matt walked over to the phonograph and turned off *The Sorcerer's Apprentice*, averting her head so the tears were not completely visible. "Were you looking for me?" Miss Matt asked finally, then added "Dear?" as the visitor was undeniably a female child.

"Marian said I could come in here," the child said.

Miss Matt collected herself and touched the handkerchief delicately to her eyes. "What did you want me for?" she asked. It was the first time in years Miss Matt had spoken to a child younger than the first year of high school, and she felt free to end a sentence with a preposition.

The child opened the door wider and slipped through, closing it behind her. She was carrying a large album of phonograph records, which she deposited carefully on Miss Matt's maple end table.

"Are those *your* records?" Miss Matt asked hesitantly.

"Marian said I could come and ask you if it is all right for me to play them here on your phonograph," the child said. "What's that?" She pointed at the Cézanne.

"It's a picture," Miss Matt said.

"We have pictures too," the child said. "We have pictures of my daddy."

"Won't you sit down?"

The child turned and looked at Miss Matt for a long minute. "All right," she said finally. "What's your name?"

"Miss Matt," Miss Matt said. "You may call me Miss Matt."

"Mine's Krishna," the child said.

"Krishna." Miss Matt sat down and picked up her cup of tea. "Krishna?"

"Krishna Raleigh," the child said. "I'm six years old and I live just downstairs and right underneath here." Both she and Miss Matt looked down at the floor, and then Krishna went on, "Marian said I could come and play my records here."

"Who is Marian?" Miss Matt asked, "and why should she give you permission to come up here?"

"That's my mother, Marian," Krishna said impatiently.

"I think it's all right." Miss Matt tried to make her voice sound a little doubtful, as though she felt enough authority to deny Krishna if she wanted to, but she realized almost immediately that all Krishna thought was that possibly Miss Matt did not own the phonograph either. "What records are they?" Miss Matt asked quickly.

"My daddy's records," Krishna said proudly. "My daddy made them for me and Marian, and you can listen to them if you want to."

Miss Matt stood up and reached for the album, but Krishna said "*I'll* do it" and ran across the room to put an arm protectingly over the album. "They're *my* records," she said.

"May I look at them?" Miss Matt asked coldly.

"No," Krishna said. She opened the album lovingly and took out the first record. "This is my daddy playing the piano," she said. "Take that other record off the phonograph." Miss Matt went silently and removed *The Sorcerer's Apprentice* and changed the needle while Krishna stood by, impatiently holding her record. "I play the phonograph all the time at home, but now it's broken," she said, "so Marian said I could come and ask you if you would let me hear my daddy's records."

The edge of Krishna's chin came just to the level of the turntable; she was forced, reluctantly, to yield the record to Miss Matt to have it put on the phonograph, and Miss Matt inspected it carefully, turning it over and over, before she placed it onto the turntable. It was a private recording, labeled TOWN HALL, and then, in ink underneath, "James Raleigh, Shostakovich Polka, June, 1940." The other side was smooth and ungrooved; Miss Matt ran her hand over it before she set it down.

"Come *on*," Krishna said finally. "This record has where my daddy talks on it." She waited, her face just at the edge of the phonograph, and when Miss Matt started to put the phonograph arm down on the record, Krishna giggled and said, "*These* records start from the inside, dopey." Miss Matt put the arm down at the center of the record and waited. First there was the sound of applause, and then a short wait, and then a man's voice said faintly ". . . by Shostakovich," and then more applause. "That's my daddy talking," Krishna said. Miss Matt waited respectfully until the piano started and then said, "Is that your father playing?"

"He played all these records," Krishna said. "He plays the piano in concerts." Her voice rose defiantly. "He's the best piano player who ever lived."

Miss Matt sat down on the straight chair next to the phonograph. "Would you like to sit on the couch?" she asked Krishna.

Krishna went over solemnly and sat down on the edge of the couch, and Miss Matt, with the music loud beside her, watched the child curiously. She was a very pretty child, with blond curls and a sweet smile; Miss Matt wondered fleetingly if her father was blond. "Where is your father now?" she asked.

"Shhh," Krishna said, pointing to the phonograph. "He's in the Army."

Miss Matt nodded sympathetically.

"He kills people," Krishna said. "He's over killing Nazis now." She sighed theatrically. "He used to play the piano, and when he's killed all the Nazis he's going to come home and play the piano again."

"He plays beautifully," Miss Matt said softly.

"It's all right," Krishna said. Her eyes wandered around the room and came to rest finally. "What's that thing?"

Miss Matt stood up and lifted the arm of the phonograph from the record. "I thought you wanted to hear your daddy playing," she said.

"What's that thing?" Krishna repeated.

Miss Matt turned. "It's a doll," she said with annoyance. "Do you want to hear the records or not?"

"I want that doll," Krishna said. She slid off the couch and scampered across the room to the doll.

"I bought that doll in a place called Panama," Miss Matt said. "I bought it from a little girl about your age whose mother made lots of dolls like that. I like that doll as well as almost anything I own." She raised her voice slightly. "Shall I continue with the records?"

Krishna was trying to reach for the doll high in the bookcase where Miss Matt kept it; finally she put her foot on the lower shelf, pushing the books back, and reached up on her toes to seize the doll triumphantly. It was a limp thing, with a gourd for a head and a scrap of red silk for a dress. "I'm going to take this doll home," Krishna said.

"That's my doll." Miss Matt forced herself to stand by the phonograph. "Your mother wouldn't like to have you take someone else's things."

"She doesn't care," Krishna said.

"Krishna," Miss Matt said, "You may not have that doll. Put it back, please."

Krishna turned and looked at Miss Matt in surprise. "I want it," she said.

"I won't let you play your daddy's records on the phonograph," Miss Matt warned.

"All right." Krishna was pulling interestedly at the doll's head, twisting the red silk dress. "I heard them lots of times."

Miss Matt walked over and put her hand firmly on the doll. "Give that to me," she demanded.

Krishna began to laugh. She snatched the doll away from Miss Matt and retreated with it across the room. "You're a crazy old woman," she said. "You're an old crazy old woman."

"Go home," Miss Matt said. She took a deep breath to calm herself, and lifted her head. "Go right home. Go home immediately."

"No," Krishna said. "You're a crazy old woman, crazy, crazy." Deliberately holding the doll out in front of her, she ripped off the silk dress and let it fall onto the floor, then snapped off the head. Miss Matt watched Krishna for a minute, her chin trembling, and then she went over to the phonograph and lifted the record off and smashed it onto the floor. "You don't deserve to have a father like that," she said.

Krishna began to laugh again. "Wait till I tell Marian," she said. "Wait till I tell Marian a crazy old woman broke my daddy's best record where he was talking."

"You can tell Marian anything you like," Miss Matt said. For the first time in her life her voice was shrill. "Now you take the rest of these records and get out." She seized Krishna quickly by the shoulder, pinching as hard as she could, and began to push her toward the door, slapping her hands to make her drop the pieces of the doll.

Krishna, still laughing, clung stubbornly to the door frame, bracing her feet against Miss Matt's furious shoving. Miss Matt finally got her into the hall and slammed the door, then took the album of records and set them quickly outside, slamming the door again before Krishna could get back in. Krishna was still laughing when Miss Matt slammed the door for the second time and turned the key, but when the child realized that the door had shut for the last time, her laughter turned suddenly into howls of anger. Miss Matt, leaning against the door on the inside, distinguished the phrase, repeated over and over, "I want that doll!" Finally Miss Matt heard the crying fade away toward the stairs, and the child's voice crying, "Mommy, make her give me that doll!"

I've got to hurry, Miss Matt thought. She stepped quickly around the broken record on the floor to the broken doll, scooped up the dress and then the other pieces, and hesitated, looking around. Finally she went into the kitchenette and opened the cupboard under the sink, and put the pieces of the doll behind the boxes of soap and the dusting cloths. I'll tell them that awful child did it, she was thinking. If I hurry, I can say that child did it all. Still hurrying, she took a brush and a dustpan and went back to the broken record. It had shattered into small pieces, and it took Miss Matt a few precious seconds to gather them up into the dustpan. I'll tell them I'll sue, she was thinking. She emptied the dustpan into a paper bag and put the bag into the sink cupboard with the doll, and then, her house straightened, with no sign left of Krishna's presence, she fluffed up the pillows of the couch and went into her little bedroom, where she dressed hurriedly and carelessly, repeating to herself incoherently: "I'll tell them the child did it, I'll say I'll sue."

She pulled on a hat over her still-damp hair, tucking the straggling ends up under the hat and holding them there with many hairpins. When she put her coat on, she turned up the collar and ducked her head down so her face would be hidden. Then she picked up her pocketbook and went out, closing the door behind her quietly. Go to the movies where it's dark, she was thinking. When she got down the first flight of stairs and was near the door of the apartment directly under hers, she hesitated for a minute before she ran down the hall to the next flight of stairs. Come back later, she thought, when they're all tired of looking for me.

Period Piece

Mrs. Van Corn had not been out of the house in seven months. She could walk perfectly well, although she disliked it; she was not particularly afraid of subways or taxis; she was not pregnant, sick, or discouraged with the things she saw. Mrs. Van Corn had simply not been out of the house because she liked staying inside. "It's the things that happen to me," she would explain seriously to her few intimate friends who were allowed inside the house to visit her. "I do so detest mud, and people, and so many ugly things happen . . . like . . ." And Mrs. Van Corn would allow her voice to trail off significantly, and whatever friend was listening would nod, and shrug sympathetically, and murmur.

Mrs. Van Corn always referred to the incident of the dog by a significant silence, and her friends always understood. The incident of the dog had been the direct cause of Mrs. Van Corn's deciding to remain inside the house. She had been outside shopping one day, with George, the chauffeur, waiting carefully outside the doors of the shops, and she had been leaving the hairdresser, displeased at something. She had almost reached the car (with George standing carefully by the open door) when a dog—not a Fifth Avenue dog—

had come up and put its head under her skirt. "His nose, you know," Mrs. Van Corn subsequently explained, faintly. It had been necessary for George to help her carefully into the car and take her home immediately. When she reached home and had been assisted to her room, Mrs. Van Corn concluded that she did not belong in the outside world, and made her decision to stay at home.

"After all," she said, "there's no need to expose oneself needlessly to these things." And so Mrs. Van Corn stayed at home. Mr. Van Corn, who went out every day, brought her back news of the outside world ("I saw Mark Carstairs the other day, and he sends his regards and asks may he call . . ."), and Mrs. Van Corn's son, Howard, who was usually away at college, brought home occasional college acquaintances to cheer his mother up.

Mrs. Van Corn was never bored. There was much to do around the house, and there were always her friends. She rested comfortably, fragile in lace, in a quiet room and waited for nice people to come to her, and nice people came, chatted, and departed. Rarely was Mrs. Van Corn disturbed by her guests. Perhaps one of them would speak loudly—this happened infrequently—and the guest would not return. "I can't bear harshness," Mrs. Van Corn would say afterward, appealingly. "I can't endure unpleasantness, you know." And so, when Howard came unexpectedly home from college to meet his mother's gracious kiss, and her charmed "Oh, is it vacation again, my dear?"—when Howard came home, he hesitated before speaking to his mother about the very urgent matter that had brought him to her. He sat instead at her feet, upon an embroidered pillow that Mrs. Van Corn kept for her lapdog, and spoke to her softly and graciously. But when conversation had died, and Mrs. Van Corn was sitting with her hands in her lap gazing wistfully upon space, Howard ventured:

"Mother . . . I'm a little worried."

"Yes, dear?" His mother's eyes rested upon him tenderly.

"I don't suppose you've heard . . . It's about conscription."

"Yes, dear?"

"You see, they want to take people about my age and make them join a sort of army . . ."

"An army, my dear?"

"Well . . . yes. A sort of army."

"But are we at war? I mean . . . I'm afraid I don't quite understand, Howard."

"Not war," Howard said, stumbling a little. "It's for peace, somehow, Mother. They take all the boys between the ages of twenty-one and thirty-one, I think, and they train them to be soldiers in case there *is* a war. Understand?"

Mrs. Van Corn nodded seriously.

"And they make them go, even if they don't want to go, and I don't want to go."

"Why not?"

"Because . . . well, I want to finish college, and I don't want to be in an army . . ."

Mrs. Van Corn was trying very hard to understand. "But, dear, I don't quite see. Won't all your young friends be with you? I mean, won't it be quite gay for you?"

"But it will be so dreadful. I'll have to drill all day, and work, and learn to shoot a gun . . ."

Mrs. Van Corn leaned back with her eyes closed, and Howard paused, contrite.

"Mother, I'm so sorry. I didn't mean to say anything to distress you. Just, about the guns . . . Well, you see why I would prefer not to go . . ."

Mrs. Van Corn lifted her hand to her cheek. "Please, Howard," she said. "Please don't discuss the details with me anymore."

"Will you make my father fix it so I don't have to go, then?"

"I prefer not to think about it," Mrs. Van Corn said.

Howard waited for a moment, and then he began again. "Mother," he said.

"Yes, my dear?"

"Mother, there's going to be a war, you know."

"Is there, dear?" asked Mrs. Van Corn, obviously believing that the subject had been changed.

"Very soon, Mother. Does it worry you?"

"Your father mentioned it. He said it would be a good thing. He said we might do worse than go to war. War, he says, is a noble thing." Mrs. Van Corn was quite tired out from the effort of remembering all this. She lay back again.

"People like my father," said Howard desperately, "believe in war as a benefit to mankind, because it solves unemployment and things."

Mrs. Van Corn nodded. "Perhaps it does," she said.

"But, Mother," Howard said, "if I were in this peacetime army thing, I would have to go to war."

"Is there a war?"

"There will be."

"And you will go to war, my dear?"

"If I am in the army I will."

Mrs. Van Corn opened her eyes, and looked seriously at Howard. "My dear," she said, "I would be proud of you."

Howard stared. "Why?"

"War is a noble thing," Mrs. Van Corn said, and closed her eyes again.

"But I might get shot, or wounded, Mother," Howard said. "Mother," he added urgently, "you wouldn't want to see me blind, would you? Or shell-shocked?"

"*Please*, Howard!" his mother said, sitting up straight.

"But you wouldn't like to have to take care of me, would you?"

"There are institutions for such cases," Mrs. Van Corn said vaguely.

Howard took a deep breath. "Suppose I was killed, Mother?"

"Your grandfather fought in the Civil War, my dear," Mrs. Van Corn said firmly. "And he was a hero."

Howard stood up. "Very well, Mother," he said. "There is only one thing for me to do. I shall get married, and so be exempt from conscription."

"Married?" Mrs. Van Corn exclaimed. "Why, Howard, my dear boy!"

"Immediately," Howard said.

"Some nice girl," Mrs. Van Corn said dreamily, "some *sweet* girl."

"Then I won't have to go," Howard said, almost tearfully.

"Bring her up to dinner *soon*," Mrs. Van Corn said.

"But, Mother—"

"After all, my dear, you are getting on to the age when a man must assume his responsibilities. And I think that a wife . . . and a grandson," Mrs. Van Corn went on rather more bleakly. "But a young wife," she added happily. "Bring her soon, really, Howard. Tomorrow?"

"But . . ." Howard began. Then: "Yes, Mother," he said, controlling his voice, and then, immediately: "Will you excuse me, please, Mother?"

"Of course, my dear boy," Mrs. Van Corn said, opening her eyes. "Run along, my dear."

As Howard left the room, Mrs. Van Corn watched him affectionately. "The dear boy," she said to herself. "A wife! Such a gay wedding. And clothes!" I shall go out to the wedding, Mrs. Van Corn decided suddenly. I am sure everything will be charming at my own son's wedding. Then: "The dear boy," she said, and let her eyes close again.

4-F Party

RICKEY PARKER WAS OUT IN THE KITCHEN COUNTING GLASSES WHEN the doorbell rang. He looked through the kitchen door, saw Pearl just putting down her cigarette preparatory to rising, and then, coming out of the kitchen holding a bottle of bourbon, he said: "I'll get it. It's probably Jillie and that cousin of hers."

Pearl rose and stood in the living room near the piano, waiting. When she saw that it was Jillie and her cousin, she stepped forward after the flurry of greetings and introductions and took Rickey by the arm. "So glad to see you," Pearl said in her best voice to the cousin. "It's nice of you to come around with Jillie."

"Pearl, darling," Jillie said, "this is Ruth. I call her Ruthie. She's adorable. You'll love her. She's without a husband now too, and I think we're going to have grand times together, all of us."

"I'm so glad you could come tonight," Pearl said to Ruth. "It must be very lonely for you at first."

"It is, a little," Ruth said. She was very small and spoke in a little voice, looking up at Pearl and barely smiling. "I guess I'll be okay, though."

Rickey had Jillie's coat and had taken her by the arm and was pulling her into the kitchen. "So that's what I was thinking," he said.

"I thought, If there are really eight women for every man, why shouldn't I be the man. . . ." They disappeared into the kitchen, and the door swung back and forth behind them.

"Come in and sit down, won't you?" Pearl said. She felt eager to be a good hostess, to see that Ruth was comfortable and warm. I imagine she has that effect on everyone, Pearl thought suddenly, men especially. "How long has your husband been gone?"

Ruth sat down on the couch and folded her hands on her lap, not looking at them. "Not long yet," she said. "Two weeks, about."

"Are you here just visiting with Jillie?" Pearl asked. "Or permanently, or what?"

"I'm going to get a job here, I think," Ruth said hopefully. "Welding, maybe."

"Ever done it before?" The doorbell rang again. Pearl half rose, waiting for Rickey.

He called from the kitchen: "Will you answer that, Pearl?"

"We're making drinks," Jillie added.

Pearl went to the door and opened it. "Audrey," she said, "hello." Why do women always look so funny alone at night? she thought. I guess you're so used to seeing them with *someone*. "How are you?" she asked.

"*Darling*," Audrey said, "such an incredible taxi driver! He was so funny; wait till you hear."

"I can't wait," Pearl said.

"I can't repeat it," Audrey said, "I'll die. Jillie here?"

"Hello," Jillie said from the kitchen doorway. "Rickey and I made you people some powerful drinks."

Rickey came into the doorway behind Jillie. "Another of my girlfriends," he said. "Meet the one man left in town, Audrey."

"He's crazy," Jillie said. "He says he's going to get eight girls for himself, because that's the ratio these days."

"I'm going to love every minute of this," Rickey said. "Everyone go sit down and I'll bring this stuff in."

Pearl led Audrey over to Ruth and introduced them. "Ruth's husband left only two weeks ago," she added.

"You poor kid," Audrey said. "Mine left seven months ago."

"Don't pay any attention to her, dear," Pearl said. "She really misses him terribly."

"Where is he now?" Ruth asked in her soft voice.

"Good Lord!" Audrey shrugged elaborately. "Would they tell me? I get letters from everywhere—he could be in Berlin!"

Ruth looked at Audrey. "Seven months is a long time," she said.

"We're all in the same boat," Pearl said, "except me. What with Rickey not being taken at all, I'm probably going to be the only wife left in town before long."

"Imagine being stuck with Rickey for the duration!" Audrey said.

"You're all stuck with Rickey for the duration," Rickey said, coming into the room with a tray. Jillie followed him, with a bowl of pretzels in each hand. "I'm the one 4-F in sight, girls, and you'd better get used to the idea now."

"Where'll I put this stuff?" Jillie asked. "You comfortable, Ruthie?"

Ruth nodded.

"Silly kid's lonesome as hell," Jillie said. "Just been married a few months."

"Really?" Pearl said to Ruth.

"Not quite a year," Ruth said softly.

"My. God." Audrey rose and stood dramatically by the piano. "Look, everyone," she said, "here's the ideal state. Married just long enough to get the fun of it, and then *grass-widowed for—*"

Pearl cut in quickly, "Where is *your* husband now?"

"He's in Texas somewhere," Ruth said. She accepted the drink Rickey held out to her. "Thank you so much," she said.

"I want all you girls to know," Rickey said, "I want all you girls to know that from now on I'm the big shot around here. From now on you girls are going to be mixing drinks for me, and bringing me my slippers, and crowding around me so thick—" He began to sing, waving a drink in his hand. "'Over hill, over dale, da-da-da-da-da-da-da, as the 4-Fs go rolling along. . . . .'"

"Rickey!" Pearl said. Rickey looked at her over his shoulder.

"Listen, dear wife," he said, "you've got to make up your mind to share me with all these charming ladies from now on. I'm just coming into my own."

"Why don't you ration yourself?" Pearl asked bitterly.

Rickey said immediately: "A young man deciding to ration—"

"Himself and his primitive passion," Audrey added.

"Himself and his primitive *elation*," Jillie insisted.

"He said, 'I can afford,'" Rickey said, "To be high and adored—"

"Because I myself am all the fashion," Audrey finished.

"*Fay*shion," Jillie said.

Pearl went over quietly to where Audrey was sitting. "What do you hear from Carl?" she asked.

"The same old thing," Audrey said. "He's working hard, and very happy to be—"

Rickey had heard them, and he interrupted with a shout: "Another man's name! Another man's name has been mentioned in my presence!"

"There, darling," Jillie said. She put her arm around Rickey. "You still have me and Ruthie."

"They ought to give me the Purple Heart for this," Rickey said. "Talk about wounded in action."

"Like to play bridge, or something?" Pearl asked Audrey. "This is liable to go on and on."

Rickey got up and went over to stand in front of Pearl. "Listen," he said, "we're just having a lot of fun, trying to make these girls forget that they're all alone and maybe show them a good time. Why do you have to go spoiling everything?"

"You can only handle one at a time, dear," Pearl said, with a smile she knew was not as kind as it might be. "We have to work in shifts, after all."

"Swing shift," Jillie said instantly.

Rickey began to laugh. "My good old Jillie," he said.

Pearl caught Ruth's eye, and Ruth went across the room to where Pearl was sitting with Audrey. "You two look so confidential," Ruth said, "I'm afraid to interrupt."

"Don't be silly." Audrey smiled. "We're just talking."

"I thought there might be something we could do," Pearl said. "Maybe even some silly game. After all, you probably didn't come to hear Rickey make a fool of himself."

"Honestly," Ruth said, leaning against the fireplace, "it's nice just being with people."

Rickey and Jillie, arm in arm, bore down on them, singing, "'As the 4-Fs go rolling along.'"

"What you girls gossiping about?" Rickey demanded.

"We were just talking to Ruth," Audrey said.

"Seems to me I barely met you," Rickey said, looking at Ruth. "You're without a husband too, aren't you?"

"Only two weeks without," Ruth said shyly.

"Wait a while," Rickey said. "Where's the old man?"

"My husband?" Ruth said. "In Texas, somewhere, typing."

"Typing?"

"He's only limited service," Ruth explained, turning to Pearl. "His eyes."

"Mrs. Limited Service," Rickey shouted, hoisting his glass. "Here's to Mrs. Limited Service." And to Ruth he prompted, "A big strong man in spite of his eyes, though?"

"He's nice and strong," Ruth admitted. She turned to Pearl again. "It's just because of his eyes," she repeated.

Jillie giggled. "If anything could keep you from missing your big strong husband," she said, putting an arm around Rickey's shoulder, "it's this big strong 4-F."

"It's my blood pressure," Rickey said. "Every time I see a lovely girl like Ruthie, it goes up and up and up and up and up—"

"That's why they won't let him in the Army," Pearl said.

"I'm sorry," Ruth said to Rickey. "That you're not in the Army, I mean."

"Dear little Ruthie," Rickey said, "she'd miss me if I went. Just pretend I'm your husband," he said to Ruth. "I'm the only man left in town, and I intend to make the most of it."

"I'm beginning to feel like a fraction of a wife," Pearl said. "Bridge—Jillie? Audrey? Ruth?"

"Honey," Audrey was saying to Ruth, "you'll find you're not so lonesome after a while. After all, he won't expect you to shut yourself away from everything."

"You think he's behaving wherever he is?" Jillie added.

"Bridge?" Pearl said insistently, her hand on Ruth's arm.

"Look," Audrey said, "mine's been gone so long. . . . I figure he doesn't want to come back to any cross old maid."

"I won't be any cross old maid," Ruth said.

"What you want to do," Jillie said helpfully, "is have a little fun. Enjoy life. Have a good time."

"I missed mine *terribly* for a while," Audrey said.

"I told you, darling," Jillie said to Ruth. "We'll cheer you up if anyone can."

"*I'll* cheer her up," Rickey said. "Who's the man around here?"

Ruth laughed. "I'm not worried," she said.

"Ruthie," Rickey said, "all my life I've been waiting for a girl like you. You're my ideal, I think. Come, kiss me."

Ruth laughed again.

"Listen," Rickey said heroically, "you'll be glad enough to find a guy like me before the war's over."

"Rickey," Pearl said, "you shouldn't talk like that."

Rickey waved one hand at Pearl. "Don't listen to her," he said. "She's a sour old woman."

"Go on, Ruth," Pearl said, "make him shut up."

Ruth looked at Pearl for a minute, then stood still while Rickey came across to her, leaned over and kissed her quickly, and stepped back. "Next shift," he said.

"Happy now?" Pearl snapped at Rickey.

"Don't rush," Rickey said. "It'll be your turn in a minute."

Ruth stood for a moment where Rickey had left her, then walked out into the hall and picked up her coat. Pearl rose to stop her just as the door closed.

"Well," Rickey said into the silence, "what a lousy sport *she* was."

Pearl sighed. "Bridge, girls?" she asked.

The Paradise

WHEN HE GOT OFF THE TRAIN, THE VAGUE FEELING OF APPREHENsion that had followed him all the way from camp turned into an acute, embarrassed terror; he stood on the station platform wondering where he could turn and run to, and someone passed him, looked at him curiously, and said, "Back again, Bert?" Then he knew it was too late, and without thinking he started down toward his home.

He passed the candy store and wondered briefly if it would be worthwhile taking her a box of toffee, but then, feeling the bulk of the bracelet in his pocket, he thought, No, that's enough, maybe I'll get her something else later. Within a block of his home he met his ten-year-old brother-in-law, and the kid grinned and said, "Hi, Bert, what you doing home?"

"Just back for a day or two," Bert said uncomfortably, hurrying past; the kid would certainly tell the whole town he was back.

"She ain't home; her and Ella's down at the Paradise," his brother-in-law bawled after him as he reached his front gate; he opened it and went up the steps two at a time. The door was unlocked. As he pushed it shut behind him, he said tentatively, "Gladys?"

There was mail on the dining room table, put down hastily: a letter for her from his mother, a couple of bills. Bert turned his mother's letter over in his hands for a minute and then put it down again; he knew what it said. He went into the kitchen; she had had a cup of coffee that afternoon; the coffeepot was still faintly warm under his hand. There was a package of bacon in the refrigerator, and a couple of eggs. Breakfast, he thought, and went on into the bedroom. The bed was mussed, and a magazine lay facedown, with half a chocolate bar on its cover. Her housecoat was on the floor of the closet. He left the bedroom and walked back through the kitchen, stopping to look into the bathroom (her powder box still open and a bath towel on the floor), and then into the living room again. "Gladys?" he called softly once more, his hand on the front door. Then he went out into the street again, walking quickly and lightly, his small feet moving with certainty along the familiar sidewalk.

The Paradise was far enough away so that by the time Bert had walked there he was quieted, and his hands were no longer shaking. He lit a cigarette, standing outside the double door, and then he went in. It was an orderly place, well swept and dark, with a bar at the front and booths in the back. It was nearly deserted by now; the respectable people who drank here had gone home to their dinners, and the unrespectable people had gone on to livelier, brighter places. He stood for a minute to get used to the darkness, and heard Gladys's voice clearly: "But I'm not *hungry.*"

She was near the back, sitting in a booth with her sister, Ella, and Ella's friend Frank, and a man Bert didn't know. Bert walked softly back and stood at the entrance of the booth, looking at them for a minute before Ella recognized him in the near dark. "It's Bertie," she shrieked. "Bertie's home again."

"Hey, soldier," Frank said cheerfully, "the war's over. Didn't they tell you out there in the sticks?" He reached out his foot and pulled a chair to the table. "Sit down, Corporal," he said. "Let's get you a beer."

They were all drinking beer. Bert looked at Gladys, and she said, "Hello, Bertie," and smiled. The man sitting next to her looked at him and said, "Hi."

"How come you're back?" Frank asked. "What you doing home again so quick? They can't stand him around that Army," he told Ella. "They keep sending him home."

"I don't blame them," Ella said, and giggled.

"You didn't write," Gladys said to him. "I would have known you were coming if you wrote me."

"Well, it's good to see you," Frank said. "You know Walter, here?" He pointed to the strange man.

"Hi," Walter said.

"Look, Gladys," Bert said, "why don't we go on home? I got a lot to talk to you about."

The corners of Gladys's mouth turned down, and she put her head back and drew up her shoulders. "I can't," she said. "I want to stay here."

"You're not going to start that again, are you, Bert?" Ella demanded. "Because if you are, I'm leaving. Frank and I'll go someplace else where we don't have to listen."

"I'm not doing anything," Bert said. "I just want to talk to my wife, is all."

"I don't want to talk," Gladys said. "I want to stay here."

"And that's that," Frank said. "Have a beer, Bert."

"He hasn't any right," Ella was saying to Walter. "He just can't stand seeing anyone have a nice time."

"Bert isn't going to be mean anymore," Gladys said. "Listen, Bert, you go along home and I'll be there in . . ." She thought. "In an hour."

"Why should he go home?" Frank put his hand affectionately on Bert's arm. "Let him stick around and have a drink."

"Go on up to Mom's," Ella said. "She'll give you something to eat."

"I saw your brother," Bert said to Gladys. "He told me where you were."

"He followed us," Gladys said. "Walter gave him a dollar." She laughed. "Like in the comics."

The waiter brought a glass of beer and put it on the table in front of Bert, and Frank paid for it. "I'm buying you a beer, Corporal," he said.

Bert hesitated for a minute, then sat down wearily. "Look, Gladys," he said, "I'm just here for a couple of days. You ought to listen to what I have to say."

"I'm listening," Gladys said. She leaned forward, her chin on her hands. "See?" she said.

"All right, dammit," Bert said. He put his hands on the table and looked at them through the glass of beer; he had small hands, hardly larger than Gladys's. That's why I don't knock one of these guys down, he thought. I'm not scared; it's just that I'm not much bigger than Gladys. He looked at her and saw that she was winking at Ella. "I guess I'm going to get a divorce," he said. "My mother thinks I ought to divorce you."

"What for?" Gladys asked blankly. When all the excitement went out of her face it was little and pale, like a rabbit's, or like the face of some small, staring fish.

"Divorce Gladys?" Ella said. "What would she do?"

"She could go back and work in the factory," Bert said. "It wouldn't have anything to do with me anymore."

"That's no way to talk," Frank said. "You're not being fair to Gladys."

"But I didn't do anything," Gladys said.

Bert looked down at his hands again instead of looking at Gladys, and he spoke very slowly and carefully so that nobody would make any mistakes about him. "My mother says our getting married was a mistake, and that when I'm out of the Army you won't settle down and we shouldn't try to stay married. And we were only married for a few days before I left, so it isn't as though . . ." He stopped helplessly, then began again: "So they gave me an emergency furlough." He looked at Gladys. "That means trouble at home. You think I like chasing you into every bar in town?" he finished desperately.

Gladys's lip trembled. "I didn't do anything," she said. "I write you every single week, and I tell you every single thing I've been doing. It's not nice to talk like that."

"Why don't we go someplace else?" Walter asked suddenly. "I want to eat."

Ella began to talk across the table to Walter again. "You know what people are going to say about a girl Gladys's age who gets divorced by her husband, and it isn't very nice to think of people talking like that about your own sister."

"You see why I wanted to go home?" Bert said. "This is no place to talk about something serious."

"Seventeen," Ella went on, her voice rising. "Only seventeen years old, my sister is. And what are people going to say?"

Walter stood up and reached for his coat on the rack. "I'm going someplace and eat," he said. Dragging his coat after him, he started for the door.

"Let's all go," Ella said. "We can talk later." She shoved impatiently at Frank to get him to let her out of the booth, and Gladys slid along the seat on her side to get out. Bert caught her by the arm. "Listen, Gladys," he said softly. "Let them go wherever they want to. We'll go home."

She pulled her arm away, not looking at him, and he said desperately, "I'll be gone by tomorrow night."

"Come *on*, Gladys," Ella said. "You can bring Bert."

"Look," Bert said to Gladys, "I thought we could go to the hotel for dinner. It's Saturday; we could dance, too, for a while."

Gladys looked at him. "I don't want to," she said.

"I brought you a bracelet," Bert said. "I didn't want to give it to you with all of them watching." He touched her arm again. "Listen, Gladys," he said, "I'm just going to be here for one night."

"Wait a minute, then," Gladys said ungraciously, and hurried to catch Ella. They talked for a minute while Walter waited impatiently at the door, and then Gladys said, "See you Monday, at my place," and came back to Bert.

"It's okay," she said. "Ella doesn't mind. They'll get someone else for Walter."

He took her coat down and held it for her to put on. "You'll like it down at the hotel."

She turned the corners of her mouth down again. "You *said . . .* " she began.

"Okay, okay," Bert said quickly.

When they got out to the street it was dark, and Ella and Frank and Walter were already out of sight. Gladys started walking toward the brighter part of town, toward the hotel, and Bert caught up with her. "We've got to talk about this, though, seriously," he said insistently.

She looked up at him and smiled. Then, as they walked along, she curled her hand under his arm and leaned up against him affectionately.

"Nice old Bert," she said.

Homecoming

JUDITH WALKED UP THE SUBWAY STAIRS AND INTO THE DAYLIGHT WITH the tired, anticlimactic feeling that comes after something exciting and final is over. She tried to make herself believe that it was because she had gone to a movie, strangely, alone in the afternoon, instead of in the evening with the girls from her office. The next movie she went to, she thought suddenly, she would be with her husband again, sitting beside him in the darkness after such a long time.

She walked quickly down the street and stopped in front of her market, watching to see if her son, Robbie, was visible. He would be wearing his little blue overalls that fit like a sailor's pants, and he would be accompanied by Judith's friend Sally, who picked him up every afternoon after nursery school and watched over him until Judith got home.

After looking around for a minute, Judith turned and entered the market, thinking that shopping early might be easier, before the market's usual six o'clock rush. The market was almost empty; no one in this neighborhood shopped at four in the afternoon; they were there either at ten in the morning, if they were home during the day, or after five-thirty, on their way back from work. At the meat counter Judith stood uninspired before the trays of meat.

The butcher came toward her cheerfully. "What can I do for you?" he asked, smiling.

Judith smiled. "I wish I knew," she said. "What shall I have for dinner?"

"Nice chops?" the butcher suggested. "Some very nice pork chops."

"No, thanks," Judith said.

"Liver?"

"Give me a little piece for the baby," Judith said. She hesitated. "I want a roast," she said. "A chicken, maybe."

The butcher was reaching into the counter, selecting a piece of liver. "Going to have company?" he said.

"Yes," Judith said. "My husband's coming home."

The butcher stood up behind the counter and said, "Isn't that fine. Now, isn't that the best news I've had today." He smiled at Judith. "You'll want a nice chicken for sure," he said. "Men like chicken."

"I guess they do," Judith said.

"Let me see," the butcher said, turning over the chickens. "He was in France, wasn't he?"

"In France," Judith said.

"About four pounds?" the butcher said.

Judith looked up and found the butcher watching her expectantly. "I don't know," she said. "It doesn't matter."

The butcher leaned across the counter. "Listen," he said, "don't you worry. He's coming back, isn't he?"

"Tomorrow, I think," Judith said.

"Then you got nothing to worry about," the butcher said. "It's the ones still over there you got to worry about. My wife," he said, putting his elbows on the counter and still watching Judith, "my wife, you ought to of heard her when she thought I was going. I got turned down," he added parenthetically. "High blood pressure. Anyway, she took on like I was being sent to jail, and I kept telling her, 'Listen,' I said to her, 'fighting the Germans is no worse than fighting you,' and she'd quiet right down. She didn't have a word to say."

"I shouldn't think so," Judith said.

"Not a word to say," the butcher said. "So you see you got nothing to worry about." He stood up and took hold of his knife. "Cut it up for frying?"

Judith stared. Then after a minute she nodded and said, "Please. Do you have any extra livers?"

"You going to save them for your husband?" the butcher demanded.

"Yes," Judith said.

"Then I got some," the butcher said.

Judith watched him put the tiny sharp knife into the chicken with a concerned expression on his face, and then she said hastily, "I'll just get my groceries," and turned away to the other side of the store. The clerk who came to wait on her was an old friend, and he greeted her cheerfully: "Got a quarter pound of butter for you," he said immediately.

Judith smiled at him. "I'll need it," she said, checking herself against the inclination to tell everyone, "My husband's coming home, you know." If I told him, I could get half a pound, she thought, and said quickly, "I'll need a dozen eggs." We'll have scrambled eggs and sausages the first morning, she thought, six eggs and one for Robbie, two to make a chocolate cake, if I haven't forgotten how; I can always throw it out before he gets home. "Do you have any cooking chocolate? And two containers of milk."

She discussed honeydew melons solemnly with the clerk: they were expensive. Were they ripe enough? Were they worth serving his first morning home, Judith wondered. She finally bought one, and a dozen oranges. Green peas to go with the chicken, carrots for her supper and Robbie's that night. Judith chose her vegetables carefully: one pound of peas—in case it was all a mistake, she thought crazily, she and Robbie could eat them; one bunch of carrots for dinner and enough left over for Robbie's lunch. "I don't want to buy too much," she said to the clerk suddenly.

The clerk was surprised. "What's the matter?" he said. "You expect your victory garden to come up all of a sudden?"

Judith realized how silly she sounded. "Loaf of rye bread," she said. "Small. And a pound of your special coffee, ground very fine." I bought the last pound less than a week ago, she thought; I must be drinking a lot.

"That all?" asked the clerk.

Judith looked at the groceries piled on the counter. "It doesn't look like very much," she said, "and yet I spend all my money every week."

"You've got to eat," the clerk said.

"Cheese," Judith said. "Give me a quarter pound of blue cheese." I'll try not to make it look fancy, she thought, but that will let him know it's an occasion, cheese and crackers with dessert.

Judith paid the clerk and gave him the points for the butter and cheese. Then, carrying the large bag, she went back to the meat counter. There were one or two other customers there now, and it was a minute before the butcher got to her. Judith could see her package waiting for her and tried to figure out how much it would cost. She had spent more than she should have, as usual. But tomorrow was an old life recommencing, and she had now a faint feeling that since he'd left, she and Robbie had gotten along somehow without shopping, without food, ration points, or money. The butcher came up to her and handed her the package.

"Little bit excited?" he asked, smiling down the counter at his other customers. "I don't blame you."

As Judith walked out the door, she could feel the other women watching her go before they turned to the butcher, who was probably telling them, "Her husband's coming home from France. Has a little boy, too, two and a half years old." They would say, "How nice," and "This is a big day for her," and then one of them would tell about her sister, she had three children, and they took her husband, who had an ulcer.

Judith went up the steps to the house, still smiling. By the time she got up the stairs, she had carried the story of the sister with three children to the point where her husband was in Kentucky and hadn't had a furlough in eight months. There was a note on the door: "Robbie and I have gone out to get tight on the money from Robbie's penny bank. See you later, Sally." Thinking gratefully of a few minutes sitting quietly by herself, Judith took the note off the door and unlocked her apartment.

Everything was standing quietly waiting for her. The furniture was still there, solid and at home with the walls and the fireplace. Beyond, through the doorway, the bedroom waited, shades at the windows drawn to exactly the same level, the blue curtains still over the windows, the bed big and restful and well made.

She set her packages down on the kitchen table and put the meat away. Almost everything went into the refrigerator. Gradually, over a period of months, her kitchen had been emptied of staples; she had bought flour and sugar and baking powder and salt in small quantities, and she and Robbie had slowly used them up. Now, with her husband coming home again, the shelves in the refrigerator and the cabinet were almost bare. Boxes of cereal for Robbie, a can or two of soup, the canisters shining and clean, looking empty from the outside. No extras; the box of candy someone had given her, standing unopened on one of the shelves, seemed suddenly like an outrage, a quiet offense against good taste. Most of these details she hardly realized, gathering from her kitchen only that it was necessary to start fresh from solid wood and plaster and enamel, to build again from there.

It was too early to start dinner. Judith went into the bedroom, wanting to take off her suit and put on something more comfortable, something that would make her seem a quiet woman in a quiet house, waiting by her son's bed for her husband to come the next day, or the next, or the one after that.

After thinking for a minute in front of her closet, she took out a dark green corduroy housecoat, clean and warm. Buttoning it down the front, she felt fresh and new. Carefully, she hung up her suit and put on low-heeled sandals in place of her dress shoes. Then, with her hair combed out and tied with a ribbon, she put away her best pocketbook and cleaned the little spot of powder off her dresser.

She felt neat and in order with her house when she walked in to straighten up Robbie's room. Robbie's heavy sweater and old blue denim overalls were gone; the clean suit he had worn to nursery school that morning was folded on the chair.

Judith put a fresh sheet on his crib, taking the old one out to the laundry hamper, and then she folded his blue blanket neatly and put it at the foot of the bed. The toys were in order, the way she and Robbie had left them when they cleaned the room together that morning. She pulled the shade halfway down and picked a thread off the floor. Everything was good.

When she had gotten Robbie's fresh sheet, she had left the door to the linen closet open; now, sitting down on the floor and looking at the neat rows, she felt that this was the center of her home. I have eight sheets, all heavy and wide, she thought, and eight pillowcases and four sheets for Robbie and four good tablecloths—everything is clean and it belongs to me.

This is the part of the house he never sees, that no one ever knows about. The laundry when it comes back, the wash on the line fresh from the tubs, belong to me and the part of the house that I live in. He will come into the kitchen, he will open the refrigerator, Robbie will climb on the furniture, but no one knows how many sheets I have but me.

These are the things that lie peacefully waiting to be picked up by someone who understands them: the sheets and the cases, the lace tablecloth set apart, wrapped like a wedding present, and the villain, a torn napkin. Women with homes live so closely with substances: bread, soap, and buttons. The crack in the kitchen linoleum is a danger to the structure; the well-spaced coolness of the sheets on the line is a sensual presentation of security. Judith knew so much about the things she owned and cared for: she knew how pleasant Robbie's bed would feel because she washed the sheets, how soft her table silver would feel to her hand because she polished it and put it away carefully. These are the things I live with, she thought suddenly, my blue dishes, my broom.

The sound of Robbie and Sally clattering up the stairs disturbed her. It would be embarrassing, she thought, if Sally came in and found me on the floor in front of the linen closet. As she rose to go into the living room to open the front door, a thought crossed her mind: I keep house like Sally, with the same ideas and the same objects, and even almost the same apartment, and I have my way of feeling about the things I own, and maybe she has hers; maybe she sits on the floor in front of her linen closet looking like a fool sometimes.

The first thing she said when she opened the door was "You ought to have a baby, Sally, really."

Sally looked up from the stairway, where she was standing behind Robbie, urging him on. "How about letting me have Robbie for good?"

Judith held out her hands to Robbie, who scrambled up the stairs shrieking happily. "Did you have a good time?" she asked him when he reached her. She picked him up and held him for a minute. "Did you have a very good time with Sally?"

"We walked miles," Sally said. "Up and down every stairway in the block. And we had a dish of ice cream at the drugstore. And we saw a dog."

"A lovely time," Judith said. Robbie had his head on her shoulder and lay there quietly. She smiled at Sally. "You were terribly nice, as always, to take such good care of him."

"He took care of me," Sally said. "Did you have a good time?"

"Lovely," Judith said. She held the door open for Sally to come in. With Robbie running in and out of the room and Sally sitting on the couch, the living room was no longer quiet; her house was being lived in. She said suddenly to Sally: "You know what I was doing when you came? I was looking at my linen closet."

Sally smiled. "I have a pink taffeta bedspread in mine," she said. "Someone gave it to us for a wedding present and I never used it; it just sits there."

"I have a lace tablecloth," Judith said.

"I think on the whole I'd rather have a pink taffeta bedspread," Sally said critically. "It's never even been unfolded but once. I'm going to give it to Robbie when he gets married." She stood up. "Well," she said. "This isn't getting my dinner cooked."

Judith rose to hold the door for her. "Thanks again," she said.

"See you tomorrow," Sally said to Robbie. He waved at her vigorously across the room. "So long," Sally said to Judith.

Judith closed the door and stood beside it quietly for a minute. Robbie was playing in his room; she could hear the sound of blocks falling. Then she realized what she was really listening to: the familiar sounds that came from an awareness of her house with only the two of them in it, the quiet in the rooms, and the waiting.

Daughter, Come Home

THE HUGE FACTORY (FORMERLY MAKING WATCHES, NOW OPERATING day and night on a new product, one that caused the manufacturers to announce "If you cannot get that new watch this year, just remember that some soldier's life might be saved by the delicate precision instruments . . .") was blacked out for the night with blinds drawn against all of the great plate glass windows, but a few steps beyond and down the block, the Bar & Grill was bright and noisy. Workers who left the factory at midnight stopped in at the bar for a beer before going on home; people were drinking coffee before going in to work, and the homely girl who went from table to table playing requests on the accordion was working overtime on "Der Fuehrer's Face" and "I've Got Sixpence." Around the circular bar some soldiers and sailors—alone for the most part, sometimes with girls—mingled with the crowding factory workers. "I'm nonessential," one of the two bartenders told a customer. "Next week I'll be working up there at the factory with you guys."

Toward one o'clock the door opened and a small, oldish, slightly drunk man entered and went directly to the bar. "Rhine wine," he said to the bartender. "What, Jack?" the bartender asked over his shoulder. "Rhine wine," the little man said. The bartender shrugged and went to the row of bottles lined along the center of the bar. He selected one, and poured a glass for the customer. "Fifteen cents, Jack," the bartender said. The little man fumbled three nickels across the bar and picked up his glass. Carrying the glass, he left the bar and began to walk up and down between the tables. Occasionally he smiled hopefully at people sitting at the tables, but no one spoke to him or, in fact, even looked at him. Finally, the little man, still carrying his glass, went over to one of the booths and stood beside it, supporting himself against the edge of the table. Then: "Mind if I sit down here a minute?" he asked.

There were two girls sitting in the booth, drinking beer. One was a fashionably dressed blonde, with orange lipstick and carefully painted eyebrows; the other was a serious-looking girl in a brown tweed coat. They had been talking earnestly, but when the man spoke to them they turned and looked at him, at the glass in his hand, and then back to his face.

"Sure," said the blonde. "You can sit down. No more tables?"

"It isn't that," the little man said carefully. "It's just that I'd like to talk to you." He spoke in the painfully clear manner of the inebriated.

"Go ahead, talk," the blonde said. She turned back to her companion. "So I think I'd better get along and see if I can get it back," she said. "After all, I don't go so good in a factory, it gets me down; I should be back in the dancehall. And he always was a good guy to work for, that jerk."

"You hadn't ought to get out of a war factory, though," the other girl said. She glanced at the little man, who was sitting quietly, holding his glass and listening, and then went on: "You ought to stay at work that's . . . you know . . . for defense."

"That's true," the little man agreed. "You ought to work at something that will help your country." Both girls looked at him silently. The little man hurried on: "I hope you girls don't mind this—my coming up here and just sitting right down without even asking you very well."

"We don't mind," the blonde said.

"I guess you just wanted to talk to someone, or something," the other girl said.

"That's right," the little man said. "Look, my name is Burton, Robbie Burton, but you can call me Robbie. What's yours?"

"Well," the blonde said, "I'm Lois, and she's Elaine."

"Pleased to meet you," the little man said. "Look, this is how it is. I wanted to talk to someone and I saw you"—he gestured at the blonde—"and I just thought, There's a girl that looks kind of like my daughter. I got a daughter as old as you are, looks something like you," he said. "And so I thought maybe you wouldn't mind if I sat down, not to start something or anything, but just because I wanted to talk, like you said." As if very tired, the little man leaned back and sipped at his wine.

"Well." Lois looked at her friend. "He says I look like his daughter."

"I'll bet," Elaine said.

"Look," the little man said, leaning forward again, "don't you do like my daughter. You look like a nice girl, don't you do like my daughter."

"What did your daughter do?" Elaine asked.

"Never mind what my daughter did," the little man said. "I'm just telling you, that's all."

"All right," Lois said, winking at her friend. "I won't. Okay?"

"Okay." The little man looked at his empty glass. "Say," he demanded, "how about I buy you girls a drink? Let me buy you two a drink, how about it?"

"We can buy our own," Elaine said quickly.

"No," the little man insisted, "let me buy you a drink. Because this girl here reminds me of my daughter and I'd certainly buy my daughter a drink. Please let me buy you a drink?" he appealed to the blonde.

"Okay, Pop," she said. He got up and went over to the bar.

"Listen, Lois," the dark girl said, "you hadn't ought to let him buy you a drink. You hadn't ought to have let him sit down here in the first place."

"Poor old guy," Lois said. "He looked so lonesome. Let him talk for a while. Doesn't hurt to be nice to a poor old guy like that. Thinks I look like his daughter, anyway."

"Don't you go doing what his daughter did," Elaine said, giggling.

Lois giggled too. "Why not?" she asked. "But shut up, here he comes."

The little man came back, laughing when he saw that they were laughing. "Now we're having a good time," he said, putting the glasses down on the table.

"Hello, Pop," Lois said.

"I guess I could buy my own daughter a drink," he said.

"You sure could, Pop," Lois said.

"Tell us about your daughter," Elaine said. "What did she do, anyway?"

The little man lifted his face to her and glared. Then he relaxed. "Nothing," he said. "I shouldn't say; I don't know. Nothing."

"Cheer up, Pop," Lois said. "Drink up." She lifted her glass and touched his with it. "Long life," she said.

The little man picked up his glass and sipped at it. "You sure do look like my daughter," he said to Lois. "Don't you ever do anything bad." He looked at Elaine for a minute and then back to Lois. "Look," he said. "When I first came here a while ago I couldn't help but hear when you said you thought you'd leave your job and go back to working in a dancehall. Don't you do it."

"Hey, look," Lois said, pained.

"Don't you go working around no men," the little man insisted. "You stay right where you belong, not in any dancehall."

"I guess she doesn't need to ask you where she's going to work," Elaine said.

"I don't want you working for that guy you called a jerk," the little man said.

"He doesn't want me working for O'Halloran, that jerk," Lois explained elaborately.

"Don't you go fooling around men," the little man said. He pounded his hand on the table so that his glass trembled. "I don't want to hear of you going around any men. You're a nice girl, now, and you're a good girl and you treat your father nice, and you bring home your money, and don't you go throwing your life away on any men."

"Well, I'd certainly tell him to mind his own business!" said Elaine.

"Your old father's never done you an evil thing and never given you any bad advice, and when he tells you you better keep right on coming home every week with that money from the factory and not go taking anything from any men and not go throwing your money away on cheap clothes and friends, he's giving you good advice. Your old father deserves for you to treat him right, and he hasn't got anybody but you and no one to help him along in his old age, so you better listen to his good advice." The little man put his hand on Lois's arm and repeated, "You better listen to his good advice."

"Well, for heaven's sakes!" said Elaine.

"Hey," Lois said, "suppose you run along out of here, Pop."

"You listen to me," the little man said desperately.

"I'll call someone to throw you out, mister," she said.

"*I'll* call someone," Elaine said. She stood up and started to look around eagerly.

The little man watched her for a minute and then sighed. Pushing his glass aside, he put both hands on the table and lifted himself up. Elaine sat back against the seat, watching him warily. The little man stood at the opening of the booth looking at the girls sadly.

"You'll be sorry some day," he said. "You'll be sorry you didn't treat your poor old father better."

Neither girl moved. The little man turned to Lois.

"And I want you home and in your own bed tonight, you hear?" he cried emphatically. Then he turned and made his way past the crowded bar and out the door. His empty glass still trembled slightly after he had gone, moving a little in the spilled wine on the table.

As High as the Sky

FOR REASONS OF HER OWN, MRS. CARRANT HAD CONCLUDED THAT the doorbell was going to ring at 8:20 exactly; the train came in at 7:55, allow him fifteen minutes to get his bag or bags (he couldn't have *much* baggage, after all), a minute or two to get a taxi, and then only the ride downtown and home—eight or nine minutes at most. Eight-twenty.

She and the girls finished dinner and started waiting shortly after six; that was when Sandra put down her spoon and remarked, "I won't eat again till Daddy comes." It was not by any means a new idea; it had lived with Mrs. Carrant for a long time ("Three more dinners alone," "Two weeks from today it will seem as though he's never been away," "The next time the Martins call they'll have to invite us both"); even the baby had awakened that morning saying, "Daddy coming today." They had postponed the baby's third birthday party until Daddy could celebrate with them. Mrs. Carrant, at dinner, had leaned over and smoothed the dark curls from Sandra's forehead. "You'd better finish your dinner now," she said, "or you'll be hungry before Daddy gets here."

By eight o'clock (the train had come five minutes ago; Mrs. Carrant had called the station and it was on time) the girls were dressed and washed and their hair was tied back with fresh ribbons. Mrs. Carrant sat them together on the couch with a picture book and ran into her room to take a last look at her own hair, slightly damp from her doing the dishes and dressing the girls so quickly, but curling as theirs did, with no gray yet. She could hear Sandra reading to the baby in a voice quickened by the excitement of being up later than usual, "How many miles to Babylon? Three score miles and ten."

"Can I get there by candlelight?" Mrs. Carrant called happily. She realized suddenly that she had been humming.

There was a pause from the living room, and then Sandra giggled and said loudly, "Yes, and back again."

Mrs. Carrant returned to the living room and inspected the picture her two daughters made on the couch with the book, with just the table lamp turned on in back of them, the light softly touching the tops of their heads and the bowl of flowers behind Sandra's shoulder.

"You look very nice, you two," she said. "If only you wouldn't move before Daddy gets here." It was five after eight.

The baby looked up from the picture in the book. "Where's Daddy?" she asked.

"He'll be here soon," Mrs. Carrant said. "If it were only colder weather," she said, "we could have a fire in the fireplace and it would look so comfortable and nice here."

"It's too hot for a fire," Sandra announced.

"It *is* too hot," Mrs. Carrant said absently. She was wondering if he would know which floor to come to; she must have another door key made.

"Daddy is coming home because it was end-of-the-war," Sandra was saying to the baby. "My daddy is as high as the sky."

"Not really, Sandra," Mrs. Carrant said. "You remember what Daddy looks like."

The baby turned around solemnly and inspected the picture on the mantel. "Daddy looks like," she said.

"He's going to touch the ceiling when he walks around," Sandra said.

"He's not so terribly tall," Mrs. Carrant said, feeling vaguely that it was important to get their father's description well established. "He's not as tall as your Uncle George." She thought. "He's taller than you are," she said. "He's taller than I am. He's about as tall as—" Mrs. Carrant hesitated, her eyes moving around the room. (I never saw him in this house, she thought anxiously; I never saw him with this furniture, even.) "He's about as tall as the grocer," she said.

"I want some cookies," the baby said immediately.

"Later," Mrs. Carrant said. "When Daddy comes." It was 8:15.

The baby's face twisted up; it was long past her bedtime. "When Daddy comes," Mrs. Carrant went on quickly, "we'll all have cookies and milk, and Daddy will have presents for you. Remember what it said in Daddy's letter?"

"It said he was going to bring us presents," Sandra explained to the baby. "In Daddy's letter it said he had presents for all of us. Mommy, too."

If he hadn't stopped for his bags, or if he'd gotten a taxi quickly, or even if the train had been early, he might be starting to ring the doorbell now; Mrs. Carrant wondered for a minute if trains were ever early. They had said at the station that it was on time; Mrs. Carrant resisted an impulse to call the station again. As soon as I get on the phone, she thought, the doorbell will be ringing. Anyway, it's silly to call the station and ask if a train is early.

"Can I get down off the couch for a minute?" Sandra asked. "To get my doll?"

"That doll's so dirty," Mrs. Carrant said. "He should be here any minute, and you wouldn't want Daddy to see you with an old dirty doll."

"I *want* my doll," Sandra said.

"I want my bear," the baby said. Both the girls were beginning to stir uneasily on the couch, moving apart from each other, the book fallen untidily between them.

"The doll is dirty, but that bear is impossible," Mrs. Carrant said firmly. "You sit still for just one minute more." She went over and picked up the book and opened it neatly. "How many miles to Babylon?" she said as cheerfully as she could. "Three score miles and ten." The doorbell rang, and suddenly Mrs. Carrant understood that it might be anything; it might be someone coming to see her, not knowing he would be here, it might be a telegram, it might be some sort of a mistake. She went to the door and pressed the downstairs buzzer.

"That's Daddy?" Sandra said, looking at the door.

"We hope it is," Mrs. Carrant said steadily, and went over to open the door.

She stood in the doorway watching him come up the last few steps. He had an embarrassed smile on his face, and Mrs. Carrant realized that she had the same embarrassed smile on her face.

"I thought I had the wrong house for a minute," he said. He came up to her and set his bag down (only one bag, after all) and put his arms around her. She could hear him say "My God," looking over her head into the living room.

Mrs. Carrant turned around. "Look at them," she said. "The two of them." Sandra and the baby were sitting perfectly still on the couch, regarding their father with wide, surprised eyes. They never dreamed anyone was really coming, Mrs. Carrant thought. Then Sandra slid down off the couch, shrieking "Daddy brought us presents!" as she ran across the floor to be picked up. He looks so tired, Mrs. Carrant thought, seeing him holding Sandra; his hair is thinning.

"Baby," Mrs. Carrant said, "here's Daddy at last."

Still holding Sandra, he went across the room to the couch. "So this is my daughter Mary?" he said. "Will you come say hello to Daddy?"

The baby's face twisted, and she screamed "Mommy!" She threw herself off the couch and ran to Mrs. Carrant, burying her face against her mother's knees. Mrs. Carrant leaned over and picked her up.

"I guess I scared her," he said uncomfortably. He reached out to touch the baby's head, but she screamed again and hid her face.

"What's the *matter* with her?" he said.

"She's never seen you before," Mrs. Carrant said sharply. "You can't really blame her."

"Baby's scared," Sandra said, leaning outward to look into her father's face. "Maybe you better give her the presents right now."

The baby had stopped crying, her head against her mother's shoulder. "Now what's wrong with you?" Mrs. Carrant asked, putting her head down against the baby's. "What's there to make a fuss about?"

"Santy Claus," the baby said. "I want to see Santy Claus." Her voice rose. "Where's Santy Claus?"

"She thinks you're Santa Claus," Sandra explained to her father, "because you were bringing presents."

"It's going to take her a little while." Mrs. Carrant looked hopefully at her husband across the baby's head. "She doesn't take to—" She stopped. "You see," she went on carefully, "it's hard for her, only knowing you from your picture." She took the baby over to the mantel where the picture was. "Look," she said. "Who's that in the picture?" she asked the baby.

The baby looked up sullenly, and then said, "Daddy." She reached over and took hold of the picture.

"It's a picture of me, isn't it?" her father said. "Do I look so different? It's a picture of me and here I am standing here." He turned to his wife. "What's the matter with her?"

"She thought Santa Claus was coming," Sandra said.

He set Sandra down on the couch and approached the baby again. "Hello, there," he said.

The baby stared at him silently, holding the picture with both hands. When he put his finger out to touch her nose, she turned her head quickly to hide in her mother's shoulder. He shrugged.

"This the new furniture?" he said. "Looks pretty good. Can't you put her to bed or something?"

"I guess I'd better," Mrs. Carrant said. "You want to take Daddy's picture to bed?" she asked the baby.

The baby nodded, holding the picture.

"Tomorrow," Mrs. Carrant said. "Tomorrow you can get acquainted, and in a day or so she'll be all over you. She's tired now anyway."

Mrs. Carrant waited for a minute, looking at her husband. "After all," she said helplessly.

Murder on Miss Lederer's Birthday

FROM THE KITCHENETTE WHERE MISS ALLISTON WAS MAKING BREAK-fast came the pleasant sound of coffee percolating and the rather flat sound of Miss Alliston humming cheerfully to herself. It was not quite nine o'clock, and the sunlight had just begun to creep along the edge of the living room carpet; a breeze came gently through the half-opened window and stirred the petals of the geranium on the windowsill. It was an apartment clearly inhabited by two maiden ladies of a certain age; an unashamed rocking chair sat next to the radiator, with a tiny needlepoint footstool in front of it; on the mantel were two matched earthenware jugs, each saying SOUVENIR OF MEXICO CITY; all the chairs were daintily antimacassared. As though extremely conscious of the fact that he was a spot of local color, a large gray tomcat sat washing his face in the patch of sunlight on the floor.

Miss Alliston and Miss Lederer were schoolteachers ("the Two Musketeers of Houston High," they called themselves privately, and they were given to wildly reckless dinners at Italian restaurants on Friday afternoons, with half a bottle of red wine and veal scallopine), and they had done their best to make their apartment homey. "I feel so sorry for those other poor girls," they were fond of observing to each other, "living in furnished rooms or private homes, with none of our comfort, and none of our . . . well, dear . . . *freedom*."

Miss Alliston was the senior by a year and a half; at forty-one, she'd given herself the position of leader. It had been Miss Alliston's idea to go to Mexico one summer. It was to Miss Alliston, too, that the one souvenir ashtray belonged; she enjoyed an occasional cigarette after their Friday evening meal, although she disapproved of the habit for Miss Lederer. "I do so enjoy my smokes," she would say sinfully, "but no one recognizes more clearly than I how filthy a habit it is."

Miss Alliston and Miss Lederer took turns on Saturday mornings getting up and making breakfast. This morning, Miss Alliston was unusually cheerful, for it was Miss Lederer's birthday and they had planned An Occasion. This morning they were going to the Museum of Modern Art, and in the afternoon to a theater matinee. The matinee was Miss Alliston's treat, a birthday present for her friend.

Miss Alliston took the cinnamon buns from the oven and put them on the table. Then, taking off her apron and hanging it on the hook on the door to the kitchenette, she went into the bedroom.

"Paula," she cried gaily, "top of the morning to you! And happy birthday!"

Miss Lederer stirred and opened her eyes. "Thank you, Evelyn," she murmured. Miss Alliston began to sing, "Lazy Paula, will you get up, will you get up, will you get up . . ."

Lazy Paula sat up in bed and sniffed. "Evelyn, weren't you sweet to make breakfast," she said. (She had said it every time Miss Alliston had made breakfast since they'd been living together. On alternate Saturdays Miss Alliston woke up and said: "Paula, you dear girl! Did you really make breakfast for me?")

"Come right away," Miss Alliston said, "or everything will get cold."

Miss Alliston threw Miss Lederer's housecoat onto the bed and went back to fuss over the table. In a moment, Miss Lederer joined her, and the two of them sat down. Immediately the big gray cat leaped onto Miss Lederer's lap, poking his head over the edge of the table experimentally.

"Good morning, dear," Miss Lederer said gaily to the cat. She broke off a tiny piece of cinnamon bun and held it out to the cat.

"Paula, you crazy girl," Miss Alliston said. "Anyway, he had his milk hours ago." There was a sound at the apartment door. "There's the paper," Miss Alliston added. "I'll get it. You sit still and finish your birthday breakfast."

Miss Alliston opened the door and picked up the paper. "What are the headlines, Evelyn?" Miss Lederer asked, pouring herself a second, and extravagant, cup of coffee.

"All about the war," Miss Alliston replied, reading the paper as she closed the door behind her and started back to the table. "The Russians are doing just marvelously, and there's good news from Africa, and Congress has done something or other. . . . We'll go over it all later."

Both Miss Alliston and Miss Lederer were intensely interested in national and international affairs. They held heated discussions over political developments and had bought themselves a small mounted map on which they earnestly and devotedly plotted the campaigns of the war, with a good deal of disagreement and spectacular generalship. After the arrival of the morning paper, however, the world and the map had always to wait upon an enthusiastic survey of advertisements, particularly for household novelties, book sales (which they never attended), and news of prime importance, which was society, gossip, and murder. There was a murder this morning on the second page.

"My dear," Miss Alliston gasped as she turned the page, "such a ghastly affair!"

Miss Lederer went to stand next to Miss Alliston while they read the story.

"And attacked her!" Miss Lederer whispered, her hand to her lips. "How fearful!"

"Horrible," Miss Alliston confirmed, sitting back in her chair at the table with the paper.

"Read it all to me," Miss Lederer said.

"There's no more than this," Miss Alliston said, turning the pages haphazardly.

"Let me see if I've got it straight," Miss Lederer said. "This girl—"

"Alice January, her name was," Miss Alliston added, referring to the paper. "A dancer, a modern dancer."

"I'm not surprised," Miss Lederer said, nodding, "the way they live. And you say she was found in her apartment?"

"Her *luxurious* apartment, in Gramercy Park."

Miss Lederer shuddered.

"My dear," Miss Alliston said, leaning over the table, "aren't you *glad* I insisted that we live in the Village?"

Miss Lederer smiled gratefully at her friend. "Who found the body?"

"'Miss January had retired early,'" Miss Alliston read, "'telling the clerk at the switchboard she did not wish to be disturbed.'"

"That's exactly what I was wondering, Evelyn," Miss Lederer said significantly. "*Why* did she say she didn't want to be disturbed?"

There was a silence as they regarded each other. Then: "I do believe you're right," Miss Alliston said, nodding. "There's certainly more to it than meets the eye."

"Exactly," Miss Lederer said. "Read me the rest."

Miss Alliston consulted the paper again. "'Her body was found by the manager. She had left word to be called at eleven o'clock in the morning, and when there was no answer to the bell he opened the door with a skeleton key, and found her lying naked in the bedroom, with thirty-one stab wounds.' Thirty-one stab wounds!" she repeated. "Dreadful! Well, he locked the door again . . ."

"There's another thing," Miss Lederer interrupted. "What was *he* doing with a key?"

Miss Alliston looked dubious. "Well, managers always have keys for all the doors. To let plumbers in, and painters, and deliveries, and things like that."

"Gracious!" Miss Lederer said. "I'm glad no one has a key to *our* home!"

"Anyway, they say she was practically . . ." Miss Alliston fanned herself with her napkin. "Heavens, I can't read it, Paula."

Miss Lederer took the paper and found Miss Alliston's place. "'Dismembered,'" she read. "I don't blame you a bit for feeling faint, Evelyn. Shall I get you a glass of water?"

"No," Miss Alliston said, recovering slightly. "Just don't read any more of the horrible part."

"Well," Miss Lederer read on, "it seems the police are looking for 'a man who was a frequent visitor to Miss January's apartment, whom she described as her manager, and a woman who is generally supposed to be a near relative of Miss January's, an elderly woman, probably an aunt.'"

"No more an aunt than I am!" said Miss Alliston vehemently.

"'She was only wearing,'" Miss Lederer went on, breathlessly absorbed, "'a pearl necklace—' Oh, my dear, imagine, a pearl necklace on the money those dancers get! And then coming to an end like that, all hacked up."

"And attacked," Miss Alliston said.

"'Sexually assaulted,'" Miss Lederer read from the paper. She looked up. "'No one has been arrested as yet,'" she said.

"If we pick up an afternoon paper on our way uptown," Miss Alliston said, "we might find out if there are any developments, whether the murderer has been caught, or anything."

"I'm interested in this man she said was her manager," Miss Lederer mused.

Miss Alliston looked at her watch. "Good heavens! Half past

ten. Paula, do you know we've been sitting here chatting for more than an hour?"

"We'll never get to the museum at this rate," Miss Lederer said, not moving.

"The museum." Miss Alliston's voice was rather flat. "We won't have much time there now, will we?"

"Evelyn," Miss Lederer said hesitantly, "do you think we really *ought* to try and crowd the museum and a matinee all into one day? I'm not too enthusiastic about just rushing through the museum, frankly."

"But, Paula, it's your birthday, and I don't want you to stay home because you think I don't want to go."

"Well, I'm not too enthusiastic about just rushing through," Miss Lederer repeated, "but if you'd like to, I'm perfectly willing to go."

"Well, personally, I'd really much rather just take my time and get to the matinee good and early."

"I'm so glad, Evelyn, because I really *was* a little tired and didn't like to say so, because I knew you were counting on it."

"If you're *sure* you don't mind not going," Miss Alliston said.

"But we mustn't miss the matinee," Miss Lederer said firmly.

"We certainly will not miss the matinee," Miss Alliston confirmed. They smiled at each other proudly. "Suppose I just run downstairs now," Miss Alliston proposed, "and see if any afternoon papers have come out yet."

Miss Lederer laughed. "You know," she confessed, "I'm surprised at myself, really I am. Letting myself get so interested in a sordid murder, I mean. It isn't *like* me, you know."

Miss Alliston said, "Well, this one interested me, especially because it took place so near here."

"I mean, I'm not one of those persons who insist on visiting the scene of a crime, or anything," Miss Lederer insisted.

"I would never dream of going near the scene of a crime,"

Miss Alliston said with dignity. "As it happens, however, this January murder was in a neighborhood I know slightly."

"Really, Evelyn?"

"I used to visit friends in the vicinity," Miss Alliston said, "but that was many years ago, naturally."

"You didn't ever know *her*, did you?"

"Alice? Certainly not!" Miss Alliston shook her head doubtfully. "I may have met her, Paula, you know; I can't be sure. Perhaps I was introduced to her at one time. You know how it is with people you meet." She got up and went into the bedroom. Miss Lederer began to reread the account in the paper.

"Dear, are you absolutely sure you don't mind about the museum?" Miss Alliston called from the bedroom.

"Absolutely," Miss Lederer said. "You know, I can't help feeling there ought to be some clues, fingerprints or something."

Miss Alliston returned with her coat on, and stood by the table snapping and unsnapping the fastener of her pocketbook. Finally she said, "Paula, why don't you just make another pot of coffee while I'm gone?"

"Do you really think we should?"

Miss Alliston was brisk. "Yes. We'll do without coffee some morning toward the end of the month, that's all. We are certainly entitled to our small pleasures, especially on your birthday." She moved to the window and looked out. "Such a lovely day; I wonder if we're not silly to spend it cooped up in a theater instead of out of doors."

Miss Lederer looked up. "You know, Evelyn, if you wanted to change the tickets for some other day, I wouldn't mind at all. Of course it's not my place to say anything, since it's your treat, but somehow the prospect of a stuffy theater . . ."

"I just don't feel in the mood for a play today, I guess," Miss Alliston said. "They're holding our tickets at the box office; I'll just call the theater."

"Get the papers after you do everything else, and then you'll probably get a later edition," Miss Lederer suggested. Miss Alliston, walking quickly, let the door slam behind her.

Miss Lederer started clearing the dishes off the table. She had the new pot of coffee percolating cheerfully when Miss Alliston returned, arms full of packages.

"It's really *dreadfully* chilly out, dear," Miss Alliston said. "You've no idea how wise we are to cancel our plans today."

"Did you get the papers?" Miss Lederer asked.

Miss Alliston put the packages down. "All the papers," she said, "and some potato salad and two codfish cakes and some rye bread, and, Paula, a tiny little bottle of Chianti! And I got myself a pack of cigarettes, too; the man said they were a very popular brand."

"Good for you," Miss Lederer said heartily. "You deserve a little treat after being so generous about giving up the matinee." She took the coffeepot from the stove and stood it on the table next to the two fresh cups, then sat down. The big gray cat leaped up on her lap, and she petted him. Then she selected a tabloid from the pile of papers Miss Alliston had brought and turned to the story of the murder.

Miss Alliston took her packages into the kitchen, then returned and sat down in her own place at the table. She opened her new pack of cigarettes carefully, lit one, and put it down beside her in the clean ashtray. Then she poured herself a cup of coffee and sat back comfortably.

"I saw in the headlines," she said, "that they've found a new secret clue." She picked up her cigarette and puffed vigorously. "Paula," she continued through the smoke, "you know, I don't think it would do any harm if we went out later for a short constitutional, and just ran over to Gramercy Park for a minute to see what we could see—"

"Dear, can I clean the turtle in there now?"

IV

. . .

Somehow Things Haven't Turned Out Quite the Way We Expected

Humor and Family

• • •

"I get a lot of unnecessary sarcasm
from the eggbeater."

• • •

Here I Am, Washing Dishes Again

HERE I AM, WASHING DISHES AGAIN. IF I WERE ANY SORT OF A PROPER housewife at all I'd start my dishwashing at a specific hour in the morning, duly aproned, trim and competent, instead of heaping the dishpan high while my neighbors and no doubt the rest of the world are off on some blissful pursuit—frying doughnuts, perhaps, or flying kites with their children. Three times a day, seven days a week, how on earth many weeks a year? What sort of look do I have on my face? The subway rider's, probably, sort of resigned and do–all–the–glasses–before–Times Square.

I don't really hate these brass faucets and the complete perfect circle of the dishpan, though; I love the things, I own them, they are so essential a part of me that I like to be near them, and when I am away from home, next to the children the thing I miss most is the sight of my own dear sink. When I wash dishes, I stare into the dishpan and at my own hands, which are the only alien things in the dishwater, the only things that don't rattle.

The green glasses from the five-and-ten love their bath; they roll luxuriously in the soapy water and seem almost to stretch. They're trying to forget their humble ten-cent origin, and they sort of hope that everyone else will forget it too. I watch them sitting on the table, holding themselves proudly; they expect that guests—they don't expect much, anymore, from members of the family—will comment on them and hold them up appreciatively. "Where did you get these lovely glasses?" someone may ask, and all along the table the glasses stiffen, not daring to glance at one another, tense until I answer, "I bought them at an auction. I expect they're quite valuable, really." Then along the table the green glasses will preen themselves, relaxing, and nod condescendingly at me. They have grown quite fond of me because of that little lie, and make a definite effort not to break when I drop them. I have noticed, too, half a dozen times, that if I forget, and confess that they did come from the five-and-ten, then inside twenty-four hours one or another of the glasses, no longer able to stand the disgrace, will plunge nobly to its death on the floor. I have only six of these glasses left, and the five-and-ten no longer carries them. My great hope is that someday I *shall* find some at an auction.

I really spend a lot more time in the kitchen than I ought, although it doesn't surprise anything in the kitchen to find me there, considering what a busybody I am, always meddling in things that are clearly none of my business. Take the forks, for instance; I'm sure I've done nothing to clear up *that* unhappy situation. I have two kitchen forks, one with four prongs and one with two prongs, and the four-pronged fork is of course my favorite because of its amiability; it is a far sweeter and more malleable character than the two-pronged fork, which was originally the fork to an inexpensive carving set, and regards this fact as an automatic entrée into the dining room.

My two forks are insanely jealous of each other, and I find that I must take a path of great caution with them, something I would not do for many of my friends. I try to keep out of their quarrels—who wouldn't be afraid of an angry fork?—but I am always fumbling the delicate balance of power that is all that keeps them from each other's throats. For instance, four-prongs is traditionally the fork for scrambling eggs, but two-prongs takes precedence in the dishwater. Four-prongs prides himself on the fact that no two-pronged fork knows how to scramble eggs adequately. There is, however, some hair-thin line between scrambling eggs and beating eggs; past that certain line the job rightly belongs to an eggbeater. If I try to force four-prongs beyond his notions of right and fitting duty, he turns limp and useless in my hands.

Then, of course, as though my life were not enough complicated, when I finally give up on four-prongs and take out the eggbeater, *that* surly character is offended in turn, and twists himself into a rigid, disobedient confusion of metal when I try to turn the handle. I get a lot of unnecessary sarcasm from that eggbeater, too. I have let cake batter stand, half-mixed, for half an hour while the eggbeater and the fork calmed down, and at least twice I have had to set them on opposite sides of the kitchen table to keep them from tangling themselves into a snarling battle. All this, while two-prongs sits sedately watching, observing that any vulgar fork with four prongs is bound to get himself into low trouble, particularly if he consorts with eggbeaters.

Two-prongs is the kitchen carving-and-roast fork, and I shall never forget the taut moment in the kitchen when I inadvertently tried to lift a roast out of the pan with four-prongs. I was in a hurry, company was waiting, the gravy was not made, and four-prongs was the nearest fork. There was a moment of absolute resistance, then the incredulous turn of four-prongs in my hand, the sudden furious clatter of two-prongs from the stove where he had been waiting, the slippery tipping of the roasting pan; even the potholder hesitated. There was nothing I could say, of course. I was at fault, so I picked the roast up off the floor, kicked the interfering roasting pan into a corner, set four-prongs pointedly in the sink, and went to work with two-prongs, who was mollified, but sullen for several days.

I do not mean to say that I am under the thumb of my forks, any more than I am honestly afraid of the meat grinder's threats, or the bullying of the coffeepot. It is simply that one cannot live a day in the middle of so many personalities without occasionally treading on some fork's toes, or sideswiping the fundamental makeup of a dishtowel. A dishtowel is, I think, the most easily cowed of all kitchen implements, excepting only the steel wool, which hides a heart of gold under its gruff exterior. My striped dishtowels take a vulgar, unholy joy in getting into the living room to clean up spilled juice. There is one dishtowel that adores my three-year-old daughter, I think because she once carried it off to her doll carriage to serve as a blanket, which is a pleasure usually beyond the reach of dishtowels. My daughter's friend is pleased to serve her now in any menial capacity, and has occasionally done service as a bib, at which it is well meaning but inefficient, as it prefers to lie back and admire her rather than catch the little bits of bacon and butter she is apt to let fall from her mouth.

When I turn my back on the sink to take up the dishtowel, the kitchen brightens and beams at me reassuringly. It rather resents being polished up, and there was quite a scene recently about the new curtains. I explained that I had made them myself, and was a little proud of them, and wanted to take the old ones down, but a great loyal voice was raised for the old curtains, and when they went into the hamper regardless, to be washed and turned into dust cloths, a vast silent resentment confronted me and my new curtains. The new curtains were edged awry, until I was persuaded I had sewn them wrong; the rods slipped down persistently. The color of the new curtains, by morning light, was made so vivid, so glaring, by the subdued martyrdom of the rest of the kitchen, that I was almost convinced that they were a mistake. But I give my kitchen time; it is primarily easygoing and friendly, and it will adapt to anything. I brought the old curtains back, in their new role as dust cloths, and left them on the table for a while, so that they might reassure their friends that they were happy and well treated. I gave the floor a wash—it hates washing, like a puppy, but, like a puppy, always feels better afterward—and promised the pantry new shelf paper, and things calmed down. There was only one morning, all things considered, when it was really *impossible* to serve breakfast in the kitchen.

My husband and son, who are gadget-happy, set up for me to use in my kitchen a magnetic metal bar, about four inches long, that takes, and keeps, a violent hold on any metal objects near it, so that I have had to pry my can openers away from it and occasionally, working too near, have had fear for the fillings in my teeth, or my wedding ring, or the tips of my shoelaces. When I moved the kitchen table over to the opposite wall, things were a little better, but I still felt, using my two forks or the can opener, the strong steady pull of the magnet against me, so that if I let go of the fork for a minute it would fly across the room to lodge securely against the magnet.

For a while I wondered about this, the advisability of having one spot in a kitchen to which all utensils would naturally gravitate, but now it reassures me. At least I can always be sure of finding my two warring forks there, nestling snugly in the broad magnetic arms of their common refuge, their maniac suspicions of each other lulled by the fact that it is big enough for both. Furthermore, I can feel through my wall magnet, even from the worktable across the room, the sure haunting echo of one magnet after another throughout the house: From the toy closet, my son's collection of magnets and small metal toys joins its siren voice to the master one in the kitchen. From beyond it, the magnets in all the various toys in the upstairs playroom call shrilly to my forks. From far above comes the thin sweet voice of the magnet in the new lock to the attic workshop. My forks tremble, look at me imploringly, and resign themselves to their work.

Sometimes, wandering as I do around my kitchen, I feel the magnetic pull myself, the urge to flatten myself against the wall and, until I am taken down for some practical purpose, lie there quiet, stilled, at rest.

Perhaps it's the magnet that holds me to my kitchen. Perhaps it's the fact that I keep my fountain pen and notebook on the shelf near the clock, so that I always have to go into the kitchen to sign letters, as well as to see what time it is, or, as a last resort, to wash dishes.

Perhaps I'll wait and dry these tomorrow after breakfast.

In Praise of Dinner Table Silence

A LONG TIME AGO, BACK IN THOSE UNBELIEVABLE DAYS WHEN I USED to buy half a pound of hamburger or four pork chops for dinner, and the living room furniture was new and I still had eight cups and eight dinner plates that matched—back in those days, if they ever did exist, my husband and I used to sit at the dinner table every night and talk to each other. I can't remember what we talked about, but I do know we could *hear* each other.

That was back in the time, too, when we had all sorts of ideas about bringing up children. We supposed that *our* children were not going to be messy all the time like other children we saw, and if we had a daughter, we assured each other, she was going to learn to like housework and sewing and cooking instead of being a drone around the house. And *our* children, we told each other happily, were going to have an intelligent share in family activities, such as sitting at the dinner table and joining in the conversation. We had a lot of these ideas.

I still can't figure out what happened. It was going to be so wonderful, all of us sitting there, lingering over coffee and hot chocolate, discussing the ballet and the good books we all had been reading. Perhaps occasionally something would come up in school that the children would care to examine a little bit more searchingly; perhaps an incident from the day would provoke a thoughtful argument. If the phone should ring (I don't know why we assumed that the chances of the phone's ringing during dinner were remote; perhaps it was because none of the people *we* knew called at that hour), a child would excuse himself gracefully and tell whoever was calling that we were dining. Compliments would be made on the food; an indulgent smile might pass between the parents at some childish quip.

As I say, I still can't figure out what happened. All I know is that somehow things haven't turned out quite the way we expected. Take that notion about lingering over hot chocolate: What we didn't know then was that the older the child, the less time spent at the dinner table.

A very small child, dawdling and playing and telling endless, giggling stories, can string out one French-fried potato until he is permitted—with some shrillness and a certain involuntary clenching of fists—to be excused from the rest of his dinner. A fifteen-year-old boy, however, can put away two lamb chops, a baked potato, a lettuce-and-tomato salad, three slices of bread and butter, and a quart of milk before his father has quite finished asking for the salt, please. Before the rest of the family has had time to compliment the cook ("String beans *again*?"), the fifteen-year-old is well on his way to the front door, jacket over one shoulder and a slab of blueberry pie in hand. If called back, he will perch unhappily on the edge of his chair, make a few perfunctory stabs at conversation, such as asking his younger sister kindly to be quiet for just one minute so other people can get a word in edgewise. He will also ask repeatedly if he can please be excused *now*, because he is really in a terrible hurry, and will answer all questions with "What?" He is in such a hurry, of course, because he has to get down to the soda shop and idle for two hours over a Coke.

The only good book that seems to be discussed at our dinner table is the checkbook, usually introduced in some such literary phrase as "I gotta have a new . . ." Conversation, which is rarely initiated by the parents, is incessant, opinionated, and personal. It is the obligation of the parents to recognize, without hesitation, the Jerrys and the Lindas, the Davises and the Old Lady Winchesters, whose names wander so freely through the social conversation. A maternal question such as "Who is Tommy? Is he that sloppy little boy who borrowed all your records?" is regarded as out-of-bounds, partly because the parent is supposed to know who Tommy is and partly because Tommy is the rage of the seventh grade and looks that way on purpose. Equally, Old Lady Winchester has been teaching the fourth grade for forty-three years, and any parent who cannot recognize her by now is hopelessly out of it.

Scientific discussions, seized upon by the father of the family in the hope of getting into the general conversation, can cause considerable chaos, with the father demonstrating the force of gravity with his butter knife or explaining what makes airplanes go, while on either side low-voiced conversations continue on topics such as whether Jimmie Smith is really the biggest drip in town or what is playing at the movies or who gets first rights at the television set at 8:30. Incidentally, a father, leaving the table to get an atlas to show someone where Alaska is, can count on losing his audience before he gets back. If the father has devoted considerable effort to telling how a camera takes pictures or how we get water out of a faucet and a child remarks that that was not at all the way Mr. Williams told it in science class, the father would be advised to get out of the conversation at once—and stay out.

As for the small daily incidents that spur conversation, there are certainly plenty of them. Opening gambits on these may vary from such provocative questions as "Guess why Jerry got kicked out of study hall again today" to "You know that three-legged dog the Johnsons got? Well, he's got four legs now." (He never was three-legged.

This was a canard, spread by Harry Johnson. All that happened was the dog got one leg cut chasing the Martins' cat up a tree. So he used to limp. Now he doesn't.) A parental attempt to introduce some small daily incident ("Who left the marbles lying on the stairs?") is usually sensibly disregarded.

The phone always rings during dinner.

Conversation about the food, although, of course, not on a gourmet level, is constant. There is surprise expressed at a new dish ("You mean I gotta *eat* this?"), personal preference indicated ("I haaaaaate liver. I hate it, I hate it, I hate it!"), and suggestions registered for improvement ("There's too much salt in this soup, and I got a black speck on my lettuce"). Occasionally a dish will provoke universal enthusiasm ("Say, this isn't bad at all") or comparison with other cooks ("Mrs. Nash doesn't make stew like this, but *she's* a real good cook"). The mother of the family naturally receives these comments graciously ("Then why don't you go eat at the Smiths' if the food's so good?") and takes preferences into consideration in her menu planning, as in telling the father after dinner that he's going to go right on getting hamburger once a week unless something is done about the housekeeping budget.

No, I can't really remember what it used to be like when we sat at the table and just talked. As I say, all I can really remember about it is that we could *hear* each other.

Questions I Wish I'd Never Asked

ALL I WANTED TO KNOW WAS WHO HAD LEFT THE GARDEN HOSE OUT in the snow to freeze.

"Who," I said to my older son, Laurie, "left the garden hose out in the snow to freeze?"

"Not me," he said at once. "I didn't do it."

"Well," I said (flank attack), "when did you last use the hose?"

"I haven't used it since last summer," he assured me. "I don't think I've even *seen* the garden hose since last summer. Or maybe even the summer before."

"What did you use to wash the car?"

"What? Oh." He thought. "Oh, *that*. You mean *that* garden hose? And *anyway* I put it back."

"Then why is it out in the snow to freeze?"

"I'll tell you," he said. "I *remember* I put it back, because I was curling it up in the garage, and I gave Joanne the frying pan—"

"The frying pan?"

"Well, yes. To wash the car."

"Why did you need a frying pan to wash the car?"

"For the soap," he said, sighing.

"I suppose," I said carefully, "it was the omelet pan?"

"We figured you didn't use that one as much as the others." He was quiet for a minute and then went on quickly, "So I gave Joanne the frying pan and the sewing scissors to take in, and I curled—"

"The sewing scissors? Mine?"

"She was cutting off the frayed edges."

"Of what? Of what?"

"There was a kind of a little hole in the upholstery."

"Of the car?"

"Well, the *dog* did that," he said desperately. "We put the car robe over it, anyway. So I was curling up the garden hose in the garage and Joanne . . ."

"Joanne," I said, "did you wash the omelet pan?"

"What?"

"Did you wash the omelet pan after you used it to wash the car?"

"Well, there was already soap *in* it. I just rinsed it out and put it back. Why?"

"Where are my sewing scissors?"

"*I* don't know. You want to cut something?"

"I am trying to find out who left the garden hose out in the snow to freeze."

"You mean when Laurie washed the car? Did the omelet taste funny?"

"Where are my sewing scissors?"

"Oh. Well, I brought them in. And Barry was doing a plane model in the kitchen. And he asked could he borrow the scissors for a minute. And I said he should put them back in your sewing table when he was through. Why," she asked, struck with an idea. "Can't you find them?"

"No. I cannot find them."

"Why don't you ask Laurie? He was washing the car."

"Did he leave the garden hose out in the snow to freeze?"

"No, that was Sally."

"Sally?"

"She had it because she was trying to ice skate."

"What?"

"On the lawn. She was going to put water on the lawn so it would freeze, but it wouldn't stretch."

"Then did Sally—"

"All I know is, it wasn't *me*."

"Barry," I said, "where are my sewing scissors?"

"What?"

"The day Laurie washed the car you were doing a plane model in the kitchen and Joanne came in with my sewing scissors and you asked to borrow them and they have not been returned."

"Oh. I don't know. Maybe Laurie took them."

"Laurie was curling up the hose."

"Then maybe Joanne took them."

"Joanne was rinsing out the omelet pan."

"Then what about Sally? Or Dad?"

"What did you do with my sewing scissors when you were through with your model plane?"

"What? Oh. Oh. Your *sewing* scissors."

"My sewing scissors."

"Oh. Well, I guess they got *in* the plane."

"In the plane? My scissors?"

"Well, I got it glued, and—I remember now—I couldn't find the scissors and then when I shook the plane it rattled but I couldn't unglue it so I guess they're still in there."

"Where is the plane now? We'll unglue it together."

"I took it to school. Dad *said* I could."

"Listen," I said to my husband. "Did you tell Barry he could take my sewing scissors to school?"

"Did I what?"

"Who left the garden hose out in the snow to freeze?"

"Well, I didn't. Why don't you ask the children? Why would I leave the garden hose—" He put down his paper abruptly. "Sewing scissors?" he demanded. "Are they making those little boys take home economics now?"

"No," I said. "They're learning safecracking."

"Progressive education," he was shouting when I closed the study door. "Good honest arithmetic was all *we* . . . "

"Sally," I said, "who left the garden hose out in the snow?"

"What?"

"Who left the garden hose out in the snow?"

"Well, I put it away."

"When?"

"I was going to ice skate because you know what Jeannie has? She has a big patch of ice right on her own lawn and she goes skating there every day and can I get new skates?"

"No. You took out the garden hose?"

"Jeannie's mother *lets* her put water on the lawn to ice skate. Jeannie can use *her* garden hose whenever she wants."

"Does she put it away afterward?"

"Put what away?"

"The garden hose."

"Can I? Get new skates?"

"Look," I said. "Did you or did you not leave the garden hose out in the snow?"

"Because if I get figure skates I can go backward."

As a matter of fact, the other day, when I was washing the dog, it occurred to me who had left the hose out in the snow. I did, the last time I washed him. Not that the question is of the slightest importance, anyway. What's important is to get it thawed out and put away. Let the dead past bury its dead, I firmly believe.

Mother, Honestly!

MOTHERS ARE HARRIED CREATURES, HAUNTED BY ALL SORTS OF TER-
rors: rusty nails, the rising cost of sneakers, rain on Class Picnic Day.
Take, for instance, the mother of the sixteen-year-old boy who is
learning to drive. Or the mother of the lead in the school play, for
whom she must create a pioneer-era costume by Monday. Or the
mother of the free-swinging third grader, who always says the other
kid started it. Most mothers are called upon, from time to time, to
endure periods of such unnerving strain that only a heroine could
meet them.

Above and beyond all those, there is another mother, who may
be met almost anywhere. Sometimes she is just sitting by herself
over a cup of coffee, staring straight ahead. Or trying to exchange a
pair of size-16 subteen Bermuda shorts for a size-14 preteen. Or
wearing gloves at a party because the bottle of polish remover has
been long and mysteriously missing. Her new white blouse has been
out to the laundry three times, and she hasn't worn it yet. She
cringes when the phone rings. She cannot endure the sight or sound
of a guitar. Any statement beginning "Everyone *else* does" sends her
into a white-faced and speechless fury. Don't get in this woman's

way. She has enough to put up with at home. She is the mother of a twelve-year-old girl.

Those mothers who have lasted till a child has reached twelve have themselves pretty well in hand. They keep telling themselves that at any rate the worst is over—except for distant headaches such as paying college bills and giving the kids wedding presents and taking a firm stand on babysitting when they are grandmothers. It might have been pretty rough the first few years, they tell themselves, what with things like chickenpox and television and stilts, but now that the girl is twelve she is practically grown up and can take care of herself and begin to be responsible.

I know mothers who keep telling themselves and telling themselves things like that, in voices getting more and more shrill, wringing their hands and grinding their teeth. Now the girl is twelve, they say, she's practically grown up. She is. She is. She *is*.

That's me.

Last year I sent my daughter, an agreeable child who liked to play baseball and thought boys were silly, off to camp. I got back— and it took only two months—a creature who slept with curlers in her hair, wore perfume from the five-and-ten, and addressed me as nothing but "Mother, *honestly!*"

By now she also calls me "Honestly, *Mother*" and "Mother, *really*" and sometimes just plain "*Mother.*" She worries constantly about her figure—usually with one hand in the refrigerator. She thinks any beardless adolescent who sings through his nose is "cute." She has perceived that in addition to being slightly behind the times in my dress and manner, I am hopelessly dated in my grasp of teenagers—especially of what "everyone else" is allowed to do. This, incidentally, is a phrase I can't even write without feeling a little chill down my back. My daughter says it without difficulty. I tell her, "I don't care what everyone else does . . ." and "No daughter of mine is going to . . ." and "When I was your age, I had to . . ." Neither of us listens to the other. She no longer thinks boys are silly.

She has compromised, oddly, with her past as a child. She no longer plays cops and robbers in and out of the treehouse; she climbs into the treehouse to read. She will spend hours riding a bike with her little brother, so long as it is understood that she is teaching him how, and not riding purely for pleasure. She has learned from her Home Ec teacher and her Scout leader how to manage perfectly well in a kitchen, but if her mother is around she drops cups of flour and burns eggs and steps on the cat. She can shut herself in the bathroom combing her hair until her mother beats feverishly and hysterically on the door, yet she is never late for school because that is where the boys are.

Punishment for a twelve-year-old may be of the "Very well, you can just go right on to the Scout meeting in a uniform that has been left lying on the floor" variety, and it is wholly ineffectual, of course. She won't go to the Scouts in the wrinkled uniform, naturally; either she'll show up at the last possible minute in the one decent dress she has left or she won't go at all; either way, it's her mother's fault, and she's going to tell the Scout leader so.

On the other hand, a mother is definitely an asset to a twelve-year-old girl. For one thing, a mother will agree to a larger clothes allowance than a father will, and she's usually a valuable ally when it comes to asking for extras, such as a new winter coat. No matter how old the female, she has an instinct that lets her know when men will be fussy about money.

A mother's no good when it comes to cooking and sewing lessons—these are properly taken care of by the Home Ec teacher, in a style diametrically opposite to anything ever seen at home. But a mother might remember enough of her college French to lend a hand with the homework, and somewhere there's always a lipstick she's forgotten to hide. She is also assumed to have a certain fund of practical knowledge ("Hello, Mom? Is this Mom? Listen, the baby's turned over on his stomach and Mrs. Banks didn't tell me whether he was supposed to or not and do you think I'd better turn him back over or can he sleep on his face?"). A mother can likewise be counted on to have errands to do in town while six giggling girls go shopping — thereby reducing the manager of the five-and-ten to near hysteria.

I must be more tolerant, I keep telling myself and telling myself. She's growing up. Pretty soon now she'll start being responsible and neat and sensible. I must be more tolerant. And there I go into her room, tripping over a Coke bottle and averting my eyes from the pictures of singers on the wall, and say through the steady beat of guitars from the record player, twisting my hands together and trying to get my voice down, "Is that my bottle of shampoo on your desk? Can't you pick up some of your magazines? It seems to me anyone would be *ashamed* to entertain her friends in a room like this. Can't you ever make your bed?" And she looks up through the tangle of drying socks and says, "Mother, *honestly!*" And then I have to go downstairs and sit by myself in the living room until I am steady again and can start telling myself to be more tolerant.

One thing really bothers me. I recently met a mother whose daughter is sixteen. When I remarked casually that I would be happy when my daughter outgrew her present stage and became more sensible and responsible, she just looked at me for one long minute and then began to laugh. She laughed and laughed and laughed. As I say, that bothers me a little.

How to Enjoy a Family Quarrel

THERE ARE GROUNDS FOR DEEP SUSPICION, I THINK, IN THE IDEA OF a family group that does not occasionally dissolve itself into a mass of screaming squabblers. I know of families where no word of dissent is ever permitted before—or from—the children, and these tend to be families where no word of tenderness either is ever permitted before—or from—the children. Not to put too fine a point on it, if two or three or four or five or six people live together in one house, sooner or later something is going to come up about which they do not see eye to eye and are prepared to say so. The children are displeased with their parents, perhaps, or displeased with one another or some outside element; it is even possible that the parents are displeased with their children. It would surely be unsafe to imagine that the average family could keep these emotions safely unspoken without some damage to the psyche, particularly the parents'.

In our family we are six—two parents and four children—and we are given to what I might call unceasing differences of opinion, more or less passionate. Almost any subject, from politics to small variations in daily dress, can find us lined up in formation on two bitterly opposed sides. Such a subject as *"Resolved,* That all allowances be trebled because of general charm and amiability" can keep us going for quite a while. This one is still current, my husband and I taking the negative.

We learned very early that it was safest to hold a united front on all major issues in front of the children. Since four of the members of our family are children, we also have learned never, never, *never* to put *anything* to a democratic vote. Time after time we found ourselves outvoted 4–2 and involved in things like going on a picnic tomorrow no matter whether it rains or not, and inviting those nice people with all the children to come for a weekend. Also we found out very early—when our older son was about six weeks old, in fact—that no parents ever got anywhere by calling in outsiders, particularly grandparents, for an impartial judgment.

Family arguments tend to be of two sorts, although one is not necessarily more peaceful than the other: the personal, or no-discussion-before-company type, and what for want of a better word might be called the impersonal—philosophical, political, or moral questions from the world at large. (The situation in the Middle East, for instance, or the probable baseball standings next fall, or whether it is fair to keep children out of certain movies, or the age at which it is proper for a girl to start wearing lipstick.)

On all general subjects, naturally, the children hold violently partisan opinions, dictated by what they saw on television, what the teacher said, or how Kathy's daddy voted. My husband and I hold opinions that are the result of reasoned, mature thought. Of course, the ending to *our* discussions often comes late at night, after the children are in bed, when my husband and I are still patiently explaining to each other in level voices the complete justice of our own views. (My husband, for instance, favors a weak answering no-trump, although I have time and again explained to him that it is a fallacious bid.)

The family argument usually takes place around the dinner table, somewhere halfway through the main course, when dessert seems impossibly remote beyond the mounds of spinach, and the novelty of eating again has largely worn off. Anyone, of course, may commence the fray, but once it's begun, certain immutable ground rules apply and may not be broken.

The ground rules may be stated as:

- The battle must be joined in a spirit of high moral indignation and a correspondingly high voice. In case of an argument on the impersonal level, some intelligent cause for an instance in the subject should be adduced, as "My old teacher made us learn all the parts of the alimentary canal." Or "What *good* is geography, anyway?"
- It is not necessary—is, in fact, reckless—to give anyone else's side of the question.
- The more vivid the detail, the more forceful the complaint. "He hit me and scratched me and pulled my hair and bit me" is clearly a finer many-angled trench to fight from than merely "He hit me."
- Once the arguable premise has been determined, counterattack may consist of flat denial ("I never did"), counteraccusation ("Well, you hit me first!"), or personal insult ("Anyway, you're nothing but a big baby"). In case of parental involvement, case histories may be admitted into evidence ("Since you are so consistently rude to members of your own family, I can see no reason why we should believe that you are civil to your sister's friends"), and dire prediction may be used as a pseudo threat ("The main part of growing up is the acceptance of responsibility, so a little girl who is going to wear lipstick and fancy shoes will naturally want to be more capable around the house and can therefore plan to wash *and* dry the dishes every night").
- If the father of the family speaks, whether in anger or not, absolute silence must be maintained, although it is not necessary to pay any particular attention to what he is saying.
- If the mother of the family speaks, by heaven everybody had better look alive.

- Any remark such as "But gosh, that was way back years ago when you were young" is regarded as dirty tactics.
- The father determines who shall have the floor by shouting "Quiet!" and half rising from his chair.
- Outside evidence (what Ernie saw, what Kathy said, the probable opinion of old Mrs. Atkins next door) is not allowed as legitimate matter of record, but there is no rule against bringing it up anyway.
- Only the father is permitted to say, "Do as I say, not as I do."
- Any apology fairly earned must be delivered as grudgingly as possible ("Yeah, so I *said* I'm sorry"), the mother and father excepted; their apologies must be graceful and complete, to teach the children manners.
- In impersonal arguments, reference books are referred to ("So go and look it up if you don't believe me") but never referred to.
- Any pronouncement by the mother or the father beginning "From this moment on, every single one of you children will . . ." can be ignored.
- Everyone must choose a side at once, as soon as the issue is brought forward, although it is not necessary to stay on the side you choose if things seem to be going the other way.

In addition to these formal ground rules, certain house rules apply in every family, differing, of course, according to the number of combatants, their several ages, and the varying vulnerabilities of the parents. In our family the basic house rules are:

- The father, who is not a man wholly without prejudice, will not suffer disorder. In his presence, pictures are to be straightened, books lined evenly on the shelves, silverware correctly placed. It is to be understood that no child of any age will tangle with Daddy on this subject. (The day when Jannie, in a fine white rage, deliberately disarranged all the objects on her father's desk is a day none of us will soon forget.)

- The mother is to be regarded as entirely unreasonable and beyond the reach of logic on such subjects as adequate clothing, riding bicycles in the street, table manners in general, and writing Christmas thank-you letters. She is not expected to make any sense with regard to underprotection rather than overprotection.
- The fourteen-year-old son will not permit his privacy to be invaded. Tidy he is not, nor clean, but no one may touch anything that belongs to him.
- The friends of the eleven-year-old daughter may not be criticized. They are her friends; she herself cannot *stand* that nasty Linda, she is never *never* going to walk home with Janet again, Millie's behavior is just simply *horrible*; but they are her friends and no one else may cast the second stone.
- The eight-year-old daughter is not to be crossed. She does things in a particular Sally way, and that way is right. Anyone who disagrees is either insane or, at best, hopelessly ignorant. In all of this she strongly resembles her father.
- The five-year-old son is adamant on personal dignity. He will listen, reason, and even consent to stop banging that gun against the wall if he is asked nicely, but at your peril lift him, set him aside, or use force against him because he is small.
- In case the teacher says one thing and the parents another, there is no question in anyone's mind who is right.

Once the ground rules are clearly established (house rules are absorbed by trial and error), the family argument should move quickly and effortlessly. Consider, for example, our family skirmish on the question of our television room, a general sore point anyway.

We have our television set in a small room furnished with a couch, two straight chairs, and three walls of bookcases full of books. In front of the couch is a small round table with two ashtrays on it and, in theory, nothing else. The television setup also includes a radio, a phonograph, and the attachments for the tape recorder. All four children watch television at some time or other during the usual day, and the couch is convenient for a parental nap after dinner. The room is, in fact, what in a less die-hard family might be called a recreation room, or even a music room, or—stretching a point—a library.

One late afternoon recently, my husband retired to lie down on the couch and watch the last quarter of the football game before dinner. He came storming out at once announcing that no one, no one, *no one* was ever going to watch television in this house again, or at least only over his dead body. The books had been knocked crooked in all the bookshelves because Barry and Sally had been roughhousing during the commercials. Jannie had left her sewing box and a book borrowed from Linda on one of the chairs. Laurie had been doing his homework in there and the ashtrays were full of torn scraps on which Latin phrases were scrawled, and the floor was covered with little pieces of thread and pencil sharpenings. I myself had left a sweater over the back of the other chair.

As I was clearly one of the sinning parties, I had no choice but to sneak my sweater out fast and attempt to modify the course of justice, at the same time making it clear to the children that Daddy and I were of one mind on everything. I chose to take the unassailable stand that I had told the children and *told* the children to pick up their things, and losing television was no more than they deserved for being so messy; but at the same time, unless something was devised to occupy all four of them during the time I was making dinner, it would very likely be impossible for me to get onto the table any of the small refinements—like deep-dish apple pie—of which my husband is very fond.

My husband said that none of that mattered at all; he would not have the television room left in disorder. Suppose, he demanded fiercely, suppose someone had dropped in to borrow a book? Would we like to have this literate stranger find the books crooked? The ashtrays full of paper? Sweaters lying around everywhere?

No, Laurie said, that was not fairly argued. In the first place, Dad never lent books to anyone, because it left spaces in the bookshelves. And Jannie had borrowed the book that caused all the disorder from Kate, and he bet that Kate's bookshelves looked even worse.

Jannie said they certainly did *not*; what did Laurie know about Kate's bookshelves, anyway, always thinking he was so smart?

I said that the sweater was mine and I had taken it off because I was going to vacuum the Venetian blinds in the television room; would my husband, I asked hotly, want his literate book borrower to find the Venetian blinds dusty?

Sally said she had not been roughhousing. Barry had pushed her and she had given him a kind of little small kick.

Barry said she had kicked him *hard*, right *here*, and anyway it was Sally who had fallen off the couch onto the bookcase.

Laurie said if he couldn't do his homework in the television room, where *could* he do it? Because how could he work in his room with Jannie playing rock-and-roll on her phonograph all day long?

My husband said now wait a minute, Jannie had every right in the world to play her own phonograph, and in any case rock-and-roll was a legitimate twelve-bar fast blues form.

Laurie said that anyone who could call that junk legitimate didn't know a tenor sax from a clarinet.

His father said that perhaps Laurie with all his education could not count as high as twelve? Because the twelve-bar blues form was exact and only an idiot could ignore it.

Laurie said he could play records that would make Jannie's records sound like a steel mill going full blast.

Sally and Barry began to fidget over their apple pie, and their father told them absently to run along and watch television, and he said to Laurie, all right, he would take Laurie's records and Jannie's records and show Laurie what was meant by a twelve-bar blues, and in Latin too, if Laurie preferred.

While they were getting out the records, I excused myself from the table and went in and straightened up the television room.

Some subjects on which we line up even are never going to be settled. Jan, Sally, and I think that I should cut my hair. My husband and Laurie say categorically that I may not, and Barry says that all haircuts are dangerous. My husband, Laurie, and Jannie think that an enormous new cabinet is necessary to hold the coin collection. Barry, Sally, and I would rather get a deep freeze, and there would be room in it for the coins, too, as well as the infinity of Popsicles that Sally and Barry believe would be kept there. I hold the most extreme position here; I think that we have too many coins anyway.

There is one argument in our family that is going to be settled out of hand. Five of us think we should get a new car; there is one hold-out who says that we cannot afford it. Four of us think that the new car should be a station wagon; Laurie thinks it should be a convertible, because they are making convertibles now that will hold six, and convertibles are the most, man! Three of us think the new station wagon should have four doors instead of two; Barry believes that if there were doors in the back he would fall out. Two of us think the new four-door station wagon should be pink, but Jannie says that that miserable Cheryl has a pink car and it's just *ugly*. One of us thinks that the new pink four-door station wagon is going to have white upholstery and chrome trimmings, and by golly that is just the kind of car we are going to get, as soon as I can talk my husband into it.

The Pleasures and Perils
of Dining Out with Children

I HAVE FOUR CHILDREN, AND I DO NOT BELIEVE THAT PARENTS WHO take children to dine in restaurants are necessarily insane. I can think of several adequate reasons for taking our children out for dinner. Perhaps the house has burned down and there are no neighbors charitable enough to take us in. Or our helicopter has crashed on the outskirts of town and the mechanic says, after the manner of mechanics, that no replacement parts can possibly be procured any nearer than Schenectady. Or dragons have invaded our kitchen and eaten everything in the refrigerator. Or I have announced, slamming the breakfast dishes around in the sink, that I am good and sick and tired of cooking meals and washing dishes and tonight I am going to have my dinner in a restaurant—although what I actually have in mind at that moment does not, of course, include the children.

I am thinking of a gracious dinner in a charming restaurant where the lights and music are soft, where if someone drops a fork the waiter brings another, where the used dishes are never seen again by me. I am beautifully gowned (nothing I have now will do, certainly), and I am going to have a crabmeat cocktail to start. Conversation is sparkling—about books, the better movies, the theater, the ballet. No mention is made of the current occupations of grade three of the local school. There is no lively banter about who was waiting around for Jimmie Brannan at recess. The names of the members of the high school football squad do not come up. All voices are quiet; there are no loud guffaws and no Dear Dollies or Precious Teddy Bears to dine with us. We will linger luxuriously at the table over coffee and brandy. I will come home from my lovely dinner, starry-eyed and in high-heeled shoes, to find the children's dinner dishes waiting in the sink. The babysitter will cost more than the restaurant. The kitchen floor will need an immediate washing, because of a butter-throwing episode that took place while the babysitter was turning out the kitchen cabinets trying to find the mustard, which I had left in plain sight on the table. The baby will not yet be in bed, the television set will have broken down, and a state of high-tension cold war will be prevailing in the living room. One of the younger children will have accepted a long-distance phone call from Grandma in California, but will be unable to remember anything Grandma said except how come we went out and left the children alone? There will be a note on the telephone pad reading "Mrs. Gbdryl called. Please call her right back." This mystery will not be solved until two days later, when Marian Williams runs into me in the supermarket and says in an icy kind of way that she is *sorry* I was too *busy* to call her but of course it wasn't the *least* bit important. It will of course have been extremely important, and if I try to explain that we went out for dinner she will say only that it certainly must be *wonderful* to be able to get out like that whenever we like. Sometime later in the week I will give up racking my brains and I will call the babysitter and ask her where she put the children's clothes when she undressed them. It will be a good long time before I make another attempt to live graciously.

However, sooner or later I am going to run again into one of those barren spells when I cannot think of anything to serve for dinner except meat loaf or tuna fish salad. Sooner or later I am going to announce that I am sick and tired of cooking meals and washing dishes and tonight I am going to have dinner in a restaurant and Daddy can take us all over to The Lake House for dinner.

The children are delighted. By five-thirty they are starving; washed and dressed in their neatest clothes, they are combed, smiling, alert. Because of this we will arrive at the restaurant somewhat earlier than most of the other diners and will, in fact, find only one waiter who is prepared to serve customers.

After a brief skirmish over seating arrangements ("Sally, if you would like to go wait in the car while the rest of us have dinner . . ."), we settle ourselves at a table that turns out to be right on the main highway from the kitchen to the bar, so that my husband and I will have to squeeze closer and closer to the table as the restaurant fills up and traffic gets heavier.

There is never any question about what the children will order. Barry would like a "peanut butter samwich." Sally wants "sperghetti." Jannie wants a well-done hamburger with lots and lots of relish. Laurie, who is fourteen, has no qualms about being in a restaurant; he has been brought here to eat and that is what he is going to do, without any foolishness of talking or playing or the small niceties of table manners. Laurie scowls ferociously at his younger brother and sisters, asks his father why we had to bring the little kids along anyway, and tells the waiter to wait a minute, he has not made up his mind yet. He concentrates sternly on the menu, pausing to ask the waiter whether the filet mignon at four dollars and seventy-five cents is bigger than the sirloin steak for four dollars and fifty cents, trying to cram the maximum amount of food into the limits of one reasonable dinner. He assures himself that he will be brought salad. He asks the waiter to be sure to remember his French-fried potatoes. He checks the desserts in advance, and while he is waiting for his steak to arrive he keeps a sharp eye on other tables to make certain that he will not be taken in by a small portion of lemon pie when the strawberry shortcake is large and lavishly whip-creamed.

It is a hard compromise between the eating habits of children and the serving habits of restaurants. When the idea of dinner is presented to a small child, he wants to see his dinner at once, all on one plate, with one spoon and one fork to eat it with. He has no patience with the fruit cups and chicken soup that precede his peanut butter sandwich. I have tried ordering Barry's peanut butter sandwich and Sally's spaghetti to be served them at once, but this only means that before I am quite through with my crabmeat cocktail, Barry and Sally will be demanding ice cream. At one end of the meal or the other, Sally and Barry are going to be without occupation while the rest of us dine. They will spend this time profitably. They may deal with the table setting, with the result that all the silverware is collected in front of me on the table, to be doled out piece by piece; napkins are trailing festively from the backs of chairs; and the vase of flowers, the salt and pepper shakers, the ashtray, and the sugar bowl all have been removed by their father to a safer table nearby.

When the attractions of the table setting are lessened ("Sally, if you would like to go and wait in the car while the rest of us have dinner . . ."), they discover that they can ease themselves from their chairs by sliding gradually under the tablecloth and popping out on the other side of the table between Laurie and Jannie, who are carrying on a conversation very loudly.

"Yeah?" Laurie is saying. "And who told *you* you were so smart, I wonder?"

"You know everything, I guess," Jannie says. "I guess you know everything, I don't *think*."

Barry and Sally locate a nice lady over there who looks as though she would be interested in hearing about the dead pigeon the dogs brought home. It is not impossible that there are other small children in the restaurant who would like to play tag in and out between the tables. At the very least they can go from one table to another examining what other people eat and asking if it tastes good. When they are brought back to the table by force ("Sally, if you would like . . ."), they settle down to various drummings, tappings, and kickings, until their father says "QUIET!" in a voice that stills the entire restaurant and, red-faced, he adds in a whisper that the next child who stirs will never see the inside of a restaurant again. He hastens to pay the check before I have quite finished my coffee. The children regard the occasion as a complete success and their behavior as exemplary. They keep referring afterward to "that time when we were so good in the restaurant."

Since we do have four children, and since there is an absolute limit to the amount of tuna fish salad my husband can regard with tolerance, and since our helicopter does break down frequently, we have finally, as a family, worked out a few simple solutions to the problem of dining out together. One of these we discovered accidentally: We went to a restaurant where the table mats were printed with a variety of jokes and puzzles. Happily, Laurie and Jannie did crossword puzzles, Sally made follow-the-dot pictures, Barry colored in all the little squares marked with an X, and my husband and I chatted about the new books and the ballet. The only disadvantage was the difficulty in getting the children to eat because they would not permit the waitress to put any plates down on the table mats.

My husband and I have also tried putting the four children at a table of their own and pretending that they have come in by themselves. This, although it requires almost supernatural acting ability, will delight the children endlessly, since they can peek around at Mommy and Daddy and giggle. Sooner or later, though, Laurie will call across the restaurant, "Hey, Dad, is Jannie allowed to have two desserts?" and the secret is out.

By far the easiest solution is to visit the restaurant of the children's choice. This will be a curb-service hamburger stand, the Elite

Café on Depot Street, or one of those roadside places that give away free balloons and lollipops and cardboard toys along with cold fried potatoes and unattractive foot-long hot dogs. The children will dine hugely, using large quantities of catsup from the fascinating plastic container, put uncounted numbers of nickels into the jukebox, visit freely a kitchen I would shudder to contemplate, and swing round and round on the stools at the counter. The coffee is usually pretty good at these places, and my husband and I can have a sandwich when we get home.

No cynicism can encompass, however, the infinite duplicity of children. Recently, because of dragons in the refrigerator, my husband and I found ourselves, with children, spending a totally unexpected weekend in an elaborate country inn. Because of a series of circumstances we found ourselves at table with an Anglican priest, a famous poet, and two jazz musicians, all of them absolute strangers. When we are dining with anyone outside the family, I always try to gather the children around me so that I can control them to some extent and conversation at the rest of the table can go on without too much competition. On this occasion I was not successful. Across the table, Jannie, looking incredibly small in her best yellow dress, sat between the priest and one of the jazz musicians, the trumpeter. Laurie, whose interest in jazz is absolute, had contrived to sit between the two musicians. Sally sat between the drummer and the poet. Barry sat between his father and the priest. I sat between the poet and my husband, with no child in reach, forced to rely upon an extemporaneous and elaborate system of signals and constant vigilance. A long, hard stare at each child in turn, moving meaningfully from child to napkin to child, finally got the napkins in the laps. My sign for put-that-water-glass-down-before-it-spills turned out to be a kind of flapping movement accompanied by a gasp. Eat-every-one-of-those-green-peas-with-a-*fork* was a baleful scowl that turned into a hasty false smile when the poet addressed me unexpectedly.

I never got much dinner, and I believe that the poet, whose good opinion I would have prized, came away with the idea that I was a kind of zany afflicted with some nervous disorder that, fortunately, had not been inherited by my children, since every child was, during the entire dinner, docile, demure, and courtly. The drummer cut Sally's roast beef (Sally dislikes meat and does not usually touch it with even the tip of her fork), and they discussed little girls while Sally ate her roast beef. The drummer said he had a little girl just Sally's age, and I distinctly heard Sally telling him that it was difficult for daddies to understand little girls, because they had invariably been little boys themselves. Laurie and the trumpet player dwelt lovingly upon the probable personnel of a band that seemed to be called Jelly Roll Morton and His Red Hot Peppers. Jannie, who was eating her salad as though she liked it, was conducting a spirited conversation with the priest over the sugary morality found in nineteenth-century children's books, a subject in which I had not suspected she was so learned, although I myself had given her *Elsie Dinsmore* to read. Barry watched wide-eyed, answered civilly when anyone asked him how old he was, finished his milk without being told, and volunteered to the table at large a brief but enthralling account of what his nursery school teacher had said about little boys who put modeling clay into the hair of little girls. My husband and the poet talked across me about baseball. Every now and then through the general conversation I could hear one of my children saying "please" or "thank you." When the children excused themselves and left the grown-ups to coffee, the priest remarked that they were far and away the best-behaved children he had ever seen. I thanked him and avoided looking at my husband.

The next night they were at home again, around their own table. Sally left her dinner in tears because she was told to eat her meat loaf or do without dessert. Jannie spilled her milk, Barry slipped all

352 • SHIRLEY JACKSON

his mashed potatoes to the dog under the table, Laurie told Jannie she was a perfect absolute idiot and ought to be kept shut in her room, and Jannie said she guessed he just thought he was pretty smart but people who had such good opinions of themselves were pretty often mistaken. Barry knocked his chair over trying to get under the table to recover his napkin, Sally wailed from upstairs that she just simply *hated* meat loaf, and Laurie left the table abruptly, remarking with his mouth full that he was going out to play catch with Rob.

I was never so relieved in my life.

Out of the Mouths of Babes

I RECENTLY MET A WOMAN WHO TOLD ME, IN THE TONE OF VOICE these women always seem to use, that she thought of her kiddies as ambassadors of goodwill. "Goodwill," she said clearly. "Ambassadors of goodwill. In everything they say and do, I want them to show just what kind of a little family we are," she said.

Most of what I wanted to say I sensibly left unsaid. For one thing, it was difficult for me to control my voice. Also, it is remotely possible that her children *are* different from mine and all others I know, and that they really might be ambassadors of goodwill, who show in everything they say and do what kind of a little family they're part of.

My children, of course, show in everything they say and do what kind of a little family *we* are. But the words that leap to mind in describing them are neither "ambassadors" nor "goodwill." "Blabbermouths" defines more exactly the term that occurs to me. As a matter of fact, they sometimes seem to me to be a mixed bag of gossip columnists, press agents, scandalmongers, and agents provocateur. Not to put too fine a point on it, they simply cannot keep their little rosebud mouths shut.

The more personal the item, the better. And they are unerring. They *know* that the neighbors and the kids at school are not the least bit interested in the serious questions we all were discussing at dinner last night. What the world *really* wants to hear is what Daddy said when he spilled coffee on his good pants. Nor is there any way to head them off. If my husband mentions incautiously that his name was misspelled on his income tax blank and I cut in hastily to say, "Let's not discuss this in front of the children," the next day everyone in town knows there is something wrong with Daddy's income tax, but it is a secret.

Some of the gabble is, of course, purely high-spirited, a genuine attempt to let the whole world in on the gay doings at our house ("You should have heard what Mommy said when the car wouldn't start"), and some of it is purely informative ("I told the teacher Daddy said she was wrong"). Occasionally the intent of the remark—this almost always to grandparents—is clearly to make trouble ("Barry broke the airplane you gave him"). It usually succeeds.

Sometimes the honor of the family is involved. Then it is the obvious duty of the children to rally round and man the barricades ("Mrs. Brown said we were certainly getting a lot of new clothes, weren't we, and I told her it was all right because you charged everything"). Sometimes the children—together and unafraid—feel compelled to defend their mother ("The kids in school didn't believe what Daddy says about being able to feed an army on what you spend").

I do not really believe that it is going to do any great harm for the neighbors to know that for Christmas, Daddy got pajamas with pictures of dancing ladies on them. As a matter of fact, if some emergency arose and he had to run into the street in the middle of the night, it would probably be just as well that the neighbors had been forewarned.

I am learning, too, to count to ten before I speak. I admit I was unwise in what I said at breakfast about Mrs. Smith and her infernal dog. But I insist that I did not say it exactly the way it was quoted to Mrs. Smith, and if she ever speaks to me again, I will tell her so.

Unraveling a knot of juvenile gossip is like getting out of an underground maze at night without a flashlight. A child comes home from school at lunchtime, quivering and furious. "I am never going to speak to my sister, Sally, ever again," she says, "or to anyone in this *whole family*, because you all said Linda looked like a chorus girl."

"Well, she does. That hair— Anyway, I never said anything of the sort."

"You did too. And Sally told Susan and Susan told *Linda* and Linda told her mother and now Linda can't invite me to her party."

"I may have said her hair was unbecomingly arranged."

"Linda told *me* her mother said I looked just as bad."

"That's ridiculous—although I do wish you'd comb back those bangs."

This does not make the aggrieved one feel any better. "And now Linda is telling everyone I'm not getting a new formal for the dance just to get *even*," she announces.

"And how does Linda know *that*?"

"Well, remember when you and Daddy were talking in the study the other night? And I couldn't sleep because you were talking so loud? And Daddy was talking about the bills?"

"And you told Linda about that, I suppose?"

"Well, she's my best *friend*."

"Susan says," Sally observes primly, "that Linda told *her* that her mother thinks it's too bad we girls dress so badly. Linda says her mother says your taste is in your feet."

"Says that about me? When her daughter goes out dressed like something from a rummage sale?"

There is a little mollified giggle. "Wait till I tell Linda *that*," Sally says.

"Now wait—wait a minute. I didn't mean it, really."

There is a remote possibility that someday Linda's mother and I may find ourselves sitting together over a friendly cup of tea, sighing over the problems of teenage daughters. But somehow I am beginning to wonder. It has come to my attention that she recently remarked that our neighbors might rather have had us put the money we spent on a new car into painting that house of ours. I have since told my daughter that she may not invite Linda to *her* party.

Anyway, I am much more interested right now in something Barry brought home from school this morning. It seems that little Jerry Allen told him that *his* mommy and daddy had a terrible argument last night, and Jerry and his sister are going to stay with their grandmother for a while. I knew Mr. Allen had business troubles, because his little girl told Sally she was going to drop out of dancing school. But I can't wait till the kids get home this afternoon to find out the rest.

The Real Me

I AM TIRED OF WRITING DAINTY LITTLE BIOGRAPHICAL THINGS THAT pretend that I am a trim little housewife in a Mother Hubbard stirring up appetizing messes over a wood stove.

I live in a dank old place with a ghost that stomps around in the attic room we've never gone into (I *think* it's walled up), and the first thing I did when we moved in was to make charms in black crayon on all the door sills and window ledges to keep out demons, and was successful in the main. There are mushrooms growing in the cellar, and a number of marble mantels that have an unexplained habit of falling down onto the heads of the neighbors' children.

At the full of the moon I can be seen out in the backyard digging for mandrakes, of which we have a little patch, along with our rhubarb and blackberries. I do not usually care for those herbal or bat wing recipes, because you can never be sure how they will turn out. I rely almost entirely on image and number magic. My most interesting experience was with a young woman who offended me and who subsequently fell down an elevator shaft and broke all the bones in her body except one, and I didn't know that one was there.

On Girls of Thirteen

SOMEWHERE IN OUR TOWN THERE IS A YOUNG LADY I AM VERY EAGER to meet. I don't know her name or where she lives, but I know just about everything else about her. She is thirteen years old. She is allowed to cut her own hair. She is also allowed to wear lipstick all the time; she uses bright red nail polish and heavily scented bath salts, and stays up as late at night as she pleases. She wears a clean blouse to school every day and she must have a great many pairs of shoes, because she does not wear overshoes or boots in any weather. Her phone calls are not restricted, and no one ever tries to make her stop giggling. She goes to all the dances at the school and she may stay out as late as she likes afterward; she may even stop off for a banana split, although this is not surprising, since she may have all the candy and sweets and toasted cheese sandwiches she wants.

She goes to the movies on school nights. If a young man invites her to walk down to the library with him in the evening and stop off for a Coke, she doesn't have to introduce him to her parents first. She wears quantities of cheap jewelry, her brother is *never* allowed to tease her, and if there is something she wants to see on television that comes on at eleven at night, or is full of shooting and screaming, she stays right up and sees it. Her mother picks up her room for her and she doesn't have to make her bed. She has a pair of high-heeled shoes; as a matter of fact, she seems to get more new clothes every day. She goes to all the basketball games, whether she has homework or not. If a book is unsuitable for her, she has read it.

As I say, I don't know her name or where she lives, but I'd like to get my hands on her. Just for about five minutes. She is the lowest common denominator, the altogether anonymous "everyone else" who rules the lives of thirteen-year-old girls and their miserable mothers. I hear more about her every day; if I point out that hot fudge sundaes are not the best thing for the digestion or the complexion of a young lady, or that there will be no ice skating until the top layer of junk is cleared out of that room, I hear, with a wail, that everyone *else* gets hot fudge sundaes, and everyone *else* gets to go ice skating without picking up their old rooms, and why does everyone *else* get all the fun instead of having cruel people around saying "work work work" all the time and she never gets a minute's peace and it just isn't *fair*. If everyone else is wearing white wool ankle socks these days, it doesn't make any difference that white woolen ankle socks get dirty fast and are wretched to wash and dry — everyone else has handed down the word and we conform, or we are *different*, which is a fate roughly equivalent to being pilloried in the public square.

My older son once remarked in a fury of exasperation that if the word "he" were dropped from the English language, his sister would be speechless. This is true as far as it goes, but in order to leave her *literally* without a thing to say, "we" would have to be dropped, too. I heard her once trying to explain this to her younger sister, who is still in the outsider stage. "*We* have a *crowd*," she said. "That means we all do the same things and don't decide things by ourselves; we all do just what the others do."

Regrettable as this sentiment may be in young people who ought by rights to be carrying around faces and minds of their own, there is no doubt about its truth. A bevy of thirteen-year-olds has only one mind, and it is the mind of everyone else. Naturally, when the mothers of thirteen-year-olds run into one another at the store, or meet at a dinner party, some of the problems can be ironed out; a simple agreement among half a dozen mothers that long black tights are not suitable for school wear can do wonders toward straightening out everyone else, and there is always the old, sometimes effective gambit "I don't care if Carole wears red nail polish right up to her elbows, no daughter of *mine* . . . " In general, however, we mothers are trapped by the oldest con game of all—I am persuaded to give in about the movies because Linda's mother has given in because I have given in because . . .

In some few areas this conformity of thought, this group identity, is valuable and fine. The group as a whole thinks college is an important objective, and so it is necessary to keep the group's school grade average on a high level. The group has firm opinions (secondhand, of course, and not infrequently handed down by some teenage idol) on such momentous subjects as drinking and smoking (bad), learning to drive (good), showing off in public (bad, particularly if there are boys around), acting on a stage (very good indeed), and going steady (all right if everyone else is doing it and if someone asks you).

These opinions are determined by a kind of mutual idea sharing, which means everyone talking at once and telephoning people who are not around to tell *them*. Sometimes such a group can be moved to action far beyond the normal capacity of any individual within it, as when they go all together to clean the house for the new Girl Scout leader, or organize and run a booth at the street fair. They are tireless, except at home. There are only two ways of getting any one of them to do anything like, say, rake the leaves off the lawn. One is to nag her ceaselessly for days until she goes sullenly and gets out the rake; the other is to say, with an air of inspiration, "Why don't we have a leaf raking party?"

Fads are not a large part of the problem. By now the teenage fad has become almost as commercial as Mother's Day, and almost any cheap novelty comes with a label attached reading "Latest Teenage Sensation." Odd gadgets of dress and language and decoration are being foisted off on the kids by people who think adolescents are a ready, quick market, but in my experience no self-respecting adolescent would be caught dead with most of this junk, hula hoops and sick jokes to the contrary. Hula hoops lasted here about two days, because they were simply not as much fun as building rafts on the lake, and sick jokes have been banned by unanimous parental decree. Or at least that is what we parents believe.

No, it is the participation in group thought that is the pattern of the thirteen-year-old life, not the group thought of manufacturers of charm bracelets, or even the makers of 45-rpm records, but the group thinking of her own crew, the Lindas and the Caroles and the Cheryls and the Barbaras, who decide by a kind of spontaneous flare that one disc jockey is preferable to another, or one television program is, as of this moment, dull and another exciting. From the time my daughter gets up in the morning to brush her hair the same number of times that Carole up the street is brushing *her* hair to the time she turns off her radio at night after listening to the same program that Cheryl three blocks away is listening to, her life is controlled, possessed, by a shifting set of laws that make your garden-variety savage initiation rite look like milk time in the nursery school. The side of the street she walks on, the shoes she wears to walk on it, the socks, the skirt, the pocketbook (and that pocketbook is a sore point; I fought against it wildly, because it was ugly, and cheap, and impractical, but Linda had one, and Cheryl, and Patty), even the jacket and the haircut are rigidly prescribed by everyone else.

I cannot remember acting this way (well, maybe; there was one terrible argument with my father that I remember, because he wanted to hear Al Smith's speech accepting the presidential nomination just at the time when my particular favorite weekly radio program was on), but then I like to think, vainly perhaps, that my life is no longer managed by the lives of my friends. What my life is really managed by is the lives of my *daughter's* friends.

Perhaps my main quarrel with this anonymous "everyone else" is her poor taste, based as it is on the lowest common denominator, the least possible thing that will suit everyone. I know by now that I am an old-fashioned, conservative, tone-deaf old fogey who doesn't know one guitar from another, and that I am heartless and a constant embarrassment to my daughter, but I cannot condone the garish, the pat, or the slovenly. I have been known to howl furiously at her to turn off that racket when all she was doing was listening to a recording of an eighteen-year-old lad singing about how he is old enough to recognize true love when he sees it. I have shuddered visibly, in public, when I have met her walking with her friends, all of them wearing dirty sneakers and swinging those hideous pocketbooks.

I snarl at the dinner table when she rattles off for the hundredth time the current popular phrase. I hunch myself over the wheel of the car, teeth clenched, when I am driving a pack of them to town so Patty can buy herself a blouse (it takes six of them to buy Patty a blouse, six giggling girls and three hours of shopping) and I hear the conversation going on behind me. I know by now that if I am putting six girls into my car the front seat beside me will always be left empty, but I can still hear them. What Ricky did, and what the teacher said, and oh, it was so *funny*, and does anyone remember what Johnny said to Cheryl when she dropped her pencil and oh, it was so *funny*, and one thing about Sandy, even though she's terribly pretty, and all the boys go for her, it's that fellow in college she really likes, even if he is almost eighteen, and Cheryl knows for a fact they're going steady. Linda heard this from Carole and Carole heard it from her big sister and her big sister says Sandy's not the one he *really* likes, and when Patty came right out and said so to her face, oh, it was so *funny*. And then Carole said that Cheryl liked Tommy, and oh, it was so . . .

It is all a kind of safety device, of course, and understandable even when most infuriating. They are making a firm bridge between being children and being grown-ups, so that they may cross together, holding hands, without terror. Nothing is ever as frightening as that first clear look at the world beyond thirteen years old, with its responsibilities and decisions and individuality, and sooner or later there is going to come a moment when what everyone else does is no protection or excuse. Her personality, evolved somehow out of what Carole said, and experiments with lipstick, and gaudy pocketbooks, and sick jokes, is going to have to stand up by itself, facing (oh, heavens!) perhaps marriage and children of her own. I hope she remembers. I only hope she remembers.

What I Want to Know Is, What Do Other People Cook With?

I HAVE AN ELECTRIC MIXER AND AN ELECTRIC BLENDER AND A TIMER on the oven and an electric skillet and an electric can opener, but what I really *cook* with is a fork. It is about five inches long, four-tined, with a black wooden handle, and my mother gave it to me when I was married. (My mother has a knack for gifts like that: when Laurie was born, everyone else showed up with pretty baby blankets and little sweaters wrapped in blue tissue paper; my mother gave me a vacuum cleaner.) I use my little fork to scramble eggs and to turn meat and to get muffins out of the toaster (I know that's wrong, but show me a better way, really better) and to poke at potatoes to see if they're done and to turn corn fritters in the pan and to hook doughnuts out of the fryer and to weasel waffles out of the waffle iron and to prick the tops of pies and to stir rice. I could really not begin to start making a meal without my fork.

It began to wear out at last. The screws that held the handle on had been replaced by my husband and my son Laurie and eventually my son Barry so many times that the holes were enormous and the handle kind of swiveled when I picked it up. And the tines were worn down on one side—I always cook right-handed—until the tip was triangular. I had better get myself a new fork, I thought reluctantly, caught for a minute in a recollection of the thousands of eggs that fork had scrambled and the pork chops it had turned and turned and turned; I had better go around to the hardware store the next time I am in town and pick up a new cooking fork.

"I would like a cooking fork, please," I said to the man in the hardware store the next time I was in town. "A fork for cooking."

"Certainly," he said, and led me to a great rack of forks.

Some of them were eight feet long and some of them were twelve inches long and they all had only two tines and the cheapest one cost four dollars. "This one is for outdoor cooking," the man said to me. "This one has an attachment that turns it into a roast baster. This one has a genuine plastic bone handle."

"No," I said, feeling silly. "I want a cooking fork with four tines and it ought to cost about a quarter and it's not for any special thing, just cooking."

"A quarter?" he said. "We don't have any forks that cost a quarter."

He didn't have any forks about five inches long, either, or any with black wooden handles and four tines. "Look," I said, holding my hands apart, wishing I had brought my little fork along with me, "about this long, four tines, and maybe it costs more these days, maybe as much as fifty cents."

"There is no such thing," he said with enormous dignity.

Well, I went to the five-and-ten and I went to the other hardware store and I looked in catalogues and I wrote to all the department stores I could think of and he was right: There *was* no such thing. I wrote to my mother and she wrote back that oh, yes, now I mentioned it she *did* remember the little black-handled kind of fork she used to cook with, but she had no idea where to get one. What did I want it for? I started asking my friends, and several of them remembered that *their* mothers or grandmothers had used just such a fork. ("Doughnuts," someone said wistfully; "you know, I haven't thought of those doughnuts for years and years; my grandmother used to get up in the morning and make them for breakfast, and I can still remember those hot fresh doughnuts on school mornings. Of course," she went on, resting one hand casually on her pressure cooker, "no one has *time* for that kind of thing now.") One of my friends thought she had seen such a fork in her aunt's kitchen not long ago, but when she called her aunt and asked, her aunt thought she was crazy. "Look, dear," her aunt said, "this is the twentieth century."

I took to hanging around people's kitchens, a habit that made me fairly unpopular and eventually got us largely not invited out to dinner anymore, trying to find out how other people did things. "Don't you scramble eggs with a fork?" I would ask. "What do you poke potatoes with to see if they're done? How about little holes on top of pies?"

Well, some people used a table fork and some people used a long two-tined fork, and I talked to a lot of people who never made scrambled eggs at all because they were too rushed for breakfast, and there were lots of gadgets for getting muffins out of toasters, and almost all of them got their pies at a bakery or frozen from the supermarket, and no one in the world but me ever used a little black-handled, four-tined, five-inch kitchen fork. I finally got so embarrassed about my little fork that I tried to use it secretly, so the children could not see and tell their friends, and I paid $5.95 for a great unwieldy thing that flipped pork chops halfway across the kitchen and short-circuited the toaster and could have been used nicely for weeding the garden. Words were passed around the dinner table about the charm of eating in restaurants, and my career as an active, participating member of the family was saved only when I finally got a new little fork.

A friend who hangs around antique shops found it for me in a basement store in Brooklyn. It was unused, authentic, and cost a dollar, because, I suppose, of its rarity. "Is this what you were looking for?" my friend asked. "I just happened to remember that you were interested in old kitchen utensils. Better boil it first if you plan to use it."

Well, I *do* plan to use it. I am starting right now to look for another one because this one ought to be wearing out in fifteen or twenty years. And unless someone lets me know what the rest of the world uses to cook with, I may even need another one after that.

Miss F. Etti Mology, Spinster

V

I'd Like to See You Get Out of *That* Sentence

Lectures About the Craft of Writing

•   •   •

"I'm teaching short story at Bennington,
and I love it. I have two classes a week.
I took the job with two conditions—one,
a hundred bucks a week, and the other,
that the College president learn to square
dance. If he doesn't learn by this coming
Saturday I quit."

•   •   •

About the End of the World
A Lecture

I FEEL THAT BEFORE I READ ANY OF MY NEW NOVEL, *THE SUNDIAL,* I would be wise to explain how it came to be written, and why, since I would not like to have any of you believe that I cook up this kind of thing in a cauldron.

I had published seven books, and was wandering around whining about writing another, considering and discarding plots, complaining that everything had already been written, and in general behaving like a novelist who needs money.

In order to reassure myself that all the best things had already been written, I took to rereading my own books, and discovered with some embarrassment that there was a kind of similarity to them, not necessarily in plot, which I could find all sorts of learned opinions to excuse, but in images and metaphors. Prominent in every book I had ever written was a little symbolic set that I think of as a heaven-wall-gate arrangement; in every book I have ever written, and, indeed, in the several outlines and rough sketches in my bottom desk drawer, I find a wall surrounding some forbidden, lovely secret, and in this wall a gate that cannot be passed. I am not going to attempt to analyze this set of images—my unconscious has been quiet for a good many years and I think I am going to keep it that way—but I found it odd that in seven books I had never succeeded in getting through the gate and inside the wall.

It occurred to me, then, that the thing to do was to write a new book, and *start* inside—write a kind of inside-out book, and maybe see what I have been writing about all these years when I have been writing outside-out books. What happened, of course, was the end of the world. I had set myself up nicely within the wall inside a big strange house I found there, locked the gates behind me, and discovered that the only way to stay there with any degree of security was to destroy, utterly, everything outside.

Concretely, the story is simple enough. A group of people are living in my big old house, which belongs to an old tyrant named Mrs. Halloran. These people are in the house more or less by chance—some of them are members of the family, one is a governess, others are guests who prefer to stay in the house rather than face destruction in the general cataclysm outside. These people believe for one reason or another in the prophecy handed down by one of their number: that the world outside is going to end, and everything will be destroyed except this house and the people inside it. After a night of horror and destruction they will come out, the only survivors, into a world of loveliness and peace, and become the first of a new race of mankind.

Nothing I have written has ever given me so much pleasure.

Memory and Delusion

A Lecture

THE CHILDREN AROUND OUR HOUSE HAVE A SAYING THAT EVERY-thing is either true, not true, or one of Mother's delusions. Now, I don't know about the true things or the not-true things, because there seem to be so many of them, but I do know about Mother's delusions, and they're solid. They range from the conviction that the waffle iron, unless watched, is going to strangle the toaster, to the delusion that electricity pours out of an empty socket onto your head, and nothing is going to change any one of them.

The very nicest thing about being a writer is that you can afford to indulge yourself endlessly with oddness, and nobody can really do anything about it, as long as you keep writing and kind of using it up, as it were. I am, this morning, endeavoring to persuade you to join me in my deluded world; it is a happy, irrational, rich world, full of fairies and ghosts and free electricity and dragons, and a world beyond all others fun to walk around in. All you have to do—and watch this carefully, please—is keep writing. As long as you write it away regularly, nothing can really hurt you.

My situation is peculiarly poignant. Not, perhaps, as sad as that of an orphan child condemned to sweep chimneys, but sadder than almost anything else. I am a writer who, due to a series of innocent and ignorant faults of judgment, finds herself with a family of four children and a husband, an eighteen-room house and no help, and two Great Danes and four cats, and—if he has survived this long— a hamster. There may also be a goldfish somewhere. Anyway, what this means is that I have at most a few hours a day to spend at the typewriter, and about sixteen—assuming that I indulge myself with a few hours of sleep—to spend wondering what to have for dinner tonight that we didn't have last night, and letting the dogs in and letting the dogs out, and trying to get the living room looking decent without actually cleaning it, and driving children to dance class and French lessons and record dances and movies and horseback riding lessons and off to town to buy a Ricky Nelson record, and then back into town to exchange it for Fats Domino, and over to a friend's house to play the record, and then off to buy new dancing shoes. . . . It's a wonder I get even four hours' sleep, it really is. Particularly, I might add, since I can't use the telephone. There is always someone *using* the telephone. The best I can manage to do is shout out the front door to the grocer's son when he drives past in his hot rod, and tell him to ask the grocer to have fourteen lamb chops ready when I come by later.

Actually, if you're a writer, the only good thing about adolescent children is that they're so easily offended. You can drive one of them out of the room with any kind of simple word or phrase—such as "Why don't you pick up your room?"—and get a little peace to write in. They go storming upstairs and don't come down again until dinner, which usually gives me plenty of time in which to write a short story.

At any rate, assuming that I am paying for my mistakes in judgment and never have enough hours in a day to spend at the typewriter, I would like to pass on a few things I have learned from those harassed, tense, welcome moments when I finally sit down to write. This, by the way, is what makes for Mother's delusions. All the time that I am making beds and doing dishes and driving to town for dancing shoes, I am telling myself stories. Stories about anything, anything at all. Just stories. After all, who can vacuum a room and concentrate on it? I tell myself stories. I have a whopper of a story about the laundry basket that I can't tell now, and stories about the missing socks, and stories about the kitchen appliances and the wastebaskets and the bushes on the road to the school, and just about everything. They keep me working, my stories. I may never write down the story about the laundry basket—as a matter of fact, I'm pretty sure I won't—but as long as I know there's a story there I can go on sorting laundry.

I cannot find any patience for those people who believe that you start writing when you sit down at your desk and pick up your pen and finish writing when you put down your pen again; a writer is always writing, seeing everything through a thin mist of words, fitting swift little descriptions to everything he sees, always noticing. Just as I believe that a painter cannot sit down to his morning coffee without noticing what color it is, so a writer cannot see an odd little gesture without putting a verbal description to it, and ought never to let a moment go by undescribed.

I was playing bridge one evening with a musician, a chemistry teacher, and a painter when, during a particularly tense hand, a large porcelain bowl that we kept on the piano suddenly shattered. After we had all calmed ourselves down, we found four completely individual reactions. Looking at all the tiny scattered pieces, I thought that I had never realized before how final a metaphor a broken bowl could be. The chemistry teacher pointed out that someone had emptied an ashtray into the bowl with a cigarette still burning, and of course the heat had shattered the bowl. The painter said that the green of the bowl was deepened when the light caught the small pieces. The musician said that the sound it made when it broke was a G sharp. Then we went back and finished our bridge hand.

Someday I know that I am going to need that broken bowl. I will keep the recollection of those scattered pieces, lying on the piano, and someday when I want a mental image of utter destruction the bowl will come back to me in one of a dozen ways. Suppose, for instance, that someday I had occasion to describe a house destroyed by an explosion; the manner of destruction would be different, of course, but what I can remember is the way the little pieces of the bowl lay there so quietly after they had been for so long parts of one unbroken whole; now, not one of them could have found its place again, and the compactness that had held them together no longer existed in this world.

Suppose I wanted to describe the effect of a sudden shock— I had just played a jack of spades when the bowl broke, and for what must have been three or four seconds I sat staring at the jack of spades uncomprehendingly before I caught my breath again. Suppose someday I want to describe the sense of loss over a treasured and valuable article—my green bowl was not particularly valuable, or I wouldn't have let people dump ashtrays into it, but I can remember how I felt when I swept up the pieces and put them in the garbage and how entirely *destroyed* the pieces looked.

The act of remembering is in itself an odd thing, of course. I had not thought of that green bowl for weeks, until I wanted a vivid image to explain how all things are potential paragraphs for the writer. I have been struggling against an odd memory effect for quite a while now; perhaps if I describe it, it may show more clearly what I mean when I say that nothing is ever useless, and certainly is never lost.

I was talking casually one evening recently to the husband of a friend of mine, and he mentioned his service in the Marines. I said, "Oh, yes, your rifle number was 804041," and then we kind of stared at each other dumbfounded, since one does not usually just happen to know the rifle numbers of the husbands of friends. We finally remembered that some months before, during a similar conversation after another bridge game, he had mentioned his Marine service, and remarked that one thing he would never forget was his rifle number, 804041. Well, it was reasonable for *him* never to forget his rifle number, but hardly likely that *I* would remember it. However, I couldn't forget it. I caught myself reciting it to myself over and over again, wondering why on earth I bothered.

I was having a good deal of trouble at the time, working over a new novel that somehow refused to go together right. I could not make my central character sound true, somehow; there was something basically at odds between her personality as I saw it and the actions she was called on to perform. One night I gave up; I shoved the typewriter away and kicked the dog and snarled that I was giving up on the book and would never write another, and furthermore it was hopeless and I might better be doing anything else in the world and who would choose such a nerve-racking profession anyway, and I was going to bed. So I stamped upstairs and went to bed, somehow forgetting to set the alarm clock.

When I came rushing downstairs the next morning, half an hour late for school, and scrambled wildly around the kitchen trying to get everybody dressed and washed, and also feeling very bad-tempered, I did not go at once into the study. As a matter of fact, it was not until much later in the morning that I went near my desk, but when I did, I got one of the really big shocks of my life. A sheet of paper had been taken from the pile of copy paper and put directly into the center of the desk, right where it would be most visible. On this sheet of paper was written, in large figures, and in my own writing with my own pencil, 804041.

Now, I have walked in my sleep frequently, particularly when I am under pressure with a book, and have often done odd things in my sleep, but I have rarely taken to writing notes to myself, and particularly not in code. What I finally did was what I should have done long before, which is get myself another cup of coffee and sit down quietly and think. Clearly, I was remembering this number as a clue to something else, and it must be something from the conversation when I first heard the number—or at least that seemed the likeliest place to start. I tried to reconstruct the conversation exactly. I could not remember what we had been talking about; I remembered the bridge table and the cards on it and that we had been waiting for the four at the other table to finish a rubber, and I remembered that except for our voices, which were low, the room was so quiet that I could hear my daughter's radio going upstairs. But I could not remember what we had been talking about. All I could remember was 804041.

I assumed that we had talked about the cards, and the game we had just finished, and then what? What do people usually talk about when they are killing time with conversation? Their children . . . small incidents that have happened . . . gossip . . . And then of course I had it, and I knew just why I had had such trouble remembering it. The former Marine had met an old friend of ours in New York, had run into him casually on the street, and had gone to have a drink with the old friend and his new wife, an Italian girl who had been in an anti-Fascist organization and had been caught and tortured. He had made some remark about being sick when he looked at her hands, and I had stopped him from saying anything more, but he had gone on to say that she spoke frankly about her experiences and particularly about a kind of schooling she had gone through to teach her to undergo torture without yielding, a schooling that trained her to withdraw her mind from her body, so that the physical pain was remote and could, by an act of superlative willpower, be endured. He had gone on from this to refer to his own war experiences, and had then remarked that he would never forget the number of his rifle, 804041.

When I remembered all of this and went back to my book again, I found that the trained ability to separate mind and body, a deliberate detachment, was the essential characteristic I had been looking for for my heroine, and was what I had been trying to tell myself by saying the number over and over again. I had made myself forget the woman's frightful experiences because the thought of them was horrible, but the important lesson, the one I needed, was there. What bothers me now is that I *still* can't forget 804041; I wonder what else he said?

That is one half of writing, of course. The lower depths, as it were. The other half is what I might delicately call information. Henry James got the idea for *The Spoils of Poynton* from a single remark heard at dinner, but he also had to find out somehow what lovely possessions looked and felt and smelled like, the tapestries splendidly toned by time, the thrilling touch of the old velvet brocade.

Among other invaluable items of useless information, I recall a book written by an English lady of the eighteenth century, which dwelt long and lovingly on the evils of education for women. This lady deplored the growing desire among the girls of her time to be educated and learn to read and write; her theory was that once a girl started filling her mind with facts instead of fancy embroidery methods and seven easy tunes on the harp, she would turn into an attic storehouse of miscellaneous knowledge, tending to decrease her matrimonial value and rendering her almost useless as a wife and mother, and even, possibly, delusional.

On Fans and Fan Mail

A Lecture

I THINK THAT THE POPULAR NOTION OF THE WRITER AS A PERSON hiding away in a garret, unable to face reality, is probably perfectly true. In my own experience, contacts with the big world outside the typewriter are puzzling and terrifying; I don't think I like reality very much. Principally, I don't understand people outside; people in books are sensible and reasonable, but outside there is no predicting what they will do.

For instance, I went the other day into our local drugstore and asked them how I would go about getting enough arsenic to poison a family of six. I had expected that they would behave as people would in any proper Agatha Christie book; one of them, I thought, would engage me in conversation in the front of the store, while someone else sneaked out back to call the cops, and I was ready with a perfectly truthful explanation about how the character in my book had to buy arsenic and I needed to find out how to go about it. Instead, though, no one really paid any attention to me. They were very nice about it; they didn't have any arsenic, actually, and would I consider potassium cyanide or an overdose of sleeping pills instead? When I said I had my heart set on arsenic, they said then I had better get in touch with a taxidermist, since no modern drugstore stocks arsenic anymore at all. Now, you have to concede that such behavior is bewildering; if someone turned up with chronic arsenic poisoning, they probably wouldn't even remember that I was in asking about it.

I actually wanted to talk, though, about the most irrational and annoying aspect of the outside world that is always infringing on a writer's life, and that is what is loosely called "fan mail." I don't answer many of the letters I get, usually, even though most of them are very kind and polite and say they liked my last book; but there is a certain type of letter that makes me wonder who is crazy these days—me or them. There is the kind of letter that asks if I am the Shirley Jackson who taught fifth grade in Toledo, Ohio, in 1902. There is the kind of letter that says I have stolen the correspondent's name for one of the characters in a book and I am going to be sued for libel unless I immediately forward all royalty payments. I got a letter recently saying that the correspondent had just noticed a picture of me in a magazine, and the picture showed me with a dog that was stolen from him several months ago; I was either to send him back his dog or a check for the dog's sentimental value, which he set at two hundred dollars. Or, consider this letter:

Dear Miss Jackson,

I am a sailor on an aircraft carrier in the South Pacific. You are my favorite author and I would appreciate it if you would answer the following questions:
　　1. Are you married?
　　2. Do you have any children?
　　3. Do you have a snapshot of yourself you would send me?
　　Hoping you will answer this letter as I enjoy literary correspondence.

Sincerely yours.

Of course the only possible answer was:

Dear sailor:

I am forty-two years old, and my oldest son is draft age. I am, however, enclosing a snapshot of my sixteen-year-old daughter, who also enjoys literary correspondence.

Sincerely.

Someday the English teachers of the world are going to be made to suffer for what they do to writers. Every spring—which is term paper time—I get, and every other writer I know gets, twenty or thirty letters, all of one kind. They vary only in the degree of misspelling, and they typically read:

Dear Miss Jackson,

Our high school English class is doing a term paper on its favorite authors. You are my favorite author, so will you please tell me the names of all your books and your best known stories and any television plays or movies you have written and also I would like to know your theories about writing and in general what you are trying to say. Also what you find in your daily life that you can use in books and stories and your likes and dislikes in other writers and if possible a small autographed picture of yourself and anything else you think may be of help to me in my paper. My paper has to be handed in this coming Friday, so I would appreciate a quick reply to this letter. Yours very truly.

As I say, I get twenty or thirty of these letters every spring, and they go into the wastebasket. In one case I had a follow-up letter from the English teacher of one of the girls who had written me; she was furious because her student had failed English for lack of a term paper. She wanted to know who did I think I was, letting that girl fail? The girl's original letter had had eleven misspellings; the teacher's had only three. I did answer several of these when they first started coming, asking to see a copy of the term paper. I finally got hold of one paper. The student had copied my letter word for word.

I would like to finish by reading you my two favorite fan letters. The first of them was sent not to me but to a friend of mine who writes children's books. It reads:

Dear Sir,

I like to read a lot of books but every time I find one I like best and write the author a letter it turns out he is dead. If you are not dead will you please answer this? I love you.

Sadly enough, it was signed only "Linda" and gave no address.

There is one letter I never tire of reading over. It was sent to me shortly after the publication of my story "The Lottery," and was addressed to *The New Yorker*, where the story first appeared. It came, naturally enough, from Los Angeles:

Dear Sirs:

The June 26 copy of your magazine fell into my hands in the Los Angeles railroad station yesterday. Although I donnot read your magazine very often I took this copy home to my folks and they had to agree with me that you speak straitforward to your readers.

My Aunt Ellise before she became priestess of the Exhalted Rollers used to tell us a story just like "The Lottery" by Shirley Jackson. I don't know if Miss Jackson is a member of the Exhalted Rollers but with her round stones sure ought to be. There is a few points in her prophecey on which Aunt Ellise and me don't agree.

The Exhalted Rollers donnot believe in the ballot box but believe that the True Gospel of the Redeeming Light will become accepted when the prophecey comes true. It does seem likely to me that our sins will bring us punishment through a great scouraging war with the devil's toy (the atomic bomb). I don't think we will have to sacrifice humin beings fore atonement.

Our brothers feel that Miss Jackson is a True Prophet and Disciple of the True Gospel of the Reedeeming Light. When will the next Revelations be published?

Yours in the Spirit.

This letter was never answered.

How I Write

A Lecture

I FIND IT VERY DIFFICULT TO DISTINGUISH BETWEEN LIFE AND FICtion. I am of course the kind of writer who, through some incredible series of coincidences, finds herself actually at the typewriter for only a few hours a day, the rest of the time being spent vacuuming the living room rug or driving the children to school or trying to find something different to serve for dinner tonight.

Most of my time, actually, is spent doing things that require no very great imaginative ability, and the only way to make these mechanical jobs more palatable is to think about something else while I am doing them. I tell myself stories all day long, and have managed to weave a fairy tale of infinite complexity around the inanimate objects in my house, so much so that no one in my family is surprised to find me putting the waffle iron away on a different shelf because in my story it has quarreled with the toaster, and if I left them together they might come to blows; they had quarreled, incidentally, over my getting some of the frozen waffles you drop in the toaster, and the waffle iron was furious. It *looks* kind of crazy, of course. But it does take the edge off cold reality. And sometimes it turns into real stories.

I remember one spring morning I was on my way to the store, pushing my daughter in her stroller, and on my way down the hill I was thinking about my neighbors, the way everyone in a small town does. The night before, I had been reading a book about choosing a victim for a sacrifice, and I was wondering who in our town would be a good choice for such a thing. Also I was wondering what would happen if they drew lots by family; would the Campbell boys, who haven't spoken to each other in nearly twenty years, have to stand up together? And I was wondering what would happen about the Garcia boy, who had married a girl his parents couldn't stand— would she have to be admitted as a member of their family? I was so fascinated by the idea of the people I knew in such a situation, I thought that when I got home I might try writing it down and seeing what happened. So after I bought my groceries and pushed my daughter back up the hill and put her in the playpen, I sat down at the typewriter and wrote down the story I had been telling myself all morning. Because I was interested in the method, I called the story "The Lottery," and after it was printed people kept writing me letters about it, saying what a frightening story it was, and how did I ever think of a horrible thing like that? For a while I tried telling them that I was just thinking about my neighbors, but no one would believe me. Incidentally, no one in our small town has ever heard of *The New Yorker*, much less read my story.

One of the nicest things about being a writer is that nothing ever gets wasted. It's a little like the frugal housewife who carefully tucks away all the odds and ends of string beans and cold bacon and serves them up magnificently in a fancy casserole dish. A writer who is serious and economical can store away small fragments of ideas and events and conversations, and even facial expressions and mannerisms, and use them all someday. It is my belief, for instance, that somewhere in the back of my own mind is a kind of storeroom where there are hundreds of small items I am going to need someday, and when I need them I will remember them. I am also sure that this storeroom must look a good deal like my desk drawers, which also contain all kinds of things I am sure I am going to need someday, such as a pair of roller skates and the curls cut off the children and an old compact and what I think is the inside lining for my heavy winter boots.

I believe that a story can be made out of any such small combination of circumstances, set up to best advantage and decorated with some use of the imagination; I began writing stories about my children because, more than any other single thing in the world, children possess a kind of magic that makes much of what they do so oddly logical and yet so incredible to grown-ups. Now that my children are old enough to read and have become more aware of themselves, I find it almost impossible to write about them without sounding artificial, because they are doing things with that unfortunate adult reasoning that takes away all the magic. Once, however, when I had spent all one rainy day wrestling with my old refrigerator, whose doors tended to jam shut, my younger daughter asked why I didn't open it by magic.

It was a lot pleasanter to abandon the refrigerator and sit down and write a story about opening it by magic than to go on being sore at it and banging it with my fist; we had to go out for dinner, but of course that's all right with me anytime. The story, by the way, paid for a new refrigerator, which is *certainly* better than trying to open the old one without magic. What I am trying to say is that with the small addition of the one element of fantasy, or unreality, or imagination, all the things that happen are fun to write about.

I am particularly interested in reality right now, because I am writing a novel in which reality is the key issue. It is a novel about a haunted house and a group of people who go to live in it and make observations upon the psychic manifestations to which they are subjected. Now, no one can get into writing a novel about a haunted house without hitting the subject of reality head-on; either I have to believe in ghosts, which I do, or I have to write another kind of novel altogether. I have found that, more than ever before, I am wandering in a kind of fairy-tale world, although right now it is full of ghosts too.

Before I started writing this, I spent several months reading nothing but ghost stories, going through volume after volume of luminous figures glimpsed floating down the garden path, or mysterious moanings in attics, and perhaps it was not altogether healthy; every now and then I had to go and read a chapter of *Little Women* again to get back my perspective.

When I start writing a book, I go around making notes, and I mean that I literally go around making them; I keep pads of paper and pencils all over the house, and when I am making beds or sorting laundry or trying to find the six odd socks that have gotten down behind the children's dressers, I am going over, endlessly, possible scenes and situations for a novel, and when anything comes out clear I race to the nearest paper and pencil and write it down, frequently addressing it to myself, in my own kind of shorthand dialect. I am apt to find, in the laundry list, a scribble reading, "Shirley, don't forget—no murder before chapter five" or, on my shopping list, "Make housekeeper go home nights" or "Shirley, have old man fall downstairs." When I am ready to write the book, I go and collect all my little scraps of paper and try to figure out what I was thinking when I wrote them.

Two weeks ago, I had written part of the beginning of the book and was having a great deal of trouble making it go together and could not find a suitable name for my secondary female character. One evening, I had been at it for a couple of hours, typing and growling and throwing pages on the floor, and finally I decided to give up. I told my husband that I was going to have to put the book aside, maybe even start another book, maybe never go back to this one again, and I stomped furiously up to bed.

The next morning, when I went to my desk, I found a sheet of typing paper; it had been taken from the pile at one side of the desk and set right in the middle. On the paper was written, "oh no oh no Shirley not dead Theodora Theodora." It was written in my own handwriting, but as though it had been written in the dark.

I have always walked in my sleep, but I don't think I have ever been so frightened. I began to think that maybe I had better get to work writing this book awake, because otherwise I was going to find myself writing it in my sleep, and I got out the typewriter and went to work as though something were chasing me, which I kind of think something was. Since then, the book has been going along nicely, thank you, and my female character is named Theodora and is turning out quite well.

Now, incidentally, you can see why a writer might be reluctant to explain where ideas for books come from. Who would ever believe it?

Garlic in Fiction
A Lecture

FAR AND AWAY THE GREATEST MENACE TO THE WRITER — ANY WRITER, beginning or otherwise — is the reader. The reader is, after all, a kind of silent partner in this whole business of writing, and a work of fiction is surely incomplete if it is never read. The reader is, in fact, the writer's only unrelenting, genuine enemy. He has everything on his side; all he has to do, after all, is shut his eyes, and any work of fiction becomes meaningless. Moreover, a reader has an advantage over a beginning writer in not being a beginning reader; before he takes up a story to read it, he can be presumed to have read everything from Shakespeare to Jack Kerouac. No matter whether he reads a story in manuscript as a great personal favor, or opens a magazine, or — kindest of all — goes into a bookstore and pays good money for a book, he is still an enemy to be defeated with any kind of dirty fighting that comes to the writer's mind.

Picture this creature, this clod, this reader, as lying comfortably in a hammock, yawning and easily distracted, a glass of iced tea by his side, half a dozen light novels and a magazine or two right where he can reach them, a portable television set well within his vision, the sun shining lazily and a golden sleepy haze surrounding him. Now ask him to select a story—a story slaved over and polished, edited and refined and perfected with infinite labor—and ask him to lie there and read. Dirty fighting is only half of it—any possible trick must be well within the rules for the writer.

Now, this unspeakable boor in his hammock may be a genuinely serious reader; he may fully intend to read the story in his hand, but it is much, much easier for any given reader *not* to read any given story. Suppose the first paragraph bores him, or the title doesn't look very promising, or he dislikes the name of the hero. Suppose there is an illustration that makes it look as though the story is going to be about love. Or he read a story once before about the same general subject and he didn't like that one. Now, of course a writer cannot go around changing the names of his heroes or the plots of his stories or an illustration or a title on the off chance that there is some reader who is going to be thrown off stride by any of them. It is, of course, the writer's job to reach out and grab this reader: If he is a reader who cannot endure a love story, it is the writer's job, no more and no less, to make him read a love story and like it. Using any device that might possibly work, the writer has to snare the reader's attention and keep it.

Here is one of the greatest pitfalls for beginning or inexperienced writers: Their stories are, far too often, just simply not very interesting. It is easy to be trapped in a story you are writing, and to suppose that the interest you feel yourself in the story is automatically communicated to the reader; this is terribly important to me, the writer tells himself, this is a matter of the most extreme importance to me, and therefore a reader will find it important, too. And the reader, opening one sleepy eye, thinks that the fellow who wrote this thing was certainly pretty worked up about something, wasn't he; funny how hard it is to stay awake while you are reading it.

Any discussion of what might or might not catch the interest of a reader is hopeless; any magazine editor can give endless meaningless platitudes about what people want to read, or what people ought to read, but in the last analysis no story of any kind for any magazine for any type of reader is going to be interesting unless the writer, using all his skill and craft, sets himself out deliberately to make it so.

I want to call this "garlic in fiction" because I cannot think of a more vivid way of describing the devices of fiction, the particular, frequently almost unnoticed tricks a writer can use to enormous advantage. Far too often we think of a short story as a simple account of something that happens, an account in which one event follows another, and the whole, limited by requirements of time and place, exists coherently and complete.

Even when writing a short story there is a tendency to discount embellishments, to feel that filigree writing does not belong: Leave the metaphors and symbols, the images and adjectives, to the poets and the composers of the Sunday supplements. Yet within the rigid framework of the short story, without in any way destroying its un-broken unity, from the first word to the last, the writer is permitted a good deal of space in which to catch at the reader and hold him with small things, used—and here is where the garlic comes in—sparingly and with great care, but used always to accent and empha-size.

Naturally, every writer has dealt in one way or another with met-aphor, and there are few more pathetic sights than a writer hope-lessly entangled in a great unwieldy metaphor that has gotten out of control and is spilling all over the story, killing off characters and snapping sentences right and left; huge metaphors, such as this one, are far better left to people with a lot more time and space to write. Adjectives are always good, of course; no short story really ought to be without adjectives, particularly odd ones—such as "fulsome"—that the reader usually has to go and look up. And of course adverbs such as "unworthily"—even if you have to make them up yourself—are always very useful.

I recently attended a symposium on folk music, and the very first words of the very first lecture so enchanted me that I left at once; the speaker began by announcing that this lecture was for "those of you who are musically oriented, banjo-wise," and since I have always wanted to use a phrase like that somewhere, let me make my present position clear by saying that I am speaking to those of you who are fictionally oriented, image-wise, and see how far I get.

I am actually going to talk about what I call images, or symbols. It seems to me that in our present great drive—fiction-wise—toward the spare, clean, direct kind of story, we are somehow leaving behind the most useful tools of the writer, the small devices that separate fiction from reporting, the work of the imagination from the everyday account. Of these the far most important, and the most neglected, is the use of symbols; I am using the word loosely, because it has altogether different meanings elsewhere, and yet I hardly know what other word to use. The thing I am talking about is best identified by reference to a theory of acting that has always seemed to me very profound, and certainly useful to the writer: Before entering upon a role, the actor, having of course familiarized himself with the character he is to portray, constructs for himself a set of images, or mental pictures, of small, unimportant things he feels belong around the character.

There must be at least one basic image, or set of images, for each character in a story, a fundamental symbol the writer keeps always in mind; as these images grow the character grows, and the accumulation of material and information about the image slowly makes up the character in the story. Various things *belong* to a character—a manner of speaking, a manner of moving, a particular emphasis, a group of small physical things—and each of these must take on, like a perfume, the essence of the character they belong to. Just as a tune or a scent can evoke for most of us an entire scene, so the basic image of the character must evoke that entire character and his place in the story. As a result of this, of course, the characters themselves grow apart in the writer's mind, become entirely separate people, and by the end of a book or a story the writer can no more mistake one for another than he can mistake a can of beans for a pearl necklace.

Suppose a story needs a male character. In the story he must further the action, although he is really a minor character. If the story requires no very definite attributes from him, suppose the writer were to assign, arbitrarily, the image of a bird to this character. He need never be named or called a bird, but his gestures and his habits are birdlike, his voice and his very words are sharp and twittering, and in his brief appearance he might select nuts, or pieces of popcorn, and pick them up like seeds from the ground, with a quick darting movement. Even if this character never appears again, he has been alive for the space of a page, perhaps, and has added depth and imagination to a story.

As I say, what I am calling images or symbols or garlic is actually a kind of shorthand, or evocative coloring, to a story. A story is, after all, made up only of words. Characters are given only the briefest physical descriptions and identities; there is really no time in a short story to examine any single person in great detail. Events are merely sketched, given clearly enough to forward the story's action but not described entirely; there is no room in a short story for more than one theme or idea.

Within these strict limits the writer must operate as vividly as he can, drawing as much as possible upon a sympathy with the reader, hoping that a single word will be enough to turn the reader inward, remind him, perhaps, of a similar emotion of his own, to bring him along willingly down the path of the story. Many experiences in life are common to all of us, and a word or two is frequently enough to enrich a story with a wealth of recollection; take, for instance, the words "income tax." There is surely a community of feeling that overwhelms us at the very sound of the words; no two people, naturally, feel exactly the same way about income taxes, but there is no question but that everyone feels *something*; a rueful or joking reference to income tax always brings a sympathetic response, and perhaps the only area where the words do not bring happy recognition is one of wholehearted approval. There are many such powerful words that work by themselves for the writer, but beyond these there must be words and phrases the writer enriches artificially for the purpose of a single story, words that have that weighting only in that story, words that must be used, in short, like garlic.

Perhaps this can best be dealt with by examples. Consider an idea for a fairly lunatic story: A silly young woman, alone in the world, falls in love with a man she has just met, and marries him without any knowledge of his history or background. On their honeymoon, which they spend in a borrowed cottage at the seashore, the wife, falling into conversation with a neighbor in the grocery store, learns that various people around the little community believe that her husband is actually a notorious murderer, one of the kind who habitually drown their wives in the bathtub and collect their insurance. This neighborhood theory is broken gently to the young wife, because no one around quite has the courage to take any action; no one is sure that he *is* the man, but with true neighborly solicitude they want to put the young wife on her guard. Suppose this silly young woman listens with her mouth open to the stories about the vicious murderer: he always persuades his wives to make wills in his favor; he drowns them, of course, while they are bathing; he always chooses a night when there is a full moon; he always brings his wife a box of candy and a bunch of roses on the day when he has decided to kill her.

Our young wife has been in the grocery because she was buying four lamb chops for their dinner. She will have to go back to their lonely cottage, carrying her four lamb chops, and wait for her husband to come home. She knows where her husband is—he has gone to take various papers, including the will she has just signed, and leave them in his safe-deposit box. She knows there is going to be a full moon because he made some romantic remark about it before he left in the morning. He is due to come home any minute. She had intended to put on one of her prettiest dresses and cook him a little dinner, just for the two of them, and then perhaps they would walk by the ocean and look at the moon. Now, with her new information, what should she do? Should she try to take a bath fast and get it over with before he comes home? Will she discover that the lock on the bathroom door is broken? Is it really worthwhile for her to bother setting the table for two or even to cook her lamb chops?

Suppose, while she is wavering, her husband comes home early. He is carrying a box of candy and a great armful of red roses. The entire story can now be brought to a conclusion without ever referring again to the rude facts. On the one hand, the wife ought in decency to thank her husband for bringing her candy and flowers; on the other hand, how can she possibly say, "Thank you, I know exactly why you brought them"? The conversation, as a matter of fact, would be extremely funny, particularly if the husband's position remained ambiguous; no one, after all, is *sure* that he is a murderer. If he is not a murderer, his reaction to his wife's terrified remark that she thought she would go without a bath might be one of considerable surprise; she would hardly be in the habit of consulting him, after all, when she wanted to take a bath. If he is very hungry and says cheerfully that the lamb chops look very small and that he could eat all four of them himself, his wife can only conclude that he intends to dine alone, afterward. I see the story as ending with the wife, maddened by suspense, shouting wildly that all right, all right, he can stop hanging around waiting; if it will make him any happier she'll go and take her old bath, and the husband would be altogether dumbfounded—or pretending to be.

Now, here there need never be a moment when the wife asks her husband point-blank if he intends to murder her, or a moment when the husband reveals himself and announces his plans; everything is taken care of by the lamb chops and the bath, the roses and the moon. If the story were broken off where I have left it, one additional sentence could give the reader a full ending. If the lamb chops were cooked at all, there must have been one place set at the table—or two. The candy might be opened—or set carefully aside for the next time.

I want to give you another example, this time from my own novel, where I had a difficult problem and found that I could solve it only by taking it out of the actual, as it were, and dealing with it symbolically. Before I use an example from my own work, I want to mention that I am the only writer whose work I am competent to discuss; it would be presumptuous of me to analyze or assign purpose to other writers. I do know how and why I do things, but with other writers I would largely be guessing, so it is not entirely from vanity that I turn to my own works for examples, and garlic.

If I say "white cat" to all of you, I daresay it would certainly, as a phrase, have some meaning in itself. Almost everyone can picture a white cat or ideas associated with a white cat; there are as many ideas about white cats, I suppose, as there are white cats in the world. The problem of a writer who wants to create a symbol, artificially endowed with a specific emotional weighting, is to invent one white cat that has a particular surrounding of emotional meaning, pertaining to one book and one character. In the book I have just finished, *The Haunting of Hill House*, the building up of a cumulative set of symbols was the only way to manage a particularly difficult passage. My problem was to take Eleanor, a woman of thirty-two, from her home in New York City to a haunted house two hundred miles away. In the course of this journey, which begins the book, she was to be built up as a wholly sympathetic character, the main character in the book; she was to be shown as infinitely lonely and unhappy. At the same time, there had to be a transition for the reader, from the sensible environment of the city to the somewhat less believable atmosphere of the haunted house, and the preparation had to be made carefully, in Eleanor's mind and the reader's, for the introduction of the horrors to come later, and Eleanor's reactions. The reader had to be persuaded to identify sufficiently with Eleanor so that when later he encounters with her the various manifestations in the haunted house he will be willing to suspend disbelief and go along with Eleanor, because she has become thoroughly believable. This was hard.

I thought that the best way to lead the reader and Eleanor into an atmosphere of unreality was by working through a kind of unreality both of them could accept readily, a kind of daydreaming fairy-tale atmosphere quite natural to Eleanor under the circumstances. She is driving alone, a trip of two hundred miles, and it is not surprising that she tells herself little stories while she travels. The fairy-tale atmosphere begins when Eleanor comes to the garage in the city where her car is kept, and accidentally stumbles against a little old lady who is quite angry, in the best old-witch tradition, but is eventually placated, and as Eleanor gets into her car the little old lady says, "I will pray for you, dearie." Eleanor thinks of this as a good omen for a journey about which she has considerable misgivings, and as she drives on, the little old lady is woven into her fantasies. Eleanor drives through a little village and sees and admires an old lovely house with two stone lions on the steps, and in the minute or so it takes for her to pass the house she has made up an entire lifetime for herself in the house with the stone lions; she has washed their faces every morning, and inside the house she has lived long quiet years, graciously, growing older in quiet elegance, with a little old lady to bring her a glass of blackberry wine each evening and help her care for the stone lions.

Before she has quite completed her dream of the lions, she passes an oleander hedge along the road, and she imagines that she might stop her car and go through the gate in the hedge and step into a castle, magically released from a spell by her coming, and she thinks that she would run down a path of jewels to a terrace before the castle, where there are fountains and stone lions and a little old lady who is actually the queen, her mother, waiting for the princess to come home and break the spell. Before she has quite unwound this story, she comes upon a little cottage almost buried in roses, and sees a white cat sunning itself on the step; she thinks that perhaps she will stop and live here forever, becoming a little old lady herself with a tiny pair of stone lions by her fireplace, oleanders and roses planted close beside her door, and she will make love potions for village maidens and dig magic herbs in the forest.

After Eleanor has driven a hundred miles, she stops at an inn for lunch, and while she is sitting in the inn a little girl at a nearby table cries out clearly that she will not drink her milk because she does not have her cup of stars. Eleanor is thinking with delight that of course a cup of stars is vital and essential for any fairy-tale heroine when the little girl's mother explains to the waitress that it is not really a cup of stars, but a cup with stars painted inside, so that when the little girl drinks her milk at home she can see the stars in the cup.

Now, the basic emphasis in the entire journey has been Eleanor's longing for a home, for a place of her own, and of course for a real cup of stars to break the spell of dullness and loneliness that she has always known. Five symbols have been set up. First there is the little old lady who is praying for Eleanor, then the two stone lions, then the oleander bushes and roses, then the white cat, then the cup of stars. Now, you see, the phrase "white cat" is beginning to take on the meaning it needs for the book. Each of these cumulative symbols dovetails with the others, each belongs absolutely to the journey between reality and unreality, and each must carry the weight of Eleanor's loneliness and longing for a place where she belongs.

Now, these artificially loaded words can only be used with extreme care, and there again is the garlic. Garlic is a splendid thing, and one that is irreplaceable, yet there is no question but that it is possible to use too much of it. This collection of weighted words can only be used like garlic, where they will do the most good, and they must never be used where they will overwhelm the flavor of another passage. They can only be used, in short, in spots where it is essential to emphasize Eleanor's loneliness, and then only in very small quantities. If one of the other characters in the book happens to remark that he dislikes cats and Eleanor says at once that she likes cats, but only white ones, what she is saying, of course, is that she likes white cats and has a dream of living alone in a little cottage covered with roses with an old lady praying for her and oleander bushes by the door. Consequently, Eleanor cannot make such a remark unless it is absolutely necessary, and the other character cannot even be made to remark that he dislikes cats unless Eleanor's entire structure of fantasy has to be evoked at that particular moment.

One side result of this, of course, is that the garlic-laden symbols cancel out any similar references. Eleanor cannot, for instance, admire a pair of Chinese porcelain lions without keying in to the whole laborious story again; she cannot have any dealings with black cats or tortoiseshell cats; she cannot admire a privet hedge or drink from a cup painted pink on the inside. Moreover, each time one of these symbols turns up, it gathers new meanings and identities; when, later in the book, Eleanor wants to make an impression on one of the other characters and says boastfully that when *she* was a child *she* used to have a cup of stars, this is supposed to act as a kind of jolt to the reader, because of course it was not Eleanor as a child who had a cup of stars, but a strange child in an inn. Eleanor's appropriating the cup of stars has become a further statement about her own lost loneliness; she has suddenly made a picture of herself as a little girl in an inn with a loving mother and father indulging her pretty whims.

Furthermore, it is beginning to appear that Eleanor is sinking into her fantasies, is moving herself into her dreamworld where she is loved and secure, and is perhaps already beginning to see herself as an enchanted princess or a happy child. Before she is through, Eleanor has made every one of her symbols her own; simply by presenting these various things as real, as belonging to her, she has come from her unhappy real life to a very happy, very dangerous, unreal life. By the end of the book, Eleanor is looking at other characters and thinking "I remember you; you dined with me once, long ago, in my home with the stone lions on the terrace." Her last sad statement—spoken as she is leaving the haunted house at the insistence of the others, who do not believe she is safe there any longer—is "But nothing can hurt me; somewhere, someone is praying for me."

It has become a statement that she is so far lost in fantasy that reality cannot touch her anymore; she is safe from danger because she no longer believes in its existence. The other characters, who believe reasonably enough what Eleanor has told them—that she has a little house where she keeps her cup of stars that she used as a child, where she has a white cat, where she has two small stone lions on the mantelpiece and roses and an oleander bush by the door—think that they are doing the right thing by sending Eleanor away; they think they are sending her home.

I would like to finish by reading two stories that demonstrate in a rather extreme fashion the idea of substituting symbols for characters; in one of them, the hero does not appear at all, and in the other, the heroine makes only the most brief token appearance.

Here she would read her short story "Charles," about an infamous first grader who never appears, and another of her short stories, "The Third Baby's the Easiest," which culminates with the birth of her third child. Both these stories appeared in magazines (Mademoiselle, Harper's Review) *before being collected into Jackson's fourth book and first family memoir,* Life Among the Savages, *published in 1953.*

"Push me again, dear—it's just like flying."

Afterword

ASSEMBLING AND EDITING THIS BOOK OF OUR MOTHER'S UNPUB-
lished and previously uncollected writing has been a great pleasure,
and an enormous challenge. Editing any world-class writer is a
daunting task, but in our case the author was so familiar to us that
the process often felt more like collaboration. Sometimes we had to
step away from the material and banish the thought that it was our
mother's writing, in order to focus on the words alone, particularly
in the stories featuring us as characters.

These stories and essays have awakened many memories from
our childhood. We literally *heard* these pieces being written: The
pounding of our mother's typewriter and its infernal ring at the end
of each flurry—then the syncopated peppering beginning again seconds later—were a constant part of our household. Now, as editors,
we have undergone an emotional experience, working with copies
of those original stories and essays as they emerged from her typewriter, many of them first drafts, with Shirley's occasional handwritten corrections, and even rare word substitutions by our father, the
literary critic Stanley Edgar Hyman.

We recall coming home from school and finding our mother
typing away upstairs or at a folding table in the dining room, or sit-

ting on her kitchen stool making notes while baking brownies. For years our parents worked side by side in their study, sitting at desks four feet apart, the sounds of their furiously fast typing rattling through the house. We easily tuned it out, but visiting friends were often shocked by the rapid-fire percussion coming from behind the closed door.

Many of the works here, especially the humorous ones, kindle recollections of dinnertime in our house, an important tradition we were not allowed to miss. Shirley would have the meal prepared, and would be sitting on her kitchen stool talking to the cats. We would all take our assigned places at the table, with one parent at either end, and after discussion of the day's events, more serious conversation would begin.

Our father would do most of the talking, with our mother adding details, color, and insight, and we all laughed a lot. Over the years we learned about mathematics, logic, ethics, history, the Greek alphabet, physics, music, comparative folklore, and religion. (One year our parents took turns reading us two chapters each night from the Old Testament, and we all explored the language and the meanings of the rituals.) We were exposed to whatever our parents were reading. We shared puzzles, songs, jokes, riddles, wordplay, and dialect humor—and we were all expected to participate. Fragments of these dinnertime conversations found their way into the many short articles and stories that Shirley wrote about our family.

One by one, we four children became characters in Shirley's work, which was published regularly in the popular magazines of the time. Some of the best of those stories were collected into memoirs, *Life Among the Savages* and *Raising Demons*. The stories were often based on actual events, but they were wonderfully embellished in Shirley's telling. She could make even the most mundane or embarrassing incidents seem funny, and we often opened magazines to find ourselves appearing as unwitting comic actors. Sometimes we were portrayed as clever and wise, sometimes foolish or mischievous, but our mother always treated us with respect and gave us some great lines.

As children, we didn't mind the attention we received. We learned to dissociate ourselves a bit from the stories, though we enjoyed them, because we recognized them to be, essentially, fiction. As adults, we proudly read them to our children and grandchildren, who love hearing them and seem to feel a connection with our younger selves and with our parents, whom most of them never met.

Laurence has been asked all his life about the much anthologized short story "Charles" and has steadfastly refused to answer questions about it, borrowing Shirley's typical response: "It's just a story." But after sixty-five years in continuous print, the story of his kindergarten nemesis refuses to die. He even received, a few years ago, a box of ninety handwritten letters from an entire fifth grade class, asking him in many admiring voices if he, "Laurie," was still mischievous, and if he had really done "all those terrible things." Laurence answered each one, as, predictably, did Charles.

Our mother's fame, though, was hardly limited to her humorous pieces. As we grew older, we read her frightening stories and novels with great, though sometimes mixed, pride. Sarah remembers that informing a new, literate friend that her mother wrote "The Lottery" could be both hilarious and terrifying. In the next few moments, she would watch herself change in their eyes.

After Shirley's early death at forty-eight, we understood, with the rest of the world, that she would write no more books. But then, one day in the mid-1990s, the manuscripts that would lead to this volume mysteriously reentered our lives when Laurence opened his front door to find a carton with no return address. After some hesitation, he peered into the box and found a stack of manuscripts, clearly identifiable by the goldenrod paper she always used and by the familiar font of her old upright Royal typewriter, as Shirley's.

Examining short stories he had never read, Laurence realized that much of the carton's contents had never been published. This prompted us to look around for more of our mother's possibly undiscovered writing. We made the first of several trips to the Library of Congress in Washington, D.C., to search through their Shirley Jackson Collection, more than fifty boxes of material our father had donated, according to our mother's wishes. We found and copied many more pieces of her writing that we had never seen. We read for months, gradually assembling and editing an anthology of fifty-four stories, which we titled *Just an Ordinary Day*.

There were many other stories that, for a variety of reasons, we chose not to include: Some ended abruptly and confusedly, some seemed too similar to other stories already slated for the collection. Some Shirley had reworked for use in one or another of her novels; sometimes there were two different drafts, both good, and it was hard to choose between them. We had decided only to include short stories, so the essays and reviews and other nonfiction pieces were kept out of the book, which was published in 1997.

For years afterward, some of the pieces we had set aside kept coming back to haunt us, and we often mused about doing another book. We knew how prolific a writer our mother had been, and we suspected there were more gems hidden in the files at the Library of Congress. Finally, in 2011, we decided to return there to search.

Again we spent long days sorting through the now much more organized Shirley Jackson Collection, photocopying hundreds of pages that looked promising, then reading through them at night, trying to make sense of them. Sometimes we were horrified to discover that the last page of a story seemed to be missing, or that, despite a promising beginning, a piece just never got itself completely written.

This was because Shirley usually worked on several things at once, often putting aside stories she had started, planning to return later to finish or rewrite them. "Mrs. Spencer and the Oberons," for instance, was begun, then restarted, then rewritten twice. In two early versions, the mysterious visitors left garbled phone messages and notes in the Spencer house while the family was out, irritating but always missing them, and then left town, so the two families never actually met. In the final version, included here, Mrs. Spencer is portrayed as a scold, obsessed with breeding and propriety, horrified that her family is abandoning her stiff standards. The addition of the popular town picnic and Mrs. Spencer's inability to "save" her husband and children created a much larger and more universal story. We feel the version we selected shows Shirley's consummate skill and dark vision as well as anything else she ever wrote.

We found that we had copies of a great number of partial stories and fragments. Sometimes we were able to match disconnected pages by noting small technical details, comparing Shirley's typewritten pages or carbon copies with others bearing similar degrees of textual clarity or fuzziness, or that had apparently been typed with the same tired ribbon, in our effort to spot missing pages and put stories back together. We tried to date pieces by guessing the general period in her life when they were written: when she had used wide margins and when narrow, when her pages were numbered and when her name was typed at the top. We tried to calculate general time periods from dated figures of speech and slang, or by how much things cost. The manuscripts that bore our father's comments showed that she had considered them complete and good enough to show to him.

Ultimately, we were able to retrieve much forgotten material, including some stories written in Shirley and Stanley's cramped, book-filled West Village apartment in the early 1940s, when our parents were both just starting to publish. We found good stories written during every period of her life. We discovered more book reviews, lectures and short essays about writing, and humorous pieces still funny decades after their original appearances in magazines. To our surprise, with our brother Barry's help, we also discovered hundreds of our mother's line drawings, cartoons, and watercolors, a few of which we remembered from our childhood, when they would appear on the refrigerator or the study door, taped up by Shirley to surprise and amuse Stanley.

Over the many months we spent poring over all this material, we found that some stories, new favorites of ours, clearly belonged in this volume, but we were forced to cull others we liked, sometimes with great reluctance. Some stories we did not fully understand at first, but the moment we did, they were transformed clearly into much more important stories than we had first thought. It took many readings for a few of the stories to sink in, and we came to understand more fully the depth and subtlety with which our mother wrote.

"The Man in the Woods," for example, at first seemed to be simply a fairy tale, or a fantasy time-travel story, but overnight it suddenly became clear to us how deeply it is grounded in mythology and iconic symbolism, with Shirley's typical hanging ending. Clues are playful and abundant, left along the way like breadcrumbs. We may not know how the story will turn out, but the mysterious Mr. Oakes clearly does when he says that he hopes that the lost traveler Christopher will care for his roses and remember that it was he who planted them. Clearly, a ritual battle is intended, and the outcome is inevitable, as foretold by the victory of Christopher's black cat, and the traditions of myth.

Shirley was raised on the classics and self-educated in the literature of the supernatural, and was fascinated by the study of myth and ritual, a driving passion of our father's, who refined his theories with Kenneth Burke and others at Bennington College in the late 1940s and '50s. After "The Lottery" was published in *The New Yorker* in 1948, bringing ancient ritual shockingly into the modern day, Burke observed that while Stanley was a serious scholar of myth and ritual, Shirley's work embodied it.

In this book we have attempted to share as many strong and varied pieces of Shirley's writing as possible. We could not keep Sossiter or Miss Lederer or Mr. Halloran Beresford to ourselves. Each story presents a new narrative voice: a rebellious teenage girl or an angry maiden schoolteacher, a slow-thinking child or an ironic reviewer. We think that this collection demonstrates the qualities that Shirley Jackson fans appreciate: her mastery of different writing styles, her pointed wit, and her ability to reveal startling truths about the darker side of our common experience.

Throughout the editing process we have come again and again to appreciate her craft: the expert use of repetition, the bare simplicity in descriptive language that is one of her trademarks, often within herculean paragraphs consisting of one very complex single sentence. Shirley herself sometimes seemed to us to be lurking among the pages as we worked, both the mother we knew and an unpredictable stranger. Here we saw her creating masterly fiction, but also meeting ghosts while we were off at school, or becoming so frustrated that she would swear off writing forever—before erupting with some masterpiece. Or she might write herself coded messages that she would discover, jarringly, in the morning, or perform some dark protective magic, just after reading us a story and putting us to bed.

While we have worked on these pieces, they have been working on us. We grew to know our mother better, and now have a much greater appreciation for the dedication that empowered her, after doing the shopping and housework and cooking and driving everyone to classes, appointments, movies, scout meetings, and the dentist, to steal a few precious hours each day to sit at her typewriter and write.

After much discussion, we titled this book *Let Me Tell You*, after the only unfinished piece we used. We included it because we think the character Shirley created for it is so memorable—almost an early Merricat, the unreliable narrator of *We Have Always Lived in the Castle*—with a voice unlike any other. We think the book's title encompasses all the material within, and it sounds almost as if Shirley were leaning confidentially toward the reader in a restaurant, whispering over the shrimp cocktail.

Shirley repeatedly said that when she wrote, she expected the reader to complete the experience of making fiction; she assumed a certain literacy from her reader, or at least the ability to pay attention, because she considered the writer and reader to be partners. With enormous care and energy, she honed her skill in a great variety of styles, with timeless characters and plots, creating memories for millions. We hope that this collection pleases her many fans, and new readers around the world.

Laurence Jackson Hyman
Sarah Hyman DeWitt

Acknowledgments

THE EDITORS WISH TO THANK OUR BROTHER, BARRY EDGAR HYMAN, for his early editorial consultation and his help in collecting the drawings; our agent, Murray Weiss of Catalyst Literary Management; biographer Ruth Franklin; Alice Birney and the Library of Congress, for their careful stewardship of our parents' extensive archives; and David Ebershoff, Caitlin McKenna, and Benjamin Dreyer at Random House for their invaluable help in refining this book.

About the Type

THIS BOOK WAS SET IN ELECTRA, A TYPEFACE DESIGNED FOR LINO-
type by W. A. Dwiggins, the renowned type designer (1880–1956).
Electra is a fluid typeface, avoiding the contrasts of thick and thin
strokes that are prevalent in most modern typefaces.